SALLY CRIED WITH AN UNRESTRAINED SADNESS

The fear and frustration of the last few weeks, the hate she'd experienced from David, and the uncertainty and tension brought on by her untenable situation supplied the fuel for her tears.

Suddenly she was acutely aware of David's nearness. More than she needed food or drink at the moment, she needed comfort. His muscular male warmth offered it. She raised her arms with a fierce desire.

Silently, David looked down at her. Lust and compassion seemed to fight a battle. With a sigh, he finally gathered the scantily clothed, irresistible temptation that was his wife into his arms, to cradle her to his own pulsating body as he carried her to the bed.

But when his black eyes met hers again, Sally knew he had still not forgiven her....

AND NOW...

SUPERROMANCES

Worldwide Library is proud to present a
sensational new series of modern love stories—
SUPERROMANCES

Written by masters of the genre, these longer,
sensuous and dramatic novels are truly in keeping
with today's changing life-styles. Full of intriguing
conflicts, the heartaches and delights of true love,
SUPERROMANCES are absorbing stories—
satisfying and sophisticated reading that lovers
of romance fiction have long been waiting for.

SUPERROMANCES
Contemporary love stories for the woman of today!

JESSICA LOGAN

JOURNEY INTO LOVE

A SUPERROMANCE FROM
WORLDWIDE

TORONTO · LONDON · NEW YORK · SYDNEY

The author wishes to thank Dr. Tom Vecchione,
plastic surgeon of San Diego, California,
for his most valuable contributions to this story.

━━━━━━━━━━◆●◆━━━━━━━━━━

Published, June 1982

First printing April, 1982

ISBN 0-373-70020-2

Printed in U.S.A.

CHAPTER ONE

THE RAIN HAD FALLEN for days. Soft, quiet, insistent, it had almost become a way of life.

The big cat looked out into the curtain of moisture, flexed her tawny coat and left the shelter of the cave, fangs bared as she hissed her disapproval of the night.

The oppressive silence of the night was suddenly shattered. Sound split the quiet, bouncing off the canyon wall and reverberating down the steep ravine. As the source neared, the din intensified.

The frightened cat, sensitive ears tight to the golden head, flattened herself to the rocky shelf and snarled viciously. The animal glared with alarmed rage, clung to the earth. . . waited.

With lightning swiftness a great object fell straight down, bounced on the narrow ledge, shed debris, then pitched over into the canyon, bound for the bottom far below. Silence rolled back across the mountainside. Filled with the whisper of the rain that slanted through the trees, the hiss of the raindrops that spattered against the rocks of the narrow ledge that led to the cat's lair, the restoration of quiet was only momentary.

A young child, part of the debris flung from the doomed automobile, cried then, the piteous whimper of a little one in great pain. Beside the child, the slender figure of a girl moved. Vaguely conscious, she had made a last effort to get herself and the child out of the hurtling car. She touched her bleeding face with numb fingers. She was not aware of broken bones or the chill slash of the falling rain.

The child whimpered, and the sound called to the girl again. She moaned, groped in the darkness, fingers moving painfully in a restless search of the rocky ledge.

Once again the child cried. The great cat roared a hiccuping protest at this invasion of her privacy.

The injured girl's search was rewarded as her questing fingers found the child. She pulled the grievously hurt little one to the warmth of her body in an instinctive gesture of protection.

An explosion rent the stillness that had followed the panther's scream. An orange red glare threw the rocky projection into stark relief. For a moment the girl's dazed eyes took in the black maw of the big cat's lair, the stunted undergrowth and the tumbled boulders that masked it.

The panther, mad with fear and outrage, launched herself. She hurled her sleek length toward the injured girl and the child she clutched.

The glare illumined the nightmare scene. The girl screamed in terror, then slipped into oblivion, the child tucked against her side. High on the mountain road a deputy sheriff on patrol cursed in astonishment as the flare of the explosion lit the canyon of the river far below. He shined his flashlight through the rain, unable to see clearly, then sent his car racing toward the scene.

The animal never attacked. Perhaps it was because of the scream or the mysterious light. But the girl was unaware of this or of the team that struggled down to the ledge to rescue her after the man sent in the call for help. She was just as unaware of the ambulance ride or the hospital to which she and the child were brought. There the child was taken from her to its own cot. Very little life remained in the child or in the girl whose last effort had been to protect the two-year-old in her care.

Men scoured the vicinity for bits of debris flung from the powerful car as it had torn a path down the side of the canyon. The burned remnant of the automobile was found far down at the bottom of the ravine in the steep mountain pass. The rain had finally drowned out that fiery explosion.

FOR DAYS the girl did not regain consciousness. Doctors went about the task of repairing her body, saving her life. Her wounds were cleansed, her ribs were taped. Her fractured skull was X-rayed thoroughly, then left to knit naturally. Teeth were repaired, her jaws were wired together, and the breaks inflicted as a result of being flung facedown onto the rocky ledge were aligned with extreme care. Her shattered left arm was immobilized in plaster. Hideously jarred internal organs accepted restored tranquillity and settled down to take up normal functions in a tentative manner.

The flesh of her face, swollen and purpled, turned into a grotesque mask that little resembled the lovely oval of the picture found in her passport. For her passport was found among the bits and pieces flung from the car as it sped to destruction. The sodden little book had been issued by the British government to one Sally Rossi, British subject, married to David Rossi, American. Included on the passport were her two children: twins, a boy and a girl, born in California two years ago.

No trace was found of the boy. The little girl slowly recovered.

Mr. David Rossi was notified. His attendance at the hospital bedside was constant and dedicated. His face a strained dark mask, he watched the girl, willed her back to consciousness. Each day he visited his little daughter, brought her things, held her gently, but the child did not know him. He did not expect her to as he hadn't seen her since shortly after her birth.

The girl had not regained consciousness. Then toward the end of her third week in the hospital, a gradual change took place. At times she became dimly aware of the hushed quiet around her. People came and went like shadows. Sometimes gentle hands touched her aching body, ministered to her, moved her. Voices would whisper in her head, call to her. Then she would slip once more into the grayness that lurked so near, that lured her back to the gentle ease of unawareness.

And one day she awoke. Soft light filtered into the room where she lay. It hurt her eyes. She murmured in protest, tried to turn from it. Pain seared through her body, set it on fire and caused her to gasp.

Instantly the man who sat beside her bed was on his feet, a bitter triumph flaring in his black and implacable eyes. He restrained her, pressed her back into the mattress, then pushed a long finger on the button of the device to summon help.

"Be still, you little fool!"

The girl blinked, turned eyes wide with wonder upon him, her attention caught by the bitterness that laced his resonant voice. She stared at him, frightened as she saw and responded to the blaze of hatred in the dark eyes fixed upon her.

The man caught the flash of pain that twisted her ashen features as her ribs moved with her agitated breath. A bleak pity stirred in his raking scrutiny.

"Lie very still, Sally. Breathe shallowly. It won't hurt so much if you do." The deep voice offered the instruction casually, without expression.

Sally! The name caught the girl's attention and held it as a nurse moved into the room on silent feet, the white-coated figure of a doctor close on her heels.

"Come around, has she, David?" The question seemed to mask the concern of the medical man. "Let me have a look at her."

The dark man with the bitter eyes was banished from the room while the doctor proceeded to examine his patient. Assisted by the able nurse, he worked with a tender speed that nevertheless was a painful experience that left the girl white as the sheet that covered her.

Every bone in her body ached. Her rib cage protested strongly when forced to rise and fall with the small breaths she rapidly learned to use. A blinding headache caused her to keep her swollen eyelids closed over eyes that rasped with dryness. Even the light weight of the sheet over her seemed too much to bear for the bruised flesh it covered.

"What happened to me?" She forced the thready whisper through immobilized lips and jaws that were firmly wired together.

The doctor considered her carefully. "You were in a bad accident, Sally," he told her quietly. "You are lucky to be alive, but you are coming along nicely."

"Wh-where am I hurt?"

"Almost everywhere you could be." His gruff murmur soothed and reassured her. "Among other things, you have a broken arm, a jawbone we have wired together, a fractured skull, a concussion and a variety of bruises that must be seen to be believed. You are making a spectacular recovery, thanks to your fine constitution and my medical skill." He grinned at her, invited her to share his little joke.

Long curved lashes fluttered up. Pain-filled eyes searched the homely face of the doctor as he bent over her. "Th-thank you." The whispered accent was distinctly British in contrast to the doctor's own American speech. "Where am I?" Her enunciation was clear through the impediment of wired jaws.

"In Cottage Hospital, in Paso Mayacama."

"Wh-where is Paso May-Mayacama?" The girl blinked as she was caught in a surge of pain, but her eyes did not waver.

The doctor saw that wave of pain, then checked the position of the plaster cast that covered one slender arm. He shifted a support, aligned a weight, and the girl sighed with relief.

"It's in California, Sally."

The girl absorbed the information, knew she did not know where that was but put the worry aside.

"How...how long have I been here?"

"Three weeks and one day."

The girl was silent a moment, eyes closed against the invasion of the sunlight into the room. It slanted across her bed in a cheerful display. The doctor noticed her discomfort, moved across to the window and pulled the draperies together.

The girl worked bravely against the pain and confusion confined in the delicate bones of her skull and came up with another question. "My name is Sally?"

Startled, the doctor turned to her. "Yes, it is. Don't you know?"

"No. I can't seem to remember it."

He looked very thoughtful indeed. "Do you remember any other name?"

"N-no. Not at all..." the thin answer trailed off. The girl was tiring; the effort of forcing speech through wired jaws, clenched teeth, was almost too much for her.

"Well, don't worry your pretty little head about it. Marion—" he turned to the attentive nurse "—stay with her. Make her comfortable. I need to talk to Dave."

Sally closed her eyes. Aching, she slipped into a deep sleep that healed and soothed.

FOR THE NEXT SPACE OF TIME the girl awoke periodically to the pained consciousness of gentle care. Liquids dripped from bottles high above her and passed through transparent tubes into needles attached to her battered body. Medicine was injected. She was kept clean and cared for. Bruises turned into ugly masses of color.

The shape of her small oval face was distorted by

swollen tissue as were the sweet curves of her body. Her head, swathed in bandages, hurt abominably and constantly. She was always aware of pain even through the masking influence of the medicines that were administered. But during her brief periods of awareness, she began to know the doctor who attended her with faithful regularity and to depend upon him as a friend. And the gentleness of the nurse, Marion, gradually became familiar to her, too.

Always she was aware of the dark and silent man who kept vigil at her bedside. He watched her with a brooding intensity, this lean and wide-shouldered man. The girl would stir restlessly in her sleep as she felt his menacing presence. Her long-lashed lids would flutter up and reveal eyes the color of pansies in the rain, sunken among the hideous bruises that covered her misshapen bandaged face. Those deeply blue eyes would meet the challenge of his. He would stare at her with a concentration that burned into her troubled mind.

What did he want? Why did he sit there, staring at her with such malevolence, such bitterness? Always she would sigh, unable to voice the questions, unable to think of the answers herself. Too spent to solve the puzzle of his presence or the reason she felt so threatened by it, she would close her eyes, and slip back into the safety of sleep.

Medical men came, examined her, murmured as they evaluated her progress, ordered adjustments in medicines and schedules and left instructions to be carried out. The girl paid little attention. She was either lost in the fog of her own agony or submerged quietly in the grip of medication.

Then one morning the pressure of the pain in her head subsided and was only a dulled memory. The sunlight that filtered into her room no longer sliced through her aching eyeballs in shafts of fire. Relieved of the horror of the headache, her broken arm, battered rib cage and other bruises became minor matters.

"Hello," she greeted the nurse who came to attend her. "You've been here with me quite often, haven't you?"

The nurse listened attentively to speech distorted by the strictures of the wire. "Yes, I've been one of your private nurses," she told her. "I'm Marion Grayson. You've been very ill for a long time. I'm glad to see you so improved. David will be pleased."

As Marion went about the task of assuring the girl's comfort, she kept up a bright chatter. She inquired if Sally could remember her name yet and was intrigued when her patient could not. "Do you remember anything about the accident?"

"No, I cannot. Was it a bad accident? Are you permitted to tell me what happened?"

"Let's leave it until you are a little stronger. Can you tell me what you do remember?"

Sally was horrified to discover that in fact she had no memory at all beyond the first time she had become aware that she was indeed in a hospital.

"Don't worry about it." Marion accepted the fact she could not remember with a minimum of fuss. She pulled the clean sheets she was putting on the bed straight and tight with expert hands, fluffed up the firm pillows and placed them in strategic spots. Truly she was so matter of fact that Sally's pulse stopped its mad race of alarm and calmed. She was able to dismiss her blank memory and concentrate upon her first conscious effort to sip her breakfast through a straw.

She had almost finished her liquid breakfast when a doctor came in.

"I am your reconstructive surgeon, little Sally. I've been engaged by Rossi to put that lovely little face of yours back in order. My name is Alan Stern."

Who is Rossi, she wondered. *Why is he concerned? And my name is Sally. How strange that should be my name.* She closed her eyes, lay still as he removed the bandages from her face and head and looked her over very thoughtfully. She paid no attention, so absorbed in thought was she about her name, about Rossi.

The shaggy-haired doctor she had begun to think of as her own came into the room and watched the specialist as he made a careful examination.

"Well, Alan. What do you think?" he asked as the other drew back from the bed with a pucker between his brows, his lower lip caught in fine white teeth.

"I agree with you, Jim." The surgeon looked at the other doctor. "She is very definitely in need of reconstructive work." Skillful fingers began the task of replacing old bandages with new. "What does Rossi wish me to do? How far is he willing to go?"

"You must do anything that is necessary to restore her features. He has set no limits. And the cost is no factor."

"I see." Stern squinted at her as he moved her chin with gentle fingers. "I'll need a couple of photos taken of her before the accident. As soon as the swelling is down, I'll get to work and see what I can do." He bade them a cheerful goodbye then and left.

"What is he going to do?" Sally's eyes were anxious beneath the bandages.

"Repair the damage to your lovely little face, my girl. At one time it was a work of mother nature's art." He smiled. "But it was never meant to be used to plow up a mountainside. And mother nature cannot repair what you did to it. Be a shame to leave it like it is. Messy."

"Oh."

The girl did not evidence any further interest in his information. The doctor watched her closely, quirked an eyebrow at the nurse, who shrugged off his puzzled inquiry, unable to answer his unspoken question about his patient's lack of interest in her appearance. The doctor scowled at her imperturbable back, then went on with his examination.

"Do you know what I looked like before I—before the accident?" The girl's curiosity had to do with the length of the doctor's acquaintance rather than with her own appearance.

"Yes, Sally. I know. Don't worry. Stern is a good man. Once he gets a couple of pictures from Rossi, he'll work his magic on you. You will look just as you once did."

"Who is Rossi?" she asked, knowing he was the dark man who had spent so much time at her bedside, but wanting to know more.

"David," the doctor replied. He watched her swollen face as he adjusted the weights controlling the movement of her injured arm.

"Oh, I see. David Rossi."

"Yes." His oblique glance questioned, saw no response to Rossi's name. He finished his adjustments and smoothed his hands carefully over the enameled rail of the bed, his face thoughtful. The nurse glanced at him, then abruptly left the room. Maclean did not see her go as he kept watchful eyes on Sally.

"My name is James Maclean," he informed her. Gray eyes searched her face for some sort of reaction. "Does that mean anything to you?"

The girl shook her head, blinked at the pain that resulted from that unwise action.

"Hmm." Maclean noticed her reaction and pulled a small penlight from the breast pocket of his white coat. "Look at that spot, please." He shined the light at the opposite wall, then swung it back to direct it into her eye. She obeyed as he bent over her for a deep and careful examination of the interior of her eye.

"You don't remember me, either, I take it?" He transferred his attention to the other eye.

"No." The girl's nostrils twitched as she registered the clean scent of his after-shave lotion, the faint odor of antiseptic that clung to him.

The doctor raised his head, stared down at her. His shaggy brows met above the clear gray of his eyes as he frowned.

"And you still don't remember who you are, eh?"

"No. You say I am Sally. David—you and David, that man—both say I am Sally." Somehow in the past two or three days the fact that the dark and brooding man who sat at her bedside was called David had sunk into some reluctant corner of her mind. She used it now in a tentative fashion.

"Do you remember David?" the doctor shot at her.

"No." The girl stared at him, wide-eyed with worry that she should ever have known the menacing man named David. "I am sure there must be some mistake if you think I should. I do not know either of you."

"There has been a mistake made, and you are the one who has made it, you whoring little bitch!" Rage twisted his dark face and glared from black eyes as the man called David strode into the room. He halted abruptly and seared her with a glance of pure hate. Stiff-legged, his booted feet wide apart, his hands clenched at his sides, he looked ready to pounce, an enraged man as full of menace as an animal.

The girl shrank from him against the unyielding bed. She flung her uninjured hand up, palm out in an instinctive gesture of self-protection.

"Easy, Dave." The big doctor's movement was smooth as he placed himself between his patient and the threat in the doorway.

"You needn't worry, Jim." David's harsh laugh cut, grated. "I wouldn't touch that filthy bit of fluff with rubber gloves and a ten-foot pole."

He shouldered the doctor aside and stalked to the bedside with the lithe easy grace of a born athlete in superb condition. Sally stared helplessly into his dark face. It was twisted with a suppressed fury. Black eyes snapped hate at her. A white line outlined his snarling mouth, stressing his ominous interest in her. His deeply tanned skin was stretched like parchment over his high cheekbones and firm jaw. A muscle twitched in one cheek as the girl stared up at him. She was unable to breathe, unable to tear her eyes away.

"Dave!" The warning was soft, and the doctor did not move as David's glance flicked him.

"The FBI has finally come up with the name of the man she traveled with." David's flat statement condemned, hated. "It was Don Lang." Strong hands closed convulsively on the rail of the bed. He took a deep breath, making an obvious effort to control the passion that ran riot through him. "Now, how the hell do you suppose she just happened to return here with Don Lang?" The whisper was bitter with an emotion that was obviously hard to handle. "She's been in this whole thing with him all the time, haven't you, Sally?"

"I don't know what you mean." Her whisper of protest was just audible in the tension-charged room. She jumped at David's bark of laughter.

"You planned to meet with him when you left here, didn't you, Sally? You have been with him all this time, just waiting, haven't you, you conniving little slut?" He leaned toward her over the rail of the bed, the rage that flickered in his intent gaze frightening in its intensity.

"Where is my son, Sally? What kind of hell have you planned to put me through this time?" Hate vibrated in his hoarse whisper. He trembled with rage and frustration, raised his hands and stared at them as if they were not his and had no right to quiver. Maclean watched him, said nothing, but his big body was tense.

The girl on the narrow hospital bed just stared at him. Frightened and confused, she felt her limbs quaking as she recognized his fury but could not know why he was so angry. Who was Don Lang?

Where had she been with him? And why did it matter? How on earth was she supposed to know where this man's son was? The questions flickered in her mind like spent candles, but she could not force a word from her lips. She gulped in oxygen and lowered silky lashes onto her battered cheeks as she heard the breath hiss from the man standing over her.

"I mean to have my son, Sally. No amount of playacting will protect you. You can forget this pretense of amnesia. And forget whatever other damn game you have come back here to play, as well. I want Charles and I will have him. You should never have come back to the area if you planned anything else!" Convulsed with fury, he had the look of one driven beyond the power of reason. His lean face twitched. He moved suddenly, then vanished through the door.

The girl named Sally lay pale and shaken on the bed. She stared at the empty doorway long seconds after Rossi had gone, uncertain, fearful.

James Maclean stood quietly a few moments, then moved a chair close to the bed and sat down. He picked up her small hand and noticed its tremble as he enclosed it in his own large warm one. "Want to talk, Sally?"

"I...I...." She stopped on a sob. Her face held a woebegone and very confused expression. "Yes, I must talk," she finally whispered distractedly. "I must know why he is so angry." She closed her eyes, shuddered. "He—that man, David—frightens me."

James Maclean nodded his shaggy head as his features twisted in a wry sympathy reluctantly given.

"Rather awesome, David," he agreed. "But I can assure you that he has good reason to be angry even if you cannot remember what it is. Most men would be insane with rage, given the same circumstances to deal with. You have my word on it."

"What have I done that was so terrible?" Her anguished whisper pleaded for information. Her jaws ached, her teeth hurt, and her head was behaving in a queer manner that caused her vision to blur, then clear. She needed to close her eyes and sink into the blessed oblivion of sleep very badly indeed, but more than that, she had to know why the passionate and angry man called David hated her so. She was unable to stop her questions as they occurred to her.

"Who is the man he is so angry about me leaving with? Don Lang, I think he said. Where did I leave from? Where did I go? What is the FBI and who is Charles? I don't know David Rossi. I'm sure I never saw him except since I've been here." A sob racked her as she gestured helplessly at the confines of the room. "How could I know his son or have anything to do with him?" The questions burst from the distraught girl. Her hoarse whisper hissed through her wired jaws and trembled as she tried to make sense of the rage of the man called David.

"Take it easy, Sally. Nothing can be gained by hysteria." The doctor sighed as he moved his fingers to stroke her slender arm and soothe her. "You were in a car accident. The car went over a cliff and burned after it exploded on its way down. You and a little girl were thrown from the car as it bounced down the mountainside. The little girl, Carla, was found in your arms when you were rescued. You apparently held her, protected her as you were thrown from the car. She has been here in the hospital and will be going home shortly. She is David's daughter. She had a twin brother, Charles. They were both kidnapped two years ago when they were infants." He watched her expression carefully. "Do you know where Charles is, Sally?"

Sally stared at the doctor's intent face in horror.

"Oh! How terrible! But...I...." The thin whisper was agonized. Her swollen and bruised lips came down and masked the pain as comprehension dawned. "He...you...both of you think I took his children!"

"Someone did, Sally. David has had no word of them for the whole two years...and now this." His eyes searched deeply when she stared back at him. "You disappeared just shortly after they did, Sally. Two days later, in fact." The timbre of his accusation left no doubt of his reluctant certainty. "It was assumed that you had a lot to do with their disappearance. You must admit the assumption must have been correct. How else could you return with Carla? And why else would you be with Don Lang? He is the one person David probably has the most reason to distrust."

He dropped her hand and arose from the chair, his own manner agitated. He took a quick turn the width of the little room and pinned her with a critical look.

"Lang was once David's import-export manager. He had control of a fairly large chunk of David's wine business. Dave caught him siphoning off money and fired him on the spot. He left, of course. The twins disappeared soon after that. Then you went.

David went through a very rough patch. And now you come back here with Lang, apparently. What's going on, Sally? What happened? You must have taken the children, or you could not have reappeared with Carla. Where is Charles?'' He bent over her suddenly, almost as intense and as threatening as his friend had been. "David has suffered enough." He spoke thickly. "He does not need this from you."

The girl moved her head in abject confusion. The onslaught of a mammoth headache blurred her vision, turned her whisper to a reedy sigh. "I don't know about any of these things. I cannot remember any of these people, these...happenings." She closed weary eyes as tears spilled through.

If the man, David, believed she had done these horrible things, he had a perfect right to hate her. She knew this with a sad resignation. One could hardly blame a man for that kind of attitude toward a person who had treated him so. But she could not remember a thing....

Why had his little daughter been with her when the accident occurred? In spite of what the doctor said, she rejected the idea that she could have been involved with the kidnapping with an inner revulsion that could not be denied. There had to be another explanation no matter what they believed. She understood the doctor's concern, however. She worked at the next question, even though the sharp pain in her head interfered with clear thought.

"Did I work for him...for David...take care of his children for him in some way? Is that how I can be blamed for...for the horrible...." A sob wrenched her. "It's unthinkable," she finished miserably. She had no doubt the man at her bedside believed she had done what she could not put into words.

Maclean looked at her carefully. He did not answer her question directly when he spoke. "You don't remember me, either, Sally? Not at all?"

"No. Should I?" She was brusque in her weariness.

"We were good friends." Regret honed a bitter edge to the words, implying a hidden content. "You once said you loved me."

The girl's eyes flew open as she took in his meaning. She stared at him in utter disbelief. "I couldn't have! I would remember."

"You did." The statement was stark, without heat. "And I am David's friend." A light flickered in his eyes as he dealt with the memory that twisted his mouth. "You are David's wife, Sally. The children were yours. Yours and David's."

CHAPTER TWO

SALLY STARED AT JAMES MACLEAN in total disbelief.

"You must be joking!" The strangled sound was barely audible. Her contused features were ashen. "My h-husband? My children? I could not forget those things if they were indeed true." The statement was a pleading question that sought an answer that would confirm the correctness of her premise. Her whole manner rejected the information she had just heard. Her eyes begged him to assure her she had misunderstood. It must be a ghastly joke that only needed a logical explanation.

Maclean's craggy face was touched with a wintry pity as he shook his head at her. "It's true. The children, Carla and Charles, are twins," he affirmed. "You are their mother. You are David's wife. There is no mistake, Sally."

The girl listened to the grim but gentle statement with a sense of shock. She was revolted, sick to her stomach. "You mean, I took the children and disappeared with them two years ago...with another m-man?"

The doctor nodded. His face was very thoughtful, very attentive.

"Do you mean to tell me that I've made no attempt at all to reassure my h-husband that the children were well and h-happy in all that time... for two whole years?"

"That's about it, Sally."

"Wh-when I did come back from wherever I was, I only had the little girl with me? Not the boy...not Charles?"

"That is the size of it. No one knows where Charles is, or where you have been. No one knows where you came from. You booked your flight in London, but according to your passport, which has been found, you were only in London a day. Just long enough to catch a plane." The quiet words fell into the stillness of the room with a startling clarity.

"What kind of a woman am I? How could I do such a horrible thing to my...husband, my children?" She choked over the word husband, knew a wild moment of disbelief. How was it possible that she was married to David Rossi and was the mother of his children? An entirely involuntary shudder racked her slender form.

"I'm not sure what kind of woman you are, Sally." The man's mouth twisted wryly. "But you earned yourself quite a reputation the year you were here. David has a younger brother. Half brother, actually. David's own mother died when he was about five, and his father couldn't stand it. He left Dave here and went to Italy. He met and married Stefano's mother there, where Steve, as we sometimes call him in America, was born." He considered her, seemed a bit uncertain of her ability to handle the information he was about to give her and came to a full stop.

Sally stared at him, the bruises standing out on the chalk whiteness of her face. Purple, blue, a greenish brown. The doctor shook his head gently and started to turn away.

"Oh, please." Her sob almost hid the hiss of the words as she struggled to make herself heard through the constriction of wired jaws. "Don't go. I must know wh-what h-happened."

"He brought them back here, Sally." Maclean spoke as if he had an extremely unpleasant taste he could neither abide nor get rid of in his mouth. "Steve grew up here. Dave loved him. And his stepmother. They were a happy family until you came along."

"I—I interfered? Wh-what did I do?"

"You seduced them both, Sally. Father and son. Mrs. Rossi took Steve home to Italy. Dave's father lost his will to live. He died six months after you disappeared."

"It isn't true! It can't be true." She cried then, utterly shocked, but Maclean's expression was hard, implacable. The doctor's grimness left her in no doubt as to his feelings about the matter. He believed his story to be true. "Sorry, Sally, you did it. David damned near went stark raving mad. And for you to turn up now with Lang—well, it is a bit much. Keep it up, and Dave may make it to madness yet. No man would blame him if he did go bonkers."

He took pity on her then and sat back down. He retrieved her undamaged hand, held it lightly in one of his own. His impulsive action comforted the girl and eased a little of the tension that had mounted in her.

"It doesn't seem possible." Sally's hopeless comment rejected the information he imparted with such calm certainty. "It is such an inhuman way to act toward anyone. What had D—David done that I should treat him so?"

James Maclean shrugged, then turned as a sound diverted his attention. Rossi came back into the room. The rigid set of his lean body attested to the degree of restraint he was maintaining over his emotions.

He moved to stand at the foot of her narrow bed and stared down at her. His obvious rage electrified her; it charged through every nerve of her body with the jolt of high-tension shock. An avenging angel, dark and implacable! She flinched, meeting the withering bitterness of his scowl as she felt his iron self-control.

"You've told her, Jim." Tight-lipped, he wasted no words.

The doctor moved deliberately to place the little hand he had been stroking rather absently back upon the white coverlet. He stood and met the other man squarely. "Yes, I did, Rossi. Someone had to tell her she was your wife." David's brow shot up and emphasized his incredulity. Maclean read his doubt with a perceptive accuracy. "She did not know that, and it does not matter what you think. She does not remember the events that resulted in this hospital stay. She has amnesia, Dave. Total amnesia, I'm afraid. So go slow, man."

The warning fell on deaf ears. David had no need to express his disbelief. Sally recoiled from the flare of condemnation in her husband's black scrutiny.

"What rot! You disgust me, Jim! You should know better than most men with whom she acquainted herself that my sweet little Sally knows exactly what she is doing at all times. Her direction may be a dead secret as far as the rest of the world is concerned, but Sally always knows."

Maclean winced at the sneer but maintained his silence. David's laugh was a travesty that stripped the other man bare in some way Sally did not understand and appeared to leave the doctor defenseless as he shoved his curled fists into the pockets of his white coat. His eyes were glued frostily to his friend's disdainful countenance.

David Rossi did not notice. He contemplated the white-faced girl with utter revulsion written boldly on his handsome features. "When do you expect her to be able to remember who she is, and what she has done." His clear baritone cut as keenly as any sharp-edged instrument.

"Very little is known about amnesia, David. I can't answer."

"Can you help her, speed up her, er, recovery?" The laconic question taunted with a sure skill.

"David, you are making this very difficult." Maclean replied with some asperity. "I just don't know. Not my line at all. I am unable to tell you anything with any degree of certainty."

Rossi smiled coldly at the G.P. "Sorry, Jim. I'm a little hacked off. Not your fault, of course. Get the best man available up here, please. Find out what has to be done." He may have apologized for his lack of patience, but his resonant voice carried a leashed passion that sent a shiver down Sally's sensitive nervous system. She closed her eyes, opened them in silent appeal as he turned his attention back to her. "Fake or

not, you are going to tell me where you left my son, I
promise you. Even if you never remember another
thing of that misbegotten mess you call your life!''

"Take it easy, for Pete's sake," Maclean interrupted forcefully. "She is my patient and is under my
care. She isn't exactly off the critical list yet. No need
to frighten her to death."

Rossi appeared entirely capable of doing just that.
He stood at the foot of the narrow white bed and
gripped the end in lean hands, his knuckles white
with tension. Did he wish he had her neck between
them, Sally wondered. How he hated her!

"She will be a damn sight better off if she dies
from fright than if she dies because she tries to cross
me again." His casual remark was delivered with
such cold contempt that neither Sally nor Maclean
doubted David's sincerity. "You know damn well
she is capable of anything, Maclean. But forewarned
is forearmed." The cliché was delivered with an impact that lent the words a formidable sense. "I'm
ready for her winsome ways this time. And I mean to
have my son."

Sally was horror-struck at the power of the hate in
the man she had just been told was her husband.
"Please," the tortured word was wrenched from her.
"I am sorry."

The despair that he concealed under his disciplined
anger cut into her sensibilities and touched her deeply.
She reached out her uninjured hand to him in an instinctive gesture to help. "I can't tell you h-how terrible I feel. . . but I assure you that there is some awful
mistake. I am not your w-wife." She stumbled over
the word. "I don't know what you are talking about."

Rossi watched with a cool detachment as tears welled into the girl's deep blue eyes and tracked a path into the bruises that concealed her beauty.

"Very pretty, Sally." Utter disdain laced his observation. "But I don't buy it. Not this time. Nor will I ever again, so you can just forget your cunning kittenish tricks. This time you are going to answer to me for everything you do. Do you understand?"

"No, I do not!" Resentment at his tone, his attitude, came to her rescue. She dashed the tears from her eyes with her free hand and scrubbed at them with her doubled fist as a child would have done. "I neither understand nor believe the ghastly things you two are telling me. I may not be able to remember who I am, but I know I am not your wife. I could never have married anyone so hateful! Surely you must be a poor father not to recognize the mother of your own children. I am not she!" She was so upset that the words hissed through her teeth. She longed to be free of the restraint of the wires, to be able to shout down the arrogant man who hated her so.

David's bark of laughter cut as neatly as a lash. "You haven't seen yourself, my girl. Your own mother wouldn't know you, had she the misfortune to still be alive. But you are my wife. That much is obvious, unfortunately." Long fingers fished into the pocket of his fitted cords. "You were wearing this when the ambulance brought you in." He swung a chunky gold bracelet before her eyes. "Remember it? It belonged to my grandmother," he informed her curtly. "She gave it to you as a wedding gift."

Sally didn't remember a thing. "There has to be some mistake," she whispered faintly. She closed her eyes as weariness and unhappiness became paramount.

"Yes," the relentless man at the foot of her bed replied dryly. "A dreadful mistake has most certainly been made. You made it, my love, when you planned the business that brought you back here. This bracelet has been in the family for over two hundred years." He held it up as she looked at him. "The family crest has been engraved upon it. Of course, it could be a fake, a reproduction. But it isn't. I've had it checked. Not that I needed to, but I wasn't sure whether you might try to deny its authenticity. Then there's this." He extracted a shabby but official-looking leather-bound booklet from the inside pocket of his tailored suede jacket.

"Your British passport, my dear. All statistics duly recorded. Including the fact that you are married to an American. Me. Charles and Carla are included on it...." He flipped the water-damaged pages and found what he sought. "Here."

She took the booklet in nerveless fingers as he thrust it at her. The ink was blurred and all but unreadable, the photograph in it ruined.

"It's yours. There's no question about it, so you need not put on an act," he stated. "I've had the number traced. You used it; make no mistake about it." He stared down at her, with a tight face. "You left London the day before you had the accident, Sally. Carla was with you. And so was Don Lang. The FBI have been investigating and assure me there is absolutely no question about the fact that you were traveling with him. So where have you been these two years? I've had the best men in the world on your trail, and they were unable to trace you...or my children.''

Instinctively Sally knew he had not sought to find her but had only been interested in locating his children. She met his penetrating gaze and flinched from it wordlessly.

''Nothing to say? Damn you, you will talk if I have to choke it out of you.'' He towered over the bed. A dangerous light that threatened her very existence sparked in his implacable stare. ''Where is Lang now? Has he gone back to Charles? I know you did not bring my boy with you. Why not? Is he ill... dead? I swear to you, Sally, I will not be responsible for my actions if I find out you have let any harm come to the child!''

''I can't answer any of those questions,'' the girl on the bed whispered helplessly. ''I—I c-can only say I am not your w-wife.'' Sally felt numbed and beaten. She did not react as his contempt-filled dark examination wandered down her sheeted figure. ''You are very obviously my sexy little wife, Sally. There are quite a few men in this town who could attest to that, given the chance.''

His laugh chilled the girl. ''They won't get it this time, my love. You're coming home with me when you leave here. You'll go nowhere, see no one unless I'm with you. You won't move, won't breathe, that I don't know about it. Is that clear?''

''For God's sake, David....'' The protest died on Maclean's lips as Rossi swung his attention to the doctor. Black eyes glittered a challenge at the medical man.

''I mean it, Jim. She knows where Charles is. I

mean to find him. I'll live in her pocket until she gets sick to death of me. When she forgets whatever damned game she is playing and tells me where my boy is, I'll be more than happy to let her go." Again the girl felt the full impact of his rage and dislike as he looked back down at her distressed white face. "Once I have Charles back, any damn man in the country can have her, and welcome." He made no attempt to disguise the deliberate insult in his words. "I don't want her."

He left then. With a muffled curse Maclean followed him from the room, his expression grim and purposeful.

Sally closed weary eyes and drifted into sleep in spite of the chaos that raged in her aching skull.

OVER THE NEXT TWO WEEKS Sally adjusted to the hospital routine.

Days came and went. Her bones knit to Maclean's satisfaction. The swollen bruises gradually subsided. Her broken ribs healed, and the headaches disappeared. She welcomed the advent of physical therapy and lived for the day her jaws would be released from the wires that bound them.

"Carla is to go home today." Marion stuck her head into the room and made the announcement. Sally liked Marion and had begun to value her as a friend. It was Marion who carried news of the child to her every day. "She will be getting dressed in an hour or so. David will be here to pick her up. Would you like to see her before she goes? I think I can arrange it."

Carla was in the children's wing of the hospital.

Sally had not been permitted to make the trip across to the children's section. Not that she would have gone. She was convinced that the sight of her battered face would only dismay the small person who was her daughter.

And so she grimaced now and shook her head. "I'm afraid she wouldn't understand the reason for my wired jaws. I think it best if I wait and see her when I resemble a human being," she murmured, regret in her clear eyes. "I don't want to give her nightmares." Marion laughed and vanished.

So David would be here to pick up their daughter. It was quite natural that he should, of course. He no longer came to visit her or to sit silently by her bedside as he had when she was unconscious. The only times Sally saw him were when the psychiatrist, John Mellon, was scheduled to see her.

Mellon was a specialist whom David had enticed up from San Francisco on Maclean's recommendation. He came twice a week and stayed for an hour each time. David Rossi always appeared with him. He would follow the doctor into the room, take the same chair in the quiet corner where he was out of Sally's line of vision and sit without speaking while Mellon asked the questions that probed gently and did not disturb.

Sally was sure David listened intently to her answers and her own questions to the doctor, but he never spoke or interrupted in any way.

Mellon always asked if she would prefer to see him alone and to have David wait outside. He assured her she could speak to him in complete privacy if she wished to do so.

Sally, without knowing why, knew she wanted David in the room; she wanted him to listen to the doctor, to her. In a vague way she hoped he would be able to evaluate the exchanges between herself and the psychiatrist and know that her claim to loss of memory was valid. Why it might be important that he realize this was a question that she did not ask herself.

David's attitude did not relax. His black eyes hard and implacable, he studied her bruised face as it returned to normal. His lean face was always emotionless, unreadable, except when his handsome mouth would twitch in an unrestrained sneer when Sally stumbled with uncertainty over details she should have known.

Sally felt his censure but ignored him as much as she was able. She concentrated on the recovery of her memory. That memory contained all the years of her life up to the present, as well as the mystery behind her husband's scornful rejection of her. She had a growing urgency to know the facts. She hoped that she would not be so defenseless once she knew the exact nature of her relationship with the dark and menacing male to whom she was married.

The girl was not greatly encouraged by her progress. As far as she was able to determine, she had made none. She remembered nothing. Regardless, David sat through each session, left when the doctor left. He made no comments in Sally's hearing.

Mellon was not scheduled to see her today. David had probably arranged to take Carla home today so the child would not have to be deprived of his presence on her first day away from her hospital bed.

Sally knew from things Marion had said in the past days that David was devoted to the child. He had cut Sally from his visiting list, but he never let a day go by without a visit to his daughter.

He did care about his children. Sally turned this small insight into his personality over in her mind. If he cared so much, why had she left him and deprived him of all access to them? Somehow a part of her rebelled at the idea that she had done such a thing. And yet, she had if James Maclean and David himself were to be believed. She did not doubt they were to be.

She worried away at the thought, then glanced up when someone entered the room.

An absolutely breathtaking specimen of manhood stood just inside her door. Tall and tanned, his blue eyes sparkled in a face of perfect proportion. Blond hair waved crisply away from his classic forehead and touched the open sports collar of a blue knit shirt that set off his coloring to perfection. His black cashmere sports jacket fitted wide shoulders and hugged his lean waist. Long legs were encased in trousers of a pearly gray that had the look of being part of him. A faint aura of aggression clung to him. He caught her astonished inquiry, then winked. His teeth flashed in his brown face. A long dimple flicked in his left cheek in a manner that was meant to demand instant attention. He stood there and exuded sex appeal, waiting for her to acknowledge him.

Sally just stared.

"Hullo, Sally!" he said finally, smiling. "Sorry I haven't been in before. I've been away. In New York. I just got back. As soon as I heard you were here, I came. With a peace offering." He moved toward her then, and Sally noticed the violets in his hand and a gaily wrapped box. "Violets, to match your eyes, candy to match your sweetness." He held them out.

"Scarletti!" The stranger whirled to face the menace in David Rossi's harsh exclamation. "Get the hell out of my wife's room."

Fists clenched at his sides, rigid with threat and a suppressed rage, David Rossi glared at the other man as he resisted an obvious desire to hurl himself at Scarletti.

"Coming on a little strong there, aren't you, old buddy?" The handsome man's insolence was pointed. "Since when did you give a damn who Sally sees, or what she does?" He turned a brazen shoulder on Rossi's smoldering anger and sauntered to Sally's bedside with a lazy grace. Laying the box upon the astounded girl's sheet-covered lap, he lowered incredible lashes over one blue eye in a distinctly provocative manner.

Sally shrank back against her pillows, confused and aghast. "Who are you? Why are you here?" the exclamation hissed through her clenched jaws as her eyes flew to David.

He reached her side in two strides. Long fingers scooped up the offerings resting on her, hurled them from the room. She heard the distinct thud as the gifts careered off the opposite wall with a spanking thump and fell to the floor.

"Get out, Scarletti, before I kill you." The hoarse dictum sounded as loud as a shout to Sally. "I'll tell you just this once. Never let me catch you around my wife again.''

The other man assessed the wild light in Rossi's dark scowl and shrugged. He settled his black jacket over his attractive frame, spread long fingers wide in a placatory gesture. ''Sorry, Dave. Didn't realize there had been a change in priorities. Bye, Sally.''

Sally did not watch him go as she kept her attention riveted upon her husband. Rossi stood there, his hands clenched into hard fists. His breath was ragged in his throat, the labored sound that of a man who has run a long way or suffered in an activity that required a tremendous expenditure of energy. His skin had the appearance of being drumhead tight, pulled over the high cheekbones and stretched to the limit. A white line circled his thin drawn mouth. He looked to be what he was—a dangerous man, pushed almost beyond self-control. An awesome sight indeed, and one that caused Sally's weakened limbs to tremble, much to her disgust.

''Who was that?'' She gripped the smooth bed cover in a desperate effort to still the tremor that caused her hand to quiver.

''Just one of your more obvious indiscretions, my love,'' he grated at her, his breath whistling through his teeth as he spat his detestation at her. ''One of the many you are finished with as long as you remain my wife! Did you send for him? Ask him to come and hold your hand?''

His expression was corrosive with abhorrence and disgust. Sally winced at the implication he sneered at her. She knew of nothing to say in her own defense and remained silent, but nausea rose in her like a tide.

What had she done? The inner cry was almost a sob that she instinctively and sternly repressed. It would not do to show the strong individual who towered over her that he had the power to hurt, to shred her sensibilities and leave her powerless. She willed herself into rigid control to face him with a white set face. "I don't even know who he is," she managed with a taut hauteur. "How dare you speak to me so, accuse me of. . . of unspeakable behavior!"

"At least, we are in agreement on that," he ground out. "Your behavior was unspeakable, but we are going to speak of it from now on, aren't we, Sally?" He swooped suddenly to lean over the bed, his long arms draped over the short rails down each of the bed's sides. "And as long as you are my wife, that behavior is going to be impeccable from now on. Isn't it?"

He was unbearably close, the heat from his body spreading over her like a mantle. Devil fires leaped in those black eyes so near to hers. Sally moaned softly and shut out what she saw by lowering her thick black lashes. David touched her face then, his fingers surprisingly gentle.

"Poor little Sally." The derision was underlain by the hint of some other emotion the girl could not define. She opened her eyes to catch it, but a shutter closed in his and masked any spontaneity in a bland opaqueness. He observed her a moment with the intentness of a marauding animal who has spotted his next victim. Sally shuddered again in spite of her attempt to control her warring nerves.

"I want to make it very clear to you, Sally." The resonant dictate spelled it out for her. "While you remain my wife. . . while I don't know what you have done with Charles. . . you will have no one in your life but me. I am sure you will find this distasteful. You may rest assured such a program is bound to try my patience to the limit." He straightened with a sigh. "But I have made up my mind, and there it is." He had no need to tell her how much he was going to hate the program he had just outlined for himself. His attitude told her quite clearly of the sacrifice it required. He went to the door and paused on the way out. "I am going to take our daughter home. I just came to let you know."

He was gone then, that willful arrogant individual who had it within his power to shatter her peace and leave her personality in shreds with the withering force of his hate for her. Sally's despair was intense. She was sure David Rossi held her destruction in his hands. She was not sure whether his control of his feelings was going to be strong enough to prevent that destruction.

Who was the man named Scarletti? Why had he come to see her? Perhaps if she found the answer to those questions, it might help. She asked Marion the next time she saw her, but the friendly young nurse did not know the man.

"I've only been here eight months, Sally," she apologized. "Shall I ask someone who knows more about the people around here?"

"No, please don't bother." Sally had a distinct intuition that she had no wish to stir sleeping dogs. "Leave it, Marion. I will ask David the next time he comes."

David did not come with him when next Dr. Mel-

lon came into her room. Sally had a troubled conversation with the man but really learned nothing about
Scarletti and his relationship to her or to David. He
knew nothing of her background and was not the
least inclined to allow it to worry him, it seemed to
her.

The next week the orthodontist appeared. Alan
Stern, the plastic surgeon, was at his heels. The
orthodontist nodded to Sally and smiled cheerfully.

"Hallo!" Sally's greeting was laced with happy
anticipation. Marion had teased her earlier about her
release from the imprisoning wires.

The nurse winked at Sally now as she pushed the
small trolley filled with sterile instruments into the
room, moving smartly to the doctor's orders. David
followed the nurse in.

Sally felt her pulse quicken at his unexpected appearance. He scowled at her before propping his long
frame against the wall at the foot of the bed. Out of
the way, he folded his arms across his broad chest
and watched the proceedings with a thoughtful
frown.

Sally stared at him a moment. Depression set in as
the orthodontist prepared an injection to numb her
jaws. He and Stern engaged in a lively technical discussion, treating her as if she were an inanimate object
in which they were interested. Sally paid no attention
to them. Her mind centered on David Rossi. He had
the ability to numb her whole being with that chilling
attitude of his. She acknowledged the fact glumly and
wondered how she was to deal with him when the time
came for her to leave the sanctuary of her hospital
room and go home with him.

The thought very definitely was one that frightened her. He seemed so hard, so cruel, so set on revenge for actions she found it impossible to recall. It was very clear to her he did not believe her inability to remember the events that made him so bitter toward her.

Where would it all end? She looked at the hard face of the man who leaned against the wall and gave up. She would just have to wait and see what the future brought. One thing she did know for sure. It held David Rossi.

Sally sighed, closed her eyes and shut out the sight of his entirely forbidding face. She concentrated upon the exchange of lighthearted banter between Marion and the two medical men, and the rumble of Stern's staccato explanation of how he expected to repair her damaged features.

The doctors moved with skill and economy of motion. They were both well pleased with the manner in which she had healed. Sally could not feel a thing. She found she was unable to utter a sound as a result of the local anesthetic administered to her. The wires were removed and dropped into the wastebasket.

At Stern's command she opened her eyes. He had scattered three large photos across her sheeted figure. Taken at different periods of time, apparently, they were different studies of a girl of breathtaking beauty.

The perfect bone structure was classic. The pansy-blue eyes were enormous. Wide apart, they were seductive, secretive. Fringed with thick and curling black lashes, they invited, offered, enticement. Perfect strokes of black brow winged over those eyes and

set them off beautifully. Her mouth was a flawless
invitation to be experienced. Blond hair that con-
trasted oddly with the smutty darkness of eyebrow
and lashes escaped the confines of the differently
shaped French knot she wore in two of the photos
and made a charming frame for the lovely face. In
the third picture the hair was loose and curled upon
the white shoulders and slender neck in an open invitation to be touched, stroked.

Sally inspected the pictured beauty. Incredulous,
she finally realized they must be of her. She shot a
glance at David. He was quiet as he watched her with
the intentness of an animal of prey about to pounce
upon his chosen victim. He met her glance with cold
contempt. Sally felt anger rise within her and tore her
eyes from his cynical features. How on earth was she
to deal with the man?

"It's not as bad as I thought it might be," Stern
told her. "I will have to do a moderate amount of
reconstructive work, but I think I can assure you the
results will be satisfactory."

Unable yet to speak, she nodded at him, her thanks
in her eyes.

"Daniel has removed all your wires. You should
find your voice again as soon as the anesthetic wears
off a bit. If Jim agrees," he added as the man in
question came through the door, "I am of the opinion you can go home. Is that okay with you, Maclean?"

Maclean gathered the photos up, a faint regret reflected in his rugged face. He glanced at his impassive
friend who remained propped against the wall. "Perhaps by the middle of the week. She still has a little

way to go with her physical therapy. It's a long way into town from Las Colinas. David will find it more convenient if he doesn't have to bring her in every day. Right, Dave?''

As Rossi nodded brusquely, Sally's heart lurched in a frantic disavowal of the fate in store for her. Rossi met the dismayed glance she sent him with one of quiet hostility.

"I'll need to take one of those profiles and the full-face photo with me so I can study it." Stern took the two pictures he wanted from Maclean. Maclean left the other on the bedside table as he made ready to accompany the two specialists from the room.

"Goodbye, Mrs. Rossi. See you the first of the week, David." Stern nodded his farewell to Rossi, then pushed the door open for Marion to leave.

The young orderly who cared for the room took advantage of the opened door and popped quickly past the doctors and the nurse. They stopped and watched with amused eyes as the young man paused, swept down in an elegant exaggeration of a courtly bow. He held a small crystalline vase that contained one perfect red rose in his fingers.

"My lady! Rumor has it that you are released this day from durance vile." He held out the rose with an extravagant gesture that was endearing. "With this token I pledge to you—"

He got no further. Lean fingers plucked the vase from his hand. Light sparkled on water and glass as the delicate object flew in a perfect arc to shatter in the wastebasket in the corner.

The boy flushed an angry red and faced the man who now towered over him, with about the same effectiveness of a bantam rooster bracing a dark and dangerous eagle. "Hey! What do you think you are doing, turkey?"

"My wife is not allowed to accept gifts from other men."

The cold statement froze out all argument. The orderly stiffened, shot a glance at Sally's shocked face and wilted. He left. Marion and the doctors vanished with equal discreetness.

Sally knew a rage such as she had seldom felt. She was consumed by a passionate desire to spring at the derisive man who stood and challenged her. She knew then that she hated him. She started to scramble out of bed, her intention clear. David caught her and thrust her back without hurting the arm that was still in the cast.

"I mean it, Sally. No man will give you gifts this time." He flung back that handsome head of his in an imperious manner as he looked down his aristocratic and arrogant nose at her. "Get back in bed."

Sally's glance was meant to wither. She pushed away his hands as they brushed the slender shape the filmy gown she wore did little to conceal. "Mel is just a boy." Even with her numbed vocal cords she managed to inject a fair degree of scorn into the whispered words.

"Since when did that make a difference to you?" Rossi flung at her sarcastically. "He's male. Males try to please you for one reason only, Sally." Icy contempt filled his expression as the girl stared at him. "No male will have the opportunity to please you this time until you tell me where I can find my son. Make up your mind to that, you little witch.

After I have Charles, I don't give a damn what you do. You are free to go to hell in your own way. You won't be around one minute longer than it takes to get you out of my sight, out of my hair." He released her and he was gone. Sally cried then, tears of rage and frustration that burned down her cheeks and left her weak.

Marion came back, took one look at her wet face and sat beside her. She tutted gently as she put a comforting arm around her thin shoulders and hugged her.

"Men are hell, aren't they?" she offered softly. "What was eating Dave? He bit my head off as he stormed out of here."

The girl only sobbed, her throat constricted with anger, her mind dulled with unhappiness. There seemed to be no way of understanding the hate and bitterness that ruled her husband and made him so cruel.

CHAPTER THREE

THE NEXT SATURDAY the cast was removed from Sally's arm. Late in the afternoon Marion came with an armload of expensive clothing.

"Lucky you. These are for you to put on." She draped wispy silk underthings and fragile hose across the bed. Holding against her waist a well-tailored skirt that fell in a swirl of pleats, she danced around the room.

"I'm being discharged?" Maclean had not visited her today and had said nothing about her release on Friday.

"Yes. It's all been arranged. That gorgeous hunk of man to whom you are married awaits without." Marion chuckled. "Without much patience, I'm sorry to say. So on your feet, Sally. Never keep a handsome man waiting." The irrepressible nurse's sigh was melodramatic. "Some people have all the luck. It must be wonderful to have a man like that adore you. How about trading him to me for this?" And she held out a fluffy little feather she picked up from the bed.

"A feather?" Sally laughed in spite of herself.

"Absolutely." Marion's grin was roguish. "Then we'd both be tickled. Me with David. You with your feather."

They laughed together and went about the task of getting Sally ready to accompany her husband. The girl recognized the nurse's attempt to lighten the depression caused by the news of her release from the hospital, and she did her best to respond to Marion's cheerful banter.

"Lost some weight, haven't you?" The comment called her attention to the fit of the obviously expensive pleated skirt in a lovely cream silk that she had just zipped over the amber silk of the demure blouse that went with it.

Sally pushed a slender hand into the waistband of the skirt, pulled a wry face. "It seems I have." She thrust silk-clad feet into slippers the same color as the blouse, then gave some attention to her hair in the room's small mirror.

Marion reached to take the hairbrush from her. "Not yet, Sally. That scalp of yours isn't ready to be brushed." She flipped it back into the small leather case she had carried into the room along with the clothes the girl was now dressed in. "You have beautiful clothes, Sally."

Sally looked down her sleek and very expensively clothed length. Her smile was wistful. "This is nice," she agreed quietly. "I just wish I could remember when I bought it." She sighed and reached into the case. Selecting a lipstick from the array of cosmetics contained on the tray, she turned to the mirror to apply a touch to her soft mouth. She tossed her hair back, ran her fingers through the springy golden brown curls. She shaped them into a cap, neatly covering the patch where her scalp had been shaved bare. Short hairs, prickly to her touch, had grown in there.

"Thank goodness my bald patch is growing back." She caught Marion's eye in the mirror, and her mouth curled in a rueful grin. "Leaves a little to be desired, doesn't it?" Sally gestured at the mirrored mess of her face.

"You are a raving beauty compared to the way you looked the night you were brought in." Marion laughed. "And it was worse the next day. Ugly wasn't the name for it, my girl. More in the order of hideous, I'd say."

Sally giggled, eyed her bruised and scarred face with a good deal of equanimity. "Dr. Stern's little repair job hasn't seemed to help much, has it? Just added a new dimension to the mess, I'd say. I hope he knows what he's doing."

"He does indeed," Marion assured her. Alan Stern had appeared three days earlier to begin the first of the series of operations meant to restore Sally's features. The process would take several months, and she was to undergo a number of sessions of facial surgery. "He has a wonderful reputation," Marion went on. "If there is anyone around who can get you into your former state of pristine loveliness, he's the man."

"I'll be happy if I just look human," Sally assured her. "I really am sort of hideous right now."

"You do yourself an injustice," Marion protested. "Your bone structure is obvious. You are quite pretty just the way you are."

Sally considered her reflection a moment. A slender, slightly misshapen small oval contained wide apart dark blue eyes set under the intriguing arch of black brows. Smudged and thick lashes swept upward and gave her expression a wide-eyed innocence. High bruised cheekbones set off a soft but determined chin that was also discolored and out of round. Gold brown curls fluffed over her forehead and grew down the nape of her slender neck. Her whole appearance was slightly off balance, out of alignment in some way.

"Wonder what I really looked like before the accident? Photographs are so deceiving."

"You were gorgeous." David's flat statement caused Sally to jerk around. He leaned against the door frame, a thoughtful scowl stamped in position. "I'm surprised you can joke about it. Hysterics are more in order if your former reactions about any minor change of appearance can be used as a guide."

"There is little one can do but joke under the circumstances." Sally felt her increased heartbeat and a rising warmth in her cheeks. Hateful man! She turned her back on him, unwilling for him to see how his caustic attitude hurt.

"Coping with circumstances has never been one of your strong points, my love," he said sarcastically. "But who knows? Perhaps your self-imposed exile has developed some laudable facets of your personality."

"Perhaps!" she snapped as her blood boiled at the challenge of his raw dislike. "Don't count on it." She fought her temper and turned to Marion to arrange a luncheon date. They agreed to meet the day she came in to see Maclean for a follow-up.

"You get on well with Marion." The flat comment quite obviously denied the existence of such a possibility. Sally threw a sharp glance at the dark face of the man whose powerful arm held open the glass door of the hospital entrance.

"Certainly!" she answered with some asperity as she followed his lead to the low-slung sports car parked under the entrance canopy. "Why ever would I not? She is a lovely person." He helped her in and closed the door before she read his expression.

"I know that. I'm just surprised you do." He crossed to his side, lowered himself into the bucket seat and slammed the door.

"Oh!" Sally turned in exasperation from the cynicism expressed in hard black eyes. "You are an impossible man. I find it very difficult to...to like you!"

"Do you?" Long fingers triggered the powerful car into life. "That's not so odd, really. I don't recall that you ever did like me."

"You must be joking!" Sally turned to blink at him in startled disbelief. "Surely one does not marry a man one does not like?"

"Ordinarily, no, I suppose not." His haughty contempt cut at her. "But you did. And to my everlasting damnation, I allowed you to—no—I begged you to do it."

Completely astonished, Sally stared at him. His unpleasant laugh seared her nerves and set off a charge of adrenaline in her system.

He changed gears and shot into the traffic with competent ease.

"I don't understand you!" The protest wrenched from the girl as he made no attempt to explain. He laughed again, the sound rough as it grated on her nerves, cut into her poise.

"Bravo! You are playing the part beautifully, my love," he sneered. "Haven't missed a trick so far. If I wasn't so well acquainted with your ability at dissembling, I might even be convinced you were actually suffering from amnesia. But your record is too long and too well remembered for me to buy it, Sally. I know you are up to something. I'm just waiting for the ax to fall."

The contempt on his strong and handsome face left Sally without a word to say. There was nothing she was able to think of to refute his judgment. "Is it possible to humor me?" she ventured mildly. "You can pretend I really don't know what you are talking about and tell me, can't you?"

He laughed then, a resonant sound of real amusement. "Better and better, Sally. Of course, I won't tell you. Why should I spoil the whole effect of your masquerade, ruin your final act, whatever it may be." The big car glided down the shaded avenue, answered a deft twist of the wheel and accelerated as they left the town on a highway that curved as it climbed.

"I am convinced you have hidden Charles for some reason of your own. I suspect it has to do with money. Since our arrangement about finance proved to be inadequate in the task of satisfying your mercenary little soul last time, I expect the attempted bite to really shake me when you get around to making the pitch. How much are you asking for my son, Sally?"

Sally did not believe what she heard. "You mean you think I am about to ask you for money in exchange for information about where your—" she stumbled over the word, remembered it was her child, too "—our child is?"

"What else?" This time his laugh was not amused. "Why else do you suppose you came back to this country with Don Lang?"

Sally sat in stunned silence as he overtook a large tanker and swept the car into a tight curve. The white safety posts supporting the protective rail blurred before her eyes. The curve straightened, the powerful car climbed. The smooth growl of the motor filled Sally's head and interfered with her scattered thought processes. All the implications of his caustic question bounced around in her mind.

Rossi cast a cruel glance at her and took in her sudden lack of color. His handsome mouth thinned. "Where is Lang hiding? Is Charles with him, Sally?" Long hands, the knuckles white and knotted, tightened on the steering wheel. "I'm not going to pay you a penny, you know." The terse words hit at her like blows.

"What are you planning to do, David?" His glance caught hers. Devil fires danced in his black eyes as his hate flared at her from his set face. Sally repressed a shudder, shrank from him.

"If I find Lang and find he has Charles, I will cripple him for life if I can control my desire to kill him." Unquestionably he meant what he said. As Sally stared at his hard profile, she knew him to be capable of doing exactly that to Lang. He felt her shocked inspection and leveled an angry glance at her. "And I shall see to it that your bread of life is kept from you, you little nympho. No men, Sally. Not a single one until you tell me what I want to know."

The girl had been shocked before. She was stupe-fied now. She stared at the hateful man at her side, distaste as bitter as gall in her mouth. "What is that thing you called me?" She knew before she asked that she had no wish to hear the answer but was un-able to stop the question.

His face tightened as his lips thinned. He turned his head then and looked at her. "A nymphomaniac, my dear Sally, is a woman who suffers from a sexual hunger that cannot be appeased by any ordinary man or by any ordinary means. Mellon tells me it is a real disease and must be treated as such. You had no in-clination to have yours treated." His black eyes stabbed into hers, tore at her defenses. "I was unaware of your proclivities when we met. By the time your actions had really spelled them out for me, it was too late. I had married you and brought you home."

Sally felt her breath gag her. She put her hands up to her face, touched it with disbelief. It was her skin. She could feel it and the bone structure underneath. It felt cold, clammy. But it was undoubtedly hers, and she was undoubtedly sitting here in this powerful automobile that was sweeping up the climbing curves of a beautiful mountain road. Into what kind of a nightmare situation was the pitiless man beside her taking her? How could he accuse her of such rotten-ness and still associate with her?

"You are saying I—I am a n-nymphomaniac? How awful! It is not true. It cannot be. You. . .you are horrible!"

"Not horrible, Sally. Just factual. You go through men with the same ease a hot knife goes through butter. Anything is grist for your mill as long as it wears trousers. Except the rules have been changed for this little caper of yours. I warned you in the hospital. No men until I know where Charles is hidden. None at all until I have him back at the ranch.''

Sally's disbelief was naked in her dazed eyes as she fastened them onto his uncompromising profile. ''You mean you l-let me go to other m-men while I was. . . while I am—'' She came to a halt in utter confusion. She was unable to force the word ''married'' through her stiff lips.

''Part of the bargain, Sally.''

His contempt was blistering. She could not make out whether it was directed at her or at himself. A little of both, she suspected. His mouth closed like a trap. He did not explain.

''What bargain?'' she ventured finally. Surely he did not mean to leave it hinted at, only half-said.

''That's all I'm saying. You know the answers. Supply them and stop this fool thing you are trying to do. Because I can assure you it is not going to work.''

Sally found herself close to tears. She turned from him and stared out the window at the rugged mountainside.

As they neared the crest of the mountain, he pulled the big car over into a cleared space cupped into the rocky shoulder that towered above them. He stopped the car, levered his long length out of his seat and went around to open Sally's door.

''Come along.''

''Why? Where are we?'' Bewildered, she could not take in his abrupt change of attitude. She stared at him in mute rebellion.

"You'll see. It's an experiment I've talked over with Mellon. He agrees it cannot harm you to try it. Over here."

His long fingers reached for her. His hard hand on her elbow insisted that she accompany him. Sally took a quick look at his determined expression and went with a murmur of protest. The lean brown hand wrapped around her slender arm and guided her across the deserted road to the edge of the vertical rock face that dropped abruptly to the streambed far below.

Sally cast a frightened glance downward, cried out as if she were wounded and collapsed at his feet in a dead faint.

CHAPTER FOUR

GLARING YELLOW EYES lit by the fires of hell threatened to engulf her. The terrifying hiccup of the animal's cry rang in her skull.

Sally sobbed in mindless terror. She burrowed into the comfort of the arms that encircled her in her effort to escape the nightmare of the attack.

She came back to consciousness to the echo of her own scream. David, down on one knee, held her quaking body in strong arms. His startled expression was a mixture of dismay and gentleness as he stroked her quivering form in an attempt to reassure her. He pressed her head into the curve of his solid shoulder, his hand spread across the back of her head, and uttered quiet soothing words.

The girl trembled, then gulped in a great lungful of air. She found herself comforted by the strong and steady beat of the heart under her cheek and the warmth of the arms holding her so surely. Her fingers clutched at him, held him close.

"What did you remember, Sally?"

The girl shuddered and was suddenly conscious of his supporting arms, the lean and very hard leg she was resting against. She straightened and pulled herself away from him.

"I beg your pardon." Her bruised and frightened

face was as white as the handkerchief she accepted from him. "I do apologize for making a fool of myself. I am not in the habit of fainting."

"Are you not, Sally? How do you know? And why did you faint this time?" The quiet command demanded an answer.

Sally swallowed convulsively and gathered her scattered forces as her nervous hands smoothed down her rumpled skirt with an odd primness. She wiped the faint sheen of moisture from her face, returned his handkerchief. "I am not sure how I know, but I don't think I faint all that often," she informed him with a quiet dignity. She took in his watchful aspect and was sure she had imagined that look of gentleness he had worn as she returned to consciousness. She pushed to the back of her mind an unexpected desire to see him look at her like that again. "I looked over the edge and saw an animal," she told him. "It was a horrid animal who glared at me and tried to pounce on me. It had yellow eyes. Huge ones."

"Interesting...." His polite murmur challenged her. "I saw nothing like that as I looked over." He rose lithely from his squat and brought her to her feet as he did so. He dropped a casual arm around her waist and turned her to face the sheer lip of the deep canyon.

"You and Carla were found on the ledge down there. The car you were driving is in the riverbed, a burned-out wreck." His spare hand indicated the shelf upon which she and the child had been found. It was a breathtaking distance below the lip of the canyon. The river sparkled far below as it wound through the trees and scrubby undergrowth that bordered its rocky banks.

Sally risked a brief glance downward, then swayed back into his steadying hold with a gasp she could not prevent. David shifted his grip to her shoulders in order to examine her wide and fearful eyes intently.

"I understand the reaction that caused you to faint, Sally. Mellon warned me you might have some sort of response to the site of the accident. Some part of your subconscious recalls the details you profess to have no memory of. You really screamed, you know. Why do you think you did that? Don't lie, Sally. Tell me."

"I don't know...." Wetness sparkled on her lashes as she shook her head. "I was frightened...."

He considered the white oval of her face, black eyes piercing. "A small overnight bag was found on the ledge with you, Sally. Your passport escaped, too. But everything else burned with the car." He watched her carefully. The girl sensed he expected to see some sort of reaction to the information he was giving her but she just stared at him in confusion. Impatient, he shook her lightly.

"Very convenient that everything burned in the wreck, wasn't it, Sally? And how do you suppose the small suitcase that just happened to have recent pictures of Charles in it escaped the same fate? Why wasn't it in the trunk of the car and burned with all the rest? Why was your handbag in the trunk? Why wasn't your passport burned? Surely it should have been in your handbag along with your personal belongings?" He gestured at the ground at her feet, his proud head moving in a tight arc. "I found it here, almost where we are standing."

"What are you saying to me?"

"I think I'm being set up, Sally," he returned tautly, dark eyes cruel and opaque with the bitter coldness of his thoughts. "I can't imagine what your plans were. But I'm sure on a gut level that the car went over the edge as part of a plan. Something misfired, and you were caught, hurt. You and Carla. How did you get caught in your own trap? You probably didn't give a damn about Carla, but I can't see you risking your precious hide."

Her face puckered, but she did not drop her gaze. She was mesmerized, caught in the trap of his powerful personality. "I don't know, David. I can't answer you." The words were wrenched from her. "How dreadful you are to believe I might risk my own child's life and not care."

He shrugged and released her, his hard mouth twisted in a caustic smile of dislike. "Okay, Sally." He turned to cross the road. "Let's go."

She followed him in a daze. Her mind refused to function as she allowed him to put her back into the car. He closed the door, went around and climbed into his own seat without another word.

He had not said anything when the car topped the crest of the mountain sometime later and glided down into the valley spread out beneath them on the opposite side. The beauty of the scene went unnoticed by the girl as she tried to sort out the confused state of her thoughts.

"I think you owe it to me to answer a few questions," she ventured. She fixed her attention on the stern profile of her husband and willed him to agree.

His quick glance held frosty amusement and a hint of reluctant admiration.

"I owe you nothing, Sally. And I refuse to play your game. You have all the answers locked in your scheming little head. Use them, for you will get none from me or from anyone else. Is that clear?"

The girl blinked away the tears over which she had no control. Her back stiffened with her own anger. In that moment came her resolve not to let this man break her.

His accusations clawed at her. They bit deep into her equanimity and threatened to destroy her sense of self. She had to accept that he believed himself justified in his attacks upon her, although her whole being rebelled against the things he threw at her with such overbearing certainty. Then her common sense came to her rescue. She did not question his belief in his assessment of her personality and her actions. He was so sure she had committed acts vindicating his attitude toward her. But what had he done to her to make such vengeful behavior viable in her mind?

Sally came up against the blank wall of her amnesia and felt stifled. Struggling with anger and frustration, she was blind to the beauty of the land through which the long sports car was being so skillfully guided. She was blind, also, to the watchful concentrated attention of the man at her side. Black eyes roved her profile, charted the change in her expression as she gave way to dejection over the untenable situation in which she found herself, then as she strengthened her resolve to fight back.

The big car rounded a curve, and the valley fell

away before them in a glory of russets, golds and browns, gentled by the autumn sunlight. Sally drew a swift breath of pure delight. "Oh, do stop," she exclaimed, enchanted. "Please stop the car."

As David applied the brakes, an expression of utter astonishment washed over his lean features. It was instantly replaced by a hard look of scorn. He guided the big car onto the shoulder of the road and cut the motor. Sally left the vehicle at speed, the door swinging unattended as she ran to the edge of the outlook. David shut the car door, followed her. His dark eyes were very thoughtful as they rested on her battered face. He could not mistake the pleasure reflected in it.

Sally leaned on the white-posted guardrail and drank in the beauty of the valley at her feet. A vast carpet of color rolled and flattened across the enormous stretch of the valley. It rolled its reds and crimsons, its golds and yellows, its dark bluish purples away from her in disciplined orderly swatches of glory bordered by the dark greens, browns and maroons of the trees that followed the streambeds and grew in the folds of the hills.

Far on the other side of the valley, the blue greens of conifers climbed slopes misted in gray. Somewhere below her a mockingbird burst into full-throated song, serenaded his heart out to the glow of the late sun. Puffs of clouds overhead caused the tapestry of the carpet to change with light and shadow as they moved in random order against the arch of the sky.

"It's so beautiful." The girl drew in a great lungful of the crisp autumn-scented air. "And it smells so good!"

With his expression masked, the man beside her

considered her. "The Indians who lived here before the white man came called it Ta-La-Ha-Lu-Si. The Beautiful Land." The explanation came from him reluctantly as if she were unworthy to know.

Sally did not notice his reserve. "Such a lovely name. Such a lovely place." Peace touched her like a benediction. She breathed deeply again, still unaware of the sharp attention she received from the man who stood behind her. "What is it that makes the perfectly beautiful color?"

Thoughtfully, David dragged his dark eyes from her glowing face and surveyed the vast vineyard that belonged to him. "Grapes, as if you didn't know, Sally. The grapes of Rancho Las Colinas de la Pantera. What have you done with your allergies?"

"Grapes?" She did not understand the question about allergies so she ignored it. "Do you mean all those beautiful patches are grapes?"

"Grapevines. You are looking at my vineyards." There was a touch of pride in his voice. "The grapes have all been harvested. The vines are resting now. As the weather changes after the harvest, the leaves of each will turn color according to the variety of grape the vine produces." His brief explanation was succinctly given, his voice hard with impatience.

"Which grape belongs to the exquisite purply blue?"

David followed the direction of her pointing finger with a bleak exasperation. "It is the Syrah. That's enough, Sally. I am a viticulturist and a wine maker. Is that one of the facts you have so conveniently forgotten? It is really useless for you to continue with this act of yours."

His bitter sarcasm cut into her pleasure in the loveliness of the land before her and jerked her back to the unpleasantness of the reality she had to face. She walked back to the car in a dignified silence, moving with a smooth grace that the man who followed her noted with a contemptuous disdain. The girl paused at the car door, took a last look at the panorama before her and sighed with the grandeur of it. "Thank you for stopping. I've never seen anything so glorious before." David closed her door with the polite attentiveness that seemed inherent to his personality, rounded the car and jackknifed impatiently into his seat.

"You've seen it all before, Sally." The statement was laced with a mocking indifference. "You just aren't choosing to 'remember.'" He sent the car down the looping highway, cast a curious glance at her incredulous countenance. "I must congratulate you upon your latest approach, my dear. It is almost a pleasure to hear you say something pleasant about the ancestral home for a change."

"You mean I've been here before and seen all of this?"

"Yes, my playacting little wife. You have."

"You are implying I did not like it before?"

"You hated it."

"That is impossible." She spoke with acrimony, sure the instinctive reaction that the sight of the beautiful valley had aroused was a true one. "I could never have hated any place as wonderful as this. I am sure I must always have had a positive response to such beauty."

Temper caused color to mount in her cheeks. Really, David was quite ridiculous. She realized at that moment that he was playing some sort of dark game with her, doing his best to keep her at a disadvantage. Well, let him get on with it. She would just ignore him and go on with her own life as best she could, she decided sensibly as she fought her temper down.

And as she did so, a resolve was born to do absolutely nothing to reinforce his low opinion of her. She would throttle her temper, do exactly as he asked her and keep out of his way as much as possible.

She would pray every day that her memory would come back so she could take his accusations and insinuations and throw them in his handsome teeth. Possibly she might then have the satisfaction of having him choke on them! There was no way they could be true. Sally turned her attention to the scenery and concentrated upon it. This allowed her to ignore the critical inspection of the dark eyes that raked her face.

David was thoughtful as he guided the car beneath the lofty arch inscribed with the legend Rancho Las Colinas de la Pantera.

"What does the name mean?" she asked. David bent a critical glance upon her as he detected the ring of genuine interest in her soft query.

"More lack of memory, Sally?" His smile mocked. She scowled at him, irritated, then remembered her resolve and smiled with a sweetness he did not miss. His mouth thinned as he recognized her change of tactic.

"Okay," he spoke irascibly. "The name is Spanish, not Italian. My great-great-grandmother was Spanish and heir to much of this valley. As my canny

Italian ancestor was well aware. He married her, and we have managed to keep it in the family since that time. The original land grant was large, and we have added to it since. Does that answer your question?''

"Yes, thank you.'' She directed a demure smile at him. Without a doubt, the imperious male beside her had shown very little softness, but she sensed his love for his land, his vulnerability where it was concerned. She wondered briefly if it might be possible to break down his icy disdain, his contemptuous hatred, through this, then dismissed the thought. She knew nothing of the land nor the art of the viticulturist. She sensed that any attempt on her part to try to learn would be met with scorn and disbelief by David. He would regard it as another ploy in the game he was positive she was engaged in. She sighed, cast a glance at him beneath lowered lashes. He was staring straight ahead, his face a bleak mask as he drove up the roadway between a stand of trees.

"You haven't told me what the ranch name means,'' she reminded him.

"Ranch of the Hills of the Panther.'' The reply was brusque, offhand. "We have always had our resident puma.''

They passed a private airstrip where a sleek executive jet rubbed shoulders with a glistening helicopter, rounded a long curve and pulled into the courtyard in an immense two-storied hacienda.

The courtyard was enclosed with large red-tiled sheds housing equipment used in the care of the vines to the far left. The adjacent garage contained two automobiles and a pickup truck. Directly in front of them a wise-eyed thoroughbred, watching them over the bottom section of a stall, whinnied softly as David left the car.

He opened her door and tossed his keys to the youngster who appeared from somewhere in the garage. He spoke to the boy in rapid Spanish, and received the flash of a sunny grin and a cheerful *sí* as he then took Sally's elbow to guide her toward the arched entrance that led from the courtyard to the patio of the hacienda.

Sally remembered her resolution not to antagonize the man and submitted meekly to the imperious hand on her arm. She went through the arch with him and stopped in utter delight.

The patio was paved with gleaming red tiles swept clean as any floor. Water danced in the late-autumn sunlight and was flung into the crystal air from the graceful central fountain. Flowers rioted everywhere, spilling from tubs and beds. They hung over walls and the delicate black fretwork of the banisters and trellises that were skillful accents to the pleasant lines of the buildings. Colorful baskets and pots swung from black chains. The vines and flowers in them tumbled in profusion and filled corners and arches of the veranda that encompassed the entire patio on both the ground floor and up a stairway to the story above.

A great hairy dog detached himself from the group of people who stood in the sunlight across the patio. The huge creature bounded across the tiles and launched itself at David in a happy greeting. David fended it off and ordered it to sit. Tongue lolling in a gay insouciance, the animal scooted close to Sally and butted his large head against her in a blatant demand to be noticed. Sally laughed and crouched down, her small face on a level with the huge beast's. The dog responded enthusiastically. Sally dodged and caught its collar, and escaped the moist tongue as the dog sought to administer a wet caress.

"Aren't you a pet!" she exclaimed. "What is his name, David?" she asked, glancing up. Her husband's dark features were a study. Nostrils pinched in, his mouth was set in a derisive sneer.

"What the hell are you playing at now, Sally?" The question was hard and accusing.

Wounded by his contempt, the girl forgot her vow not to arouse him for the moment. She jumped to her feet, battle ready. "How dare you use that tone to me?"

With black hostility David searched her upturned and aggressive little face, then shrugged. "The dog's name is Quito. We slightly altered the Spanish form of God forbid, which would have been Quita." He turned from her and snapped his fingers at the dog, who came to heel instantly to follow his master across the patio. "I might use the same term to you," he tossed back over his shoulder bitterly. "God forbid!"

Sally pelted after him and caught his arm. David stopped in his tracks and considered her confused wrathfulness with a blistering lack of concern. Quito sat down and watched them, his teeth showing in a grin of complete satisfaction.

"Just what are you getting on about?" The girl was prickly with indignation. "Why are you being so hateful?" If he did not give a damn about the interested spectators across the patio, neither did she.

She longed for a good fast argument, a chance to clear the air. If only she could once get him to talk about the trouble between them!

"Your ordinarily hysterical reaction to Quito's presence is well documented, my love." His black eyes were calmly attentive, but he had no intention of arguing with her, and his attitude made it clear. "There is no sense in wasting your acting talents. The present company will not be impressed. We all know you hate the dog." His hand turned her toward the little knot of people and compelled her along.

Hysterical reaction! What hysterical reaction? The girl skimmed a quick glance at the large animal cavorting at her heels, then glared up at the arrogant male who hustled her along. If only he were not such an obstinate person! Why had he become so determined not to answer her questions, not to let her defend herself?

The impossible man halted in front of the small group who awaited him.

The disapproval on the faces of those assembled by the steps to the veranda was a tangible force that cooled the warmth of the sunlight. They watched her as she hesitated to a halt beside David. Hostility reached out, engulfed her. The girl swallowed nervously and turned to the tall man beside her in mute appeal. David's black eyes swept down to assess her uncertainty. A smile flickered and turned his dark face into a mocking unreadable mask. He reached out and dropped a muscular arm about her slender shoulders in a gesture that did not reassure her.

"Ladies and gentlemen," his mockery deepened as he spoke. "My wife has been in an accident as you all know by this time. You will recognize her, but she will not be able to recall that she has ever seen you before." Derisive ridicule ran a lazy thread through the pleasantly deep voice. Sally felt her color rise as she heard his challenge to her claim to loss of memory. She nodded shortly, almost overcome with an urgent need to strike him, to wipe the disbelief from his dark face.

David, his eyes intent, read her thoughts and grinned. Impish mischief crinkled the corners of his eyes, altering his looks. Suddenly he epitomized pure devastating charm. Sally caught her breath and stared at him, conscious of the heartbeat that thudded in her ears in a disconcerting manner.

"She has come home and is mistress of my house once more," he continued smoothly. "It will please me if each of you make an effort to help her in any way you can as she tries to regain her memory. I'm counting on you." His black eyes pierced each member of the little group. The warning to them was subtle, but it was there. He expected them to accept her back, treat her as his wife. He would brook no insolence, no censure on their part, no matter how they might feel about her. His dealings with his wife were strictly his affair, and he meant it to stay that way.

His glance challenged them. The silent acquiescence he received to his unexpressed demand caused his charming grin to twitch at the corners of his mouth again. He nodded to them, then turned to his wife. "Come, Sally. We will go in to grandmama, then we must visit the office." Firm fingers grasped her elbow and steered her across to the wide double doors opening onto the veranda. He flashed a smile over his shoulder at someone she did not see as he reached the entrance. "Please come with us, Irma."

A slender dark girl in her middle teens detached herself and followed them through the door into the interior of the house.

Its graciousness was unexpected. As she followed the dictate of the iron grip on her elbow and allowed herself to be piloted across the luxurious entrance hall, Sally had little time to take it in. The entrance was impressive. It soared the two stories of the interior and was paneled with mellow wood that glowed with a patina of age and care. A graceful stair curved up to the balcony serving the rooms on the top floor. A domed ceiling lit the entry.

Sally moved at David's side, crossed the deep-piled carpet of mustardy gold that led through the arch opposite the entrance door and down a wide passage. She noticed the glass doors at the end of the passage, the huge swimming pool just beyond, nestled, jewel-toned, in the lush green of the lawn. The untamed mountainside foliage rose steeply from the lawns, forming a backdrop of spectacular beauty. There seemed to be flowers everywhere. In borders and beds, on the mountainside, as well, they spilled color with lavish carelessness.

Sally sighed with pleasure at the panorama. The little sound earned her a sharp scrutiny from her husband as he tapped quick knuckles against the oak of a closed doorway halfway down the passage. The girl took a swift gulp of air and, squaring her shoulders, marched in beside him as they were bidden enter.

They went into a small and exquisitely appointed sitting room. And dominating the room was the small and exquisite gray-haired person who was David's grandmother. Sally needed no introduction. The family resemblance was too strong to be mistaken.

She had the same fine black eyes under straight black brows penciled by the hand of a master. And there was the same proud classic nose in a very feminine version, but nonetheless just as arrogant. Her mouth was as beautifully shaped as his and was set almost as cruelly as she surveyed the girl at her grandson's side. Hair that had probably been as dark as his fell in vigorous and untamed life, curling where it would as it defied her attempt to confine it in a French roll at the back. Oh, yes. This petite woman in rustling black taffeta was definitely part of his family.

David turned, bade Irma wait and closed the door firmly behind them. Those relentless fingers maintained their grip on Sally's left elbow. He exerted enough pressure to propel his reluctant spouse across the room to the woman who waited with a still displeasure.

"You did not come out to greet us, *nonna*." David's comment was wry as he stooped to drop a kiss on the softly crumpled cheek.

"No, David, I did not." The old voice was accentless but had the intriguing lilt of one who had spoken another language as a mother tongue when she was young. "I did not wish to appear a hypocrite. I cannot welcome Sally home."

"*Nonna*, I have explained to you the conditions that make it necessary for Sally to be here." His stern declaration left no doubt that he expected his grandmother to agree to his decision to bring his wife home.

That lady's small chin jutted out as her face reflected firm disapproval. "Yes. It is your right to have her here. After all, this is your home, and you may do as you please." She gestured impatiently and continued quickly as though unwilling to be interrupted, "But I think it only right that Sally know exactly how I feel. She had caused you great unhappiness and brought unnecessary shame and disgrace upon you. You are my grandson, my family." Black eyes glittered as the old lady subjected Sally to the bitter frankness of her inspection. "She has robbed me of the pleasure of seeing my great-grandchildren, of knowing them as they grew. I am human. She cannot expect me to forgive her for what she has done. I will be civil to her as long as she is in your home. But I do not welcome her. She cannot expect that."

Sally looked into those hostile black eyes and knew in truth she could not expect more. There was sorrow in the depths of the older woman's gaze, but it was a fierce and proud sorrow. It condemned, sought to castigate. Humbled and unhappy in the awareness of the grief her selfish actions had caused, the girl's expression was softly contrite.

"I do beg your pardon, Mrs. Rossi," she whispered. "I am truly sorry my thoughtlessness has caused you so much pain. I understand, and I wish I could put it right."

They stared at her as she finished the little speech, the grandmother in a kind of startled disbelief as if she had never expected to hear such words from the young woman facing her, and David with a skeptical cynicism written clearly on his tanned face.

"I wish I could believe you." The older woman allowed her skepticism to color her voice. Her doubts that the person before her could actually regret an action were very clear indeed. She transferred her black eyes to the face of her grandson, the bleak look softening. "Have you decided to take my advice about Carla, David?"

Alerted by the tone of voice in which she spoke, Sally glanced upward and met her husband's eyes. He stared down at her a moment, his feelings masked.

"I have thought about it, *nonna*," he allowed. "But we both know Carla is dreadfully unhappy. Contrary to what you believe, I think Sally must see her and even take care of her if that is what Carla seems to want." He sighed and shook his head as a spasm of strong emotion caught at him.

"You were thinking of keeping my... my daughter from me?" Sally pulled her elbow from his restraint, faced him, her fists clenched at her sides. "How cruel! And how dare you? As the child's mother, I surely have the right to care for her!"

"You have no rights except those I give you." His reminder was irritable. He sounded tired all at once and sick to death of her. "I assure you, she will be watched every minute she is here, *nonna*. I will not give her the chance to disappear with Carla this time."

Mrs. Rossi was very clearly upset by this decision. "I have to disagree with you, but of course, you must do what you think best. You are generally right. I hope you will not regret this." She issued the reproach in her clear voice, then called to Irma. When the young girl entered, she asked her to go and have Carla brought to the sitting room. She sighed then and lowered herself into the high-backed upholstered wing chair, her penetrating black eyes never leaving the face of her grandson's wife.

Sally's thoughts tumbled about in her head as she tried to keep a tight rein on her emotions. How hard these people were, how implacable in their righteousness. To think they had considered keeping the child from her! And yet it probably seemed a natural reaction to them. Oh, what had she done to make them hate her so? To have taken the children and vanished was bad enough. Horrible, in fact. But she sensed that even this was only the tip of the iceberg, so to speak, the culmination of a series of things that damned her irredeemably in their eyes.

She stood quietly beside David, her eyes on the door, a sense of unbearable suspense seizing her as she heard the soft rustle of someone's approach. Her heart jolted painfully as she waited for the first glimpse of the daughter she was unable to remember.

Irma opened the door and stood there with the child in her slender arms. The little girl turned enormous black eyes, took one look at the adults who watched her so intently and struggled to get out of Irma's encircling clasp.

"Mum-mum!" she cried as she wriggled down. "Mum-mum!" She escaped from Irma and rocketed across the space toward Sally. Sally sank to her knees, her arms out to welcome the fragrant small bundle of humanity that hurtled toward her.

CHAPTER FIVE

SALLY CAUGHT the child's flying figure, cradled her in her arms. Her heart sank even as she crooned soft words of reassurance to the ecstatic child. She did not know the joyful bit of humanity, but there could be no mistake about the child's reception. Carla did know her and did love her.

God, she must really be David's wife! Since she had regained consciousness and been told she was married to the hostile tall man who was a stranger to her, she had been inwardly convinced it was all a mistake that would sort itself out, given time. Carla's instant recognition, her joyous greeting, put paid to her lingering hope that she was not married to David Rossi.

The child clung to her, wildly exultant to have found her beloved mum-mum. Sally choked back tears that were threatening to spill over. She was not sure whether those unshed tears were for herself, for her shattered hope that she was in no way connected with the man who stared so stonily down at the two at his feet, or for the happy little girl in her arms.

She smoothed curls exactly the same color as David's back from the flushed little face and kissed the child. As she glanced up, she surprised an expression of amazed incredulity on the soft and wrinkled features of David's grandparent.

David himself wore a masked look of coldness. Pinpoints of light flared in his eyes and challenged her to deny his assertion that she was indeed his wife, the mother of his children. She was also the woman he hated because of her treatment of him. The thought that he was more than justified in his attitude made her feel ill.

Sally hugged the squirming bundle of energy to her and rose to her feet. Her mind seethed with confusion. It was clear that the little child in her arms knew and loved her, and expected her love in return. And it was equally obvious the baby's eager reaction to her was a total surprise, at least to David's grandmother. The girl was not too sure of David's own response to the clear evidence of the child's love for her. He watched the interplay between them with a censorious expression in his black eyes. His face might have been carved of stone for all it gave away.

Sally extracted tiny fingers from her short curls and kissed them as she bounced the happy child in her arms. The little girl gurgled and settled happily into her arms. An absurd sense of happiness lit her own face. Carla loved her if no one else did. It made no difference to the baby that her mother did not remember her. Sally hugged the thought to her and glanced sharply at the tall man who frowned down upon her.

"Give the child to Irma, Sally. We must go to the office." He issued the command, then turned to his grandmother. "*Nonna*, has the new man shown up?"

The baby understood David's words and threw chubby small arms around Sally's neck and clung like a limpet.

"Yes, he is here." Mrs. Rossi's reply was interrupted by the child's wail of protest as Irma came close, her young features soft as she invited the baby to go with her. Carla screamed in protest.

"Mum-mum, mum-mum. Want mum-mum!"

"Irma, get that child out of here!" the older woman instructed harshly. "Sally, you must allow Irma to take Carla back to the nursery."

Sally backed away from Irma, her face determined. She held Carla with a gentleness that reassured the baby, then faced David as she crooned love to the little girl. "Don't allow her to be taken from me, David," she pleaded. "Can't you see she is afraid I will disappear again? She must have been terrified when she regained consciousness in the hospital. So alone and among strangers. Let her stay with me now. It may be very bad for her to have to be parted from me again. Please, David."

"It's impossible!" Mrs. Rossi spoke incisively. "You must go with David. He promised me! Carla will only be in the way."

Sally ignored the grandmother, kept her eyes fastened on David's.

He reached out a long finger, touched his daughter's cheek. "Ah, *piccolina*! Come to your daddy, *sí*?" He chucked the baby under her chin, and the charming smile that transformed his grim expression caused Sally's heart to do a disconcerting flip.

The baby refused to be deterred. She buried her hot little face against her precious mum-mum's slender neck, the pressure of her small arms interfering with Sally's breathing.

If David was chagrined at his firm rebuff, he hid it

well. He shrugged powerful shoulders and turned to leave the room. "Bring her along, then. You will have to mind her, keep her out of the way. We must go to the office."

Sally did not understand why her presence was demanded in the office, wherever that might be. It seemed much more logical for her to stay in the house, to soothe and comfort Carla here, rather than have the child deal with a completely new environment when she was obviously so distraught. She opened her mouth to say so, then closed it as David stopped at the door and turned around impatiently.

"Get a move on!" The instruction was imperious, arrogant. "I have a new general foreman I must confer with immediately." He held the door for her, and Sally went through it without a protest. She did not know why it was necessary that she accompany him, but she realized he had just made a compromise, and he did not feel the least inclined to compromise further.

They left the house, crossed the entrance patio and went into the courtyard where David had left his car. The car was visible in a stall of the garage. A four-wheel-drive vehicle awaited. David marched her around to the passenger's side, scooped her, child and all into his arms before she had an inkling of his intent and deposited her on the hard seat.

With no attempt at conversation, he drove the powerful small machine back down the road that curved in front of the hacienda to a left turning, then climbed another curving road before pulling up in front of a huge complex.

The buildings were massed together and screened

from view of the hacienda by a magnificent stand of conifers and the slope of the mountain shoulder. White and very utilitarian-looking, they hummed with activity. The large parking lot to the left and down slope was full of vehicles of various types. The mountains rose sharply directly behind the buildings and so close that they towered over them with a sense of brooding presence.

David came around to Sally and held up his arms. "Let daddy carry you, Carla. Come, *cara mia*."

The child looked down at the man whose dark eyes matched her own, decided he did not mean to separate her from her beloved mum-mum and went to him. He kissed the curls on the top of his baby's head while his imperturbable gaze fastened on Sally. She blushed under that keen inspection, tossed her head in irritation at her response and climbed nimbly down from the high seat.

THE DAY PASSED. Sally paid strict attention to the little girl and kept her out of trouble. As the child explored the busy office, she lost her awe of machines that clattered away and made friends with the interested office staff. Carla would scoot away to inspect a new thing as it caught her notice but always returned to touch Sally and make sure she was still within reach.

The child charmed the office staff with her quick acceptance of them, her lack of shyness. She had an amazing self-possession, obeyed without hesitation when asked not to touch but left no doubt in anyone's mind of her attachment to her mother.

Sally watched her with a growing wonder. It was

incredible that the child could be hers and that she should have absolutely no memory of her. There was no uncertainty in Carla's manner. Her mum-mum had returned to her. Her life was complete.

Carla's very confidence shattered Sally's. The little girl was the picture of her father. Crisp black hair, baby fine, framed delicate features that bore the stamp of his paternity. Black eyes twinkled from the attractive frame of lush and curling black lashes. Her straight little nose was as patrician as his. Mischief danced in her dark eyes, in the charm of her baby smile. David was the child's father. Sally was not fool enough to deny it. And she was the child's mother. There was no other explanation for Carla's instant and total acceptance of her.

So she was also David's wife. The confirmation of this filled the girl with trepidation. She did not want to be his wife. Secretly she had refused to believe it. This belief had served as her sheet anchor to sanity since Maclean had told her who she was. To find out she was wrong, that she was indeed married to the formidable man whose baritone dictates she could hear from the opened door of his private office, was almost too much to bear. She shuddered, pushed the thought from her and concentrated on her little daughter.

David kept them in the office the rest of the working day and did not seem concerned about them. Sally smarted under his offhand manner, and lack of communication, but decided not to create a fuss in front of his employees. Her determination built as she suffered through the weary afternoon. She longed for a warm bath, a chance to lay her head down, but contented herself with flipping through the attractive magazines scattered around the reception area of the big outer office.

There were several bulletins on viticulture printed by a university among the magazines. Intrigued, Sally picked one up, started to read it. Carla came to her finally, climbed on her lap and promptly fell asleep.

That is how David found them when the time came to leave the office. He stood in the door of his office for long moments, his eyes masked and thoughtful as he scrutinized the picture they made, the sleeping child cuddled against the slender form of the girl who was his wife, the girl herself immersed in the informative bulletin she was reading.

When Sally felt his eyes on her and looked up, he moved to her side, picked up the child and without a word went out to the car.

He still said nothing as he took Carla from Sally's arms when they reached the hacienda. He crossed the patio, Sally at his heels, and ran lightly up the curving stairs to the balcony that circled the entry hall. He pushed open a door and entered his daughter's dainty room. Irma was there with the child's food, which was kept warm under silver covers. He gave Carla into Sally's arms and dismissed the teenager, leaned against the door and watched while Sally coaxed the baby awake, then coaxed food down her. He still did not speak but just observed critically as Sally ignored him and crooned to her daughter, washed her sleepy little face and got her ready for bed.

David took the child then and put her in her dainty bed, his lips gentle on the child's already unconscious little face. "Come on, Sally." His order was almost lenient, as if the sight of her care with his daughter touched a spring of humanity in him she had not been able to reach before.

"Where are we going?" Sally asked the question in all innocence as they left the child's room.

"To our room, to change for dinner, of course." He turned a frosty glance of amusement on her as he noted the instant whip of color into her cheeks. "We generally dine about eight, and we dress for it as it pleases my grandmother, who is quite old-fashioned in many ways. In here."

He pushed open the door to a magnificent room that obviously stretched across the front of the hacienda. It was enormous. Carpeted in the mustardy gold of the passageways, it was tastefully done in golds and ivories and browns, with sharp accents of green. The room was furnished both as a bedroom and sitting room, with the mammoth bed taking pride of place. A lovely cherry-wood desk sat against one wall. Beautiful antique chairs, chests and tables were scattered about in tasteful groupings.

Floor-to-ceiling windows opened to the soft evening stars. The view across the valley to the mountains must be arresting in daylight, Sally thought. It was spectacular in the moonlight. The balcony outside the long windows was filled with comfortable-looking furnishings and potted plants.

"Go through the dressing room, and you will find the bath, Sally." He eyed her, his mouth curling. "Just in case you have forgotten. And your closet is to the right. You will be using this room with me instead of the one beyond the bath as you once did. I hope you understand."

"I don't understand," she declared wrathfully, her resolution in shreds as a result of her afternoon of enforced inactivity. "Are you implying I am to share this room as your wife, and is this something I have not done before?"

"You will share the room with me, Sally, but not as my wife. As a captive, perhaps. As the blue chip I mean to use to win whatever game you and Lang are playing. But as my wife, never. You have never shared it as my wife, nor shall you now."

His scorn lashed at her, cut her to the quick. She winced, marched through the dressing-room door, determined too late to maintain an aloof silence. She remembered his declaration on the awful day in the hospital when he had discovered she was suffering from amnesia. He was going to live in her pocket, he had said. She would not be able to move or breathe unless he knew about it. So this was what he meant. This was why she had been forced to spend the afternoon cooling her heels in his office. And Carla had spent it there, too, instead of in the sunshine where she belonged, just so he could assure himself that his selfish dictate was carried out! This, then, was the kind of life his grandmother also expected her to live until her memory returned! She was a woman. How could she be so cruel, so heartless?

Sally slammed the dressing-room door behind her and stripped off her clothing with little attention to the needs of the lovely things. Naked, she tramped through the fluffy ankle-deep carpet into the bathroom, almost too angry to take in the luxurious appointments of the room. Lined with marble, with a sunken tub and a crystalline shower stall reflected in the tall mirrors that threw back her image, the room was a delight. Tall colored bottles of intriguing sizes and shapes gave accents to the room as did pots of vines. A long louvered window looked out on the moonlit valley she had glimpsed through the bedroom windows.

Sally sighed as she took it all in. Well, if she was to be a captive, at least she was to be denied no luxury except her freedom. As she turned on the shower and stepped into the steaming needles that cascaded down, she suspected her freedom might mean more to her than all of this.

She was in for another surprise when she finished her shower and went into the dressing room. She opened the closet David had indicated was hers and found it chock-full of exquisite and very expensive clothing. Built-in drawers down one side of the large area proved to be bursting with dainty silk underthings and gossamer tights. A rack, also built-in, held enough shoes in serried ranks to start a shoe store, she was sure. Cashmere sweaters, jackets of all descriptions, street clothing, cocktail gowns, evening gowns—name it and it was represented.

What on earth had caused her to buy so many fabulous things, then abandon them? Sally shook her head, then started to sort through the long evening gowns. She selected a black silk organdy with a scattering of white polka dots. It had a closely fitted bodice that was double-breasted with ridiculously large white pearl buttons fastened beneath her uplifted high breasts. A huge white organza collar was frilled with dainty lace and spread wide across her slender shoulders. Filmy sleeves ended in demure white cuffs frilled to match the extravagant collar.

The dress looked delightful on her. It fit her shoulders but missed the mark at the waist where it was designed to hug closely before it flared into the full circle of the skirt, which was lined with white and hung in enticing folds just at her ankles. Sally searched through a drawer of silk scarves, found a long black one and solved the problem by passing it twice around her waist and tying it in a cummerbund. She found some black satin pumps that looked as though they went with the outfit. As she bent over to slip them onto her feet, she heard David enter the dressing room.

Sally swallowed convulsively as his critical glance swept over her, his expression bland and uncommunicative. He unbuttoned his white shirt, pulled it off and threw it at a laundry hamper set against the wall. Sally took one look at that muscular masculine chest and bolted to the sound of his amused chuckle. Incensed at her own lack of poise, she sat down at the dressing table and picked up a lipstick. She carefully applied a light coat of color to her lips.

Why on earth were they trembling? She didn't know. And she didn't care, she told herself with some heat as she ran uncertain fingers through her short curly locks and tried to arrange them in some order. Several bottles of perfume ranged across the center of the dressing table. Sally sniffed them all, chose one she liked and applied a few lavish splashes with a fine feeling of defiance.

She was seated in one of the comfortable chairs, gazing out at the moonlit scene spread before her, when David came back into the room. Sally turned her head as he entered and looked at him. He was magnificent. Long legs encased in slim black silk trousers, his wide shoulders covered by a perfectly fitted white dinner jacket over a white frilled shirt, he was handsome enough to take her breath away. She watched as he moved lithely to the tall mirror over his dresser and fiddled with a recalcitrant bow tie. He muttered under his breath, then bit off an oath.

Sally grinned and went to him. "Here. Let me do it," she offered easily.

He stared at her, momentarily taken aback, then his hands fell away from the bit of silk. Sally took a deep breath and was very aware of the fragrance of his toiletries and the clean scent of his freshly showered body. As she touched him, she felt the beginnings of a flush deep down. But she fought the awareness that stabbed through her nerves, flipped the silk ends of the tie with an instinctive ease and patted the perfect bow that was the end result. David caught her hand as she withdrew it and held it as he looked at her with a dark interest.

"Where did you learn to tie a proper bow, Sally?" His brow lifted while he reviewed the expressions that chased each other across her still slightly misshapen face.

Sally pulled her hand from his fingers and maintained a willful silence. There was no reason for him to keep on about the things she was unable to recall, she thought tartly. He could just go stuff them for all the answers he would get from her from now on.

David's low laugh was unpleasant as he seized her hand, tucked it under his arm. "Let's go have a drink, shall we? And see if we can bury the hatchet for this evening. Somewhere other than in my ribs, preferably.''

''Why can't we talk, David? There is so much I need to know. You know exactly what you are talking about all the time, but you force me to guess. Then, when I guess incorrectly, you turn on a black rage and...and just let me dangle. I wonder why, but you never help, never give me a chance. I feel so terribly inadequate.''

He bent his proud head, stared down at her as he escorted her down the graceful stairway. ''Do you know that is the first time since I've known you that you've given any indication you might even want to understand me?''

Sally halted two stairs up from the floor of the hall, her face incredulous. ''I cannot believe you,'' she ventured crossly. ''Surely any woman needs to talk to her husband, needs to learn to understand him.''

''Not you, Sally.'' He continued to the bottom, then turned to face her, black eyes on a level with hers. ''Never you. As a person, I simply did not exist for you before you went away.'' He inspected her confusion with a tight-lipped smile, his mouth curved with self-derision. ''Makes quite a change, you acting as if you were concerned in any way about my personal reactions, my personal feelings. You will pardon me if I find it hard to believe that you really have any interest in anyone's comfort except your own. I will admit, however, to the fact that you have been putting on a good show. As long as you continue to act as though you are actually worried about me, about Carla, I intend to reap the benefits.'' He closed a large and long-fingered hand over her wrist and applied enough pressure to ensure she joined him.

"You can go straight to hell, David Rossi!" she muttered, her lips stiff with anger. What an obstinate domineering man he was! Well, if he thought she would ask him again to talk to her, he had another think coming. She had offered to try to put their relationship on a firmer footing. It was very obvious he wanted no part of it. She would keep herself to herself, and he could go...go fly a kite, she decided in a fit of temper.

It was just as well she had been able to make that decision was her rueful thought as they sat at the lavish dining table in the long dining room. They were joined by his grandmother at the candle-lit beautifully set table. The soft light reflected in the highly polished surfaces of the priceless antique furniture. A fire crackled softly in the handsome fireplace as the late evening was cool.

Tall soft-footed Franco served the delicious food as he moved around the linen-draped table and crossed the thick carpet with an unconscious grace. Ilena, who was Irma's sister as Sally found out later, came in occasionally to help him. Franco was the older brother. The mother, Theresa, cooked the wonderful meals and ran the household with all the confidence of a top sergeant.

David sat at the head of the splendidly appointed table, his expression cool, withdrawn. Sally took no part in the conversation between David and his grandmother. The old lady, her back straight and imperious, sat on the tall dining chair at her grandson's left. She ignored the presence of the girl across from

her as if she were invisible. David talked to his grandparent, discussed the happenings of the day, the state
of the vineyards and the business affairs of the vast
corporation of which he was the head.

Mrs. Rossi seemed very conversant with the operations of the giant complex. David did the old lady the
courtesy of asking her opinion on various points. He
listened carefully to her, weighed her answers and
then discussed with her any difference to his own tentative decisions. It seemed to Sally that he took genuine heed of all his grandmother said. He certainly
showed her a good deal of indulgence.

Sally watched him under lowered lids. His face was
shadowed in the candlelight. The dark austere planes
of his high cheekbones, his square and determined
jaw and broad forehead were cast in a soft relief.
Black short-cropped curls lay in an attractive dis-
order on his well-shaped head, just touching the collar of his evening shirt. His lashes were long enough
to mask his eyes, to keep his secrets to himself. Firm
slashes ran from the corners of his thin and imperious nose, creasing appealingly when he smiled. His
mouth was wide and sensuous. He certainly was a
handsome brute, Sally allowed herself to think for a
moment, her senses stirring. Then she sighed and
straightened resolutely against the back of her chair.

It was a hopeless situation. She did not belong to
their world. The sooner she learned this and stopped
beating her head against a brick wall, the easier her
life would be, she decided. David wanted only one
thing from her. As soon as she was able to tell him
the whereabouts of his son, she could expect to be
ejected firmly from this lovely place she had left with

such a cavalier attitude once before. Why had she done so? She was beginning to suspect she would never be able to find the answer to that question. She moved her shoulders irritably against the silk of her gown, cross because she could not leave her situation alone. She kept returning to it, worried at it as a puppy might worry at a bone. The image caught at her fancy and made her smile.

"Well?" David's authoritative query startled her. Her long lashes swept up as she emerged from her reverie, and she found herself staring into his dark eyes.

"I'm sorry," she apologized. "I wasn't listening."

"*Nonna* will not consider having Carla spend her days in the office with you." He watched her with a quiet speculation. "Since the child is obviously attached to you and does not want to let you out of her sight now that you have reappeared, how do you plan to handle the situation?"

Sally glanced from his quizzical face to his grandmother's disapproving one. She bit her lip and asked the only question that occurred to her. "Why can't I stay in the house and take care of her?"

"I've already told you why you go to the office, Sally," he frowned. "Stop being obtuse. I meant it when I said you will spend every minute, twenty-four hours a day, with me."

"That is impossible," she whispered bleakly. Suddenly the fear that he planned to enforce his threat and do exactly as he stated became a reality to her for the first time. "You must be joking."

"I assure you I am not." He assessed her rebellious rejection of his declaration with calmness, then gave her an arrogant smile. "You will soon find I mean exactly what I have said."

His grandmother made a motion to rise, and he was on his feet instantly. He assisted her with her chair as she arose and excused herself. "I shall leave you now. You must sort out your own differences. Good night, David. Sleep well, Sally." The old woman gave the girl a quick glance in which there was a faint stirring of compassion, quickly hidden. Surprised and unsure whether she had truly seen the grandmother's softened look, the girl murmured a polite phrase and found herself alone with the formidable male who was her husband.

He looked at her thoughtfully, came around and pulled her chair back. "We will solve the problem of Carla in the morning, I think. You have had a long day. You look quite exhausted. Come with me." And he took her hand, then led her from the room and back up the stairs.

Sally accompanied him without word. Her heart hammered in her throat like a trapped wild thing. She was conscious of the soft whisper of their shoes on the luxurious carpet of the stairs, the murmur of the grandfather clock as it ticked away beneath them, and the discreet clatter of china and silver as Franco cleared away in the dining room. Her senses sharpened so she almost felt the shift of the light as it played across her back and tangled in the gold brown of her curls. David walked up beside her, his shoulder above her ear, his lithe stride taking the stairs easily. He continued around the balcony at her side, and quite suddenly she knew beyond a shadow of a doubt he had meant exactly what he said. He planned to go to bed with her.

Her blood froze, and her mind refused to accept the idea as she looked wildly for a place to run to, a place to hide.

He glanced at her, caught her frozen look and slid a powerful hand down her arm in time to stop her bolt for safety. He thrust the door to the big bedroom open with a long and lazy arm. "You don't really expect me to allow you to be on your own for all the hours of the night, do you, my sweet?" The smile he gave her was cruel, and it meant to insult. He watched her expression, laughed. "I've been that route, or is this another facet of your personality you cannot remember? All those late-night trips that you were accustomed to in order to meet other men must surely have left some impression. How about it, Sally? Want to talk about it yet?"

Sally shivered and stared at him with dislike. She was unable to move through the doorway into the threat of what lay beyond.

"I n-need to look in on Carla," she muttered. Her lips felt stiff, alien. "She may need t-tucking in." She peeped at him through lowered lashes, her panic obvious.

David grinned at her as his eyes mocked her discomfiture. "Okay, Sally. We'll look in on her. But rest assured, there is no escape for you. I will sleep in my own bed tonight, and you will keep me company."

Speechless, her throat suddenly so dry it ached and her heart squeezing in her breast in great convulsive

jerks, Sally walked ahead of him into Carla's room.
It was lit by a soft night-light. Carla was curled in a
ball. She had kicked off the covers. Her little hands
were flung out, curled toward the palms like rosebuds. Sally crooned softly, dropped to her knees beside the child's bed and tucked the baby in. She
touched the tumbling curls with gentle fingers, a
piercing sorrow bringing tears to her eyes. How could
she give birth to such a delectable morsel of humanity
and then completely and absolutely forget it?

A sound whispered into the room, and Sally
looked up as Irma came through the connecting door
into Carla's nursery. "I thought I heard Carla," the
teenager breathed. "I was just coming to check."

"Thank you, Irma." Sally dashed the tears from
her eyes as she rose. She cast a quick glance at David,
but his face was hidden in the shadows. "I didn't realize you were so near."

"Oh, yes," the girl answered softly, smiling.
"David moved me next to Carla's room the day he
brought her home. I have been looking after her."

"I am so grateful. You have done an excellent job.
I'm sorry we disturbed you. Good night."

Sally faced the inevitable and turned to the dark
stranger who awaited her. She sought desperately for
a means to delay the moment she must enter the enormous room across the passageway and close herself
in with the silent man at her side, but nothing came.
Mindlessly she stepped in. The door closed with a
smooth click, and Sally's heart threatened to choke
her.

Hysteria hit her like a shock wave. She turned on
her tormentor with the mindless drive of a cornered

animal fighting for its life, as the control she had maintained so carefully all during the past few weeks of stress snapped. Clawing, kicking, screaming her hate, she attacked with a clear intent to destroy.

David caught her flailing figure and tried to protect himself without hurting her. It was impossible. Buttons flew as her hands grabbed at him and ripped down his shirtfront. She slashed at his face, squirmed from his grip like quicksilver, then gouged a great path down the side of his face. He manhandled her, turning her so one arm held her writhing back against his chest, but she got away. Grimly he caught the back of her gown, but it couldn't stand the stress of her movement and tore. With an oath he lunged and caught her, fell on her as the door to the room burst open. If the aroused household had bothered to knock, the noise of the girl's passionate screams had drowned the sound.

She was not screaming now. The breath had been knocked out of her. She lay under her husband, air sobbing in and out of her lungs, the sound mingled with his own labored breathing. He held her wrists above her head in a grip of iron, his face so close to hers she was sure she would suffocate. Her eyes wild, she stared her hate at him. The only sound was the tormented stridency of their breathing. Then David turned his head.

"Get the hell out of here!" he stormed. "And shut that goddamned door!"

As the door closed, Sally started to cry. Great racking sobs caused her slender body to shudder under the weight of his. Tears cascaded down her ravaged face. She was deathly white, but the hysteria as such was gone. She was completely drained and without energy or will.

David held her wrists above her head, kept her body captive beneath the long length of his and watched her as an animal of prey might watch its intended victim. His eyes hooded, his face brooding, he did not move for a long time. The bloody scratches on his tanned cheeks and broad forehead had dried when he finally shifted. But he didn't intend to release the still sobbing girl even then. He lowered his handsome head with a groan and buried his face in her slender neck. Sally, mindless with exertion and the shock brought on by her fear, turned to the comfort of his kisses as her confused instincts sought for closeness with another human.

He released her arms to enfold her pliant slenderness, an unnoticed sob in his own throat as he pulled the ruined gown from between them and threw it into the corner. He lay against her a long moment then and savored the feel of her warm loveliness. Temptation quivered through him, tightening his muscles. Aroused, he raised his head, passion flaring as his black eyes raked her tearstained face.

Sally cried with an unrestrained sadness. The fear and frustration of the past few weeks, the hate she had experienced and the uncertainty and tension brought on by her untenable situation supplied the fuel for her tears. She felt David move, and the tears flowed faster. She needed comfort, needed closeness more than she needed food or drink at the moment. His muscular male warmth offered it. She raised her arms with a fierce desire as she felt his withdrawal.

David looked at her and understood her need for

what it was. Lust and compassion fought a battle. It was a battle destined to be short-lived. With a sigh he came to his knees and gathered the scantily clothed irresistible temptation that was his wife into his arms, to cradle her to his own pulsating body as he carried her to the bed.

SALLY AWOKE sometime in the night to the pressure of his arm locked around her slender waist. She burrowed more closely into the curve of his shoulder and dropped back into blissful sleep.

CHAPTER SIX

SHE AWOKE TO THE FEEL of David's hand on her shoulder. He shook her lightly.

"Wake up, sleepyhead. Time to rise and shine."

"Well, the sun certainly hasn't," she answered smartly as she came instantly awake, the remembrance of her evening performance flooding back to embarrass her. "What time is it, for goodness' sake?" The lamps were on against the darkness outside.

"I've just told you. Time to get up. Hustle, please. I want to eat in a quarter of an hour. You will need to wear jeans and something warm. I inspect the vineyards at first light every day." He did not seem the least inclined to bring up the events of the night before. Sally breathed a sigh of thankfulness, accepted the thick warm robe he tossed to her and slipped into it as he turned to the windows to pull the draperies back.

He was dressed in biscuit-colored jeans and a workman's rugged shirt in the same material. He had shaved, and his thick black curls were combed into rebellious order. His after-shave lotion tingled pleasantly in her nostrils. It intensified her awareness of the energy and drive that crackled around him.

Vexed by a persistent, if somewhat fuzzy, memory

of her behavior the night before, she was bothered by a very muddled recollection of David's actions. Dimly she recalled his bellow at the amazed audience in the open doorway, the comfort of his kisses and his murmured words as he held her close during the night.

She dashed for the bathroom, glad of the necessity to take care of morning needs as she found she had no wish to explore further into the ramifications of her first night as David's wife. She blushed as she shed her underthings and dumped them in the hamper. At least *he* hadn't removed them. She found a brand-new toothbrush left thoughtfully on the cabinet of the washbasin. After using it vigorously, she ducked into the powerful needle-sharp shower for a long two minutes, toweled herself as she dripped water and then walked into her dressing closet.

She sorted through a variety of pants and pantsuits, but the nearest thing she came upon that resembled working jeans was a black shirt and matching pants. Both were fringed with white leather and absurdly studded with fake jewels and steel worked into intricate patterns. Sally shrugged and pulled the pants on over silk undergarments, then buttoned the ridiculous shirt. She heard David still moving about in the bedroom and went out to face the inevitable study.

"There is nothing appropriate for me to wear," she protested. "These are absurd, but everything else is fit only to lounge in or to wear to parties. And there are no shoes for me at all unless you are planning to drive through the vineyards in a limousine. Anyway, all the shoes are too big for me."

David surveyed her thoughtfully. "Is that a fact?"

One eyebrow hooked into the curls that had already escaped the effects of his severe brushing. "The shoes being too large, I mean."

"Well, they are not much too large," she acknowledged. "Just enough to allow them to slide around a bit uncomfortably on my feet. I've lost weight, I expect. The clothes don't really fit as they should, either." She pushed her thumb into the waistband of the ornate black pants and pulled it away from her body to illustrate her point.

"Hmm. I see." He went back with her into the closet, surveyed the rack of shoes and reached for a pair. "These are the ones you were in the habit of wearing with that outfit, I believe."

Sally looked at the pair he held out to her and giggled. "It's obvious I didn't accompany you on very many early-morning jaunts if I wore those," she returned. The shoes, if they could be called that, had heels like spikes and a thick wood platform daintily shaped to hold a small foot comfortably. The black leather bands designed to cross the instep were only held in place by jeweled studs matching those on the pants and shirt she wore.

"You are right." He tossed the footwear into the corner near the rack. After rummaging in the bottom drawer of the built-in chest, he came up with a pair of white tennis shoes. "You were never known to get up before noon. You have never gone with me." His bland expression said clearly that he expected her to reject the tennis shoes. "Wear these for now. We will get you something more appropriate when we go in to see John Mellon next week."

"I didn't know we were going to see him." Sally

busied herself with the laces on the tennis shoes. "I thought he was from San Francisco." David's nearness in the close confines of the closet set her nerves to singing. She fumbled with the laces, the residual stiffness in her mended bones adding to her awkward effort.

"Let me do that." David brushed her fingers away to take over.

Sally held her breath, her pulse stirring with a thunder she did not understand. She stared at the black crispness of the curls so close to her face and pushed a desire to touch them as far out of her mind as she could.

"He is in Frisco." David finished and stood, bringing her to her feet as he did so. "We are scheduled for a visit once a week. I will fly you down. Let's go." Brusqueness had taken over again. It was as if he, derisive of himself, felt a little ridiculous because he had weakened and lowered his barrier against her enough to offer to help.

He was very probably regretting the comfort he had wasted on her during the night. Sally was surprised to find the thought gave her a good deal of bitterness. She did not care in the least how he felt about her, she told herself sternly. He was an arrogant unhappy man, too accustomed to having his world work exactly as he demanded it work. And she wanted no part of him.

She followed him as he ran down the stairs, her nostrils twitching to the delicious aroma of coffee. She drew up short as he pushed open the door to the charming breakfast room that opened off the kitchen. His grandmother was seated at the linen-covered

breakfast table. Dressed in black, she was eating a
flaky roll, crumbs from it scattered at her place.

She nodded gravely at Sally but showed no surprise
at the sight of her. She smiled at her grandson.
"*Buon giorno, nipote.* Sally. Did you sleep well?"

Nothing in the old woman's demeanor indicated
knowledge of the events of the night before. Sally
breathed a prayer of thanks for small favors and
slipped into the chair David held for her. But his
grandmother must surely be well aware of the unfor-
tunate burst of hysteria. After all, the noise had electrified the household. A swift amusement caught at
her and caused her to muffle an undeniable chuckle by
tucking in her lower lip. Teeth clamped down severely,
she cast a mischievous glance at David as she wondered what the staff had thought as they opened the
door to find them on the floor. She met the stern glint
in his eye and throttled her amusement.

"You are up very early," she said, turning quickly
to the older woman.

"I am up early every morning." The note of pride in
her old voice was unmistakable. "Since I came as a
bride to this valley, it has been my custom to rise with
the dawn and ride with my men across the vineyards."

From the clear note of censure in the brittle voice,
Sally gained the very clear information that her own
failure to do this was a very black mark against her in
nonna's books.

"Sally has decided to make up for her former lack
of interest," David put in smoothly. "She will go
with us each morning."

Until I tell him where Charles is, the girl remembered. What had he said? He would live in her pocket

until she gave him the information he sought, then any man in the country could have her and welcome. She winced inwardly as she swallowed coffee that was too hot. So getting her up before dawn was part of the campaign to keep her under constant vigilance, she realized.

Well, if he thought to punish her by his insistence on her presence during his early-morning survey of his kingdom, he really did need to revise his tactics. It was not a hardship to get up so early. In fact, as she thought it over, she did not know why she had refused to go with him before. She buttered her roll and ate it, drank her juice as she concentrated on her former attitude and tried to understand it. She did not believe she would enjoy the luxury of bed until noon, except on rare occasions. Still, she must have been guilty of just that as a regular part of her behavior. Neither David nor his grandmother was in the least doubt about it, and obviously neither of them felt it a trait to be condoned.

If it did not feel natural to her, and they did not like it, why had she done it? No answer occurred. She sighed and put the notion from her as another of those imponderables she had no solution for until her memory returned.

David watched her with a curiously intent look. He stood as soon as she finished her coffee, helped his grandmother from the chair, then held the door for the two women.

Sally followed them out of the house and across the patio. The sky had lightened considerably. A cock crowed his head off somewhere to the left as they entered the courtyard. He was challenged by another some distance away. The liquid notes of a redwing blackbird dropped into the stillness that followed.

Sally listened and suddenly gave a happy little skip. It was such a beautiful morning, crisp, clear, invigorating. She took a deep breath, savoring it as she turned to face the rising sun and watch it work quick magic. It rolled up behind the mountain range far to the east, where gleaming bands of light sliced bright paths through the morning mists that clung to the peaks. She was entirely unaware of the keen black eyes that dismissed her enjoyment with a caustic cynicism, a cynicism destined to win an easy victory over the stir of a gentler emotion that lived for a secret moment in the dark attentiveness of her husband.

A sleek palomino stallion nickered softly and champed his curved bit as David approached. The animal was magnificent. His hide rippled in the soft sunlight in a delightful golden beige. He tossed a pure white forelock out of his intelligent eyes and shook a beautiful white mane as David patted his arched neck and ran lean fingers down the length of his slender leg. He nuzzled at the man, his white-stockinged legs beating a quick and impatient tattoo on the pavement of the courtyard. The boy who held the reins responded with a flow of Spanish that soothed. The animal stood quiet then, head high, his ears pointed as he watched the humans with interest.

Sally thrilled to the beauty of the picture he made as he stood there. He was a thoroughbred from the tips of his aristocratic ears to the end of the gorgeous tail that so nearly swept the ground.

"May I pet him, David?" she breathed, quite in awe of the splendid creature.

"You had best confine your petting to Quito at the moment." The laconic comment approached rudeness. "No need to stretch your acting ability to the limit." He turned to help his grandmother into the small four-wheeled open buggy standing beside the saddled stallion.

Sally had no time for a reply as Quito bounded through the courtyard arch and assaulted her with enthusiasm. His huge muzzle was damp with dew, tangled with debris. He had apparently been off on an early-morning jaunt of his own and returned to join the party. She ordered him to sit with considerable sternness and then climbed into the buggy and seated herself beside David's grandparent as he requested.

They set out then, David in the saddle and at the head of the expedition, his grandmother handling with an easy expertise the reins of the small bay harnessed to the vehicle.

They were gone almost two hours. Sally spent a good deal of the time wondering just what the sarcastic man in the saddle ahead of them had meant by his caustic remark about her acting ability. If she did not regain her memory soon, she would just quietly go out of her mind, she decided recklessly. Just how would Mr. Know-It-All handle that? Probably lock her away in a dungeon and beat her every day to rid her of evil spirits, she decided and giggled. He certainly was medieval enough in his ideas of the treatment of amnesia. He had to be a primitive if he thought subjecting her to his constant presence might supply sufficient pressure to bring on a sudden confession that she knew the whereabouts of their son.

She was ready to allow that she would not have

been able to withstand him if she had not truly had amnesia. He did not believe her, of course. So he expected his tactics to work. What would become of her if they did not? More importantly, what would become of the little boy she had so callously left somewhere? What if she were never able to assist David in his search for his child? Had she left him with someone who would love him and supply him with the things a little boy needed to become a fulfilled adult? Whatever the conditions that had driven her to such action, Sally could find no way to forgive herself for what she had done. Surely there must be better ways of handling a man than using an innocent baby as hostage to her own desires.

She looked at the straight back of the man riding ahead of the buggy. There was no way to rationalize such an act. She surely did not deserve any compassion or any consideration from him. If she did not regain her memory, she would merit any punishment he might deal her. And she must take it without a cry of any kind for his mercy, she decided grimly.

She knew he had men on her trail now, trying to backtrack her movements before she'd arrived at Heathrow for the flight to the States with Carla and Don Lang. She did not know how the investigation progressed. England was large and filled with people. And she had heard him mention that a citizen of Britain did not necessarily have to have his or her passport stamped to travel in western Europe. She might have left the child anywhere on that vast continent.

If only she had left some clue the men could pick up! Or if only she could recover from this frustrating amnesia that blocked her memory. David would use his wealth and his drive to find the child if he could, but she wished profoundly she were more able to help him.

They were high on the slopes now. The vineyards fell away from them, down onto the valley floor where they stretched straight across to the high rim rising above. The vines were bare, denuded for the most part of leaf, as well as fruit. Men were working in the vines, stripping remaining leaves and growth, piling them high at the ends of the steeply rising rows. Other men worked transferring the debris onto small wagons pulled by tractors. The tractors moved carefully on the narrow roadways, which were little more than paths. These roadways were the means of access to the vines.

Each row of vines was marked by stakes. The wires that stretched from stake to stake glinted dully in the early-morning light. They offered support to the grapevines during the growing season, Sally surmised.

David and his grandmother discussed the pruning that had to be done once the workmen had finished clearing the present tangle of withered leaves and woody stems away. The old lady seemed as aware of the care of the vines as David. They talked about the ongoing work with the deference of equals. Sally listened and found she was interested in their discussions. Several questions occurred to her, but she was not willing to call attention to herself.

She was completely fascinated. The workers moved busily in a landscape of real beauty, the tree-lined mountains a startling backdrop to the scene. As she looked around, Sally caught the odor of newly turned earth. She found it all so invigorating. She sat beside the old lady, alert, engrossed and idiotically enough, with a sense of fulfillment.

If only she were able to remember her life in this delightful place! She must have loved it in spite of David's attitude. She became convinced of this as the morning went on.

David's grandmother drove the buggy. She would stop it and look over a specific section of the vineyard or an operation of the workers and make comments to David. She did not address a word to the girl beside her in the two-hour period they were gone from the hacienda.

They left the horses at the stable. Quito followed them to the doorway of the hacienda, clinging to Sally's footsteps in a manner she found endearing. If no one else on this vast estate approved of her, she at least had won the affection of the big dog.

She went through the big double doors ahead of David and ran lightly up the curve of the staircase, her husband at her heels. He was still there when she reached her dressing-room door.

"How am I to dress?" She turned and faced him, her question cool.

"You will be in the office all day. I want you to leave Carla with Irma today. She is quite capable of taking care of the child, and I don't think it is good for Carla to be cooped up in the office. She needs fresh air and sunshine."

"Surely I am better able to take charge of my own child than a teenager," Sally came back tartly. "And I certainly don't look forward to being cooped up all day, either, David."

"You may not." His gentle smile was not pleasant.

"But I intend to see that you are, my love. Get ready, please." And he turned to vanish into his own dressing room.

Sally's anger flared. It was still boiling two hours later as she followed him out to the Land Rover, the velvet skirt she wore flicking to the rhythm of her long and lovely legs, her silk shirt rustling.

Carla's sobs were ringing in her ears. It seemed a needless exercise in cruelty to leave the child when she wanted her mum-mum's presence so badly. Sally had done her best to reassure the child. She had cuddled and cosseted her, insisted upon feeding her breakfast to her. And she had told her quietly and endlessly that she was just going to work with her daddy, that she would come back when he did.

Carla had accepted her assurances with some misgiving but had finally let her go, her small body shaken with the storm of her protest. The crumpled tearstained little face she held up to be kissed stabbed at Sally. David, a silent witness to his daughter's upset, had kissed the child, too, and murmured soothingly to her in Italian.

He held open the door of the Land Rover, then took Sally's arm to help her into the high seat.

"Don't touch me!" Sally shook him off wrathfully. "You are abominable! How can you make your own daughter so unhappy? I hate you!"

"Be quiet, Sally." He closed her door forcibly before rounding the vehicle to swing up into his own seat. "I know you hate me. I'd be an idiot if I didn't. Carla has formed a deep attachment to you that I still cannot understand. Never in the six months you were here after the birth of the twins did you so much as look at them." His glance seared her, critical, embittered. "I am happy that leaving here meant you took time to form some sort of a relationship with the child, let her love you, loved her, as well. I can only hope you included Charles in your love." He twisted the key, and the motor roared to life. They shot through the archway of the courtyard and sped down the road.

Muscular arms across the top of the steering wheel, he glanced at her thoughtfully, turned up the driveway to the huge winery and the cluster of buildings attendant upon it.

"I cannot deny the evidence that Carla loves you," he finally said. "And a baby gives love because it receives love. In that case I cannot deny you have shown our daughter love." He drew up in front of the office building and stopped. "And that, my love, is completely out of character." Dark eyes accented his position. "What made you change, Sally? In this I have to allow you must have been sincere. It's hard to fool a child. So what happened?"

Sally stared into his curious dark eyes, her own tormented, confused. "I don't believe you, you know." She was aghast that he should think it impossible for her to love her own child. And yet, what had she done with Charles? The specter of her son's disappearance troubled her. It held her silent in the fear that David might have been right in his original assessment of her inability to love her children and him.

He sat there, arrogant, assured. A handsome devil sent to torment her, to drive her mad with unanswerable queries. It just wasn't fair. She shook her head at him, her golden brown hair catching the early sun, glinting.

David straightened from his indolent position and reached out a long finger against her hair, his thumb stroking the strands of silk around his finger. "When did you cut your hair, Sally?"

A thrill struck through her at his unexpected touch, left her without breath and rendered her speechless.

"I like it," he murmured softly. "It fits your face, makes you look like a Grecian boy. And the color is lovely. I never did care for the bleached-blond look you insisted on before."

"I am not a boy," she reminded him tartly, unable to keep up with his change of mood. When had she cut her hair? It had been very long and very blond in the photos given to Stern.

"You certainly don't feel like a boy," he said laughingly.

Sally slapped his hand away. It was the first time he had referred to the events of the night before, and she knew she was skating on dangerous ground. "I told you I don't want you to touch me!"

David moved then, his lazy indulgence wiped out in a flare of passion. He seized her by her silk-clad shoulders and hauled her across the division of the seats into his arms. "I'll touch you any damn time I choose," he informed her coldly.

Sally was still as she did her best to hide her quiver of fright. Some hard object pressed into her thigh and caused a persistent pain. The girl ignored it as she sought to reject the very evident intention written clearly on David's hard face. "Please, David. Let me go."

"Not this time."

He kissed her then, and light exploded in her head. She struggled, gripped by an unknown and unwanted sensation that ran down her nerves in an electrical shock. She lifted her fists to beat against the implacable strength of the man whose kiss seared into her and aroused emotions she had no idea existed.

"So early in the morning, David. And in front of the office, too. Is that any kind of an example to set?" The cold scorn in the woman's voice sluiced through Sally's vibrating nerves with all the effectiveness of a bucket of ice water expertly administered.

David's head came up slowly. His dark eyes narrowed as he glanced down at the newcomer who stood at the side of the vehicle. "Get the hell out of here, Alicia," he rasped. "Mind your own business. You were due at your desk ten minutes ago." He turned back to the girl in his arms, his eyes intent upon the soft mouth he had just ravished.

Sally was too distracted to hear the other woman's breath hiss as she left. But she read David's intent clearly and struggled like mad. "Let me go, you... you bastard!" She gasped the tormented demand at him as she fiercely moved, risking a black-and-blue mark from the gear lever or whatever pressed into her thigh. "L-let me go. Please, David." The plea squeaked from her as she surrendered to the inevitable and begged for freedom from his arms.

He laughed at her then and kissed her with a lingering sweetness that did little for her self-possession. Sally stared up at him. The fact they might just possibly have an interested audience did not register with her at all.

"Why did you do that, David?" she finally asked with a confused bitterness. "What are you trying to do to me?"

"Just doing my best to make sure you enjoy your period of captivity, Sally." His smile mocked her. "I happened to remember your fondness for contact with the nearest available male." Hard hands gripped her waist as he swung her easily across the seat and deposited her on the ground on his side of the Land Rover. "Since I was close, I decided to indulge you." He landed beside her, feet widespread, hands on his own neat waist.

Sally scrubbed her fist across her indignant mouth, her eyes flashing fire. "Well, thank you very much...for nothing. I will thank you to leave me alone from now on. I don't need any help from you. And there is no need for you to make a spectacle of me in front of th-those people."

The people had disappeared discreetly. David stood there, arms akimbo as he considered her, a wicked look in the black depths of his eyes. Sally did not flinch from the probing curiosity in his dark glance. But she found it took a considerable amount of control to kill the impulse to fly at him and pummel his mocking handsome face. She hated him, and he frightened her just a bit.

David appeared to be teasing. Sally was sure it was more than that. Buried beneath his suave and taunting exterior she sensed a far deeper motive. His actions were deliberate. He expected them to trigger some sort of behavior in her, and he watched carefully for it to appear.

Lion and mouse. The concept came to her suddenly out of nowhere. David was like a very big and dangerous lion watching a very small and helpless mouse. And he did not think she had any chance in the world to escape. She wondered if he would ever be caught in a trap and need this small mouse to gnaw his ropes and free him. Not David, she allowed. Then her eyes widened in shock as she realized what the fleeting mental picture meant. She had remembered a story she knew. Something from the past!

"What is it, Sally?" David pounced with the quickness of the cat she had likened him to, his hands urgent on her shoulders. "You've remembered something. What is it? Tell me."

"Nothing, David. Let me go!" She winced under the strength of his hands, her face drained of color.

"Tell me!"

Fire danced in those black eyes and consumed her will. So she told him. He released her with a suddenness that caused her to stagger and turned from her to stride across the attractive bricked walkway that led into the offices, his broad-shouldered figure taut in the beautifully tailored black suit he had changed into.

Sally followed in silent misery, trim in the velvet suit and midnight-blue silk blouse she had chosen from the fabulous wardrobe. They represented the nearest thing to that which one would wear to a business office.

Not that it really mattered in her case. David gave her a curt nod and left her in the reception area. *After his performance outside, his cool attitude must really be setting curiosity on the boil,* she thought. She sat down, crossed her nice ankles and went back to the government bulletins.

They interested her. She read carefully and absorbed as much of the knowledge as she could. She made a mental list of things she did not understand to ask David about if he ever decided to talk to her as one human to another.

It was some time later when the feeling of being watched impinged itself upon her. The woman was standing by the door Sally knew led to David's inner sanctum. She was stunning.

Dark hair swept upward in a perfect French chignon that crowned the shape of her lovely head in delicate beauty. Her features were flawless, large dark eyes set wide apart over high cheekbones, an imperious nose of classic loveliness, a curved and sensuous mouth that at the moment was stretched in a line of grim dislike. Her skin was white, with a translucence, a glow, that was arresting, and her figure was faultless as Sally could clearly see. She wore a silk dress meant to look demurely businesslike. It was set off with several expensive gold chains.

Sally met her eyes and almost gasped aloud at the loathing in them. More than loathing. Hatred. The woman looked at her with no attempt to hide her animosity, then turned with an air of deliberate discourtesy and vanished into the office behind her.

CHAPTER SEVEN

SALLY BLINKED, SIGHED, hardly had time to wonder about the woman and who she might be when David came through into the outer office.

He glanced at her, put the sheaf of papers he held down upon the desk of one of the three girls working away behind typewriters and came through the swinging door of the barrier toward her. She came to her feet as he approached, not at all willing to have him tower over her. Her pulse fluttered uncontrollably.

He darted a look at the bulletin she had in her fingers, a frosty amusement quickly masked as he read the title. He took it from her, tossed it onto the low table.

"Come along, Sally. You might as well meet the rest of the gang since you will be required to spend so much of your time here."

Ann Evans, the receptionist who operated the complex switchboard, was a tall and efficient blonde who greeted her coolly and did not seem particularly pleased to meet her.

Tammi Thomas had a freckled sweet face and a mop of rusty hair. She was as exuberant as a puppy and clasped Sally's hand enthusiastically. "I'm so happy to meet you, Mrs. Rossi," she bubbled. "I've heard so much about you, but I really didn't expect you to be so pretty!" she laughed as she was introduced.

Considering the amount of reconstructive work still to be done on her, the reaction surprised Sally. She was aware of her husband's wry expression. What had the girl heard? Apparently it had not put her off. She smiled at the girl.

"Isn't gossip awful?" the irrepressible girl rushed on. "They made you out such a monster, and you don't look like that at all...." She faltered to a halt as the steely regard of her employer impaled her. "Oops! Sorry. I bet I've done it again."

"Yes, Tammi. You have. Go back to work, there's a good girl. I'll see you later."

"Yes, David." The girl picked up the papers he had deposited upon her desk and headed toward the big file cabinets that lined the back of the room.

Jackie Haines was a gentle dark-eyed girl who watched as David and Sally approached her desk, an odd little smile on her face. She stood as they neared her, a stack of invoices in her hand. When David introduced his wife, Jackie's reply was polite, yet restrained.

"I was just going to the warehouse to check out this shipment, David," she excused herself. She smiled briefly at Sally and left.

"She is Jack Haines's daughter," David remarked. Apparently the brief statement was supposed to explain the girl's evident reluctance to prolong the contact with Sally.

"Should that mean something to me?" Sally asked

with some irritation. "I can assure you I don't know who Jack Haines might be."

David guided her toward the door to the inner office, his fingers firm on her elbow. "It will probably be quite a blow to him to hear you have said that," he remarked. "He was. . . is one of your less laudable conquests, my love. His wife was a cripple who committed suicide."

"Because of me?" The question forced itself out.

"Because of you," he agreed acidly. Sally swallowed convulsively, a hard band constricting her heartbeat.

"I don't believe you," she protested in a stricken whisper as she struggled in his unyielding grasp. David thrust her through the door and kicked it closed behind him. He dropped his hand from her arm at the same moment.

Sally glared at him as she rubbed her aching arm. He returned her look with a piercing glance, a nasty quirk to the edge of his firm mouth. Aghast, Sally realized he did believe her capable of conducting an affair with a married man. A married man, moreover, who had a crippled wife dependent upon him. She stood there, an angry flush spreading into her hairline, her breathing constricted with her loathing of the man watching her.

"I—I couldn't do such a thing!"

"You could and you did," he assured her grimly. "Barbara Haines had an incurable disease, granted. But she was coping with it until you decided you'd have a little fling with Jack." His sneer conveyed his disgust quite adequately. "She found it impossible to cope with her disease and compete with your, er,

charms. She told him as much in the note she left,"
he finished relentlessly.

For an awful moment Sally fought down a wave of
sickness. She dropped her eyes then, no longer able
to meet the accusation in the dark gaze of her tormentor. Wordlessly, she stared at the floor, unable to
believe herself capable of such a thing, but equally
unable to deny David Rossi believed it of her. David
towered over her, his eyes bitter, his face hard and
uncompromising.

Then as the door across the room opened, he
turned, his hand going to his wife's shoulder. "This
is Alicia Ricci. She is my private secretary," he commented briefly. "Alicia, my wife."

Sally gathered she had not known the secretary before. She raised her head with an effort, forcing a
smile onto stiff lips. "Hello, Alicia. I'm glad to meet
you," she murmured miserably.

The other woman did not answer. She just drew
herself up and stood there, her eyes on David's hand
where it rested on the girl's shoulder.

David did not seem to notice. He loosened his grip,
went to his big desk. Sally felt curiously vulnerable as
she stood there quite alone and waited for Alicia to
take her eyes off David and acknowledge her presence.

It took a little time for her to do so. Sally stared at
her, unprepared for the woman's deliberate rudeness, momentarily put off by it. Belatedly recognition came, and Sally felt her color rise once again.
Alicia Ricci was the gorgeous creature who had
watched her with such venom in her eyes across the
distance of the outer office a few moments ago, Sally

realized. She was also the person David had spoken so sharply to when she had interrupted the scene in the Land Rover.

The hatred Sally had seen so clearly in the office was masked now, hidden from David. However, Sally could feel it as a palpable force. It flowed out at her and grated upon her senses, although it was concealed in the bright false smile the woman had pinned on her perfect features for the benefit of the man standing by the big desk.

In that instant Sally knew why the woman hated her. Alicia Ricci wanted David and wanted him with a strength of purpose that would regard any means as fair as long as she obtained him. She stood there, beautiful, sure of her indispensability in David Rossi's life. Her challenge to Sally was undeniable.

Sally's head came up proudly, and her blue eyes darkened, a black ring suddenly appearing around her irises. She nodded to the woman, then turned quite deliberately to David. "May we go to lunch now, David?" She asked, knowing somehow that she had met the challenge thrown out by the other woman. She forced a smile into her voice. "I am really starved, and I would like to check on Carla to see that she is not pining for us."

She heard the other's indrawn breath as she staked her claim. Sally smiled inwardly, linked her arm through Rossi's as he bent a glance upon her that questioned, analyzed. But he bade the secretary a brief farewell and went with his wife.

CARLA GREETED THEM with a glow of happiness. To David's obvious surprise, she broke out into speech, stringing together chattering sentences.

"She has not talked before," he told Sally seriously. "I had not realized she could." Sally remembered now that the child had only used syllables the day before.

"Carry me, daddy," the little tyrant demanded as she held up plump arms. She had been with Irma in the patio when they arrived. David, down on one knee, poked a long finger into her rib cage and sent her off into a spate of giggles.

"Never," he told her solemnly. "Not unless you say please."

"Please, daddy," she answered promptly. He rose, tossed the child in the air and caught her as she squealed in delighted fear.

"Perhaps she is happy now," Sally murmured softly. "Perhaps that is why she has decided to talk."

"Perhaps," David agreed.

Sally saw to the child's lunch, getting pleasure from feeding the little girl, then took her up to her bed and tucked her in for a nap. Carla seemed perfectly at ease with her world as she sighed, cuddled the fluffy rag doll she had taken to bed with her to her soft little cheek and proceeded to go to sleep.

Sally went down to her own lunch, her face thoughtful. David ate with her, but he was withdrawn and busy with his own concerns. Sally watched him and wondered about his relationship with the beauteous Alicia.

"Make a list of the clothes you need," he ordered abruptly. "We have to go to San Francisco tomorrow afternoon. We can do some shopping after you see Mellon."

"May I stay here and make it?" she inquired. "I

can't see any reason for me to go back to that office and just sit.''

"You may not see any sense in it, Sally," he returned. "But your presence is absolutely necessary to my peace of mind. You will be there each day."

And that, his attitude said quite plainly, was that.

Sally looked at him, knew he would not be moved from the impossible stand he had taken and sighed audibly. "Then if I must go, give me something to do, for goodness' sake. I cannot just waste my days sitting in your anteroom like a—a toad in a hole. That is just plain stupid." She flushed angrily, the glint in her eyes aggressive.

"You are offering to work?" he questioned skeptically. "Your time away from here really has worked a miraculous change in your personality."

"If you say so," she agreed pertly. "I wouldn't know." David's look said volumes about his lack of faith in her memory loss.

However, he did hand her over to Tammi when they returned to the office complex, and Sally began to learn the filing system that kept the huge corporation in order.

She worked with Tammi all afternoon and enjoyed it. Tammi was twenty and full of the devil. Joie de vivre bubbled from her, sparkled in everything she did. There was no question of her intelligence. She knew exactly what she was doing, why she was doing it and how to do it very well. Sally was relieved to find she learned easily. She did not often have to have her young teacher repeat a bit of information.

Alicia Ricci passed through the office a couple of times and subjected Sally to looks dipped in pure venom each time she did.

"D'you know what?" Tammi asked conversationally as the door closed behind Alicia the last time it happened. "I bet that old serpent in the Garden of Eden wasn't a snake at all. It was just a dame who hated Eve because she got to Adam first." She giggled. "Probably a witch who changed herself into a snake. And we now work with her in her natural form."

"Tammi, you are impossible," Sally declared.

Tammi slanted a glance at her. "She was really working on David before you turned up in his life again, you know. And she has always reminded me of a snake with those glittering yellow eyes of hers. A beautiful slithery boa constrictor, trying to sneak up on David and wrap herself around him so he couldn't escape. I've a notion you came back just as she was moving in for the kill." And Tammi put her hands around her throat, tightened her fingers, rolled her eyes and stuck her tongue out. She looked absolutely horrible.

Ann Evans raised cool eyebrows as they indulged in a gale of laughter, but Jackie Haines just went on working quietly. David came through the door Alicia had closed behind her.

"I'll be ready to leave in ten minutes," he announced. "Tammi, will you check these invoices before ten tomorrow, please? I need to know if they are correct by then, but you will have time to do them in the morning."

"Okay, David. Do you want me to be here early?"

She lived with her parents in a small town a few miles away, she had told Sally.

"No. Just stir your stumps when you do arrive," he answered casually as he turned back into his private office. Sally felt a twinge of envy at the easy manner he had with his staff.

"Does he always deliver his orders personally?" she asked.

"If he wants a special thing done. He's super to work for. You have to get the things done and have them right, but he always appreciates it."

"Hmm." Sally was still pensive when David reappeared to collect her and hand her into the Land Rover. She thought of the lovely Alicia and her obvious resentment, and of Tammi's coolly dropped information about Alicia's hopes.

Undoubtedly Alicia Ricci was accustomed to getting things done for David and doing them right. She did not allow herself to think of the form David's appreciation might have taken if Tammi's hints meant anything.

Serpent in the Garden of Eden indeed! If so, then she and David had certainly bitten into the bitter apple of dissension. She grinned ruefully, and David glanced at her sharply as he pulled up in the courtyard. He was quick, Sally allowed to herself. Thank goodness he wasn't up to mind reading.

SHE MANAGED THE EVENING rather well, first by getting down to dinner in good time, dressed again in a gown whose waist she cinched with a matching scarf. This time it was a midnight-blue silk whose hem was embroidered with an elaborate foot-deep scroll of gold thread. The color became her, and the scarf set off her narrow waist very nicely.

Nonna greeted her politely and even addressed a remark or two to her during the course of the meal. Carla had been no problem. She had accepted her good-night kiss with angelic complacency and had settled in for the night.

But Sally was not managing so well now. As the meal drew to a close, her mind switched back and forth with a desperation that grew as the inevitable approached.

David stood to push back his grandmother's chair, and Sally shot him a look of craven despair. He hooked speculative brows into the tumble of dark hair on his forehead, then grinned with a sardonic understanding of her stormy expression as he bent his head to kiss his relative's wrinkled cheek. *Nonna* reached up and patted his brown face as she bade him a fond good-night. She nodded to Sally and closed the door as she left the room.

Sally stood hastily as David turned to her. "I'm tired. I think I need to go to bed, too." She despised the slight quaver hidden in the words and hoped he did not hear it.

"Shall I come help?"

Sally swallowed quickly, the image of David's aid last night all too vivid. "I think not," she got out. "Even the extensive wardrobe upstairs will not stand up long to your brand of undressing a person." Her blush was painful.

David watched it stain her face with considerable interest as he stood aside for her to pass.

"Pity," she thought she heard him murmur as she

fled the room and sped up the stairs. She did hear distinctly as he requested Franco to bring a pot of coffee into his study. Good. That probably meant he would be working. She might even be fast asleep before he decided to come up.

She undressed at speed, searched frantically through the drawers until she found the one that contained a selection of silken nightwear. Shifting to the bottom of the neat piles, she found a pair of apricot silk pajamas that she snatched with a sigh of relief.

She heard David come into his dressing room then. Very hastily she stepped back into the lace-and-silk confection she had worn for panties and pulled the pajamas on over them in a frantic rush. Her fingers trembled so she was scarcely able to deal with the small buttons that closed the top of the set, but she managed as she dashed into the bathroom to splash water over her face. She washed her teeth, steeled herself and marched through to the bedroom, ready to do battle.

David Rossi would have war on his hands if he so much as laid a finger on her, she decided grimly. If the hysterical outburst she had indulged in last night had brought the household to the door to witness her screaming performance when she was in shock, he could jolly well expect to have the roof shouted down around his ears tonight when she was conscious of exactly what was going on. She shivered when the direction that those goings-on might take presented a vague, but nonetheless frightening, picture to her vivid imagination.

Well, just let him try. He might be able to insist she

shared his bed with him. But that was as far as she was prepared to let it go!

She clicked off the bedside lamp and dived beneath the covers. With nervous fingers she pulled up the silky sheet and the fluffy coverlet, her eyes glued to the crack of light she could see under David's dressing-room door. She made sure she was on the narrowest margin of the mattress as possible, a far reach from the other side of the bed. Stiff as a board, she waited, trying to get her heartbeat and her breath under control. Her eyes were huge, frightened, in the soft light of the lamp on his side of the bed. And her efforts to control her shaking body were expended in a lost cause. She was not able to be still.

He opened the door to the dressing room, and adrenaline shot through her system, demanding action. But Sally forced herself to be quiet, to lie still, as he advanced across the enormous room toward the bed. She didn't die as he came to her. But she wanted to.

David was naked to the waist. His muscles rippled under the tanned skin of his torso as he reached for the light on the table beside the king-sized bed and snapped it off. As the well-sprung mattress yielded to his weight, Sally's nerves quivered a response that translated itself into a wild lurch of her stomach muscles. Wishing to disappear into the mattress, she went rigid, unblinking in the darkness and waited for him to move.

By the time her heart had given up the absurd attempt to deafen her with its thunder and steadied to a more normal throb, the only sound in the room was

David's easy regular breathing. He had fallen instantly asleep, apparently.

Listening to the gentle sound of his breathing, she wafted up a heartfelt prayer of thanksgiving that he was one of those amazing individuals who was able to do this. Her sigh of relief was tempered by the realization that he probably also possessed the faculty to be instantly awake. She lay rigid as a mummy and waited for the night to pass. It did. And sometime in the early-morning hours, she fell asleep, too.

BUT DAVID WOKE HER before first light again with his demand that she ride out with him.

Quito joined them as they walked through the early dawn to the courtyard. He was in his usual good spirits and cheered Sally considerably. She had had a bad night and was feeling the effects.

The splendid palomino flicked his ears at them as they entered the courtyard. His reins were held by a stocky well-built individual whose eyes were shadowed by the brim of a cowboy hat.

"Morning, Robert. Nice to see you." The deep and urbane voice of her husband was edged with a sarcasm Sally's sensitized ears had no difficulty discerning. "Is Juan ill?"

"I let him sleep in this morning," the man called Robert replied.

Sally, who had just caught a glimpse of the youngster who had greeted them yesterday morning when they came out for their jaunt, looked at him in faint surprise. He seemed to be watching her, but she could not be sure. His eyes were hidden by the slant of his big hat brim.

Nonna rattled off a spate of Italian as David helped her into the buggy and handed her the reins. Sally went around to her side, to find the man called Robert at her elbow.

"Nice to see you back, Sally," he remarked casually. "Let me help you up."

A quiver of apprehension shot through the girl's nerves. There was something about the man's greeting that sounded impossibly intimate. She withdrew from him instinctively, unaware of her husband's intent look.

"Thank you very much. I can manage," she said. And she scrambled in, causing the buggy to rock in her haste. David watched her from where he stood on the other side of the carriage, his face a mirror of his cynicism. *Nonna* flicked the reins against the sleek animal between the buggy shafts. The bay responded, and they clattered out of the courtyard.

Sally heard David's quick flow of Spanish behind her and the creak of saddle leather as he mounted. She felt embarrassed, unhappy, and paid little attention to the section of vineyard they covered that morning. Her mind was fixed on the way the man called Robert had greeted her. David's own greeting and his words to him had implied that the man's appearance was unexpected. And she knew he had lied about the boy. Why? Who was he?

Much as she would have liked to ignore the situation, she asked about Robert when they returned to the hacienda from the early-morning inspection.

"He's my trainer. He has charge of my racehorses," David answered. "And he is a good one. I would hate to lose him." The threat was implicit in his tone. He would be sacked without regret if the dark man beside her decided to do it.

"Is he. ... was he someone I knew be-before?"

"Yes, Sally. He was." David thrust open the bedroom door, then closed it behind them. He wrapped a long hand around her arm to stop her in her tracks. "I didn't give a damn what you did before." His soft tone was deadly in its intensity. "I figured you weren't worth losing a good man over. But the stakes have changed, Sally. Charles means more to me than anything in the world. I will fire Sandman if you see him once. You will have no men in your life until you tell me where Charles is, so if you want any relief, you had best remember." His meaning was very clear indeed. A knot tightened in the pit of Sally's stomach.

"You are foul! How can you be so abominable as to suggest I cannot live without...without men. I hate you! Don't touch me! And I think your Robert Sandman is horrid. I could never be attracted to a man like that." Truly offended, she glared like a wild thing, hated him with a passion.

"You think not?" he sneered at her. "He's a knight in shining armor compared to some you, er, entertained."

Tears burned unshed in Sally's eyes, and gall seared the back of her throat, which felt as if it were on fire. A charged silence fell between them. Sally stared up at the man who towered over her. His angry eyes flared with a deep passion. Then he sighed as though it hurt him and dropped her arm as if it had suddenly gone too hot to handle.

"Get changed, Sally." He broke the tense silence

irritably. "We will have a busy morning. We have to fly out of here before noon if we are to make your appointment with Mellon in good time." He unbuttoned his khaki work shirt and pulled it out of the brown jeans he had worn for the morning ride. The muscles in his back gleamed as he vanished into his dressing room, the discarded shirt in his hand.

Sally stared after him, rooted to the spot by the sharp reaction the sight of his muscular back sent charging about her system. "Dear God!" she muttered with a distracted and very horrified awareness of the strange tingle that coursed down her nerve paths. *Is it possible I really do react the way he thinks I do? What if I really must have a man about all the time?*

She was very thoughtful as she dressed in the same blue velvet skirt she had worn yesterday. She pulled on a cashmere sweater with long sleeves and a cuffed neck, tied a gay scarf under the roll of the neck and looked for footwear. The shoes she had worn yesterday had chafed her feet. She doubted she would have a chance to change before they left for San Francisco and knew she needed to wear something comfortable. She finally settled on a pair of blue suede boots. They were a little too large, but she zipped them up over thick cotton socks she found in the drawer with the tennis things and found they fit perfectly.

She applied a little makeup and fluffed up her hair, still distracted by the strength of her reaction to David as a man. As she thought about it, she realized she was aware of him every moment of the day. If he entered a room or left it, she knew without seeing him do it. When he looked at her with those dark and unfriendly eyes of his, her nerves would tingle a warning whether she herself was looking at him or not.

And she had caught herself watching him when she was sure he was not watching her. This had happened several times in the past couple of days. What did it mean? Was she truly the kind of woman he so callously believed her to be, a woman unable to live without the constant sexual companionship of a man? Or rather, of men, the more the better?

To the other men she had met—James Maclean, John Mellon, Alan Stern and that nice orthodontist—her only reaction had been a sort of friendly gratitude. As for the man this morning, the man David said trained his racehorses, she had only felt a quiver of dislike for him.

Still, she could not deny David was beginning to affect her powerfully. Her constant awareness of him and the state of tension of her nerves was something she could not ignore as much as she would have liked to do just that.

It's just because of this silly campaign he is on, she told herself. He was forcing himself on her, forcing her to be aware of him by his insistence upon her constant presence. He had set out to make himself the center of her attention, and he was certainly succeeding.

She gave up her fruitless analysis of the situation and went down to meet David in the hall below. As she looked into those dark and cynical eyes of his, she had the distinct feeling she might be living a nightmare.

THE NIGHTMARE GOT WORSE as the morning went on.

"I didn't know you kept racehorses," she remarked as they drove toward the office complex.

"Did you not, Sally?" He sounded skeptical. "I seem to recall that you followed the racing season with dedication during the time you were here. You made quite a hit in the owners' boxes of the racecourses of the state as I remember. With various other owners, of course. And my trainer." That was the end of that conversation.

Sally went into the office in a flaming temper. She pitched into the work Tammi had to do with a fierce concentration. After the invoices David wanted were finally checked and in order, she went to the huge warehouse with Tammi to count the items each invoice called for and make sure everything was delivered.

They had been working ten minutes when David came into the building. He crossed to them, reached down and removed the clipboard Sally had in her hands and gave it to Tammi.

"I will send Jackie out to help you," he told Tammi, his lips twisted with displeasure. "I need Sally in the office at the moment." His hand closed over his wife's arm, viselike.

"Okay, David." Tammi shrugged, unspoken curiosity in her voice. "I'm about finished. Sally has been a great help. She catches on quickly."

David smiled coldly at Tammi and hurried Sally out of the building and back to the office. He did not say a word to her until he had closed the door to his private office behind them. "And just what the hell are you up to, Sally?'' He stood over her, threat in his attitude.

"I'm not sure what you mean." The girl was breathless from the fast trip back into his inner sanctum. She stared up at him, affronted and wide-eyed.

His lips thinned with his exasperation, he stared down at her, put his other hand on her free arm and gave her a disconcerting little shake. "Sally, I told you very clearly that you are to spend all of your time where I can see you. You will not disappear for any reason. Do you understand?"

"No, I don't." She squirmed like an eel, trying to shake him off. "Let me go! I will not be treated so."

"You will be treated any way I see fit." Again that little shake. "Do I make myself clear?"

"Just who do you think you are? You make conditions, try to control me, say dreadful things about me, and I am supposed to just take it." She continued her struggle in spite of the warning flare in the black depths of his eyes. "Well, I won't, you know. I am not your slave, no matter what you think."

"Oh, but you are, Sally," he breathed dangerously. "You are. My amoral hateful little slave." Color rose under his tan, darkened it. Sally did not take the warning, flailed out at him. He muttered an oath, caught her to his hard length and buried his face in her neck. Sally went still as a stone in outraged surprise. His lips moved against the sensitive cord of the white column under them, and Sally quivered, her body trembling with the unexpectedness of the sensation that shot through her nervous system.

David laughed sarcastically and raised his dark head to return her agitated stare of incredulity with a hard lack of sentiment. As she looked into the darkness of his bitter gaze, she knew she had no hope of concealing her reaction from him. He understood exactly how his nearness affected her.

"Give up this damned charade, Sally." The demand was soft, deadly. "You can't win. Your body demands male attention as it demands food and drink, my little wife. It calls to men." Disgust registered on his lean features. "And with your looks, every man who sees you wants to answer the call." He laughed then, and the quality of the sound made a mockery of any softer feeling a man might have for a woman.

Sally shivered. Black despair hit her in a shock wave. She sobbed, a wrenching, shuddering convulsion that tore through her slender body and left her helpless. David's hands tightened on her instinctively and prevented her from falling. As she hung there, suspended between two hard hands that punished rather than held her, she became conscious of the woman standing in the doorway beyond David's shoulder.

Alicia Ricci clung to the ornate knob of that door, her face as white as a sheet. Sally had not heard her knock, and David did not glance around. He had not heard her or was ignoring her if he had done so. Her dark eyes flamed like an angry cat's, and hate distorted her handsome features, twisted them in a mask of vengeance. Her lips drew back in a snarl. And then she was gone, the door closing as silently as it had opened.

David did not allow the distraction. He shook Sally lightly again. "I'm the only man around, Sally.

And I shall not answer. I am gambling that your need will drive you to tell me where Charles is so I will let you go. Until that time I plan to keep you under constant surveillance. And you are slave to my plan. Is that finally clear to you?''

Sally just stared at him. She could not have uttered a sound for any reason. Her thoughts were rioting in bitter chaos. There was no way for her to deny to herself the effect David's nearness had upon her. Her body thrilled, throbbed to his touch. She wanted, more than she had ever wanted anything, she was sure, to sink against him and drown in his warmth. Fiercely resentful, she was sure he knew exactly how she felt.

The cold amusement in his dark look knifed through her, causing her eyes to smolder with rage. He released her, and Sally sank into the nearest chair. *Oh, God!* she cried in a silent frenzy. *All those things he has been telling me about myself must be true.*

She wanted David. She wanted him to hold her, wanted him to love and caress her. She wanted him with a passion that shocked her.

Yet, how much she hated him, she told herself. The ambivalence of her feelings made her very uncertain of David, very wary. How could one hate a person and still have such a need to be close to him, to want his love? White-faced, she dropped her head in her hands and gave in to a mindless kind of grief. David watched her, an odd expression hidden in his dark eyes. Then with a sigh, he turned and went from the room.

Sally did not go back out into the outer office the rest of the morning. David went to his meeting in the big boardroom on the next floor of the office complex and took his hateful and very beautiful secretary with him.

Sally stayed in the luxurious and silent bolt hole where he had left her and tried to recover her equanimity. She relaxed in the deep chair and sought for the peace that she found so hard to come by.

Stark realization of her position was clear to her. She was here with the man she had married. She had wronged him as no woman has a right to wrong her husband. And in doing so, she had turned him into an implacable enemy who, considering, had no wish to harm her. He only wanted his child. He was willing to wreck her to get Charles, and he would not let her go until he did.

In all fairness, she knew his feeling toward her was justified. It was up to her to cause him no worry and to do all in her power to regain her memory. Then she could leave his disturbing presence and get on with her own life.

How would she feel if her children were gone from it? She could not answer that question, but she knew very well David was not tolerant enough to allow her to share the children with him. He considered her a plague to be eliminated from the lives of the little ones before she infected them in some permanent way. In the light of his evidence she might be just that, she acknowledged.

So she would go, she decided. As soon as she could remember where it was she should go to for the rest of her life. Yet a future that did not include the proud and arrogant man who was her husband seemed impossibly bleak.

THAT AFTERNOON David flew her to San Francisco in the sleek executive jet parked on his airstrip. When they arrived at the busy airport south of the city, a silver Jaguar, parked in a private bay, waited for them.

David whisked her into town in time for her appointment with Mellon. He had been morose and taciturn throughout the brief flight. He was still unapproachable when they reached the psychiatrist's office. High in a tower overlooking the Golden Gate, Mellon's consultation room was furnished with deep-piled carpet that stretched wall to wall and hugged the sills of the floor-to-ceiling windows that framed the spectacular view. Huge cushions were scattered about. Upholstered in lovely earth colors, each had a small table beside it that contained an intriguing work of art.

David took one look from the entrance to the equally plush waiting room that was much more conventionally furnished and opted to stay there.

Sally, knotted with misery, was not sure whether she missed his quiet presence in the room as she talked to the doctor or not. She was a little relieved he was not there to hear her tell Mellon she thought his attitude toward her was entirely understandable.

"Why is that, Sally?" Mellon asked quietly.

Sally looked at him miserably, swallowed the sob in her throat and told him what she had found out about herself.

"And you are sure David is right in what he is doing to you now?"

"Yes. How else can he be expected to handle me?"

She discussed the sleeping arrangement with him

without any vestige of rancor, told him of *nonna*'s
justified rejection of her and little Carla's evident
love. And she told him of her recollection of the story
of the lion and the mouse. He was extremely interested in this and amused at her explanation of how it
had come about. She left the session with a sense of a
vague relief from the tension that knotted her nerves
and filled her with apathy.

Then they went shopping. David took the short list
she had made, looked at it and laughed it to scorn.
He thrust it into the pocket of the fitted black suede
pants he wore and proceeded to take charge of the expedition. He paid no attention to his wife's lack of
interest. She was just too drained of emotion to do
battle with him.

She sat back without a murmur and watched him
assemble the intrigued shop assistants and get them
moving in the direction he wished them to go. He
looked as arrogant as some high-riding buccaneer,
she decided, with his proud dark head and his masculine physique. His suede trousers fit like a second
skin. The matching black suede jacket ended at his
trim waist. He wore a black cashmere sweater under
the jacket, the high ribbed neck close around his
muscular throat.

He was undoubtedly the best-looking man she had
ever seen, his Mediterranean ancestry obvious in the
color of his skin, the blackness of his eyes and hair.
And he was full of charm when he wanted to be. He
wanted to be now.

Sally was scandalized and quite worn out by the
time David called a halt to the buying spree. He had
the eye of a connoisseur and put together outfits, ac-

cessories and all the bits and pieces that go to make up high fashion with the ease of an expert. The only thing he had allowed her a voice in was the purchase of jeans. But he insisted on buying the outrageously expensive designer kind, although he did allow her to get the regulation blue color. Sally bought three pairs, then insisted on having plain shirts, as well.

They finally left for the airport with the Jaguar loaded with boxes and bags full of beautiful things.

"You spent a fortune on me," she accused him as they sped south down the wide freeway. "I do not need so many clothes."

"I can afford it," he told her briefly. "And the holidays are coming up. You will need them."

"The holidays?"

He gave her a dark look, his disbelief in her blocked memory clear in his eyes. "Yes, Sally. The holidays. Thanksgiving. Christmas. New Year's Eve." His smile was sarcastic. "We do a lot of entertaining over the holidays. It is traditional and expected of us. I can't have you running around in shoes that are too big, clothes that do not fit you. Bad for my image."

"Oh." She registered his real reason for his extravagance with a sense of hurt. For a while there she had entertained the thought he might be outfitting her because he wanted to please her. She should have known differently, but his real reason stung, anyway. "Have you been shopping with me before?"

"No, I haven't, Sally. That's why you have a closet full of inappropriate clothing. Your taste runs strictly to party things and the like." His glance flicked over the blue velvet suit she wore under the knee-length fur. Sally realized he was right. There was really nothing in the huge and bulging closet that was suitable for ordinary everyday wear.

It was dark when David landed the jet, bringing it down with consummate skill. Miguel Sanchez met them with the big station wagon. The two men stowed the packages in the rear of the big vehicle, and Miguel drove them to the hacienda. Sanchez was a mechanic. He took care of the complicated machinery of the Rancho and doubled as chauffeur, Sally knew.

They had no time to dress for dinner. Franco helped Sally off with her fur as they entered the door. They washed in the delightful half bath just off the entry hall and went directly to the dining room.

They were late, and David apologized to his grandmother, who was already seated. She accepted the apology with a faintly disapproving frown and watched as he seated Sally.

Dinner proceeded in much the same manner as it had the night before. David and his grandmother talked while Sally listened. It would take time, the girl knew, for *nonna* to accept her back in the household. If she ever did.

"You have had a good effect on Carla," *nonna* offered suddenly. Surprised, Sally smiled at her.

"I am glad," she answered with a simple sincerity.

"Already, she is happy," the old lady continued. "She talked to me today for the first time." A small frown gathered on her wrinkled forehead. David watched the two of them with a masked interest. "I really cannot understand it." His grandmother appeared truly perplexed. "You cared nothing for the child or for Charles before. But you care now."

Sally breathed a sigh of thankfulness. Perhaps *nonna*'s words meant she was about to relax toward her. The girl caught David's critical gaze and tensed. His smile mocked. It told her as plainly as words that she might be going up in his grandmother's estimation, but she was not in his. Not by a long chalk!

Her spirits sank as she realized any courtesy he showed, any variance in his attitude, was done in an effort to cause only one thing—the quick restoration of her memory and his son. He would go to any lengths to bring this about. His every move was a ploy with which he meant to wear her down and break through the blank wall of her amnesia.

Oh, God, she prayed silently, *please let my memory return soon. Else I shall lose my mind and allow him to eliminate me without a struggle.*

Nonna excused herself as usual when they had finished dinner. David held the door for Sally, then escorted her across the hall into the big room he used for a study. Book-lined, with comfortable leather wing chairs scattered about and a large leather sofa under the windows, it was definitely a man's room. A fire crackled cozily in the large hearth at one end of the long room. An enormous desk occupied pride of place at the other.

"Would you like to sit by the fire?" he asked quietly. "I have some work to do before we go to bed. You may watch television if you like." He gestured to the electronic equipment built into the cabinets to the left of the fireplace. "Or read."

Just like that! She bit back the retort as it rose, gave him a speaking glance of dislike and marched to a big leather chair drawn up to the fireplace. It had the advantage of being placed so that its back was to the end of the room where the desk stood. At least, she could sit in peace and not have to look at the difficult man who expected to rule her every waking moment.

"Accept it, Sally," he warned softly. "I am entirely sincere when I say you shall not draw a breath I do not know about until you tell me where Charles is. It is the only damn thing I want from you, and I shall have it. I might as well warn you I almost always get what I want. In this case, I am not prepared to put up with failure."

He moved across the deep-piled carpet then to the equipment on the cupboards near the fireplace. The girl closed her eyes against the ache caused by her awareness of him.

Music flowed around her as he activated a stereo with a rich full sound. She did not recognize the music, but it was tender, throbbing with sweetness. It filled the room with soft sound and soothed her. She kept her eyes closed and tried to relax into the support of the big chair. She was sure no woman had ever felt more miserable.

Whatever would she do if her memory never came back? What lay in her future then?

CHAPTER EIGHT

SALLY WENT THROUGH THE ORDEAL of the sleeping arrangement with much the same trepidation as she had the night before. She found, on going into her dressing room, that the clothes it had contained were removed, as were the shoes. The results of the day's shopping hung as neat replacements. The several pairs of shoes David had insisted upon buying were neatly arranged on the shoe rack. The drawer of silk scarves had been emptied and now contained the few that matched the outfits purchased during the day. Even the drawers full of lingerie had been cleaned out to make way for the day's loot.

Sally climbed into a set of the pajamas she had asked for, buttoned them and zipped up a fleecy housecoat over them.

"What happened to all the other clothes?" she asked as she encountered David on his way from the bath to his dressing room.

The sight of him was unexpected. She threw the question at him in an effort to divert her thoughts from his appearance. He had a towel tossed over black curls damp from the shower. A short terry wrap, which fell to mid-thigh, was fastened around his lean waist. He looked, she thought, like an ancient Roman gladiator who had just left his steam bath. And he had probably had an ancient Roman gladiator for an ancestor. The lineage showed clearly in his muscled chest, in the powerful length of his legs.

His physical effect was like a heady wine that struck at her senses and made them reel. And what did she know of Roman gladiators? She clutched at the thought in wonder. Another memory from her past.

David watched the expressions as they chased themselves across her face, his own careful, withdrawn.

"I figured you would not need the old clothes with the new type of life you will be leading, Sally. Since your life-style will be so different, I did not think it a good idea to leave them around to remind you of your good old days. I gave them to the Salvation Army. If we overlooked anything today, you can get it next week when you go to see Mellon."

He turned then and vanished into his dressing room. Sally scrambled quickly into the far side of the bed, too tired and upset to react to his implication. She turned out the light and experienced the same horror of anticipation she had the night before.

David came in, and was asleep without comment before her heartbeat stilled. She huddled in the dark, the fresh clean scent of his cologne tickling her nostrils, with her ears alert for a change in his soft breathing.

Three weeks or so were to go by before she accepted the sleeping arrangement with any sort of equanimity. David would send her in to shower first, shower himself while she got into bed, then come in, get into bed, turn out the light and go instantly and deeply asleep. Sally did learn that he never snored and lay quietly in his sleep.

Several times she did awaken to find his arm around her body as though he had sought and found her in his sleep. After trying gingerly to remove it and almost causing him to awaken, she just gave up and lay awake, tense and quiet until he removed it. Always he awakened her in the morning. And he never commented on the fact that he himself sometimes awoke to find her in his arms.

The morning after the first trip to San Francisco, Sally asked him at breakfast for her own horse to ride. "I'm sure *nonna* would be relieved not to have me so close to her," she pleaded. "And I really would enjoy riding. . . ."

David looked at her, a curious light in his dark eyes. "Are you sure you know how?" he asked skeptically.

"You must know whether or not I can ride," she answered with some heat. "After all, I was. . . am your wife!"

"I knew very little about you, Sally." He considered her bleakly. "It didn't seem worth my while to find out."

He watched with interest as she flushed with annoyance. Sally bit her tongue and glared at him. She was determined not to arouse him, determined to keep their present relationship on an even keel if it was at all possible. But he would keep making provocative remarks that irritated and challenged her.

"Well," she tried to sound reasonable, "if it isn't too much trouble, I would like to try and ride each morning."

"If you think you can handle it..." his voice trailed off. He glanced at his grandmother. That old lady shrugged. Her expression was watchful as she took in the girl's mutinous face.

David looked dubious, but he reached for the telephone on the stand against the wall behind his chair and dialed. He ordered a horse by name to be saddled for her.

Finished with breakfast, Sally hurried across the patio as she rushed to see the horse he had chosen for her. David and his grandmother followed at a more sedate pace.

A pert little mare stood beside the great palomino. Black as satin and as gleaming, she tossed her head and eyed the girl who advanced toward her in an interested friendliness.

Sally skipped across the forecourt and touched the lovely creature's shining neck. "Oh, you beauty," she breathed. "What is her name, David?"

He laughed. "As you say. Bella, for beauty."

The little mare nuzzled her, and Sally's eyes sparkled. "Thank you for letting me ride her, David." She gathered up the reins from Sandman, barely noticing him in her pleasure. She thrust her toe into the stirrup and was ready to swing up when she felt his hands at her waist. She became rigid as a poker as the revulsion she had felt the day before came into full flower.

"I can mount myself," she exclaimed coldly. "Please allow me to do so."

He stepped back instantly, his expression hidden by the wide brim of the hat he wore. David, who had taken a step forward, said nothing as Sally lifted herself into the saddle with a motion that said she was accustomed to doing so. He moved to the mare's side, checked her stirrups and left them long so her legs were at stretch. He swung into his own saddle, said a brief thanks to Sandman and nodded to his grandmother.

Young Juan was there to care for the horses when they returned and from then on brought them their mounts.

Sally thoroughly enjoyed these morning rides. She felt quite natural in the saddle and had no fear of the motion. Once, when they first broke into a trot, David told her sharply to settle into the saddle. She had been about to rise with the rhythm of the animal under her but found it very comfortable to allow her weight to hold her to the horse's movement. Her husband observed coolly but made no comment.

Sally wondered where she had learned to ride, and why David was not aware of the fact that she could. She soon gave up the puzzle in the enjoyment of the early morning.

Days settled down into a routine then. Every morning they would breakfast, then have their early-morning survey of a portion of the vineyards. Sally loved that time of the day.

After changing into businesslike clothing, they would go to the office. Sally worked with Tammi, ignored Ann's unfriendliness and respected Jackie Haines and her seeming wish for aloofness.

Alicia Ricci was another matter. The woman always looked at her in a manner that projected a vitriolic dislike. She pounced on any small error she could charge to Sally as the girl learned the office routine from Tammi. Sally was quick and rarely had to be told twice about a thing, but Alicia took a gleeful delight in pointing out any fault.

Sally took it for several days, then fed up, she decided her intention not to arouse David's wrath by pertness or self-defense had nothing to do with the attacks launched at her by his personal assistant.

One day David came through over the intercom and asked Tammi to retrieve a special report he needed from the files. Tammi was in the warehouse, checking some new invoices. Jackie Haines had gone with her to help. Sally explained but said she would find the report and bring it in. He thanked her and clicked off.

She went to the files, happy she was able to be of use to David Rossi in a small way. Her fingers had just closed over the report when it was jerked out of them. Her head snapped up in amazed protest, and she found herself staring into Alicia's dark hate-filled eyes.

"You are not authorized to go into the personal files of this corporation," the woman hissed.

Sally reacted with an involuntary speed. She snatched the folder back, her own eyes a blaze of blue.

"Miss Ricci, I would remind you that you are an employee of my husband. I understand he is the chief stockholder of this corporation. As such, he has just requested that I find this report and bring it to him. I assure you I intend to do just that. I would think," she added tightly, "it would behoove you to conceal your obvious dislike of me. I shall be forced to bring your discourtesy to his attention if you do not."

"You don't think Dave gives a damn about how I treat you, do you?" The other's laugh was not pleasant. "He doesn't care how you are treated!"

With swift dismay Sally recognized the truth of the thrust, but her head rose proudly. "I would not want to put it to the test if I were you," she managed defiantly as she marched through Ricci's office and tapped on David's door. She tossed off his hard look at her flushed face as she crossed to his desk and put the folder on it. She turned then and marched smartly back past Alicia and returned to work.

Inside she died a little. She knew Alicia Ricci spoke the truth. David didn't give a damn how she was treated. All she represented to him was the pathway back to his son. The knowledge was fast becoming almost more than she could bear. She dared not ask why this was so. Her anger abated, to be replaced by a hurtful misery. She assuaged it by hard work. Alicia backed off, gave her a little peace.

THE WEATHER, which had been misty with occasional showers, turned fine. Thanksgiving came, and the Rancho donned holiday dress. The hacienda was filled with the scents of good cooking. Pies and cakes were baked, and lovely crusty loaves of bread. On the morning of Thanksgiving Day, great turkeys, plump with dressing, found their way into the large kitchen oven, along with delicious-looking hams. Sauces and vegetables were bubbling away, melding exotic flavors.

People swarmed into the house. Sally met aunts and uncles, cousins and kinfolk. All the workers who lived on the ranch were invited to come to the feast, and many did. Among them were Jack Haines and his daughter. They were withdrawn and unfriendly.

Haines finally flashed a glance at Sally. It was strange, distraught. Then he retired morosely into a wicker chair removed from the main body of people who laughed and chattered around him without much interest in him. He showed little in them.

Sally looked at his slender withdrawn face and was moved to pity. He appeared haunted, and he certainly was not a happy man. Why did he stay here, she wondered. He was an excellent wine maker according to all reports. It would be easy for him to find another vintner eager to use his talents. Surely it would be easier on him to put his bitter memories behind him and move on.

Long tables had been set up in the pleasant patio. These were draped with thick white damask linen with an autumn arrangement of flowers in the center of each table. The sun was bright and added to the spirit of the festivities. Although the day was cool, the patio trapped the warmth of the sun and blocked the wind in a manner that allowed one to go about in shirt sleeves in perfect comfort.

Carla was enthralled by all the company and activity. After tentative advances, which were recognized and encouraged by her cousins and the other little ones of the huge party, she joined in the fun and tumbled about the feet of the adults with a joyous disregard of life and limb.

David was something of a favorite with the young ones. Sally watched as he took pains to address each child personally. He handled them so well, listening to them with attention, teasing and talking with them. He was serious or laughing as each occasion demanded, and Sally knew before the day was very old that he was a man who truly loved children. She sighed at her inhumanity in depriving him of his own little ones. How could she have been so hardhearted?

She did not know and went back to the business of being hostess. *Nonna* watched from the high-backed chair in which she sat, the dowager queen of all she surveyed.

The women chattered around her yet watched Sally from the corners of dark eyes. Twice she came upon groups, interrupting rapid spates of Italian that she could not understand. She was conscious of a flow of overt hostility from them. From the look in their eyes she knew they talked about her.

The men, too, cast covert glances at her, eyes coolly speculative as they assessed her still misshapen but undeniably lovely features, then slid over her equally undeniably perfect form.

Sally, fed up, gave up all pretense of an attempt to be sociable and joined the frolicking children.

"Come with me, Sally." David came and extracted her from a shrieking cluster of preschoolers with whom she was playing a game of monster. He looked at her in a way that was oddly possessive, as well as puzzled. The children objected strenuously at the loss of their playmate, but he removed her, anyway.

He kept her at his side then with an arrogant air about him few could miss. His attitude offered a challenge to the others Sally could not misread. It said quite plainly that he expected them to realize she was his wife and was to be treated as such. It caused her to glow with an inner happiness she did not suppress.

Just before the dinner bell rang, James Maclean walked under the arch with Marion at his side.

"I am so glad to see you, Marion." Sally greeted her friend with a heartfelt relief. *One really has difficulty when one lives with constant disapproval,* she thought wryly as she hugged Maclean's companion with a glow of happiness.

"Hey, save a little of that for me!" Maclean commanded.

Sally cast a laughing glance at David and stretched up to kiss Jim's rugged chin. The doctor hugged her, his arms convulsing slightly as she pulled hurriedly away.

David did not seem upset at her impulsive action. He linked his arm in his friend's and moved him in the direction of the bar. Sally turned to Marion, not sure why she felt such stark relief at her husband's acceptance of her show of affection.

"Are you and James dating?" Sally asked as she steered Marion around the dish-laden tables.

"Well, in a way...." Marion hesitated, looked carefully at Sally. "I'm a widow, you see. Recently enough so that it's hard for me to actually think of another man as a date...."

Sally had not known of her friend's widowhood. It had not been discussed during her stay in hospital. She turned to Marion now, quick sympathy in her eyes as she drew her down upon the cushions of a wicker lounge just vacated. "I'm sorry, Marion. You never mentioned it before."

"I know. It's not something I talk about." The nurse's eyes glistened with an unshed tear. She smiled hastily. "But Jim knows. He's been kind enough to ask me out a few times. He's so sweet," she smiled. Sally hadn't thought of the rugged doctor as sweet. She gave Marion a thoughtful look and returned her smile.

"I think he's a fine man," she declared softly. "But I didn't realize he wasn't married." She looked to where he stood with David. Carla had spotted him and propelled herself at his legs as Sally watched. Maclean picked her up and kissed her, his attention diverted from his conversation with David. "I thought he must be married, with a house full of happy kids and a doting wife. He looks the type." Carla's eager acceptance of the big doctor only confirmed Sally's firmly expressed opinion.

"He is the type," Marion spoke mildly, an odd note ringing in the words. "His wife divorced him and left, taking his two sons with her."

Sally's quick ear picked up the hint of censure, and she examined Marion's quiet features. Was she critical of Maclean for allowing the divorce? Something in the nurse's expression warned her to let sleeping dogs lie, not to pry, but she was unable to leave it. She asked the question even as she guessed the answer.

"Oh, Marion," she whispered reluctantly, "you surely don't mean I was the cause of his d-divorce?" She didn't need to hear the words to know this was exactly what Marion did mean.

"They used to come here, Sally," she murmured, a deep feeling in her tone. "He says you professed to be in love with him. He and Linda weren't very happy together, but he wanted no part of you. So you framed him, compromised him and made sure his wife was on hand to misunderstand. He swears you did him a favor, but your motive was revenge because he ignored you.''

Sally went white as a sheet. She froze there in the sunshine, unable to move under the onslaught of emotion that gripped her. Shame tore through her. She shook as she forced herself to remain seated but resisted the impulse to leap to her feet and scream she was not like that, could not do such a revolting thing. She sobbed suddenly, and Marion's arm came around her shoulders.

"Don't cry, Sally,'' she whispered. "People are looking. Anyway,'' she continued stoutly, "no one will ever be able to convince me you could do something like that!''

"Oh, Marion, I do thank you, but I am afraid your loyalty is sadly misplaced.'' She raised her head in a kind of proud sorrow. "I keep finding out things about myself. And everything I find out only seems to dig my grave deeper.'' She caught her breath, stopped a sob. "I think I probably did exactly as he has told you.''

"Nonsense. You couldn't have. Here comes David.''

Sally glanced beyond Marion's dark head and saw that he was approaching, his black eyes riveted to her wan face. Carla rode his arm as a giggling passenger.

"What are you two up to?'' His question was entirely casual, but Sally caught the sharp alertness behind it. She reached for her daughter, buried her white face in the little girl's black curls to hide it from her husband's discerning scrutiny.

"Girl talk,'' Marion answered laconically. David

stared down at his wife a moment, but before he could question further, the dinner bell rang, and they were swept up in the excitement of the mob hunting places and seating themselves.

When all were seated and hushed, David opened the meal with a prayer of thanksgiving. Then he stood, wineglass in hand and offered up a toast. Adults and children alike rose with him, glasses in hand.

"A toast, my friends, to those brave and farsighted men and women who celebrated the first Thanksgiving at Plymouth Colony in 1621." Everyone grinned and responded to the toast, then looked at David expectantly. He did not fail them. "And to the intrepid capitano who made it all possible by his discovery of this country in 1492! To Cristoforo Colombo!"

The company shouted with approval, drank and settled to the serious business of consuming the food before them. The dinner proved to be a gourmet delight.

Sally could not eat a thing. Miserably she sat beside David, Carla on a high chair between them, and picked at her food. She knew without much doubt that she was fast approaching the end of her endurance, and she could see no help in sight. David's grandmother was seated on his left, with Maclean and then Marion beside her. The person to Sally's right was an ancient and garrulous Italian cousin of David, who spoke little English and spared little time from his consumption of the delicious food. When he did, he chattered politely to her in his native tongue for which blessing Sally was duly grateful. She need only move her stiffened uncooperative mouth a fraction to achieve enough of a smile to satisfy him.

Carla grew sleepy before the feast was half-over. Sally excused herself, clutched her small daughter to her and fled up the stairs. Eyes bright and strained with unshed tears, she sent Irma back to the patio when the teenager appeared to assist her. She bathed and powdered the sleepy little girl, got her into her pajamas and then sat with the delectable child tucked against her and rocked her to sleep.

It was an unnecessary action. Carla was groggy with drowsiness and, in any case, never did fuss when put down for her daily nap. But Sally needed desperately to be close to someone who loved her. She could accept the fact that she did not deserve love, but she was completely unable to deny her need for it.

There was no way she could return to the noisy happy crowd on the patio. They despised her for what she had done. She could not blame them, but she had only one friend down there, and Marion's knowledge of her abominable and heartless attack on Jim Maclean's happiness, her deliberate wrecking of his family, was more than Sally could bear at the moment.

Her mind a seething chaos of emotion, Sally retraced her way down the curved and graceful staircase and went out through the kitchen. She gave the kitchen staff an unhappy ghost of a smile, picked up a great rosy apple from the pile in a basket and closed the door behind her.

Dazed by her unhappiness and her disgust at herself, she headed for the stables. The autumn sun was warm on the russet silk of the lovely dress she wore.

Her delicate shoes were an exact match to the color of her dress and hardly the thing one wore to a stable no matter how clean and swept it was. But Sally did not notice nor would have cared if she had.

If she were to survive, she knew she had to find some peace and quiet for herself, some time to order her confused emotions and get back on an even keel.

Bella welcomed her with a soft whicker. Sally let herself into the little mare's stall and fed her the apple, her tears barely contained.

"Oh, Bella," she whispered dejectedly, her face a mirror of suffering. "What am I to do? Everyone hates me and I hate myself. I have ruined so many lives." She leaned her face against the satiny hide of the horse's neck, feeling utterly weary. "And I don't even know what I have done with Charles. What if I left him in a place where he is not receiving proper care?"

At one time she would not have considered such a thing possible. Now, she doubted very much whether she could have cared one way or another. True, Carla loved her, but the other things she had done so callously to people weighed heavily against the odds that she might have provided decently for Charles before leaving him.

She stood there with her face against the patient mare for a long time. Thoughts and emotions chased themselves around in her mind like squirrels in a barrel but gave her no rest, no peace. With a real ache in her heart, she finally gave up. It was useless. There was no way out of her situation, no solution as long as she could not remember her past.

She sighed, patted the sleek hide of the warm little

creature and turned to leave the comfort she had found there, as infinitesimal as it was. At least, Bella did not reject her outright, she thought sadly as she turned to go.

Robert Sandman was standing at the half door of the stall, eyes narrowed and glittering under the brim of his big hat.

"Hello." Sally's greeting was uncertain. She knew he had not come to the feast, wondered why. "I-I've just been giving Bella an apple."

"I know," he agreed softly. "I saw you come in."

"Oh!" Sally was startled. "I didn't see you. Why didn't you say something?"

He moved aside, opened the stall door for her, his eyes never leaving her face. "I wanted to talk to you, but I thought I'd wait until you were through... feeding your horse." The last phrase grated on Sally's raw nerves, and she looked at him sharply.

"Yes... well, I must get back to our guests. I can't speak with you now."

"Yes, you can, Sally. Now. In here." And his fingers fastened on her shoulder like a vise. He thrust her into an empty stall containing bales of hay and slammed the door behind them.

Sally wrenched her shoulder from his grasp with a convulsive action that caused her to stumble. She clutched at the side of a bale of hay and turned to face the man who had accosted her.

"How dare you!" she exclaimed fiercely. "Get away from the door at once and let me out of here."

"Oh, I'll let you out, Sally." His sneer was a threat. "Once I am through with you, I'll let you out, and you can go to the devil for all I care. But first I am going to have my due.''

"What do you mean? Are you crazy?'' Sally could not believe what she had heard and kept her eyes on his with a tormented horror. "David will fire you if you touch me. You know that!'' she wailed as he advanced on her.

"David can take his damn job and shove it,'' he bit out, his mouth twisted in grim purpose. "No dame gives herself to me, then acts the way you have since you managed to get yourself back into your lap of luxury. You are mine, by God, and you will stay mine until *I* tell you otherwise. And no dame runs out on me, Sally. Not even you.''

Sally gave a frightened gasp and ducked under his reach, but he caught her and dragged her back against the baled alfalfa behind her. "Let me go,'' she stormed. "I won't have you touching me like this.''

He thrust his muscular body against her and pinned her back relentlessly, the heat of his sexual arousal searing through her clothing.

"I'm going to touch you, you little bitch. I'm going to touch you like you've never been touched before. Is that clear?''

The hate and lust of his purpose was written in his eyes. Sally stared up at him in wide-eyed fear, paralyzed as she read his intent. He stared at her for a long moment, then hooked the fingers of one powerful hand in the neckline of her dress and yanked.

Sally screamed once, a high piercing sound of fright as the dress parted to her waist. He yanked again, clawing at her undergarments. Recovering from the failure of her nerves, Sally fought like a wildcat. Strength she did not know she possessed turned her outraged body into a biting, kicking, slithering machine that kept escaping from his superior strength.

Hot breath terrified her as it rasped from his throat. His strength was too much for her slender reserves, but the thought of surrender never entered her head. He fought her to the floor and succeeded in snapping the fastening of her bra. Sally went for his eyes, hands slashing, her nails ripping bloody gashes in his face.

He laughed at her, a horrible sneering laugh, and pinned her body down with hard muscle honed by years of active physical labor. Sally sobbed with disgust as he captured one of her punishing hands, then lowered his disgusting mouth. She twisted her head to one side to avoid him and gather what breath she could to scream again.

At that moment help arrived. Quito cleared the closed bottom of the stall door and landed beside the writhing figures on the floor, his lips drawn back, teeth bared. He sank them into Sandman's biceps without a pause in his forward motion.

Sandman yelled with pain as the big animal turned his body and held on like grim death.

The man cursed with fervor and released his grip on Sally's arm, to cuff the dog with his fist. Quito took the blow to his head and hung on. Sandman drew back his fist again to deliver another punishing blow to the animal. Sally sobbed in terror but grabbed for his arm and clung to it grimly as she tried to prevent injury to the snarling dog.

David burst through the door of the box with the speed of an avenging angel. He straddled the struggling bodies, raised his interlaced fists above his head and brought them down with the drive of a sledge-hammer.

Sandman collapsed on the girl beneath him. Quito released his hold, retired a little distance and let his master take charge. David kicked the inert trainer away. He reached for the girl and gathered her into arms that trembled.

Sally cried then. Great deep sobs wrenched her slender body and caused her to shake in his arms. She was entirely out of control.

David raked the scarred face of the unconscious man at his feet with a bitter glance, then read the signs of Sally's attempt to defend herself in the long scratches she'd gouged into Sandman's coarse features. He stood with his distraught wife and carried her into the tack room where he wrapped her almost nude body in a clean but scratchy horse blanket.

Sally was too riven with humiliation and unhappiness to note such a small discomfort as a prickly wool blanket. She burrowed into David's shoulder and sought the warmth it offered without shame or question.

David sat on a rough bench and held her against him in a gentle understanding she would find it hard to credit later on. He moved a tender hand through her burnished curls in a manner that soothed and reassured her. And while she sobbed so bitterly, he crooned soft words to her in Italian, his fine eyes smoldering with a light that had been entirely foreign to them until quite recently.

Sally was mindless in her need for comfort. Cut off
from all love and approval, denied even the bracing
effect of the knowledge that everyone else was mistaken and she was right, she had accepted the image
of herself others had given her over the many weeks
since the accident. With no memory to help her
understand the corrosive power of the guilt she had
to accept, along with the growing list of the vile
things she had done, she needed help to endure.

Guilt and remorse had bitten deep, leaving her
with no reserves in her being. She cried without caring whether she ever stopped. She needed the con-
solation of David's arms about her, the restoration
his soothing words were bringing to her, more than
she had ever needed anything in her life. She drank it
up with a blaze of thirst, then finally quieted against
his strength.

"I—I'm s-sorry, D-David," she wailed against the
wall of his chest.

"Shh," he admonished gently. "Don't cry, Sally.
It will make you ill."

"I—I d-don't care. I de-deserve t-to be i-ill. I—I
am a h-horrible per-person." The last words were
almost drowned in sobs.

"Shh. Stop crying. There's a good girl."

"Good-good g-girl!" Her attempt at a laugh
wrenched through her, causing a flare in the eyes of
the man holding her. "Th-that m-man didn't th-think
so."

David hugged her to him in an aggressive movement. He looked stunned at the strength of feeling
that moved through his own muscular frame.
"Want to tell me about it?" His rich baritone was

strained with an emotion he was doing his best to repress.

Sally was too distressed to notice. She wished with a quiet lucidity she could die but knew she must not until she recovered her memory and told David where she had left their son.

And so, held safely in his arms, she told him how she felt, an occasional sob weighed with the loneliness of her grief and unhappiness wrenching her stricken body.

When she was finished, David stood, picked her up and started for the house. Sally was exhausted, too tired to notice that he strode purposefully toward the joyous noises that came from the patio, too tired to have protested, anyway. She relaxed in the blissful strength of his arms like a child come home to safety.

She was asleep before he crossed the courtyard and passed under the arch to the patio. He carried her through the silence that fell on the crowd of friends and relatives, brushed aside all offers to help and took her up to the room they shared.

SALLY WOKE IN THE MORNING, Sandman's blood washed from her body, the alfalfa brushed from her mop of curls, her bruised body naked between the sheets. David's arm was around her slender waist, his breath sweet on her cheek.

CHAPTER NINE

SHE STIFFENED IN FRIGHT, then forced herself to be still as he stirred against her. His arm tightened possessively, tucked her closer to his side, but he did not awaken.

Sensation ran through the girl, electrical in its intensity. She relaxed then into absolute bliss, secure in the circle of his arms, her mind refusing to function beyond the glory of the feel of his embrace, the soft warmth of his body, the sweetness of his breath as it stirred her hair and thrilled her.

She felt him tense after a mindless haunting interlude that could have been two minutes or two hours long. Nothing mattered until his movement shook her out of her dreamy ecstasy and landed her back in present reality. Her husband was awake.

David went rigid. He rolled across to his own side of the bed and kicked off the eiderdown. He sat up then, his back to her. "Are you awake, Sally?"

"Yes." The brief monosyllable sounded breathless in her ears.

"Good. Dress for San Francisco. We're going there directly after breakfast." He stood, stretched his lithe body. "You have an appointment with Mellon." He headed for his dressing room.

"I have?" Sally sat up, clutching the sheet to her.

As far as she knew, she had no appointment with the psychiatrist until next week.

"I called him last night," David informed her abruptly. "He has agreed to see you this morning."

"But, David," she protested. "I've already seen him this week. I really have no need...."

"Don't argue with me, Sally. You went into shock after the events of yesterday. Get up and dress," he commanded.

Her mind seethed suddenly with disjointed bits of pictures. Sandman wrestling her to the floor of the stall, Quito's big furry length hurtling over the closed bottom of the door, the man's yell of agony as the big dog set his teeth.

David paused at his dressing-room door, the knuckles white on the hand that clutched the knob, his other fist clenched. He watched as expressions chased one another across Sally's sad face. His own was bleak, withdrawn.

"What happened to Sandman?" she whispered finally.

"I hit him. He's in the hospital."

"Oh, David. I'm s-sorry." Sally knew she was in some way responsible for the man's outrageous attack upon her. She sat there in the wide bed and felt her insides crumble in self-hate. "It's all my fault."

"Nonsense." David rejected her offer to take the responsibility for Sandman's actions with a brusque impatience. "You have been a model of decorum since you have returned. I cannot fault your behavior. The bastard attacked you with no provocation. I should have killed him. I will if he touches you again. He will not return here."

Abruptly he disappeared into the dressing room. Sally stared after him in confused disbelief. She was unable to take in his sudden shift in attitude. Always before, he had thrust the burden of blame on her and refused to believe she did not seek the attentions of the men she encountered. Sally was very thoughtful as she dressed in a lovely red gold wool dress. It was one David had insisted she buy when they had shopped. A mandarin collar hugged her slender neck. The bodice fitted closely, the neckline piped with brown velvet that followed the plunge of the opening, then crossed demurely at the valley between her high and pointed breasts on the way to the banded waist. The skirt was fitted and smoothed over her slim curved hips with beautiful ease. Sally tucked a silk scarf in lovely browns and golds into the plunge of the neckline, fastened on a chunky chain of gold that David had also insisted on buying and zipped on soft leather boots of the same color as the dress.

She picked up a brown leather handbag, dropped her things into it and went out to find David waiting for her in the big bedroom. He watched her carefully as she came toward him, his black eyes masked.

SALLY HAD a painful two-hour session with Mellon. He forced her to reveal her sense of guilt, her terrible frustration. In the end he wrote out a prescription for her, demanded she take it as directed. When she asked him what it was for, he told her it was just to relax her and aid in the return of her memory. The girl agreed to do as he said, but she could not fully believe him.

He escorted her to the waiting room. "Dave, will

you come in for a few minutes? I need a word with you," he asked casually.

"Sure." David Rossi fixed an attentive gaze on his wife's troubled face. "Be right with you, John." He crossed to Sally. "Are you all right, *cara mia*?"

His concern sounded genuine. He took her arm, guided her to a seat. Sally stared up at him. She did not understand his evident anxiety for her. She remembered he had called her *cara mia* while she was still in the hospital. His voice had been angry then, the words spat out in hate. The words sounded different now—soothing, melodious, in some way almost seductive. What did it all mean?

She waited almost an hour for David to reappear. When he did, he was thoughtful, withdrawn.

"Let's go." He assisted her into the soft fur he had not sent to the Salvation Army with the other things she had once worn.

"It's almost lunchtime," he remarked as he opened the car door for her. "Want some?" He bent that proud head of his and leaned his forehead against the top of the low-slung car. His tanned face was so close Sally's heart performed an errant little flip.

She smiled at him with an uncertain shyness. "I could eat just a little."

"Right!" He smiled a charming unexpected smile and shut the door with a thud.

Sally felt her heart thud, too. She watched him as he steered the powerful car, her eyes intent under lowered lashes. His mood puzzled her. Whatever he had talked about to Mellon appeared to have lifted a load from his shoulders and put him in a holiday spirit. He parked the car high on a street crowded with narrow houses that formed a solid front down toward the bay far at the bottom. Then he took her into an intimate little restaurant filled with exquisite odors.

After they had eaten a delicious luncheon, he escorted her on a personal tour of the city of San Francisco. They rode the cable cars up and down the steep grades, visited Fisherman's Wharf, wandered through Chinatown, climbed stairways built into sidewalks and ended up at Union Square, where David filled her arms with flowers from a vendor's cart.

All afternoon he had teased her and entertained her with a running commentary on the history and significance of the points of interest he took her to see.

Sally was unable to believe his change in attitude toward her. She was awkward with him at first and very uncertain. But she was unable to resist the charm of his manner. Her natural optimism soon bubbled to the surface, and she joined his lighthearted frame of mind with a feeling of thankful relief. If only it lasted!

"Shall we spend the night in town?" he queried suddenly, dark eyes intent on her glowing face.

"Oh, could we, David?" she breathed. It would be heavenly to be away from the oppressive atmosphere of disapproval that hung so heavily over her at Las Colinas. And to spend the night with David while he was in such a relaxed mood! "It would be super. But don't you have to get back to the ranch?"

"I don't have to do anything, *cara mia*. I run the damn thing, remember? Come on."

They crossed Powell Street and entered the ornate lobby of the St. Francis Hotel. Sally stood by his side as he arranged a suite for them high atop the old and very plush hotel. David took the flowers from her and gave them to a bellman to be arranged into a vase, sent someone else to pick up his car and then escorted her to their rooms.

They were beautiful. Two bedrooms opened off the lounge that separated them. Each bedroom had its own bath with an inviting sunken tub. All three rooms looked out over Union Square and on down the hill. They were high enough that their view of the sparkling bay was unimpeded. Sally was enchanted.

David insisted she take a bath, then have a short rest.

"I am not an invalid," she protested. " I don't need a rest."

He took off her fur, tossed it across the back of a chair upholstered in blue velvet and grinned down at her.

"At the risk of sounding autocratic, *cara mia*, I want you to do as I say. You've had a bad shock. You need rest to ensure that you get over it without any aftereffects. Please?"

She found she was unable to resist him when he turned up the volume of his charm in such a manner. She stared up at him as she was still faintly distrustful of him. What was he up to? He smiled down at her, his handsome face bland. Sally surrendered.

"Yes. All right, if you really think I should. Why do you call me *cara mia*?" She suddenly recognized the phrase to be an Italian endearment and thrilled to the possibilities.

"It is your new name," he declared solemnly. "I have just christened you. It shall be my private name for you from now on. I shall call you *cara* because you are a darling."

Sally considered the light that danced in his dark eyes, decided he was in a mood to tease her and smiled at him. If he only knew how much it meant to her to see something besides stark rejection and hate in his handsome face when he looked at her. Her heart sang a quiet song. Darling!

Sally smiled, counted her blessings and turned to her room. "I rather like it." She was prim, afraid of happiness. "It is such a contrast to the way you usually say my name."

"Glad you approve. Will you be okay if I go out on a bit of business?"

"I'll be fine. I'll follow your suggestion and soak awhile, then take a nap."

"Okay. I'll see if I can get some tickets to something. If I can, we will go to the theater first and dine later."

Sally was willing to do anything to keep him in his newfound mood. She suspected his long session with Mellon had something to do with it and was grateful to the psychiatrist for whatever he had done to bring it about. *Let it last,* she prayed silently. *Let it last.*

SHE AWOKE FROM HER NAP to find the small lamp on the elaborate dressing table had been turned on against the darkness outside. A crystalline gown lay draped across the bench of the table. It shimmered and sparkled in the soft glow of the lamp. Silver slippers, little more than straps and spiky heels, sat on the floor beside it. A drift of delicate underthings was heaped on the surface of the dressing table.

Sally got up, went to them and touched them in wonder. She dressed in the lovely things and stared at the image of gleaming perfection that looked back at her from the dressing-table mirror.

Knuckles tapped lightly at her door, and David came in, immaculate in the dark suit he had worn to bring her to town, a fresh shirt setting off his tanned and striking face.

"Thank you, David," she exclaimed huskily. "It is the most beautiful dress I have ever seen."

"It does look good on you, doesn't it? I thought it would."

And Sally understood then what his business had been that afternoon. He had gone out and found the fabulous gown she wore, the accessories that went with it. She felt a small glow of pleased satisfaction. He had remembered her sizes from the shopping expedition he had taken her on previously. It was a small thing, perhaps, for a man of his capabilities, but he had remembered.

David Rossi's expression did not give away a thing, but it seemed softer somehow, easier.

"Curtain time in a few minutes, *cara mia*. We'd better go." He smiled at her suddenly, and her breath caught in her throat. She allowed him to assist her putting the fur on, and they went.

All evening the girl watched him warily. Surely he must be launched on another phase of his campaign to break down her defenses, bend her to his will and pry the whereabouts of their small son from her blocked memory. She did not understand or trust his new easy attitude toward her, but she joined in with a deep feeling of gratitude and decided she might as well enjoy him while she could.

Enjoy him she did. He took her to a lighthearted comedy, laughed with her at the cheerful nonsense of the actors. Afterward they dined in a plush restaurant perched high above the earth, it seemed, on top of a slender column of a tower whose elevators ran up the outside of the building and presented a breathless view of the city below. They ate above the light cloud cover that drifted over the city, a fluffy torn blanket that allowed intermittent glimpses of the fairy lights beneath their window table.

Later, David danced with her to the fast throb of modern rhythms, the intricate patterns of Latin dances, the slow and seductive movements of waltzes.

Sally floated in his arms idiotically happy. She discovered she could dance. With David it was easy. His muscular body telegraphed his motion to her and left her in no doubt as to what he required. She moved in his embrace as the perfect complement to his easy grace.

By the time he left her at the door to her bedroom, she was absolutely bewitched. Sally spent the first night since her release from the hospital alone in a bed. Snuggling down, enchanted, she had no need to take one of the pills Mellon had prescribed for her with the stern instruction to take one each night. She hugged her delight to her and sank into a dreamless sleep.

IT WAS THE BEGINNING of a time of sheer happiness for Sally. David took her home to a changed household. She was not aware of his phone call home after his long talk with Mellon.

His grandmother held little brief with Sally, of course. She probably cared not at all whether Sally lost her mind. The girl had brought too much sorrow and disgrace upon her beloved grandson for the old lady to forgive easily. But she did care about the return of her great-grandchild. She wanted him returned with a passion surpassed only by David's. And so she followed David's careful instructions, issued orders to her household that they dared not disobey. And she did try to extend a frosty cordiality to the girl.

To Sally, it was as if she returned to Rancho Las Colinas de la Pantera and found it to be the land of bliss. She responded as a flower responds to the sun. She blossomed.

David removed himself from her bed, using the room on the other side of the suite. Relieved of that tension, Sally began to sleep with the healthy need of a youngster. She awakened each morning before David could arouse her, took a quick shower and slipped into her dressing room.

By the time he showered and shaved, she was down in the breakfast room, tucking into the huge breakfast she found necessary to sustain her strenuous morning. They would go into the morning mists then, her stirring interest focused upon the things he looked for and the reasons he looked for them.

She found she was entirely happy as he shared his knowledge, his expertise, with her. His grandmother listened to her eager questions, the discussions that showed plainly that she was truly interested in the work of the vineyards and gave a reluctant sort of approval to the changed person she found David's wife to be. Her memory was long, though, and she found it difficult to reconcile the old image of Sally with the new one the girl presented, but she did try.

Carla was an absolute joy. Sally teased her, played with her, taught her. David watched, a wary disbelief lurking in the depths of his handsome black eyes. At times he joined the fun, to Carla's intense delight and Sally's amazement. He possessed the Italian's natural love of children, and it showed in the way he handled the little girl. He disciplined her, indulged her, steadied her in an easy manner that fascinated Sally.

As the days went by, she fell under his spell herself. Without the least glimmer of what she was doing, she sought him out. If he was gone from the room, she missed him. His firm tread as he approached was a sound she instantly recognized. She would feel his eyes on her in that curious assessing way he had of looking at her, and her heart would leap in an excited manner that she considered quite ridiculous. Sometimes she would meet his intent black glance, and her color would rise in a way and for reasons she could not explain to herself.

He was a disturbing man, and he stirred her deeply. It did not impede her happiness. Quite the contrary. It seemed to add to it.

She still went every day to the office with David. Things were not so easy there. Ann Evans did little to respond to her advances. Jackie Haines remained coolly impersonal.

The real problem was Alicia Ricci. Cool, beautiful, efficient, she was the perfect secretary to David. Bitchy and vindictive, she did her best to make Sally's life uncomfortable and put her in the wrong.

She knew about David's edict that his wife should stay in the office, of course. Small situations kept arising that Sally would have given her attention to under normal circumstances. She would have gone out among the workers of the vast complex and done whatever was necessary to solve the problems. But the girl was wary. Not inclined to risk the newfound peace between David and herself, she managed to sidestep the situations with an adroitness that supplied Tammi with continuous amusement. The other girl did not understand why David was so adamant about having his wife stay strictly in the office, but she was entirely supportive of Sally's efforts to do so.

Sally proved to be a valuable addition to the office staff. Nothing escaped David's sharp intellect. She even received a paycheck for a rather large amount when the staff was next paid, but she protested. She did not need to be paid and did not want the money.

"You are my wife, Sally. Not a slave to the corporation," David warned her. "Your work is valuable. You have earned the money."

Sally flushed with delight at his offhand praise, took the check and stuffed it into her handbag.

She had gathered two more by the time the staff and crew locked up for the long Christmas holiday. She went to Paso Mayacama with David and spent them in a gift-buying spree.

Sally had been filled with dread as the holiday approached. The thought of having to withstand the speculative eyes and the overt curiosity of David Rossi's relatives so soon after the horrible fiasco of the last gathering would not bear consideration. She asked her husband about it. "Will we give a big party for Christmas, David?"

They had finished dinner. She and David were alone in the big study. A fire crackled in the fireplace as one did in each room of the house. There was an extremely efficient central-heating system, but the hacienda had been constructed with fireplaces long before that particular luxury became a necessity. Fires were kept burning each day now that winter had arrived.

Sally sat tucked in a large wing chair, a book in her fingers. David glanced up from the papers he was dealing with at his desk. She made a fetching picture. Her feet were curled under her, the long russet velvet of her gown flowing over them. Firelight danced on her face, turned her wide velvet blue eyes into dark and mysterious pools, glinted off the brown gold of her mass of curls. David's sigh, his look of regret, passed, unnoticed by the girl across the room.

"No, *cara*." His reply was soft, thoughtful. "We will have no guests at all. Just family. Christmas is a time for one's immediate family, I think."

"You mean. . . no relatives?"

"No relatives, little one. Only the four of us."

"Oh, David! How wonderful!"

Sally's relief at not having to endure the pressure of his enormous extended family or their intrusion into her new happiness was so great that it took considerable restraint for her to remain in her chair. Her most immediate impulse was to run to him and hug him in gratitude.

Gratitude? She stared at him, a slow and sure knowledge rising to the surface of her mind. It wasn't gratitude she felt for the man across the room from her, his features hidden in the deep shadow cast by the lamp on his desk.

It was love. Sally sat there, transfixed. Oh, no! It couldn't be! She shot out of the wing chair as if it were suddenly on fire. David watched her with considerable interest as she beat a hasty retreat toward the door.

"G'night, David," she mumbled with a great deal of incoherence. "I—I must get to bed." And she ran, an arrant coward in flight from her feelings and the man who had evoked them.

Sally did not sleep well that night. She tossed and turned in the enormous bed and succeeded in churning the bedcovers into a chaotic tangle she eventually had to climb out of and pull into some semblance of order.

How could she have been so stupid? She raged at her wayward heart, but she did not change it. She was irrevocably and absolutely in love with David Rossi, the man she had wronged so grievously that he could do nothing but hate her with an abiding passion.

She was sure she must have hated him before. But unable to remember the previous emotion and the reasons that had caused it, she had committed the unpardonable idiocy. There was no way she could deny her present feeling. It flamed in her, consumed her, put all her attempts at rational argument to rout.

What on earth was she going to do? Rossi was not

the kind of man to lose sight of his goal. He wanted Charles. The only reason he tolerated her presence at all was because he did not yet have his son. As soon as he did find the little boy, Sally expected to have to go.

She wrestled with the problem until the early-morning hours. "You fool," she lectured herself severely. "You stupid fool. How could you have been so mindless? David hates the ground you walk on. So just get busy and get that dumb memory of yours to work. Tell him what he wants to know and get out of here." She knew with a grim certainty that David Rossi could use her love to destroy her completely if he found out about it.

She buried her face in the pillow with a sob but faced the fact that it was the only thing to do. David's attitude had changed toward her. Fair enough. Mellon had told him he must change, she imagined, if he did not wish to drive her around the bend and render the chance of finding Charles impossible. He had been able to put his natural feelings aside, to become gentle and caring toward her when it was brought forcibly home to him that his caustic cynicism was not going to work.

She had been crazy enough, needed kindness enough, to fall into the trap. She had fallen in love with him and sown the seeds of her own destruction. Her only hope was to win her release by remembering where the boy was and to leave Las Colinas before that steel-trap mind of David Rossi discovered the truth about her feelings for him.

She finally went to sleep after vowing that she would never betray herself to him.

CARLA WOKE HER in the morning. The little girl bounced on the bed and squealed with delight at finding her mother still asleep. "Mum-mum, mum-mum, get up," she chortled. "Daddy wants to eat b'kfast."

Sally pulled the sweet little body into her arms and hugged her soundly. "Go away, you little monster. Can't you see your mum needs a little extra beauty sleep this morning?"

"It isn't obvious." David tossed the comment from where he leaned against the door frame. "You look good enough to eat."

Sally took one frightened look at his lean and muscular length and buried her confusion in the child's soft curls that were so nearly the color of his.

David watched the picture they made, his gleaming eyes appreciative. Sally flicked a glance at him from the corner of her eye, and he took the hint.

"If you ladies will excuse me, I'll wander on down," he stated, his deep voice a little slurred. "Don't be too long. I'll be lonely and starved."

Sally sighed and scrambled out of bed. She did not know how she would get through the day with her new knowledge so heavy on her heart.

She soldiered on a bit grimly, but she made it. And she made many more days just like it. David turned the full power of his charm on her. He was humorous, teasing, serious. Always he acted as if he were fully aware of her and needed her presence. He stopped monitoring her movements, allowed her to wander freely wherever she wished. Sally, unwilling to risk another encounter such as the one at Thanksgiving, stayed close to the hacienda except when David accompanied her.

She might have contained herself around David, kept knowledge of her love of him a secret he did not penetrate, but she was not so successful with John Mellon. He weaseled it out of her on her next visit and appeared quite happy with the turn of events. He did not encourage or discourage her but just looked to her to make her own decisions and heal her own wounds. John Mellon was looking for something, Sally knew. He was convinced that she was hiding from a traumatic emotional upheaval she did not yet dare face. That was the thing that blocked her memory, he told her, and not the blow on her head alone. Sally fretted, but there was no way she could refute his opinion.

Nonna watched her with a silent and restrained carefulness. She offered neither approval nor disapproval of the way David handled the situation. Occasionally she would smile with a cool amusement when Sally and Carla played together. She was invariably courteous to Sally. However she was distant with the girl, as though her judgment was withheld, bottled up within.

They went nowhere during the holidays. Sally even begged off from the New Year's Eve party and dance held at a country club somewhere. She knew she was taking unfair advantage of her husband's new and surprising leniency toward her, but she did not feel up to it. The thought of a crowd of unfriendly women, of running across another man whose attitude said clearly he expected a response from her such as she did not even want to think about, was too much to bear.

David threw her a keenly assessing glance and

agreed she need not go. He was obliged to do so, however, as part of the governing board of the club.

He left around ten that evening. Sally thought he was the best-looking creature on the face of the earth as he crossed the hall in an impeccable black tuxedo and a ruffled shirt.

He came to her as she stood in the doorway to the study, raised a long finger and ran it down the side of her cheek. The gesture caused the girl to shudder and drop her eyelids in a frantic effort to mask the surge of sensation his light-touch sent down her nerve paths.

"Go to bed, Sally. I shan't be too long." He hooked his long finger under her chin, then raised her face. Sally did not dare look at him. "Your scars have healed beautifully," he remarked quietly. And then he went, leaving the girl to cling to the doorjamb as she stilled the thrust of emotion his unexpected action caused to race around her system.

As she climbed the stairs in the quiet of the night, a small worry that she should have pocketed her pride and gone with David was niggling at her. Trying to ignore it, she went to the windows of the big room and pushed the draperies back. Moonlight lay over the valley, shadowing the folds of the hills and the stands of trees. The far mountains were mysterious, beckoning. On impulse Sally went to the closet and put on a warm robe.

She opened the window then and stepped out onto the long balcony that ranged across all the rooms on this side of the hacienda. She did not sit but went to the railing and looked out across the rolling acres of vineyards that stretched as far as she could see in the soft moonlight.

What did this beautiful land hold for her in this new year? She stood there in the cold and clear last night of the year she could not remember and knew she must face those days ahead.

A scream struck down from the mountain then. An unforgettable bloodcurdling sound in the night. It was answered by the sound that tore from Sally's throat as she hurled herself back into the protection of her room. She slammed the French windows closed and jerked the draperies in place with fingers she was not able to control. She dived under the covers, lay there and thought bitterly of David. She needed him. . . .

But he was late. Very late. She had recovered by the time his Jaguar came up the hill, and she did not look at the clock at her bedside. She did not want to know how long he had stayed away or the reason he had done so.

BUT ALICIA RICCI supplied the answer on the first day back at the office.

"Goodness, Alicia!" Tammi exclaimed as David's private secretary delivered a stack of invoices to her desk. "Ol' Santa must have held up a Brink's truck to be able to afford to leave that in your stocking!"

Sally had her own desk now. She glanced across the space between her desk and Tammi's in time to see the absolutely exquisite jeweled watch on Alicia's slender wrist. The woman shot back the cuff of her fine wool dress, looked at the beautiful diamond band that circled her wrist and smiled with a secret malice.

"Well, one does expect rather nice gifts when one works for a man as rich as David is," she murmured. "He is too kind to me, but I must say I enjoy it."

Tammi looked shocked as her gaze flew to Sally's suddenly taut face. "David did not give you that!" Sally heard the incredulity in Tammi's voice.

"No?" Alicia's wide almond-shaped eyes narrowed in mockery. "He was a little late with it, I must say. But he apologized so nicely New Year's Eve." She sighed in evident happiness. "And my corsage was so beautiful. White orchids, with this enchanting little watch tucked away in them."

Sally felt her blood drain away. She would not have been surprised if it never returned. Each word Alicia Ricci uttered was a coffin nail driven into the spirit of her newfound peace and contentment. She picked up the ledger in front of her and went up to the big accounting office on the next floor. If she did not stagger, it was only through a grimly determined effort to hold her pride to her. Never would the woman know the effect of her deliberate little revelation. Sally's new sweet world lay in a shambles around her, but Alicia and David would be in hell before she would let them know her hurt or see her vulnerability.

To take Alicia out, to give her such a fabulous gift! It spelled the death knell for the respect Sally had for her husband and moved her a million miles away from him emotionally. Her heart encased in ice, she returned to her desk and her work with the blind expertise of an automaton.

But Alicia Ricci was not through with her yet. . . .

Sally went back to the hacienda with David for lunch. They had made a habit of it since she began to work in the office. It made a pleasant break in the day and gave her a chance to play with Carla. She would feed the little girl, listen to her nonstop chatter and put her down for her nap before going down to the breakfast room for the delicious meal Theresa set before them each day.

Nonna did not appear to eat with them usually, and she was not there this day. Sally would have welcomed her company.

"I have to go to Los Angeles, *cara*," David remarked as they were eating. "I must attend a rather important symposium on market procedures." He grinned at her, his teeth a slash of white in his dark face. "I'm to be one of the speakers."

"Will you be away long?"

"At least a week. Maybe ten days. I have to leave this afternoon."

"Isn't it rather sudden?" she asked uncertainly as a sense of foreboding struck at her. "Why have you not told me about it before now?" She hated the thought of his absence, she found.

"I've known about it for months. I finished my paper for my talk before Thanksgiving." His dry tone held a faint note of censure. "And I was not telling you anything much at that time."

"No." Sally felt her color rise. "You weren't, were you?"

"That time is past, *cara*," he stated flatly. "I have no wish to bring it up. You prefer our present relationship, I imagine?"

Hurt lurked in Sally's eyes. She kept her lashes lowered. "Yes, David. I do."

"Look at me, *cara*. Let me see what you are thinking."

When she did not comply with his request, David made a disgusted sound and pushed his chair back with an impatient motion. "Sometimes I feel as if I want to beat you, Sally. Come. I will take you back to the office."

He retrieved a soft leather bag and a small suitcase from the closet in the passageway. He had apparently packed his clothes for the trip earlier in the day. Hustling Sally out to the Land Rover, he helped her in and threw his luggage on the back seat.

"You have changed so much even I am beginning to believe you, little one," he informed her as he switched on the motor. "At first I was going to insist you come with me." He considered her a moment before he set the car in motion. "But I have decided something has happened to you to change you. So I am taking a risk, leaving you here. Don't change back into the way you were while I am gone. Or ever again."

The threat in his command was implicit. Sally shivered, glanced away. How could she possibly love such an implacable man? Thank heavens, he did not know she was in love with him. He and Alicia Ricci would really have a ball if they ever found that out.

"I am just me," she told him flatly. "I have not changed, nor do I expect to."

He was a good one to talk. First he acted as if he hated the sight of her. Then all this smarmy charm he had been using to persuade her he had decided she was fit to be admitted to the human race. And all the time he had been carrying on with that witch in the office. Her silence was very self-righteous.

David pulled off to the side of the road and turned to face her, danger signals in the depths of his eyes. Sally glanced at him sharply, turned away quite deliberately.

Strong hands caught her shoulders, turned her back to him again. When she still did not meet his critical gaze, he dropped one arm around her, pinned her to him and raised her rebellious face with his other hand. "Look at me, *cara mia*. Now!"

Sally raised her smudgy lashes irritably. What an autocratic bastard he was. Her sense of humor got the better of her anger, though, and she smiled.

David's breath hissed. "God, *cara*. You drive me to my limits." A spark flared deep in his black eyes and was instantly gone.

Sally watched a nerve jump in his temple and knew he was fighting a battle to control dark emotions. Her treacherous heart began to bang about in her chest with great painful thumps. She squirmed but was unable to break his hold so she quieted in his embrace. "What do you want from me, David?" she whispered, eyes wide and dark on his.

"What do I want from you?" he groaned, looked shocked. He released her, pushed her roughly into her seat. A ragged breath tore from him, and he dropped his head on the steering wheel a moment. Sally watched him with consternation. He turned that proud dark head of his then and pierced her with a look that seemed to strip her bare. "I just want you to promise me you will stay here on the ranch until I return. Will you do that?''

"Of course," she answered instantly. "But do you think you can trust me to keep my word?''

"I am banking my sanity on it, *cara mia*," he murmured softly, his eyes an intimate caress. "I am betting the future, all of it, and leaving it in your hands. Think you can handle it?''

There was a promise in his dark eyes, a glint of passion. Sally glimpsed a glory of some sort. A tremor shot through her in answer to the call of his unspoken demand. She dropped her lashes in swift defense, but she was not quick enough. David read her answer.

He laughed deep in his throat and lowered his head. His lips touched hers. His kiss was feather light. Velvety, sensuous, sweetly aggressive, it was wholly seductive. Sally stiffened, then surrendered without a struggle. Soft arms found the way around his neck, and she gave in to her need as it seared her nerves, demanded alleviation. She surfaced when David pulled back, his hands on her arms as he pushed her away and straightened.

Sally went rosy with embarrassment. David held her hands a moment in his, intense satisfaction reflected in his face as he narrowed those fine eyes and assessed her reaction with a disturbing accuracy.

"I think the future is in safe hands," he murmured complacently as he returned her hands to her lap and started the car.

Sally had no reply to that. He let her off in front of the office complex and waved to her. "Goodbye, *cara*. Think of me."

And then the alarming man was gone, the large vehicle hurtling back the way they had come, toward the airstrip, Sally knew. She turned and entered the office complex and encountered Alicia Ricci on the way out. The woman had on her outdoor clothing, and her handbag was in her hand.

Alicia saw Sally and turned to Ann Evans as she closed the hinged part of the barrier that acted as a division between the office and the reception room.

"Oh, Ann. I am so thrilled!" Her laughter ran gaily up the scale. It grated horribly on Sally's sensitized nerves. "David just insisted that I take the rest of the day off and go find some new ski togs." Those slanted amber eyes touched Sally with a hint of insolent malice. Sally sighed and continued on her way through the barrier. It seemed to her everyone on the ranch and everyone who worked in the winery knew how to ski except her. They were always going on about it.

"How nice for you," Ann came in on cue, a little of that malice in her tone, as well. Tammi glanced up, frowning. She made a little sound that caused Ann to glance at her from the corner of her eyes. The other girl considered Tammi coolly but ignored the warning. "Where are you planning to go, Alicia?"

"We shall go to Aspen," Alicia trilled. "David has the most delightful chalet there, as you know. We haven't used it much at all this year." The look she threw at Sally said quite clearly who was responsible for the chalet's lack of occupancy. Sally had stopped at the mention of David's name and was staring at Alicia with a slowly mounting outrage. "The snowpack is perfect this week, and so he thought it would be a good time to go.''

"But David just left for Los Angeles...." The words were out before Sally could stop her anguished protest.

Alicia swung around on her in malevolent triumph. "Yes, isn't he clever? He's arranged to be away at just the time I want to go to Colorado." She laughed with a throaty complacency. "But of course, you realize David always knows how to get exactly what he wants. And he does manage to get it when he wants it."

She left the counter then and swung out the door, her head turned as she stared back at the white face of David's wife.

Tammi came away from her desk with a muttered curse. "God, Sally, what a bitch." She threw a comforting arm around Sally's shoulders, her look a silent threat to the unruffled Ann who grinned with some satisfaction and went back to her switchboard.

"The witch of Las Colinas is just itching to have her eyes scratched out," Tammi hissed grimly. "And I am just itching to do it for her. What a foul thing to say about David. Just wait till he hears. She's gone too far this time."

Sally used all the willpower she owned and sat down at her desk. The rosy dreams she did not know she had entertained crumbled into dust. She appreciated Tammi's support, but knew David would not lift his hand to correct Alicia Ricci.

Oh, David, she mourned. *How could you?* And yet in her heart she knew he had every right. She had no claim upon him, no way to stop him from doing anything he wished with whomever he wished.

So much for the childish hope she had buried so successfully from herself. David might be treating her with a careless ease that she had mistaken for the beginning of a different feeling toward her, but he hadn't changed. His mistress would not have dared to humiliate her so in front of the girls in the office had his attitude toward her altered.

Her heart a knot of misery, she got on with her work.

CHAPTER TEN

DAVID HAD LEFT on the Wednesday. Alicia Ricci did not return to the office the next day, nor did she show up on Friday. By then Sally was in a sorry state.

She retired into herself, and Carla alone was able to bring a smile to her face. She went to the office and worked with a dull efficiency, but the former joy she had felt as she learned about the problems and techniques of keeping the huge enterprise in business was gone.

Sally admitted she did not understand herself. She knew she loved David Rossi, but she was also realistic enough to realize that gave her little claim on him. And many businessmen gave personal secretaries expensive gifts, she supposed. But to take her to the dance, to arrange to meet her in Colorado! That was just too much!

The girl stopped eating, an act that peeled weight off at an astonishing rate. By the end of the next week her weight loss had really become apparent.

Tammi was all confused, warm sympathy. She thought the increased office load was partly responsible. "The witch of Las Colinas is really asking for it this time," she muttered one day. "David is going to go through the overhead when he finds she has just abandoned the office."

"He knows exactly where she is, and what is going on, Tammi. He is with her, remember?"

"Oh, Sally! You can't believe that," Tammi protested with a really shocked look. "David isn't like that, you know. Alicia was just trying to get at you. He would never do such a thing." ——

"He has done it," Sally answered with resignation.

Tammi shook her head. "I know better. David was friends with her brother, Victor. Vic was killed in Vietnam, and David took Alicia on to help out the family. She is always taking advantage of David's affection for her brother and her mother. She comes on the great and indispensable lady, but she has skated near the edge several times as far as David is concerned." Her red curls bounced in indignation. "I hope to God she has gone too far this time, and we are rid of her!"

The girl was wrong, of course. Sally had already accepted the fact that Alicia Ricci meant far more to David than just a secretary. She could not imagine David engaging in a lighthearted affair, so he must love her. Heartsick, she buried her nose in her work.

"Aren't you eating anything at all, Sally?" Tammi was not about to shelve the issue yet, and they had the room to themselves. Tammi was worried; she meant to have answers.

"Some. Don't fuss at me, Tammi. I'm all right." *Nonna* had looked at her with some concern at the breakfast table that morning and with worry in her dark eyes, too, had asked the same question. As soon as breakfast was finished, Sally had gone back upstairs and weighed herself. She had lost ten pounds in the ten days since David left with the declared intention of going to the meeting in L.A. as a cover-up for his assignation with Alicia in Aspen.

"Maybe. But you are getting to be as thin as a rail." Her pixie face was fretful. "David is going to have a fit when he sees you."

"He doesn't worry about me, Tammi. Nor do I expect he should."

"Uh-huh." Tammi's pause said she knew something about the situation between David and his wife. Indeed, everyone between the ranch and San Francisco apparently knew about them and knew the reasons for the strange relationship, as well, Sally thought bitterly. Really, it was like living in a fishbowl.

Tammi considered her bent head with a sympathy Sally was able to feel. "I thought for a little while there...." Her voice trailed off, and she looked embarrassed.

"Don't be a romantic, Tammi. Things will never be different between David and me." Sally spoke sharply and was immediately sorry. She reached across and patted her friend's hand and felt a sense of relief as Jackie came back to her desk and shut off the conversation.

Franco was waiting for her in the big Rolls as he had been every morning and afternoon since David went away. Sally was glad enough to see him. Winter had come to the lovely valley. But it was winter, northern California style, a season of rains. These varied from misting fine curtains sweeping down from the north to pelting rains that obscured everything.

It was raining hard that afternoon by the time they

reached the hacienda. Franco pulled up close to the patio arch and came around with an umbrella that they shared as they darted through the downpour to the glowing warmth of the house, Quito splashing gaily after them.

The next day was Saturday. Rain sheeted down all day. There was no word from David. He'd been gone ten days. Sally nursed her hurt and managed to live through the endless hours. She arose to weeping skies on Sunday. Would the rain never end?

It was almost noon before it did stop. Although the skies remained a sullen threatening gray, Sally could no longer abide staying in. *Nonna*, who had watched her restlessness with a hidden sympathy, offered no opposition when the girl announced her intention to go for a ride. Sally stamped into her boots and shrugged on a denim jacket. She fled from the house and her bitter thoughts of David with a sense of relief. Skipping over puddles of water, she dashed out to the stables, Quito at her heels. She saddled the little mare, who seemed as eager as the girl to get away from the close confines of the buildings. The two animals slopped gaily through mud and water as they followed paths, crossed tumbling creeks and wove in and out of wooded areas. Quito spent a great deal of the time charging away on interests of his own, loping back to horse and rider as the impulse took him.

He had climbed a ridge and dropped out of sight on some intriguing enterprise. Sally crested the ridge and pulled the mare to a halt, patting her damp coat with gentle fingers. She straightened in the saddle as she dropped the reins across the saddle horn and stretched. She felt more at peace with the world than she had for days, the thought of David and Alicia far back in the reaches of her mind.

Surely no one was expected to feel bad on such a glorious day in such a superb place. Granted, the sun was not shining, the clouds were assuming a posture of threat, and there was no way she would ever be able to solve the problem of her love for David. Still, there was too much in the world to be constantly in a state of upset. She would just make the best of it.

She heard Quito bay far back in the ravine in which he had disappeared. Then a scream split the stillness that followed. High, enraged, bloodcurdling, the sound froze Sally.

Bella reared and spun, dashed down the slope and away from the fearsome sound. Sally clung like a limpet to the saddle, unable even to scrabble for the reins she had so incautiously draped across the little mare's neck in those first few minutes up there on the ridge.

She found them finally. It did her little good. Bella did not respond, her panic sending her peeling down toward the valley floor. Quito caught up to them and raced along at the mare's side as Sally sought to calm the frightened animal.

The surefooted little mare made it through the rougher country of the slopes and was down into cultivated land when Sally finally calmed her. Bella stopped then, her wary eyes rolling back, her lathered sides heaving as her labored lungs acted as bellows, pumping in and out.

Sally slid from the saddle, her own legs trembling. "Bella, Bella. Poor baby," she murmured reassuringly as her fingers stroked the animal's hot neck. She cast a reproving glance at Quito, who was grinning up at her.

"What were you doing, you monster?" Sally asked as severely as she could. "You should have more sense than to take on an animal who has the ability to scream like that. What was it? A mountain lion?"

Quito thumped his tail in the gravel he sat upon, quite willing to agree with anything. Sally felt a stirring of memory. Somehow the panther's scream had struck a chord deep within. She remembered the incident from New Year's Eve and knew that was not what she was trying to recall, but the memory of the first time she had heard the scream did not come.

Pensive, she stood beside the little mare, petting her and rubbing her until she was entirely calm. Then she mounted and rode slowly back to the ranch. Both Quito and Bella were considerably subdued and showed none of the high spirits in which they had left the stables for the ramble into the foothills.

When Sally took the mare into the stable, Miguel met them, his face a mirror of the disquiet he felt as he noted the mare's condition.

"I am so sorry, Miguel," Sally told him earnestly. "We were riding in the foothills, and a panther screamed from somewhere above us. It was very frightening. Bella bolted before I was able to stop her. She is very tired." She swung out of the saddle, more than a little tired herself. "Can you tend her, please?"

"*Sí, señora*. You must go and rest yourself." He squatted and ran knowing fingers down the mare's slender legs. "No harm has been done, I think. Please do not worry."

She smiled gratefully and headed for a hot bath. The rain that had been a threat as she had returned to the stables began with a vengeance as she crossed the patio.

AFTER DINNER Sally sat alone in the study. The fire snapped in the big hearth, and she could hear the hiss of the rain against the windows hidden behind the drawn draperies. She sat in a pool of light cast by the only lamp she had lit, a book in her hand, curled into the big chair she so often sat in when she was in this comfortable room.

A restlessness stirred in her and made it impossible for her to concentrate on the text in her fingers although she was interested in the subject. The book was one David had made available to her. It discussed the factors contributing to the magic of fine wines and man's attempts to bring these to bear on his wines.

David would not be able to fly in with the weather as it was. So even if he had planned his return to coincide with the close of the convention in Los Angeles, he had a perfect excuse for another night with his love. The thought squeezed the blood from the girl's heart, and she sat there, the book in her lap, tears spilling over and scorching down her cheeks, a figure of misery in her small island of light.

Quito lay at the edge of the heat, his sober eyes fastened on her woebegone wet face. Sally had insisted he come in out of the rain. She and Carla had spent a hilarious few minutes toweling him dry, and Sally had brought him into the study for company when *nonna* retired just after the evening meal as was her habit.

The big dog rose and shook himself, cast an interested glance at the closed door to the room, then went to Sally and lowered his huge head into her lap and snuffled for attention or in sympathy. Sally gave a little laugh and fondled his shaggy ears. She closed her eyes then and leaned back into the wing of the big chair. The dog's mute gesture touched and comforted her. If only her relationships with people could be so uncomplicated!

David opened the door and found them thus. Quito cocked an eye at him, but was not about to give up the pleasure of having slim fingers stir gently through his rough coat. He was not often allowed in the house, and he meant to enjoy his time to the fullest.

Rossi came into the room and closed the door softly, his dark eyes on the tearstained pale face shadowed by the light of the burning lamp. He was aware of the crackle of the fire, the hiss of the rain against the glass, the faint smell of wood smoke.

"You've been crying, *cara*." The comment teased, but his features were tense, vulnerable for an instant of time. "May I hope your tears are for me?"

Sally jumped to her feet as if stung, paying no attention to Quito's reproachful look. The book thumped to the floor, and she bent automatically to retrieve it.

David beat her to it, knelt and handed it to her, his expression shadowed from her as he stared up at her in a curious seeking manner. Sally took the book and clutched it to her breast in a defensive gesture.

"Are they for me, little one? Have you missed me? Hmm?"

Sally stood as if transfixed, unable to tear her eyes from his proud dark face. The man rose lithely to his feet with a muffled sound of impatience. He reached for the girl, and she moved back quickly. The back of her knees hit the edge of the chair she had been in and caused her to collapse into it. David followed her down, his arms across the upholstered chair, his eyes on a level with hers as he came to his knees in front of her.

Quito moved lazily back to the edge of the hearth, made a couple of turns and relaxed with a profound sigh, his eyes on the two humans as he observed their antics with a good-natured benevolence. Neither of them knew he was in the room.

"Go away, David. D-don't t-touch me....." How she ached for the very thing she was rejecting so strenuously!

He laughed, reached up to touch her soft curls where they glowed like brown gold in the flicker of the firelight. "I want to touch you, *cara*," he breathed softly. "I've dreamed of nothing else for ten miserable days. And that played hell with my concentration." His fingers left her hair, moved down her arm and captured her hand. He lifted it, stared at it as if he had never seen one before. "We must talk, you and I."

Sally heard the call of seduction in the deep timbre of his voice. It vibrated in her ears, sped through her body in a shock wave of warning. She shrank back in the chair. How dare he come from Alicia Ricci and speak to her so!

"I think not." She was inordinately proud of the

little note of cool disdain she managed to inject into the words. "I am not in the mood to discuss Alicia Ricci and your entertainment for the past few days." David flinched as though she had struck him, then shook his head slightly and dropped her hand as if it had become slimy. He rocked back on his heels, drew the whole proud and arrogant length of him to his feet and loomed over her with a haughty expression.

Sally kept her eyes on his face, dimly aware of his swift flush of color as she rushed on with her reckless speech. "Do you mean to pretend you were in Los Angeles attending a meeting?" Hands clenched at her sides, face white, she was barely able to restrain the impulse to launch an attack, to pummel him in an effort to deal some of the hurt she had suffered in the past ten days back to him.

"Be quiet, you stupid little girl." David's command lashed her raw nerves. He fixed her with a narrow-eyed stare. "What are you telling me? What has Alicia done? What has she told you?"

"As if you don't know!" Sally's fury mounted as his shadowed face hardened. "Oh, I have to agree with her that it was clever of you to arrange your... your illicit meeting in that filthy ch-chalet of yours so it looked as if you were attending a conference! But you should teach your mistress not to b-brag so much. Especially in front of an off-office full of people."

Hard hands descended upon her shoulders. David swore passionately in Italian as he pushed her into the chair, with Quito an interested onlooker. Sally flopped down like a crumpled rag doll, her hands over her eyes, tears seeping through her fingers.

David's long finger punched a dialing code with an enraged efficiency. He barked Alicia's name into the instrument with a volume guaranteed to make the unwary recipient on the other end of the line fear for his hearing. He did not take his eyes off Sally's huddled figure.

"I see," he remarked into the phone. "So she broke her leg, did she?... And where is she in hospital?... Why was I not notified?... That is no excuse, *signora*. No, I am sorry. I have had to find a replacement for her. Yes, I realize that. When she is on her feet again, I may be able to help her find a new position, but I will not have her back."

Sally scrubbed her tears away, relief flooding into her. Alicia had been lying! Happiness sang through her as the need to escape David's undoubted displeasure caused her to stand with the vague notion of escape in her mind. David's hand came up in an imperative gesture. Sally wavered an instant, and the impulse to leave was lost.

"I am sorry to hear that, *signora*." He paused, listened, his face cold. "I will have her things sent to you. Let me know of any additional expenses you have, and I will attend to them for you. No, I am sorry. She may not come back. *Buona notte, signora.*"

He replaced the phone in its cradle and moved toward Sally with a silent grace she found extremely threatening. She trembled as he came to a stop, so close that she felt the warmth of his body. His masculinity engulfed her, challenged her, declared war on her. She was absolutely unable to move.

Neither of them heard the discreet knock at the

door. Franco opened it, and Marion Grayson entered the room to be met by two pairs of eyes that were dazed, unfocused for a moment in time. The nurse looked uncertain, not sure what she had interrupted.

David recovered first. "Marion! What the devil are you doing here in this kind of weather?" He put his arm around the slim nurse and kissed her damp cheek. Sally calmed herself, ran to her friend and hugged her, wet raincoat and all. She had never in her life been so glad to see anyone. Things, she realized unhappily, had been about to get out of hand.

Marion laughed, happiness bubbling in it. "I just had to come," she told them as David helped her out of her raincoat. "I had no idea how bad the weather was. It was raining in Paso Mayacama, but there was an element of reasonableness in it. That downpour out there seems determined to eliminate the mountains around here." She fluffed her hair and threw her arms around Sally again.

"I am so happy! Jim and I are going to be married! Next Saturday. I wanted Sally to help me choose a gown and my trousseau." She blushed, laughed up into David's eyes. "Jim wants you for best man, Dave. Sally shall stand up for me."

"I'm surprised he let you make the trip out here on your own." David led her to the sofa at right angles to the fireplace, then went to get a drink to warm her. Quito stayed on the edge of the rug, without bothering to move. David grinned and walked around him.

"I didn't ask him," she admitted. "Tomorrow's the only day I have for shopping, so I just came to beg Sally to come to town and help. She has such wonderful taste. And I would never be able to finish on my own. Not in one day.''

"I see." David considered the two of them, his gaze lingering on Sally's avid features. "I expect you are right. Why don't you and Jim bring her back out in the evening and join us for dinner.''

"That will be delightful. I'll have to check with Jim and make sure he's free. Can we let you know?''

And so it was arranged. Marion stayed the night, happy with her arrangements. Sally went to bed without finding out about Alicia Ricci or the ski trip to Colorado. David was in the house, though, so her sleep was not as restless that night.

THE NEXT MORNING she went with Marion to Paso Mayacama. It rained in great drenching sheets of water all day long, but the two girls barely noticed as they laughed and chatted their way from shop to shop. Marion tried things on, bought those things she liked. They matched colors, fabrics, accessories and had a wonderful time spending money.

She decided she would be married in a lovely silk suit that fit her as if the designer had her figure in mind. She did not want a white wedding gown because she did not want James Maclean to go through a traditional wedding.

"After all," she told Sally quietly, "he did go through that once and suffered a broken heart. This is a whole new ball game. I want him to know.''

Sally was saddened as she thought of her part in wrecking the life of James Maclean. She was ashamed and sorry, but there was little she was able to do to repair the damage now.

"Are you sure James will want me as a part of the wedding party?" She knew she could not bear the thought of causing the kind man she liked so well any additional unhappiness.

"Don't be silly." Marion's reassurance was instant. "He knows Linda just wasn't in love with him as much as he was with her. She would not have used what you said as an excuse to leave if she had been. She married six months after she left him." Marion touched her cheek with affectionate fingers. "Besides," she stated flatly, "there has to be something wrong in this whole mess. Of course, men like David and Jim don't lie, but I sure wish you would get your memory back so we could have your version of some of the things they seem to accept as gospel. There has to be another explanation there. You can't possibly be as black as you are painted."

Sally felt the tears in her eyes. She blinked, but a couple escaped, anyway. "I can't tell you what it means to me to have your friendship, Marion. I'm so lonely sometimes."

Then, confessions over, they dashed back out into the rain and went to look for shoes to go with Marion's clothing.

IT WAS LATE when they left the last shopping center on the far outskirts of the town, the car full of delectable packages. They were tired, but happy.

"We're to meet Jim at my place at seven." Marion made it sound like an adventure as she directed the car onto the deserted street. "Looks as though we are the only ninnies still wandering around in this rain."

Sally was laughing with her when the car lurched

and began to bump along with a disconcerting determination.

"Oh, no!" Marion wailed. "We've got a flat!"

"Flat?" Sally questioned. Marion explained.

"You've got to be joking." Sally laughed. "What
does one do in weather like this when one has a
flat?"

"One pulls into the nearest bar's parking lot and
goes in for a drink to sustain one's soul in such a time
of dire need. Like so." And she twisted the steering
wheel, guided the limping car into the parking lot of
a tavern. Rain blasted down in torrents as they raced
for the entrance. They laughed breathlessly as they
scrambled through the doors.

"See if you can find your way to a seat," Marion
instructed her. The interior of the place was as dark
as a cave, but full of people, mostly male to judge
from the murmur of deep voices, the sound of shouted laughter. "I'll go call the auto club. I'll have a gin
and tonic if you can manage to get waited on."

Sally's eyes adjusted to the darkness, and she followed as the waitress guided her to a small booth.
She ordered two drinks and relaxed against the imita-
tion red leather of the seat. The dim interior was full
of men, with the occasional woman in the crowd. It
was too dark to see much, and she was really not interested in the occupants of the smoky noisy room. A
man detached himself from a group around the long
bar and came toward her.

"Hullo, Sally."

The girl inspected his handsome blond face and returned his greeting warily. Unbidden, the scene in the
hospital rose in her mind. This man had brought her

violets and candy, and caused David to react with a violence he could barely contain.

"How are you, Mr. Scarletti?" she forced the polite query, sure David would not want her associating with this man. Not that she wanted to as he created a sense of deep unease in her.

"Mr. Scarletti!" he repeated the name with a bark of laughter. "Really, Sally! Darling, lover, *caro*, Vince. But never have you called me Mr. Scarletti."

"I truly do not know what you are getting on about," she told him tartly, the old hopeless feeling of unhappiness taking over. Why on earth had she agreed to come in with Marion? It was almost inevitable she would be reminded of past transgressions of which she had no memory. "I would appreciate it if you would go back to your friends and just leave me alone."

His narrowed blue eyes glittered in his handsome face. "Oh, you would, would you. Well, let me tell you, Sally Rossi—"

"I don't want you to tell me anything," she cut in, temper rising. "Go away."

He stared at her with a mounting disbelief, then swung around and went back to the bar just as Marion approached.

"Well, that's done." She slid into the curved shape of the seat. "I called Jim and told him what had happened. What a ridiculous time to have a flat. Thanks," she said as she accepted a frosty glass from the waitress and sipped gratefully. "It's still raining fit to drown a goose out there. It will be a good half hour before help arrives, so we will just stay here where it's dry."

They sat and chatted about the coming wedding and the satisfactory purchases of the day as they waited for the repairman to appear. Sally did not mention Scarletti and kept her eyes from straying to the portion of the bar where he leaned his handsome length. The fact that she could not remember him and did not know what relationship she had once had with him disturbed her greatly. Once Marion was safely married, she vowed, she would never set foot in Paso Mayacama again.

Not that she would have much of a chance, she knew. Once her memory returned and Charles was found, David would want her as far away from this part of the world as he was able to send her. Timbuktu, she thought bitterly, then wondered where and why such a peculiar word had surfaced.

"Marion, where's Timbuktu?" she asked, her curiosity aroused. For some reason she was sure it was a place-name.

"Timbuktu?" Marion laughed, astonished. "I'm not too sure of its exact location, but it is somewhere in darkest Africa, if one may call Africa dark in these enlightened days. One is usually consigned there by those wishing to see the back of you forever. Why? What brought that up?"

"I haven't a clue," Sally admitted ruefully. "I was thinking of faraway places, and the name popped into my head."

Marion considered her carefully, but before she could pursue her interest in her friend's strange recall of the name, a slicker-clad repairman arrived at the table. Marion told him where the car was, and he left to see to the flat tire.

Sally then used Marion's natural interest in her own coming change of status to divert her friend's attention from her own strange small recall of an unknown word. She had a cowardly feeling that was most uncomfortable. She *had* to remember where she had left Charles. But how could she, when it meant she must leave and never see David again? Oh, God! How had she managed to make such a mess of her life?

Marion chatted happily away. The light was so dim she didn't notice Sally's pained and bitter expression. The girl was glad when the repairman returned, and Marion went with him to settle his charges.

She stood and shook out her raincoat. Gathering up her handbag, she left a tip for the waitress and went into the small lobby of the bar. She placed her handbag on the carpet at her feet, intent upon shrugging into the damp rainwear.

Helpful hands reached out from behind her and took the raincoat. Startled, Sally glanced over her shoulder. Scarletti stood there, the raincoat held ready for her to slide her arms into the limp sleeves.

"Allow me." His amused look mocked her annoyance.

Sally resisted an impulse to snatch the garment away from him. She was unsure of the reason for her definite dislike of this handsome man, but her instinct was to keep as much distance as possible between him and her person. She cast an irritated glance at him and slipped her hands into the sleeves, then pulled the raincoat upward to thrust her arms on through and free them.

Before she succeeded in doing so, Scarletti seized

her and jerked her against his hard chest. His head swooped, and Sally was shocked into immobility as she felt his mouth hard on her soft lips. Sally heard an outraged sound from Marion as an accompaniment to her own muffled cry of anger. She reacted instinctively, her fists raised, but caught in the sleeves of her coat. Then she was dragged away from the man and pushed against Marion. Scarletti landed on the floor with enough noise to disturb the rowdy crowd around the bar.

David stood over him, white with rage. "Get up, Vince. You have a beating coming."

But Scarletti stayed where he was, a welt already appearing on the side of his face where Rossi's blow landed.

David looked intense, dangerous, as he fought to control himself. Marion moved to pull Sally's coat up, free her arms. Sally buttoned it wordlessly, turned away from the spectacle of her husband standing over the man he had floored. The room beyond had gone quiet. Interested heads turned toward the small lobby. Sally met Marion's understanding regard and went with her toward the door. She did not need to express her wish to leave this place to the nurse.

"Allow me." Sally had to choke an impulse to giggle wildly as David pushed the outer door open for them with the same phrase Scarletti used when he seized her coat with the ostensible intent of assistance.

They halted in the tiny vestibule while Marion struggled with her umbrella.

"I'll do that." David took it from her. "I've come

to take Sally home before the rain washes half the mountain slopes down over the roads and makes them impassable," he continued.

"How did you know where we were?" Marion asked him as she gave up the umbrella.

"Called Jim. He told me where to find you. I came over to lend a hand." He cast a look at his wife that would have quelled a riot. "I expected to fight the elements, not an eager lover."

Sally froze inside, stood in silent misery as he escorted Marion to her repaired car with the only umbrella. No one came into the lobby while she waited for him to return for her. Scarletti had picked himself up from the floor and was no longer visible. Sally was duly grateful.

David was driving the big four-wheel drive ranch vehicle. He put Sally into it, threw Marion's umbrella into the back and climbed in beside her. It was a silent trip back across the winding road to the valley called Ta-La-Ha-Lu-Si. The rain was a blinding gray obstruction that the windshield wipers were able to do little to disperse.

David sat hunched over the steering wheel, his features grim. Sally could sense his alertness. He was apparently as tightly wound as a fine watch spring. He watched the road intently, ready to release his enormous energy into instant action.

When they reached the first mud slide, the girl understood why he was so tense. Mud and rock had been loosened from the slope of the mountain that towered over the road. The debris lay across the powerful vehicle's path in a knee-high barrier.

David left the car and tramped through the sheeting rain, barely visible in the headlights. Sally peered through the blurred glass and watched him as he took a careful survey. He stood a moment in the rain, his head thrown back as he stared up at the mountain slope. He came back into the machine then, his head soaked, his black hair clinging to his skull in a curling dark cap, and eased the vehicle into motion with judicious care.

Sally concentrated on David's impassive features as he negotiated the tricky business of crossing the mud slide without loosing destruction upon them. The dim light of the dash revealed his grim look. He was sure of his judgment, confident of his assessment of the danger.

Sally relaxed in the warmth of the big vehicle. He was going to go through the mud slide. He knew it was possible. Her acceptance of his belief in himself and his ability was complete. If he thought he could do it, then he would.

The thought that he had come after her through such weather lit a small and happy flame somewhere deep within her consciousness. Her common sense told her he had probably done so because he distrusted her and didn't want her to have the opportunity to disappear. Still, he had made a tremendous effort to get to her. She hugged her tiny bit of comfort close and dropped into a soft daydream of what it might be like if he were motivated by a real concern for her well-being. It would be nice to remember when he sent her away at last.

With that thought haunting her, the daydream flew out into the wet darkness and vanished. She must be more realistic, or she would turn into a pite-

ous whimpering blob. She shook herself out of her
soft mood and straightened her spine. She was far
too independent to give in to self-pity.

They crossed three mud slides before they reached
the edge of the valley in which the vineyards grew.
David pulled the big ranch vehicle onto the shoulder
of the road from where she had first glimpsed the
valley in which his ranch lay.

The darkness was Stygian. It invaded the car as
David killed the motor and doused the headlights.
Rain hammered against the roof of the vehicle and
hissed against the windows. David turned to her,
muttered a muffled curse and switched on the interior lights. "There. That's more like it. Shall we
have our little talk now, my love?"

"What talk?" Sally temporized.

"The one I meant us to have when I hurried home
last evening." He reached into his clothing, dug out
the stubby pipe and tobacco he had begun to smoke
with a concentrated regularity the past few weeks.

Sally watched abstractedly as he lit it. Her
thoughts raced around in a chaotic mess as she remembered the scene Marion had interrupted the
night before. She did know that the angry and brief
phone call he made had been to Alicia Ricci's. But
she wasn't sure exactly what kind of information he
had gained, or why he had wanted it.

But it had been evident to her that David Rossi did
not know where his secretary was when he made the
call. The possibility had lightened her day, and made
the discomfort of an intensive shopping trip in the
rain a thing not worth noticing. With a hope in her
heart she was not able to suppress, she watched her

husband's face in the tiny glow of the tobacco he was puffing into life. It was all she could do to keep from reaching out and touching his proud damp head.

He snapped his lighter off and straightened, then looked at her in what appeared to be a grim sort of amusement. "You are the most exasperating female I have ever met." Dark eyes searched the oval of her face in the dim light. "Do you know that, Sally Rossi?"

Sally trembled at an odd note in his voice and shook her head.

"Well, you are. And I am just about to break one of my cardinal principles for you."

"Oh?" Sally tried for coolness, but the small syllable sounded breathless even to her ears.

"Yes, 'oh?'" he mimicked. "I make it a rule to never complain, never explain. And now I find myself about to explain something to you. I have come to the conclusion that it is probably essential to your mental health and perhaps to the recovery of your memory, as well, if you can understand what went on between us before this whole disaster started. So I shall explain."

Sally made a small sound of negation. In the past weeks she had come to hate the idea that one day she must face the reality of what had happened between them to turn him into such a pitiless enemy. He was a man who cared about people, about things. And she had been surrounded by the evidence that he knew how to love with a deep commitment. Her past held no attraction for her, and it could be the complete destruction of any hope she might have of remaining with the man she loved. She did not want to know.

His pipe apparently acted up. David applied the flame of the lighter again, his face a grim study. "First, about Alicia." He raised his arrogant head and stared down his haughty nose at her. "I shall say this once only. I went to Los Angeles and attended a symposium on the marketing of fine wines. I was there for ten days as I had expected to be. I returned home, driving through six hundred miles of pouring rain because I wanted to talk to you." He shook his head in silent wonder at his own misguided tolerance. "And I get home, to be treated to a helping of scornful accusations that concerned a stupid rendezvous with my secretary."

"Yes, but. . . ."

"No, 'yes, but' about it. It happened. You may even have thought you were justified. But I don't want to hear about it. I am quite capable of arranging a rendezvous, or anything else I damn well please, whenever I wish. I am, however, quite unaccustomed to having to sneak around should I choose to make such an arrangement. And I am certainly unaccustomed to being called a liar by a chit of a girl!"

He scowled at her with a suspicious intensity, but the near darkness of the car's interior prevented him from seeing the idiotic relief in her dark blue eyes. For Sally was suddenly and joyously convinced David spoke the truth. He had not been with Alicia Ricci. Her heart skipped away, as carefree as if it had miraculously escaped from under one of the gigantic boulders strewn so carelessly around the mountains. Nothing else could matter very much to her at the moment, but she did her best to still the happy tumult in her head and concentrate on the sound of his serious voice.

"I've done a bit of thinking," he told her in a rather severe way. He was silent for an inordinately long moment, then he struck the wheel in front of him with his closed fist. Sally, startled, moved away instinctively.

"Sorry. I didn't mean to frighten you. It's just that I find this a little hard to say." Sally, who could not imagine David ever found anything he wanted to say in the least difficult, just sat in the dark and looked at him. "I've decided I am almost equally to blame for this damn mess we find ourselves in."

His voice was a little hoarse, the usual deep tone ragged with suppressed feeling. Sally resisted the impulse to reach out and touch him. He wasn't looking for sympathy, but something was certainly bothering him. He sighed deeply, turned his head so he was able to see her face as he talked.

"I was ill about three years ago. When I recovered, the doctor insisted I have a long holiday. So I went to the Mediterranean. It gave me a chance to visit my father's people and our wine interests there. So my time away was not altogether wasted."

"I am sure it was not," the girl murmured in polite interest.

"Don't patronize me, Miss Goody-Two-Shoes," he retorted. "Anyway, for the record, it wasn't all play, you see. But a lot of it was." He moved his head, stared down at his hands where they rested on the steering wheel. "I had my yacht over there. She had been chartered to various wealthy businessmen. I decided to use it myself for a while. When I went to see about it, you were on board."

Sally gasped, incredulous. "I was on your yacht, in the Mediterranean? How could that have been?"

He shrugged. "Just an exceptionally attractive bit of baggage left over from the last party as it turned out. You did not tell me the truth about your presence on my property, of course. It didn't matter much. I wasn't interested in how you got there, or where you came from. I only wanted you to stay."

"And did I, David?" She was still as a statue as she waited for his answer.

"Oh, you stayed, Sally." His laugh was a lash with which he flailed her. Or perhaps himself. "You stayed. For a whole month you stayed. And we lived the sensual life of proper Sybarites. You lapped up luxury as a starved kitten laps up cream. It amused me, and you were a partner whose thirst never was slaked. I knew better, but I used your very evident willingness quite freely."

Sally realized just exactly what he was implying and stared at him in an aghast disbelief. "You mean I lived with you on your boat?"

"For four weeks, Sally."

"And I don't remember something like that?"

"So you say."

"I don't believe you!" She barely got the words past her throat. It had suddenly gone dry and ached with the effort of getting the protest out.

"The twins were the result. We got careless. You were hysterical and spoke wildly, I thought. You told me you hated me for doing such a thing to you. You were dead set on an abortion." His laugh was bitter. "I refused to allow you to do it and forced you to marry me. Against your wishes and my better judgment.... And I've paid for it every day I have lived since. You set out to make very sure I suffered, and you managed quite well."

"How did you force me to marry you? You could not have made me go through a ceremony unless I agreed. . . ."

"You agreed," he returned tautly. "I made it worth your while. You agreed to have the child and stay with me for three years until the little one was old enough to get along without his mother. And I gave you an unlimited expense account in return, as well as a healthy cash settlement. But it didn't work. The child turned out to be twins, and you set out to wreak your revenge for your months of discomfort, your hated motherhood."

"H-how?"

"You used your sex appeal and your beauty. I had found you irresistible at first. God help me. But I proved to be only one of a crowd. No man was safe from you."

His laugh struck at her again, making her want to shrink through the floorboards and vanish from his sight.

"Friend, ranch hand, busboy. It didn't seem to matter to you as long as they were male. You got a response from them all, made them want you. And you made sure I found out about each little, er, indiscretion, shall we call it?"

He heard her shocked protest, turned to search her scandalized expression in the dim illumination of the car's light.

"When you decided to take on the men of my family, you went too far. I learned the real depth of your depravity and realized you were not fit to be around my children. So I made plans to send you away." His deep voice plowed on relentlessly despite Sally's exclamation, which pleaded with him to stop. Her hands twitched with the effort it took to keep them in her lap. She wanted to clap them over her ears, to shut out the hateful words.

"I had worked something out, which you appeared to agree to. And then the children were kidnapped. I was convinced you knew all about that kidnapping, Sally. I still am. It could not have been carried out without your help. I came down on you pretty hard, and you disappeared." She had no trouble interpreting the suppressed fury in his words. "I don't know where you went, or how you managed to hide. You had help of some kind. And the best men available were not able to find you. Nor could the FBI or Interpol."

"You make me sound h-horrible," she ventured into the loaded pause. "I guess perhaps I was."

"Yes. You were. But as I look at it now, I was not entirely blameless. I insisted you marry me. You did not want to. You said you could never love me. You wanted an abortion and would have been quite willing to accept much less than it has finally cost me. But I thought there might be some hope. I did not see how a woman could have a child and not love it. But you managed to discount that theory without any trouble. You hated the children and me. When you had them taken and then ran, I almost lost my mind because I knew how you felt about them. That is why it is hard for me to understand your present attitude toward Carla. I have watched you. Your love is genuine. What happened, Sally? What made you change?"

Sally was silent, a quivering mass of hurt. She was not able to think of a thing to say in her own defense. His treatment of her, his lack of charity, seemed totally justified. How he must hate himself for the brief passion that led to their marriage!

She sensed in him the feeling of responsibility that had driven him to insist upon marriage with her to fulfill his obligations to the unborn children. He would want any child for whom he was responsible to have the proper parentage and care.

"Would you have married me if I hadn't become pregnant?" Sally forced the question out and tried to will a steadiness into her words. Somehow her breath stopped, her heart listened, as she awaited his answer.

"No. Never."

The girl sat in stunned silence, hurt welling up. And then anger surged through her. "How dare you speak to me the way you have, then? How dare you treat me as you have?" The fury rushed out in full spate as his unfairness became apparent to her. "If I am correct, you kept me on your yacht—oh, I'll agree I may have been willing to stay—" She refused to let him interrupt. "You used me for your pleasure, then denied me the right to decide whether or not I wished to have your accidentally conceived offspring. You forced me to marry you, then had the nerve to protest because I dared to dislike you and defy you."

"I was prepared to put up with your dislike," he broke in with the dry comment. "It was the form of your defiance I was unable to handle. No man could have done so."

Backbone stiff as a poker, Sally stared at the rain sheeting down the windshield. "Well, I can tell you one thing, David Rossi. Whatever I've done, you certainly brought it upon yourself."

"That's why we are having this little talk, remember? I created my own hell. You only made sure I enjoyed it." He reached out, touched the curve of her soft cheek. "I want it to change, Sally. You seem so different. I would like to call a truce. And who knows? Maybe we can work something out, try again."

Sally, tormented and confused, turned on him in fierce anger. It was her turn to refuse now, and she did. "Never, never, never." Her heart had shriveled up and died within her. Hateful, hateful man. She clamped her lips shut and refused to allow a sob to escape.

David considered her set face a moment, then chuckled in the most infuriating manner. "My way is not always the best way, *cara*." He flicked the key in the ignition and started the car. "I make my mistakes. But this is no mistake, and I mean to have my way. I must warn you I seldom fail once my mind is made up."

"Not this time, David Rossi," she spat at him. "I will always hate you!"

"We'll wait and see, shall we, *cara mia*? Do I get my truce?"

He sat there in the softly lit darkness, his hands on the steering wheel, his eyes on her dimly illumined face and waited for her answer. Sally inspected his shadowed features and knew she was not capable of sustaining her anger against this aggravating individual who was her husband. She had no wish to in the first place. The prospect of an association with him that was free of wary restraint was almost too heady to contemplate. Her nerves tingled as she drew a deep breath and took the plunge.

"I expect one of us will live to regret it, but yes, David. Let's have a truce." She offered him her hand on it with a fair idea of which one might come to those regrets, but she did not care.

David shook hands solemnly, then raised her fingers to his lips and kissed them with an odd gentleness. He released them and sent the car down the rain-swept road toward the ranch Sally now thought of as home.

CHAPTER ELEVEN

HAPPINESS SPRANG TO LIFE, living in Sally as the effervescence lives in fine champagne. She was scarcely aware of the rain that pelted down all week and caused slides to tumble down the slopes between the ranch and the town.

When she got to the office on Tuesday, someone had already cleared the desk Alicia Ricci used in the plush anteroom to David's office. The woman's personal things were jumbled into a cardboard box. David walked through to his office with a brisk command to Ann Evans to store the box until such time as someone came to retrieve the contents. Tammi, with a look of absolute contentment, confided that Ricci had been fired. Sally glowed.

A young woman whose name was Lisa Taylor came down from the big accounting floor and went into David's office. Sally knew she was a typist and supposed she had been given Alicia's position.

She was busy with her own work a couple of hours later when the poor woman flung open the door and stamped up the stairs, her head erect with anger. "I was not hired as a secretary, Mr. Rossi," she cried over her shoulder. "I'm sorry if I don't come up to your standards. I'll just go back to the job I was hired to do, thank you." She vanished up the staircase.

David stood in the door and watched her go. He had a sheaf of letters in his hand. His tie was loosened, his collar unbuttoned, his sleeves rolled up to the elbow and his hair raked into chaos by impatient fingers.

"Tammi, are you able to take shorthand or type from a Dictaphone?" he questioned abruptly. "I can't get anyone here to do this damn work with the road closed, and Lisa is hopeless." He eyed Tammi Thomas in desperation.

"Sorry, David. Not one of my talents."

Sally sat at her desk. The odd conviction that she was able to do the work he needed grew in her mind. She listened to him put hopeful queries to both Ann and Jackie. They were regretful but did not have the skills.

He rattled the letters and went back to his office. Sally got up and followed him. He watched her as she came in and closed the door behind her.

"Will you let me try, David? I have the strangest feeling I know how to do those things."

One eyebrow hooked into his tumbled black thatch. "You must be joking, Sally."

"I don't think so. May I have a pad?"

He bent over, picked up the one Lisa Taylor had left behind in her flight to familiar territory. Sally took it and the sharpened pencil he handed her.

David sat down behind his rather enormous littered desk and scanned the first letter in the pile in his hand. He raised his eyes then, fastened them on his wife and began to dictate in concise sentences. Sally's pencil flew over the steno pad, filling the slender columns of the page with squiggles. She didn't have a clue about her source of knowledge, but she knew what she wrote.

David watched her take his dictation with an incredulity that grew as the page filled. "Read it back to me," he commanded her softly as he finished the letter.

After Sally did so, David stood up and rounded the corner of the desk. "Where did you learn to do this, *cara mia*? Did you know how when you were here before?"

"I don't know, David." She met the dark penetration of his gaze without artifice. "I just knew I could do it when you were asking the other girls for help." She tapped her pencil thoughtfully against her pad. "It feels as if I have known how for a long time. I don't know where the symbols came from, but they were automatic."

"My God!" David raked through his hair again. "I wonder what Mellon will make of this. Do you think you can type, as well?"

She shrugged. "Shall we see?"

He took her into the secretary's room, uncovered the typewriter and switched it on for her, then indicated where the paper was stored.

Sally backed a sheet with another, rolled them into the machine. After taking a deep breath, she started. Her fingers seemed to fly over the keys, and in very little time she handed David a perfectly typed letter.

He scanned it, shaking his head in disbelief. "Come, little godsend. We've work to do."

AND SO BEGAN a period of a brilliant joy of living for Sally. David worked with the energy of a demon as he strove to catch up on the backlog of work his absence at the conference had caused. Undoubtedly his task was made harder by Alicia Ricci's absence from the office when he had expected her to be there, but he never mentioned it. Sally worked with him contentedly.

She would tumble into bed at night with a wonderful exhaustion and drop into deep sleep. If she dreamed, she did not remember it in the morning. Working so closely with David imparted such a bliss to her that she felt she was walking on air.

All week long they plowed through the work. And all week it rained. By Wednesday the phone lines were down, cut off by a slide somewhere. Sally began to think they would miss the wedding. Then Friday afternoon the cloud cover broke, and David's pilot flew the jet in from Los Angeles. They were able to get to San Francisco in time for her appointment with Alan Stern. He did the last bit of reconstructive surgery, said she would not need any more, thereby adding to Sally's gladness.

The small discomfort she felt from Stern's final work was soon forgotten as they flew back to Paso Mayacama for the joyful wedding. Marion and James said their vows to a judge who was a friend of both James Maclean and David. Marion sparkled and the rugged doctor laughed with a gruff happiness that reassured Sally. Afterward, she quietly offered her apology for her role in the break-up of his marriage.

"Oh, Sally, don't be a goose." He hugged her with unabashed goodwill. "It was all for the best. Linda had no love for me. What you told her was just an excuse she used. I miss my kids, sure. But she wouldn't have stayed with me under any conditions. And if she had, what would I have done when I met and fell in love with Marion?"

Sally looked at him a little uncertainly, then kissed him quickly. "You deserve to be happy, James Maclean. I'm glad you have Marion. Take good care of her."

"I plan to do just that. C'mon, Mrs. Maclean. Let's go start our honeymoon."

The newlyweds went to San Francisco with David and Sally. They were leaving that afternoon for Hawaii and points west. David flew them in just in time for their flight. After waving them off, David and Sally went to Mellon's office to talk over the surfacing of Sally's latest knowledge. David had been unable to rearrange the appointments when Marion announced the wedding date.

Mellon was convinced she had acquired the skills earlier in life and used them enough to make them an automatic response. He theorized that she must have been someone's secretary at some time and probably a good one from David's analysis of her efficiency.

They came no closer to unlocking her memory. But it no longer mattered to Sally. She went back to the ranch with David and lost herself in the bliss of being with him each day.

She loved him. This she already knew. Now she began to need him. Hunger grew in her with a deep and undeniable insistence. It refused to be ignored.

If he left the room, her ears strained to hear his steps as he returned, and her body tingled with the necessity of his presence. She was tuned like a fine instrument to his changes of mood, the thrust of his personality. She was barely able to put up with the least separation from him nor to restrain her impulse to follow him like a shadow as he went from place to place around the vast complex that was the working winery.

She tried to mask this wild and growing need of hers by endless attention to the task at hand. She seldom looked up at David when she knew he might be watching her. And as she bent to her tasks with a dedication that threatened to give her round shoulders, David watched her with a quiet amusement in his fine eyes. At times he would stare at her until she was forced to meet those dark eyes. The unexpected expression in them puzzled her, kept her off balance.

He began to tease her then as he teased his grandmother and Carla with little jabs of humor that challenged her quick mind to find snappy retorts. They laughed a lot and were easy with each other in a way Sally loved.

He never touched her. Sally began to long for this. Her dreams at night became softly erotic. She would wake in the morning and flush in embarrassment at the things she remembered. The bed covers were churned into a hopeless mess by her seeking restless body.

THE WEATHER CLEARED as the spring of the year drew closer. David spent all of his days in the vineyards now. His long absence every day whetted Sally's longing for him. He did most of the business at hand in his study at night. Sally helped him, and the hours they spent together did little to assuage her need.

Once the evening meal was finished, he generally asked if she minded going over the things that had come up during the day and needed his attention. Sally could not have denied herself the pleasure those evenings gave her. Alone with him in the cozy intimate room, she took dictation, typed his letters on the electric machine, which he had moved in for her, in a glowing fog of happiness. She did the work with an automatic efficiency, but her whole being was alive with the sheer sensuous euphoria his nearness gave to her.

David watched her, knowledge in his eyes, knowledge and something more. He watched her with a deep and hidden feeling he did not share with anyone. His grandmother watched them both, an inexpressible sadness in her eyes.

So it was that Sally worked through the days of late winter on the ranch called Las Colinas de la Pantera. She rode her mare each morning, laughed and played with her daughter, ran David's office with calm competence while he worked with his men in the fields, and she suffered sweet agony in the long hours spent with him in the intimacy of his study each evening.

The bruises left by the last work on the repair of her facial structure were fading. They still went to San Francisco once a week to see Mellon, but Sally gained little hope from the interviews. She did not suggest the visits cease, however. The time she spent alone with David was too precious to her. She gathered every moment to her as if it were a jewel and hoarded it against the time he would send her away.

Twice he took her to Paso Mayacama. Once was on the occasion of the Macleans' return from their honeymoon. And one time they made a fast trip in for a machine part he needed. Both times road crews were still working to clear the debris left by the earth slides. In a couple of places long piles were driven into the roadside to hold back the encroachment of the mountain slope loosened by the torrential downpours.

In March the bare bones of the vines suddenly developed patchy irregular splotches of green, which quickly broke into pale leaves gleaming in the morning sun.

And before Sally's very eyes, it seemed, the whole valley blazed forth in the exquisite yellow gold of wild mustard. The plants grew chest high on the horses as they waded through the fragrant sea of gold that drowned the stubby wood of the vines in a heady beauty.

Sally was entranced. David told her the wild mustard grew each year, only to be plowed back into the earth for the elements it contained. The girl refused to believe anything that produced such loveliness could be classed as a weed.

Then it was plowed under, and the workers got down to the serious annual business of preparing the vineyards for the coming season of growth. The helicopter chopped up the air over the valley as it moved tirelessly up and down, back and forth, performing tasks assigned to it with the ponderous lack of grace of a very large bumblebee.

Sally often watched its flight with amusement. She knew David frequently flew it himself as he went about the work of the vineyard. She saw it come down this day close to the hacienda and thought perhaps David had come in for an early lunch as he did sometimes if his presence was required some distance away, and it was nearly lunchtime. In this case she was denied her secret pleasure in the noon meal he normally shared with her. Distinctly disappointed, she returned to the job before her to look up later in happy surprise as David came into her office.

"Leave that and come with me, *cara*. I have something special to show you."

Sally looked up at him. He stood in the doorway with an arm high against the frame, his lean weight on it. He was dressed in the tan twill of a workman's clothes, the cuffs of his shirt turned back against strong forearms. The shirttail was tucked securely into snuggly fitting pants, hugging his muscular chest, which gave him a primitively virile image that stirred her errant heart.

"Will we be gone long?" She smiled at him as she stood. He narrowed his black eyes at her and grinned lazily.

"Long enough," he murmured with a softness in his reply that caused her to shoot him a glance of startled inquiry.

He just leaned there, his expression bland, uncommunicative, his eyes hooded and unreadable. Sally's heart tripped over itself, then resumed a rhythm that felt decidedly bumpy and caused the girl to go breathless.

She pulled the typewriter cover on with a jerky motion and heard her husband's amused chuckle. And just what was he getting up to now, she wondered stormily as she shot him a glance that she hoped quite vainly would put him in his place.

A heady sensation flooded her, warned her. Sally gulped as adrenaline hit her system, but even riches wouldn't have made her refuse to go. Her need to be with him was too great.

She glanced hastily at the clock on the wall. Ten o'clock. Much too early for lunch. Again David laughed deep in his throat as he caught her inquiring look.

"Frightened, little one?" He captured her hand as she came to the door. Sally's breath fluttered at the provocative sound of those ordinary words. She risked a swift glance upward and was caught by the intentness of his black eyes on her upturned face. They stood a moment and stared at each other, then David moved abruptly, breaking the spell.

"Come along," he demanded imperiously and left the office. "You haven't been for a ride in the chopper yet."

"I didn't know I had the option."

"You are the owner's wife, young lady, and don't you forget it. You can have any option you damn well choose."

"Well!" To say Sally was startled was to put it mildly. "That is a change! But my options must always coincide with your lordship's wishes, I presume?" she teased.

"You presume correctly." He opened the door of the pickup he had evidently driven from the hacienda to the office, saw her in and closed the door smartly.

Sally settled back and tried to sort out his new attitude toward her. She had not made much progress by the time they reached the big helicopter that was used on the ranch for spraying, fertilizing and a variety of other jobs.

David strapped her into the passenger bucket seat,

went back to the pickup and returned with an enormous wicker picnic basket and a couple of blankets. Sally looked at them curiously as he heaved them into the space behind her. He came around and got into the other seat.

"We're going on a picnic, *cara*. On my own particular mountaintop."

"I didn't know you had a mountaintop, David."

He grinned at her, that secret look in his eyes. "Not many people have been privileged to know of it, *diletta mia*. It is not a place I take people as a rule."

"Why are you taking me?"

"I want you to know about it, to share it with me." Sally was dumbfounded. What was in his mind now? Her intellect struggled with reasons why this amazing man wanted to share anything with her at the same time as her instincts thrilled to the knowledge that he was about to do so. "Besides, I want to talk to you where we cannot be interrupted."

He reached, started the whirl of the blades, and they were airborne. He spoke briefly into the microphone of a two-way radio, received an answer she did not understand, then they were off.

After a swift moment of near panic, Sally relaxed, fascinated at the bird's-eye view of the undulating slopes of the vineyard below. She remembered the phrase he had used. *Diletta mia*. She wondered what it meant, then forgot to ask as she leaned forward and enjoyed the experience.

David crossed the valley to the north and came to the range that cut off the northward reach of the gorge that flattened and widened as it went south.

The helicopter moved toward the mountain that blocked the pass, rose steadily, then flew across the top to the western edge and settled down gently.

David cut the motor, climbed down and came around to help Sally. If his hands lingered on her waist longer than necessary, the girl was too enthralled to notice.

"It is beautiful, David," she declared enthusiastically. "Just look at it." She threw her arms out, her delight sparkling from her radiant face and her laughing eyes.

"Told you it was special." David piled the basket and the blankets in the shade of the only tree on the flat mountaintop and went back to the helicopter. Sally heard him speak into the two-way radio to give their location. A faint crackle remained in the air as he finished speaking, but Sally was scarcely aware of it. Amused, he watched her as he spread out the blankets and set the basket firmly in the shade. She ran to the edge of the area and exclaimed in wonder as she looked across slumbering peaks to the ocean, miles away. A mist was creeping in from the north, stitching lace around shadowed crags. As far as she could see to the south and the east, mountains rose in serried ranks. It was breathtaking. The temperature was cooler atop the mountain than below, but the morning sunlight had warmed the air, and there was only a faint breeze.

She viewed David's vineyards in the valley that lay to the south, the buildings of Rancho Las Colinas de la Pantera dwarfed by the distance and the mountain that towered behind them.

He came to stand beside her then, his muscular frame so near she gradually became aware of the strength of it. The faint familiar fragrance of his after-shave mingled with the tobacco he smoked and the hint of something else that set her senses on edge. It became impossible to listen and make sense of the information he was imparting to her in his deep baritone.

Hypnotized by his nearness, she did realize he told her about his discovery of this place, how he came here when he needed to get away from everyone. He pointed out deer moving on the slopes of the mountain. Sally made an effort to be attentive.

"They are something of a pest. We have to watch them carefully as they will strip a section of vineyard in a night if they are allowed to do so. It is a good thing we have our resident panther. She helps keep them down."

"Panther?" Sally was unable to withstand the searching look in his gaze and quickly dropped her own eyes.

"Well, actually maybe a mountain lion," David allowed. "Although I am not sure there is a difference."

"How do you know it is a she?" she questioned.

"The male generally comes to the female at mating time. We have heard them on the mountain. And we see evidence of the cubs at times."

Sally told him then of the scream she had heard New Year's Eve and of the time Bella had bolted.

"You might have been killed." David's taut features spoke of his very evident concern. Her eyes on the distant scene, Sally reassured him carelessly. David fell silent, his attention riveted to the curve of her mouth, his manner tense and expectant.

Sally noticed David's concentration quite suddenly. He was just a little behind her, his imperious head bent as he focused his total attention on her lips as she spoke. Long lashes shielded his eyes and kept her from reading his intention. Her pulse leaped, beat madly in the sweet column of her neck as her alerted senses responded to the challenge of those dark eyes staring at her lips. She moved away in a confused sort of retreat.

"What's in the basket? Shall I unpack the lunch?"

"Come here, *cara mia*."

"No. I—I . . . ."

"Come here."

She could not help it. She went.

David stood there, a soft fire in his dark eyes as he took in her tremulous uncertainty. Sally was immersed in total awareness. She felt the warm spring sun on her face, heard the breeze that stirred the grass at her feet, smelled the fragrance of the fresh warm earth, was aware of a joy that whispered to her as the man reached for her.

She went into his arms with a sweet eagerness, with nothing held back. David held her close a moment, his eyes on her face as he searched it with a bemused wonder. Sally clung to him. Her longing for his embrace burned through her with the speed of a prairie fire and consumed her just as thoroughly. There was no existence for her outside the arms of the man who held her so tightly against his muscular frame.

A tremor ran through him, and he snatched her

closer to bury his face against the pulse throbbing in her throat. "I want you, *cara*. God, how I want you," he muttered hoarsely, his lips against her neck.

A thrill such as she had never dreamed existed coursed through Sally. She arched in his arms, driven to distraction under those lips that sought and found delicate points of pleasure on her neck, lips that awoke erotic desire and engulfed her in it. She moaned the delight she was unable to speak, and David raised his dark head, his look questing, teasing.

Sally's eyes flew open, pansy dark and filled with the love she had been so careful to hide from him. David drank in what he saw there, lost in his own need for her response.

He kissed her then, and the world exploded in glory for the girl in his arms. He explored the honeyed softness of her mouth, and Sally lost all sense of time, of place. Her only awareness was of the arms that held her, the strength of the body against her, the fierce beat of his heart and the sweetness, the completeness, of his mouth on hers. She abandoned herself into the fire of his passion and fed it with her own.

He stepped back suddenly, his hands hard on her arms as he held her away. "Go unpack the lunch." His muttered command was thick, harsh. Sally recoiled, and she stared at him in a wide-eyed lack of comprehension. He turned his back on her, his head rigidly held. "Go, *cara*!"

Denied the opportunity to see his face and read his expression, she went. She moved through the warmth of the spring sun, her body as light as the air through which it passed. Music welled up within, lending deftness to her movement, happiness to her being. She knew with every atom in her that she was hovering on the brink of ecstasy, was about to become whole.

There was no question about the instrument of her transformation. She watched as he approached the picnic lunch she had distractedly spread on the snowy cloth the basket had contained.

He sat away from her, separated from her by the width of the white square. His expression was controlled, his eyes masked. Sally's smile was sweetly indulgent as she handed him the plate of sandwiches. His voices murmuring his need for her sang in her ears and made the distance he strove to maintain a lie. She loved him and knew he wanted her. It was the stuff of which her dreams were made.

"I wanted to talk to you about the changes in you." He reached into the basket and extracted the chilled bottle of white wine she had left there to stay cool. "These are profound differences, *cara*, and they confuse me."

"Brought on by my amnesia, I expect." She was very careful to watch everything but his face. Taking the glass, she sniffed the contents with appreciation. Wine had become very much a part of her experience in the recent months. It was always served with their late dinners and generally with lunch.

"I don't think so. There are so many things. Your love for Carla. And Quito, for that matter. You could not stand the beast before, and he did not like you. Now he does." Quito was a devoted companion. Sally was amazed he should think she had ever disliked the animal, but it seemed of little consequence at the moment. She stared at him as though intent on memorizing every line in his handsome face. "A dog doesn't change like that."

Her heart was in her eyes as she made no attempt to conceal the depth of her feeling. She scarcely heard his words. She was absolutely unable to concentrate upon anything except her love for him. He drew a ragged breath and thrust the sandwich he was about to sink his white teeth into back on the plate. He closed his eyes a moment, lashes black against the tan of his cheeks. Sally went still as he opened those dark eyes again, transfixed by the flame of passion he did nothing to hide.

"I want you to do something for me." His whisper reached her, seductive, demanding, commanding. He rose to his knees, swept the picnic things aside. "I want to see you, *cara mia*. All of you. Now."

He was beside her then, his fingers insistent upon her. Sally shuddered with delight and anticipation as he undressed her. His hands moved over her, delicate in their movements. He wooed her, gentled and aroused her as he stripped the clothing from her body.

And when she knelt naked before him, the sun a benediction on the sweet curves and hollows of her, on the delicate flush of blood spreading upward from her firm and uptilted breasts with crested nipples hard with the passion she felt for him, desire exploded in David.

He touched her, tender rapture in his eyes, in the planes of his hard handsome face. He gathered her to him, his hands exploring the lines of her body, his mouth seeking and finding the centers of erotic pleasure.

Sally went mad with enchanted sensuality. Her slender form became a living flame in his arms. She moved with a mindless exhilaration, intent only on the man who held her, on the gratification of a need so great that the bright sun above and the hard earth upon which she lay seemed nonexistent.

And David moved with her, his superb body held in exquisite control, his hands and lips filled with the exalted knowledge as old as mankind. His skin warm velvet against the heat of hers, he controlled her movement, controlled her passion and led the way to fulfillment.

Sally cried out sharply in sudden pain as he completed their union, then sank into a glorious golden vortex of delight, her whole being an instrument of pleasure. Her small outcry was already forgotten. Even though she had not completely understood the reason for that cry, now was not the time to search her constantly elusive memory.

Sun and sky mixed with the wonderful scents of the awakening spring earth, and all became part of her exquisite fulfillment. She was vaguely aware of the sudden and absolute stillness of her husband's muscular frame for an instant, but so acute was her joy that she chose not to dwell on whatever it was that quieted him for the lost moment. Then in the beauty of their sharing and the glorious aftermath all else paled into insignificance for her.

It was not so for David. A sob she did not hear caught in the long column of his tanned neck, and he moved, his eyes raking the contented and flushed face of the woman in his arms. The color washed from his sun-browned features as he stared down at her with a bleak expression that, curiously enough, was strangely mixed with a guarded happiness.

Sally reached for him as he pulled away, her eyes closed, her skin glowing, dewed with moisture. "I love you so, David. Don't go."

"I must."

He rose to his knees, wrapped her in the soft blanket under her, then swept her back into his arms, his eyes tormented.

"Oh, *cara mia*! What have I done?" There was despair in the hoarse whisper.

Sally came back to earth with a jolt and gazed up at him with consummate happiness, but she was unable to understand the lingering unrest in the depths of his black eyes.

"I'm not sure what it was." She smiled saucily, radiant. "But I can assure you that it was done very well, David Rossi. May we do it some more?"

Black humor lit a response he instantly suppressed. He smoothed her golden brown cap of curls with gentle fingers, then buried his face in them with a sudden motion.

Sally lay still in his arms, the thrill that shot through her filling her very cells with ecstasy. She throbbed with passion, with longing, but dared not utter a sound in fear of shattering the perfection of the moment.

David raised his head then and stared at her as if he had never really seen her before. "Oh, *cara*, what am I to do with you? You don't realize what I have just discovered, do you?"

She shook her head, felt him tremble against her and moved her face from the hollow of his shoulder to inspect the tough angle of his jaw with love and longing. He looked down at her, closed his eyes as if in pain and brought his proud head down to nuzzle her soft cheek.

"My poor darling. Something else you can't remember.... You are so lovely, so sweet. I should have known.... I should have known weeks ago."

Sally wriggled in exasperation. David had folded the blanket around her, trapping her arms beneath it. She wanted her arms free. She needed to throw them around his neck and kiss away the deep furrows of stress etched on his features.

"You aren't making one bit of sense," she told him severely. "You—"

The speaker in the helicopter suddenly came to life. "David, contact us at once," it commanded.

The sound startled Sally, causing her to jump in her blanket cocoon. Her husband tightened his arms, his face brooding, intent. For a moment or two, with sadness in his eyes he gazed down at her. Then he kissed her gently and deposited her amid the ruins of the picnic. He seemed almost to welcome the interruption, she thought idly, her eyes slumberous.

Lazy, still, in her blanket wrap, she watched as he pulled on silk shorts. The formfitting underwear covered his body as closely as a second skin, which caused a thrill of pleasure to strike deep into the girl. Wide-shouldered, lean-hipped, his legs long and muscular, he was arresting in his handsome male beauty. He jerked on trousers, stamped into his short-topped boots and strode to the aircraft, his skin a gold that glistened in the warm sunlight.

Sally hugged her lovely contentment to her and closed her eyes in blissful happiness. Surely her world would be wonderful now. She loved David and he knew it. She belonged to him. He had not said he loved her, but she knew he did. She did understand it must be difficult for him to say so. The change from his former feelings had to be drastic.

But she knew instinctively that no man was able to give the sheer glory to a woman that David had given her unless he was deeply in love. David loved her. He must.

Sally drifted into dreamy sleep there on the sun-kissed mountaintop as the mist like a silver sea crept down the steep slopes and isolated them above. A few minutes later, she awakened to the heady sense of well-being it gave her as she watched David return from the aircraft.

Her lovely eyes wide with the wonder of her love for David, the splendor of this lovely place, she spoke of it in a hushed murmur. "It is so peaceful, so beautiful, David. I love your special mountaintop."

"Glad it appeals to you," he said, shrugging. "Get your things on. We must go," he added brusquely. His abrupt change of attitude stunned the girl, left her off balance.

He began repacking the picnic basket. Sally sat on her legs, fought off confusion and hurt. He sounded grim and looked strained.

"What is wrong, David? Have I offended you?"

"Don't be ridiculous," he retorted, his irritation obvious. "You've done nothing at all. It's just that

Steve has arrived, and I must go at once.'' He tossed her things at her with an impatient gesture, his long mouth twisted with what was surely distaste. He finished with the basket, expression guarded, seemed about to say something, then stood and went away with his burden.

Sally flushed deeply. She was suddenly painfully shy. She struggled to keep the blanket around her, struggled to climb back into the clothing she had shed with such joyous abandon. Her fingers felt thick as she made a mess of the fastening of her bra and fumbled with the buttons of her blouse. She finally zipped up her skirt, pulled on her panty hose and shoes, and joined him.

He glanced at her, eyes moody as she approached the helicopter. Taking the blanket from her, he handed her a comb. She was helped into the aircraft without a word.

The craft roared down the valley, leaving the silver cloud that had turned the mountaintop into an island of magic far behind.

''Who is Steve?'' Sally ventured finally into the icy silence David had pulled about himself.

''Stefano. My half brother.'' It was a flat statement, without emphasis, without feeling.

''I thought he lived in Italy.'' Sally was surprised. ''Did you know he was coming?''

''He does live in Italy,'' he returned, tone caustic. ''And I did not know he was coming.'' He turned his head, his long mouth twisting a fraction. ''Something just occurred to me when I found out. I was just wondering if it were possible you might have known.''

"I? I don't even know him," she protested, shocked.

"That is also possible," he allowed dryly. "We will just have to wait and see, won't we?"

Sally searched his features. David had had the wary look of the hunter about him. She stared at him soberly and then realized he was different in some subtle way. She had almost been able to hope he had begun to accept that she had been truthful with him. But now there was a tension in him, a strained kind of expectancy she had not seen before.

"What will happen if your brother knows me, and I don't know him?" She had to know.

"I expect him to know you, *cara*. And I don't think you will know him."

The answer dumbfounded her.

"And what if I know him?" She breathed the words, her eyes wide with apprehension.

"Then I expect I shall want to kill you," he answered with a calm certainty, and she froze in her seat.

CHAPTER TWELVE

HE KEPT HIS EYES on her, his expression icy, unreadable. Sally felt confused and aghast, but she knew that David meant exactly what he had said. If she recognized his brother, it would in some way confirm a suspicion he was doing his best to overcome. His eyes narrowed, glinted, as the aircraft approached the airstrip. "I hope to God you do not know him," he said simply.

David set the craft down on the tarmac. Franco met them and tossed the picnic things in the trunk of the big car. He sat beside his boss as David drove to the hacienda. Sally was stunned. She could think of nothing to say.

Nonna met them on the patio. "Bianca is resting, my grandson. She is *incinta*, with child—" the aside was for Sally's benefit "—and Stefano is frightened for her. She is ill." The crusty old woman seemed softer somehow, a plea in her dark eyes as if she sought her grandson's understanding.

"Where is Steve?" The cool question gave away nothing.

"He has gone to the winery."

"Stay here, Sally. We will work no more today." He swung around and left her on the sunlit patio. Sally stared after him, lost and forlorn.

"He is disturbed because Stefano has returned."
Nonna touched her arm softly. "He is remembering
old hurts, Sally."

"I know he is, *nonna*." The girl had used the easy
form of address with David's grandmother for a
number of weeks. The matriarch had unbent toward
her and had come to the point where she appeared to
like Sally. She never put it into words but seemed to
approve of the girl and of the way she handled Carla
and dealt with David. In many ways she was almost
affectionate toward her grandson's wife. Sally
looked at the old woman now, a bleak unhappiness
in her own expression. "I wish he had none to remember."

"Things happen." The old lady patted the girl's
arm. "Those things cannot always be pleasant as
much as we wish they might be. It is the way we deal
with such things that make us what we are. You have
been dealing with your troubles very well, my child.
David is aware of your change."

"Thank you." Sally flushed with pleasure. It was
the first time *nonna* had praised her. "It means a
great deal to me to have you say so."

"I mean it, child. You are so different." She
tucked a veined hand into Sally's arm and guided her
toward the house. "You love David very much, do
you not?" Wise black eyes examined the girl's expression. "And he has learned to love you. I have
seen it. Do not let Stefano's presence destroy David's
love for you."

"I—I am not sure what you mean."

"You... went with many while you were here before, Sally. I do not mean to disturb you, but it is

true." She sank into a cushioned wicker chaise longue and indicated Sally should sit on the same chaise. "You seemed only to be genuinely attracted to one. Stefano." She sighed, her face sad with memories. "David sent him away to Italy because of your involvement with him. I missed him a great deal. David is the center of life here at Las Colinas. Stefano was the sunshine."

The sick shock that washed through Sally each time an episode of her previous way of life was brought to her attention arrived with its wry bitterness. This stern but rather sweet old lady had been denied the presence of a beloved grandson because of her selfishness.

"I am sorry," she apologized contritely. "It must have been very difficult for you."

"Yes, Sally, it was. But things are better now, and I am much happier." Again her old hand reached out, and she patted the girl's arm in a forgiving gesture. "Stefano is back now, and he requires help. The girl he married is delicate and needs special care if she is to carry her child to term. Stefano wanted the very best medical attention for her. Bianca was quite willing to accept she could get it in Italy, but Stefano grew up here and is much more at home with American physicians. So he has brought her home to be seen by specialists in this country."

"I am sorry she is in danger." Sally spoke with a real feeling of regret. "If I am able to help in any way, please let me know at once."

"Keep David happy, child. This will be of inestimable value in assuring the peace of the hacienda." Keen old eyes searched the soft contours of the girl's

features and lit up with a knowing gleam. "This will
not be hard for you?"

The exquisite ecstasy of David's lovemaking was a
living memory. It brought an attractive flush to her
lovely face. Quito came up to her, demanded attention, and Sally rubbed his coat with a dedication he
appreciated as she avoided meeting *nonna*'s penetrating eyes.

"It will not be hard," she whispered the agreement
as she tried to put from her mind David's cold withdrawal when he had learned of his half brother's arrival.

SALLY DRESSED FOR DINNER with extreme care. She
was filled with foreboding as she attended to the light
makeup she generally wore in the evenings. She
brushed her hair until it lay in a cap of burnished
golden brown curls that glinted in the light of the
dressing table.

After careful consideration she chose a lacy black
skirt, ankle length and nicely flared over its own stiff
black petticoat. The matching top was of silk geor-
gette and had wide four-inch cuffs that matched the
high lace collar that hugged her slender neck. She
cinched the crushed-lace belt around her small waist
and stood up. Finally she smoothed on gossamer
tights and put on the black satin slippers that completed the stunning outfit. It was one that David had
insisted on buying during the shopping spree he had
taken her on. She knew it had cost him a fortune. But
she had to admit now that it was certainly worth it. It
really suited her.

David, spectacular in evening dress, came into the

passage as she left her room. He paused to run a critical eye over the slender girl who was his wife. Sally did not hear his breath as it caught in his throat. She missed the flare of passion that he instantly masked in those dark eyes as he took in her appearance. His hooded inspection raked her glowing face, then shifted to take in her delightfully curving body.

She did see the muscle twitch along his thrust of jawline, though. She realized he was critical of her and felt a deep regret. Their truce, it was apparent, was at an end.

He offered his arm and she took it. He ignored her silent appeal and seemed entirely unaware of the warm love in her eyes as she turned her face up to his. Sally gave him a reproachful look and let him lead her down the stairs to the meeting with his brother. She was not looking forward to the inevitable confrontation, but she knew of no way to avoid it.

David had something else in mind, however. He led her into his study. To her complete astonishment, a studio photographer had set up his equipment and was busily fussing over a large camera supported by a tripod.

"This is Thomas Avila, *cara*. He is the best of Paso Mayacama's photographers. I want him to take your photo."

"Whatever for, David?" Sally's protest was automatic. "You already have all those others."

The seductive photos they had shown her in the hospital came to mind. They had been beautifully done by an expert well accustomed to pandering to lovely women and finding their best angles.

"I want some of you as you look now." David

hooded his eyes with his long black lashes. "I like you much better without the bleached-blond long hair you once insisted upon." The flashing smile that always charmed her touched his tanned features. It wrenched at her heartstrings, causing her pulse to race. Enthralled with the happiness shooting through her, Sally went and sat in the upholstered chair Avila had arranged under the gleaming spotlights. He had positioned it against the silvery reflection screen he was using as a background. Absorbed in her feeling for David, Sally allowed the photographer to pose her. He took several shots of her, without the girl murmuring a protest of any kind. If David wanted them, then David should have them. It was as simple as that.

"You will see to these immediately?" David's question was a command to Thomas Avila as he reached for his wife.

"I'll process them as soon as I get back to my studio," he was assured as Avila began at once to dismantle his equipment.

"As soon as you pack up, Franco will take you to the airstrip. My pilot is waiting to fly you back."

Sally's brow wrinkled as she stared at the tall and very impassive owner of the Ranch of the Hills of the Panther in amazement. Such extravagance, and just for a photo!

"You're going to fly him back?"

David smiled at her stunned reaction. "I had him flown here," he returned imperturbably. "Seems only fair I should fly him back."

"But...why on earth...."

David chuckled deep in his throat, guided her deftly out of Avila's hearing and into the hall. The door shut softly behind them.

"I decided that what I wanted most in this world were some photos of you, my love." He stopped her, stared down into her incredulous face. "While we were on the mountaintop," he added softly.

His murmur brought a tide of glorious color into her upturned features. David caught his breath, fastened his attention upon her lips and seemed about to lower his dark head to her. Sally waited an endless second, but then felt a shameless disappointment as the moment was shattered by Franco clearing his throat behind them.

"Sorry, David, but that phone call you want has just come through."

"Thanks, Franco. I'll take it in the study." He surfaced from his intent regard of the flushed loveliness offered him so freely and turned back into the room they had just left as Avila came out the door, loaded with cases. "Help Tom, will you, Franco? I won't be long," he added as an afterthought to his bemused wife. The door closed firmly behind him.

Well! Nothing, it seemed, was allowed to interfere with David Rossi's business! Not even a pending and much desired kiss!

Feeling decidedly piqued, Sally went to the huge oak entrance door and opened it for the two men. After thanking her, they stowed the photographer's bulky equipment into the back of the big station wagon parked near the patio. They slammed the doors. Avila's "Good night, Mrs. Rossi" drifted through the scented spring air as he climbed in beside Franco and went about his business.

Sally stood in the open doorway, slender and quiet in her lovely black gown. She was aware of a strange peace as she stood there, a deep sensation of belonging, of being home in this delightful valley the Indians had named beautiful. She drank deeply of the fresh air, heady with the fragrance of the awakening blooming earth. Her face was glowing with her contentment when David joined her there, his long fingers resting an instant on her rounded shoulder, then sliding down her arm to entwine with her hand. He had an extremely satisfied look about him.

"Shall we put you to the test and let you see Steve, *cara*?" The sardonic query apparently mocked them both.

Pray God I don't know him, have never seen him. Sally stilled the shiver as it threatened her body, squared her shoulders and raised her chin. She marched beside the tall figure of her husband with an unconscious aggressiveness that caused his mouth to quirk in a sudden amusement that she did not notice.

The man she assumed to be Stefano was in the luxurious sitting room, talking to his grandmother with animation. He turned as she entered with David. *"Cara mia!"*

He turned from his grandmother and swept Sally into strong arms, crushing her against his immaculate shirtfront. Bending his head, he dropped a kiss upon her startled mouth, then held her away and laughed at her expression, his eyes probing. "I was surprised when my brother said you were here. It's nice you've come home. I'm glad to see you." Something in his manner contradicted his hearty words.

Sally resisted the impulse to shrink away from the

attentive coldness that lurked in the depths of his tawny eyes. His mouth curved in a winning smile. David watched them with a cynical hostility that belied his passionate lovemaking high on his mountain. Oh, why had he changed so? Sally was miserable as she turned away.

"You are Stefano?" she offered, preferring to call him by his more formal-sounding Italian name. David's brother was a handsome well-built man of her own age, she thought, his personality elusive and hidden behind his easy facade of glamorous good looks. For he was good-looking, with the classic features of a Michelangelo statue. High cheekbones and wide-apart tawny eyes were set off by a thick head of well-cut black hair that hugged his head in a manner attesting to the skill of his barber. His nose was thin and a perfect foil for the sensuously cut mouth above the firm cleft chin. His lean body in the confines of his evening suit exuded power, confidence and energy. He was not as tall as David. Sally decided rather quickly that she much preferred David's rugged handsomeness to this man's classic beauty. She did not recognize him and doubted she had ever known him.

She backed out of Stefano's restrictive grasp and moved toward her husband. David gave her a little mocking bow and handed her a glass of sherry. She wondered if she passed muster. Was David convinced she did not know his brother? She could not tell.

"Yes, I am Steve. As you very well know, Sally." His statement teased. "You could not forget me even if you have amnesia as my brother says. I do not forget you, and you could not forget me, I think."

"Where is your wife?" Sally disliked the provocative note in his smooth remark and sought to change the subject. David and *nonna* watched and listened, but did not seem inclined to intervene.

"Bianca is ill, poor sweet. She does not feel as if it would be wise to join us this evening. I am worried about her." He made an appealing picture as he stood there with his glass in his hand and spoke of his wife. Sally knew in a curious way that she did not believe him to be as concerned with his wife as he sounded, and wondered why not.

"I shall be glad to meet her." Her doubt of Steve's sincerity troubled her, causing her to move close to David in an instinctive effort to gain reassurance from him. David looked down at her and suggested another drink. Sally declined but stayed near him as Steve gaily took over and performed as host.

They talked then of Italy and the events that had taken place since Stefano had departed. He had gone, she learned from the conversation, to become familiar with the management of the vast corporation's Italian interests and now was head of the European branch of the business.

David still controlled the whole operation, she gathered as the evening wore on. Stefano would not be a full partner until after the birth of his first child.

"Isn't that a rather odd requirement in a business venture?" Sally could not contain her curiosity as this point was attacked with some heat by Stefano when they sat down to eat.

Nonna threw her a glance that begged her for silence. David's look was decidedly derisive. Stefano shut up as tight as a clam, his shuttered scowl as petulant as that of a small boy caught at some well-planned mischief.

Franco soft-footed into the strained interval and murmured something to David who came to his feet at once and excused himself.

The silence in which he left the room still existed when he returned. Once seated, he raised his wine-glass to Stefano and smiled at his grandmother.

"To the prodigal's return and to your happiness, *nonna*."

"I'm very happy, grandson. Stefano is back, and I'll soon have another great-grandchild to hold."

Her glance at Sally did not seem to condemn, but the girl still sensed the old lady's loving concern for her great-grandson who was missing. The bleak unhappiness Sally always felt when she wondered where she had left the little boy engulfed her.

David watched her across the table, read her unhappy discontent with herself and was well satisfied.

"Come, *cara*." He was at her elbow as they finished the meal. "Excuse me, please. A friend of mine has arrived and wishes to meet my wife. We will join you shortly."

Nonna and Stefano were curious, but David escorted Sally from the room, his manner impeccable yet noticeably imperious. They crossed to the study and entered as a large man heaved himself up from the wing chair Sally usually used when she sat in this room with David.

"Good evening, Mrs. Rossi."

He was a powerfully built individual who exuded command and intelligence. His name, David told her, was Roger Dickson. David gave her no indication of the man's profession, nor was any mention made of it in the chatty session that followed.

Dickson, it seemed, had been at university with David Rossi. They apparently had not seen each other for years. They reminisced over pranks, triumphs and heartaches of those years in a manner inviting Sally's laughter.

Dickson left without making an effort to see the elder Mrs. Rossi or Stefano.

"They don't know him," David told her when she raised the question. "He was one of my friends who never had the time to come home with me. Always too busy working."

When they returned to the big salon, *nonna* and her grandson were laughing happily. Sally hovered uncertainly, bothered by something in the younger man's attitude that she could not clearly define. Expansively he included them in the conversation.

Sally was soon most uncomfortable. Stefano would make a quick sly reference to an incident in which she could only imagine she must have shared with him from the embarrassed expression each of his recollections brought to *nonna*'s face.

David watched her like a hawk, gauging her reaction. He made no attempt to interfere as she did her best to answer Stefano's sly innuendos. She railed silently at her lack of ability to recall the incidents.

Why didn't David defend her against Stefano's insidious attack? She knew, of course. David still thought her capable of all the things of which he had accused her. Her thoughts started to twist strangely.

He believed her to be despicable. His lovemaking had meant nothing except that he had found himself alone with her and had taken his frustration out upon her. He had taken her to his mountain and used her quite deliberately. He was as callous and as hard-hearted as ever. The episode of the afternoon was just another attempt on his part to break the shell of her amnesia, she decided. She was foolish to have thought anything else.

Stefano continued to bait her with a deliberate provocativeness all evening. Sally finally had enough of his snide attempts to get at her. She flung her head up in an irritation that she didn't bother to control. David's watchful inspection aroused her almost as much as his brother's efforts to goad her memory back to normal, whatever that might have been. She jumped to her feet, the black lace of her gown clinging to her sweet curves.

"I'm exhausted. Are you ready to go up, *nonna*?" But it seemed the old lady was enjoying the company of her restored grandson too much to wish to retire.

Sally said good-night as politely as a good child and quickly sought the sanctuary of her room. She didn't, she decided, like Stefano Rossi one little bit. It was very apparent to her she could never have liked him, no matter what others said. He was a nasty man, mealymouthed and hurtful for all his good looks. He was not a person she could have associated with at all under any circumstances! She dismissed all thought of him with no difficulty and concentrated on David.

Lying in a froth of bubbles, she dwelt on the exquisite fulfillment of David's lovemaking. Her body was filled with longing, sensitive even to the touch of the thick fluff of the bath sheet she wrapped herself in as she left the tub. She trembled as she reached for a whisper-soft white nightgown and its matching negligee. It floated around her, reminded her of the silver drift of mist she had looked down upon from the top of David's mountain.

Would he come to her tonight? She sprayed a delicate scent on wrists and throat and knew he must if life was to be worthwhile.

Too restless to sleep, she turned out the light in her bedroom and went onto the balcony. It was chilly in the spring night, but Sally did not notice. As she sat quietly in the cushioned chair, her exhilaration slowly turned to bitterness when she realized she was to be denied her husband's presence and the arms she wanted so badly. Finally she went to bed, cold and disappointed. And sometime later she drifted into an unhappy dream-filled sleep.

"SALLY! SALLY!"

She jolted awake in a rush of happiness. "David!" She reached for him in a fog of sleepy joy and instantly realized it was not her husband who bent over her.

"Stefano!" She tore out of his grasp and catapulted away from him, twisting out of bed and landing on her feet on the opposite side. "What are you doing here? Get out at once!"

"Shh, Sally. Do not wake the sleeping devil." She knew the reference was to his brother, and it made her shiver. She moved her hand against the wall, and the room flooded with light.

Stefano cursed and glared at her. "Don't be a fool! Turn out the light. I must talk to you. David will kill us both if he finds out what's going on."

Sally stared at him, stricken. What was he implying? "I've nothing to say to you. Will you please leave my room and go back to your wife before David comes and finds you here!" She resisted the impulse to clap her hands over her ears. Suddenly she didn't want to know any more about her past.

"My wife!" His laugh was bitter. "You can taunt me with that! You who knows why she is my wife, why she bears my child. I will not have such talk from you, Sally. And David is asleep. I made sure of that before I came."

He left the bed and made his way around the end, his manner menacing. Sally measured the determination in his face and backed away a little before she realized the folly of retreat.

"If you come one step closer," she hissed at him, "I do assure you I'll scream loud enough to shout the house down." She almost sighed aloud as he stopped, gauged her resolution. "I mean it," she threatened as he hesitated a moment too long, which advertised the fact that he did not wish to be found in her room.

He did not retreat but stood down at her end of the bed and fixed a charming smile upon her. "Come, Sally. We are in this together. We shouldn't quarrel."

"I can't believe I've anything to do with your concerns, your plans. I've never seen you before as far as I know. Get out of here!" A primitive fear tingled a warning along her nerves. Stefano glared at her. She saw a muscle jerk in his tensed jaw.

"Where is Don Lang, Sally? What is he up to?"

The question astonished the girl. She had forgotten about Lang. She had also forgotten she'd crossed the Atlantic with him. How did Stefano know about the man? From David, perhaps?

"I don't know where he is. I don't remember a thing about him."

"Come on, Sally." Again the winning smile he turned on so easily. "This is Steve you are talking to. Steve." He touched the chest of the white toweling robe he wore with a long forefinger. "We planned this together, and we can't quit now. You can pretend with everyone else. Even David. But let's knock it off with old Steve, okay?"

Quite the American when it suited him, Sally noticed as she looked at him in silent dismay. She shook her head, unable to mask her dislike of him. They stood there in the stark bright light of the overhead chandelier, and Sally felt a wave of animosity as it swept from him and engulfed her. His tawny eyes darkened with a leaping fire of hate. The skin tightened over his lean and handsome facial bones, and he stared at her from a mask of livid anger.

She was frightened as she had never been frightened before. "I d-don't understand you!"

"You understand all right, Sally, my girl. This amnesia junk is a good cover. Brings out the old protective spirit in my sappy brother, doesn't it? And it sure as hell is a good cover for whatever plan you and Don have in those tiny minds of yours. But it's not good enough for me." The charm of his smile was lost in the animal snarl of his mouth. "I know better, don't I? And you had best come clean before I decide to hurt you. I'll give you twenty-four hours, Sally.

Contact him, and tell him I've bought into his game. Get his answer here, or I won't be responsible for your safety. Do I make myself clear?''

Sally stared at him in frozen amazement. She was unable to reply. He sneered at her and left the room through the French doors. Sally stood and trembled. Long minutes later she put out the light and crawled back into her bed.

She knew she was in real danger, but had no idea what she must do to save herself. She lay for hours, her thoughts scrambling around in her head. Her longing for David was swamping her common sense and making logical thought near impossible.

However, she was faced with two incontrovertible facts: she did not know who Don Lang was; nor did she have any idea of how to contact the man.

As the hours ticked by, she hungered for David's presence beside her in the great bed. She sobbed a bitter regret at the memory of the days he had slept with her here in this charming room. It was with real difficulty that she prevented her treacherous and demanding body from forcing her out of the bed and through the dressing room to him.

It was far into the morning before Sally finally closed her eyes in exhausted sleep.

CHAPTER THIRTEEN

SHE WENT TO BREAKFAST with a bruised look on the soft skin under her eyes—the badge of her sleepless night.

David fastened his black eyes upon her as she entered the cheerful room, his expression withdrawn but faintly regretful. Stefano was there, his brash charm filling the room as he recounted youthful pranks for his grandmother's amusement.

Sally perched on the edge of her chair, her longing for David's touch, his kiss, riding her. She kept her lashes lowered in a shy aloof manner as she sought to protect herself and hide her feelings.

"You look ill, *diletta mia*. Perhaps you should rest this morning." There was quiet command in David's statement.

"I'm okay. I just didn't sleep well."

"No?" His smile mocked a little. "Then get some sleep now, *cara*. Steve can ride with me."

"You do look tired, Sally," *nonna* put in, real concern in her observation. "We cannot have you ill, as well as poor little Bianca."

"I am sure Bianca will be fine now that she is here." Stefano was decidedly casual, his bland smile unperturbed. "She will be down to meet you later, Sally. I agree you should stay here. You must have many things to think about." His bold tawny eyes dared her. Sally moved restlessly, aware of her husband's dark interest in Stefano's attitude toward her.

Standing abruptly, David helped his grandmother to her feet. *Nonna* went to the door with Stefano. David paused beside Sally's chair, his eyes on the down-bent shiny curls.

"Go get some rest, *cara mia*." She heard him take a deep breath, heard the catch in it. "You had a restless night, I think. Bianca must stay in bed until noon, and Irma will care for Carla. You look so—unhappy."

The note of concern caught at Sally, searing her. She tossed her head up and surprised a fire of passion in the dark eyes above her. Shaken, she stared at him, a thrill shooting through her.

A laugh grated in his throat, and he swooped and kissed her with a hard thoroughness that stopped her breath. Then he was gone, the echo of his laugh an agony in her mind. Never would she understand David Rossi.

She went to her room but could not sleep, her need for David a passionate fever in her blood. It went far beyond her ability to control it, raging in her, consuming her.

In desperation she collected Carla, much to her small daughter's delight, and they went for a long and rambling walk that consisted of a jumbled series of stops and starts. Carla was at the age when the whole world was a wonderful place she must find out about at all costs.

The child directed an insatiable stream of questions at her mum-mum. Sally abandoned her abstraction and surrendered to Carla's need to know. They spent several hours in solemn discussion of the whys and wherefores of stones, bugs, worms, clouds and various other phenomena of nature.

Quito joined them and nosed dutifully at the various items that attracted the child's sharp attention. Then, tired out, Carla nodded in Sally's arms as they returned to the hacienda.

Sally gave the sleepy child over to Irma's care and was surprised to find she had enjoyed the morning. The tension had drained from her, taking with it the residue of fear her contact with Stefano had left. How could he harm her? He could not force her memory to return.

She showered and changed and went down to her lunch with an easygoing calmness, looking lovely in a softly flowered print dress.

After all, David had kissed her. She hugged the thought to her and knew nothing else really mattered at all.

Bianca was tucked into the corner of a vast sofa in the sitting room, her tiny form, softly rounded by pregnancy, dwarfed by the huge piece of furniture. She stood as Sally entered the room, her dark eyes huge.

"I am so glad to see you." Sally took her hands gently as she introduced herself. "I hope you are feeling better."

The girl smiled shyly and assured her in broken English that she did indeed feel much better.

"Please sit down." Sally invited, patting the sofa as she did so herself.

They carried on a stilted conversation, Bianca

apologizing for her accented English, a painful blush staining her cheeks as she acknowledged her inadequacy. Sally brushed the effort aside and tried a little Italian, just to put the girl at ease. She was little more than a child, Sally thought. Probably eighteen or nineteen at the most, with homesickness to deal with on top of her extreme shyness and worry about her unborn child.

They were laughing gaily when the rest of the household put in an appearance. Sally's efforts at Italian had touched the girl's sense of fun and relieved her tension to a degree.

Stefano crossed to his wife at once. He raised her small hand to his lips, then kissed it with a lingering charm. It embarrassed Bianca. A delicate flush stole up her smooth creamy cheek and climbed into the line of her luxurious black hair. She peeped up at her handsome husband, then dropped her lashes in a quick confusion Sally found endearing.

She smiled, then felt David's eyes on her. Glancing at him, she met his assessing gaze. She caught a glimpse of some deep feeling he instantly repressed and sighed quietly. The cold fact that he meant to keep her at arm's length was quite apparent to her. It hurt deeply, and she was not yet able to handle her growing despair.

Slowly she was coming to the conclusion that she had been wrong about David. Could it be that the wonderful experience on the mountaintop had just been another of his experiments to test her, to break through her stupid amnesia?

He could never love her, she admitted. But she blamed herself, the way she had treated him before.

After all, what else could she expect? She had tried his patience, scorned his manhood, lived wildly. He had taken her to the mountaintop, made love to her with a passion she could never forget, but he was only getting his own back. The bitter thought lay in her consciousness as unpalatable as gall, and she did not have an antidote.

David was watching her now, a careful calculated sort of inspection that she resented strongly. *"A quelle heure est le déjeuner?"* he asked her suddenly.

"Dans un instant," Sally answered easily, translating his request to know when they would eat, without hesitating. David's eyebrow shot up, and he grinned at her.

. Bianca stared, then clapped her hands in delight. "I did not know you could understand French, Sallee," she chortled in that language. "How wonderful. We can talk!"

"How did you know I could?" Sally asked David, startled at her unknown ability, wondering that he should have discovered it.

"You read a letter from Paris this week and answered it without even realizing you had done it," he answered complacently. "And while you do not know Italian or Spanish, I have seen how quickly since your return you have picked up phrases from both languages. Let us speak in French. Bianca will be much more comfortable."

Sally was intrigued by her own fluency in French. She laughed and joked with Bianca. Both men were extremely competent in the language. *Nonna* understood it and threw in the occasional dry comment of her own.

Lunch was an interesting experience. It was nearly over when Stefano brought up the reason for his unexpected appearance. Bianca was having trouble with her pregnancy and must be seen at once. The discussion embarrassed Bianca, but Stefano plowed ahead.

"I'll need to take Bianca in to see the gynecologist on Wednesday, David. It's the best he could do in the way of a first appointment. We took it, of course."

"Sally goes to see Mellon that day," David replied briefly. "I'll fly you down to San Francisco."

"Fantastic." Stefano leaned back in his chair, fingering his coffee cup. "I'd like to show Bianca a little of San Francisco if she is up to it. Where's your yacht at present?" The glance he shot at David seemed carefully veiled to Sally. She happened to be looking at him and caught an expression on his face that he was quick to hide.

"She's just out of dry dock. She's been completely overhauled since I've had her returned from the Mediterranean."

"Hey, man. That is just great. It's the Easter weekend next week, isn't it? How about taking her out for a short haul? We could have a super time, stay on her four or five days. Be like a short vacation. Bianca needs one. She has been so upset."

David looked him over, glanced at Bianca's pained expression and Sally's uncertain one.

Sally looked at Stefano, a little surprised at his show of concern for his delicate wife. She had gained the impression somehow that Bianca was not his prime worry, but she wondered where she had picked up the notion, saw the warm smile he turned on her now and decided she had been wrong.

"I have only two men on board. Skeleton crew. My captain and my chef are on leave for two weeks, as well as the rest of the gang. We'd have to shift for ourselves."

"We can handle her." Stefano sounded eager. "She's a sweet craft. Needs very little attention as I remember, with all the sophisticated gear you have on board."

"True," David mused. "Think you can cook, *cara mia*?"

His endearment was oddly intimate. Sally looked at him through dark lashes, a flush stealing up her soft cheeks. What would it be like to be confined to the small space of a yacht for several days with the dynamic person who was her husband?

"I can try," she murmured, her throat suddenly dry. A shy kind of eagerness shot through her. "I would like to," she added. She stared studiously into the dregs of her coffee cup as she said the words. She did not dare glance up, although she could feel his gaze upon her.

"I suppose I can afford to take a few days off," David agreed. "There is nothing pressing here at the moment. We could use the yacht as a hotel, do some sight-seeing." His dark eyes remained on his wife's bent head. "It might prove interesting at that."

His voice held a teasing note. Sally stole a quick look at him, but his face was entirely bland, his eyes unreadable. Her slight shiver was caused by the exquisite panic that raced around her nerves at the thought of the shared intimacy of space on a small boat. An endless variety of possibilities came to mind. She repressed them with commendable sternness and tried to smile without a blush. She did not do too well.

BIANCA'S APPOINTMENT was at nine Wednesday morning. Sally's was not until one, so she volunteered to remain with the girl as Stefano seemed to have pretty well lost interest in his wife's state of health. Sally wondered about his change of attitude since he had seemed so keen to place her in the best hands. However, she realized it was really not her business as she accompanied the shy girl into the doctor's examination room and sat with her while the doctor gave her a thorough going-over. She was able to translate his remarks to Bianca in a reassuring flow of French the girl appreciated.

After, the gynecologist sat with them in his consulting room. "Well, Mrs. Rossi, I will want to see you in two weeks. I do not think at this time you stand any chance of losing your baby, but we will keep an eye on you and make sure you do not."

Bianca thanked him in her heavily accented English and breathed a sigh of relief, glad to have the examination finished, glad to have his assurance. She asked if it might be wise to return to her own country.

"I want you to stay here," he told her severely. "You must not be junketing off around the world. Time enough when you have your child."

She promised to stay, sad eyed. The doctor gave her a printed list of his requirements for her and dismissed her.

Sally's visit with Mellon was as uneventful as usual. He was extremely intrigued with the fact that she found herself to be fluent in French, but it did not seem to surprise him.

"Many British treat French as a second language, you know," he told her. "Since you are apparently a top-flight secretary, as well, it is not really surprising you know the language. Have you tried any others?"

"I can't speak Italian or Spanish." She shrugged. "David speaks those around the ranch quite frequently. I only know a smattering of words in each of those languages, although I am improving in my use of them."

Stefano was interested in Mellon's opinion of Sally. Once back in the car and heading for the yacht club where David kept his seagoing vessel, he questioned her closely.

"I am truly concerned that my beautiful sister-in-law should be so affected." He managed to get a note of sincerity in his smooth tone, which Sally thought to be quite specious, although David answered him readily enough.

"Mellon is of the opinion that Sally's amnesia has little to do with the blow she received to her head," he informed his brother. "It may have induced temporary amnesia, but he feels she sustained another kind of shock, and this is what blocks her memory."

"And he considers this loss of memory to be genuine?"

"It's real enough." David's crisp reply warned his brother to back off. "Small things are occurring, such as this discovery that she speaks French and the fortunate stroke of luck that allowed her secretarial training to express itself. That might not have been revealed had I not lost my temper and chewed out a poor and very inadequate typist," he added with a gleam of humor flashed at Sally. "Felt sorry for her, did you not, *cara mia*?"

"You were being a beast," she protested. "I offered to help in a fit of insanity."

"You have not enjoyed working with me since the unveiling of your remarkable talent?"

Sally laughed at the mischief in the dark glance he turned on her. "I shall not feed the fire of your ego, David Rossi. The way I feel about my golden opportunity to be associated with so exalted a personage as yourself goes with me to my grave."

"You may very well live long enough to regret such a blatant neglect of my finer feelings, Mrs. Rossi," he assured her, something in the way he said it catching at her.

"Is there no way to help her?" Stefano was plainly impatient with the teasing exchange in the front seats. Bianca touched his arm, disturbed by his attitude, and he shook off her touch with a frown. "Isn't there a way to shake her up, get her mind back into the groove?" They had been speaking French, but he shifted into English to ask the question.

"We will speak French so Bianca may follow our conversation." David issued the command sharply.

"Sorry, my little wife." Stefano dropped back into French. "But doesn't this shrink have any recommendations to speed up her recovery?"

"He thinks it best to let her relax in her own way," David informed his brother with a conciseness that once again warned Stefano not to encroach. "I followed his suggestion and stopped at the scene of the accident when she left the hospital. It was hard on her and proved nothing."

"What happened?" Stefano's curiosity was avid.

"I fainted." Sally shuddered as she recalled the nightmarish incident. "I would rather not talk about it if you please, Stefano." Surprisingly he did not press the issue.

David drove through the gates of an exclusive club and parked. The gleaming white yacht was an enormous structure. Sally followed David down into the luxuriously finished teak-and-leather main saloon. The small and exquisite dining room led into a spacious modern galley, a model of spanking efficiency. David opened cupboard doors, showed her the well-stocked pantry and refrigerator.

"Think you can find enough for our breakfasts while we are on board?"

"If toast and orange juice will do, I'm sure I can cope," she retorted smartly in answer to his teasing question.

"I'm sure you can, my love." He smiled. "We'll go ashore for dinner this evening, then spend a couple of days just cruising around the bay. Can't go far with only an engineer and radioman on board, but we should have a good time."

He guided her back through the saloon and into the passageway beyond. "You will sleep here." He opened the door to the master suite. Sally drew an appreciative breath. It was a beautiful room with a master bath glimpsed through the half-opened door across the way.

"It is as big as a room in a house," she murmured in surprise. "How large is your boat, David?"

"Hardly a boat," he corrected her dryly. "*Sea Breeze* carries a full crew of fifteen and is quite capable of sailing anywhere in the world. She often does, in fact.''

"Is... is this the yacht you met me on?'' She didn't want to know, but the question could not be stopped.

"It is.'' He shrugged dismissively. "It has six private rooms with bath, Sally. It can accommodate quite a party. I take it you have no memory of it?'' She glanced into his hard face, the fleeting impression passing through her mind that he no longer expected such remembrances from her. Shaking her head, she was conscious of the throb of the yacht's engines as the ship got under way.

David stared down at her a moment, then smiled and caused her heart to flip and resume a ragged beat that she found to be most uncomfortable.

"Have a rest, Sally. We'll go ashore about seven. I'll call you.'' And he shut the door on her and left.

WHEN SHE CAME ON DECK, dressed for the evening, the yacht was anchored far out in the bay. They went across to San Francisco in the yacht's powerboat and spent a pleasant evening on the town. Bianca, relieved of her anxiety about her pregnancy, chattered away in French, admiring and exclaiming on everything she saw.

Stefano was withdrawn and short in his answers as if Bianca annoyed him. He evinced a distinct lack of interest in the needs of the timid girl who was his wife and was to bear his child.

Sally was irritated by his lack of sensitivity. She marched recklessly into the breach and tried to give Bianca an extra amount of attention, to make her feel at home in this strange land in which she found herself. She was determined not to let Stefano's boorishness ruin Bianca's newfound contentment.

Occasionally Sally caught her brother-in-law's eyes upon her, his look dark and intense. Was he remembering his threat to her about Lang?

David didn't seem to notice Stefano's interest in her. He blandly ignored Sally's unease, while appearing to be almost totally absorbed in the scene around them. Before the night was very old, Sally began to chafe under the studied indifference David directed toward her. Shielding his thoughts behind his long lashes, his narrowed eyes touched the three of them impersonally. What was going on in that keen brain? Sally only wished she knew.

His dark face at times looked thoughtful as if he were contemplating all kinds of options. Sally felt a healthy urge to kick him in the shins to evoke some sort of response from him. He was solicitous of Bianca, however, smoothly making up for Stefano's apparent lack of concern.

They ate in a restaurant famous for its Italian food, David told them. The consensus of opinion was that the fame was well deserved. Bianca assured them she had not thought to find such delicious fare outside her own country.

A small but excellent orchestra was tucked away next to the pint-sized floor. The music enticed patrons onto the dance area. Sally watched the circling couples as she tried to imagine what it would be like to have David hold her closely again. Would he rest that strong chin of his in her hair? She flicked a veiled glance at him and caught him watching her.

He smiled. Annoyed at her instant reaction to him,

she stared back at the dancers. David rose with lazy grace, his dark eyes intent.

"Dance with me, *mi' amora*."

Sally wanted to refuse, but his fingers wrapped themselves around her slender wrist, and she was unable to resist his insistence. She went into his arms, fighting the demands of her body. It wasn't easy.

He wrapped one strong arm around her, captured her free hand and held it against his chest as he laughed down at her. The glint in his eyes caused her lashes to fall at once. David made a contented sound as he pulled her closer, the firmness of his body moving against hers to the slow beat of the music.

"Happy, *cara*?"

How could he treat her with such apparent indifference and then pretend to be concerned as to her happiness? Sally held herself rigidly and allowed her temper to flare.

"I'm happy enough, David," she shot the brittle declaration at him. "Please don't worry about me. I can take care of myself, thank you very much." She was really fed up with the man. To make love to her as he had...and then to have acted in the indifferent way he'd shown since Stefano's arrival! It was just too much to bear.

"Perhaps." The word mocked her. Long fingers moved down her spine, and Sally gasped as she fought the treacherous desire his movement evoked. David laughed then, a completely masculine sound fraught with a completely masculine understanding of his effect upon her.

"I rather fancy the thought of taking on the job myself," he murmured softly. "Surely you wouldn't deny me the pleasure? You may depend on me to do it well, I think.''

''I've learned not to depend upon you for anything,'' she retorted flatly. ''You have no interest in me, nor have I any in you.''

''I beg to dispute that statement.'' His eyes flashed, and his voice was deliberately provocative. ''I'm very much interested in certain, er, aspects of you, my little hellcat. I would seriously advise you not to push your luck with me unless you are willing to face the consequences.'' His hand slid down her back and forced his full meaning into her consciousness. Sally gasped and blushed painfully, then tried to pull away from the intimate heat of his aroused body.

''No, *cara mia*. I want to hold you, to dance with you.'' And so they danced, circling the floor slowly, and Sally felt her treacherous body respond to the powerful force of his masculinity. The sensations he induced acted as a spell, and she was lost, lured into a poignant desire in which only he existed. He led her from the floor finally, a satisfied expression on his lean face as he took in her dazed enchanted bemusement.

BUT HE SHOWED HER to the master suite of the boat without offering to kiss her. Confused, she realized the door had closed firmly. The man she was having so much trouble living without stayed on the other side of the frustrating barrier that the closed door represented. How was she ever to break that barrier down?

Sally spent another very restless night in a big bed meant for two. With every atom of her being she yearned for David. But he did not come.

In the morning she was in the galley, scrambling eggs and frying bacon when Stefano put in his appearance.

"What have you done about contacting Don Lang?" he asked abruptly, not bothering with a greeting.

"Nothing," she assured him as she poured freshly squeezed orange juice into large glasses. "There is nothing I can do. I have explained the problem to you. You will just have to accept it."

"Never, Sally." His snarl was vicious. "I mean to know exactly what kind of a game you and Lang are up to, and how you plan to double-cross me. Are you sure Charles is stashed safely away?"

Sally stared at him aghast. The whole world was convinced she knew where the little boy was, it seemed. "Are you suggesting I have deliberately hidden my own son away for some reason?"

"You've got to be joking! The whole blasted idea was yours. Don't come on the innocent with me, my girl." He looked as though he was about to spring on her and choke the life from her.

Sally was speechless as she stared at him, her thoughts racing around in her head in horrified confusion.

"You know how we planned to use the boy to force my dear brother's hand. It was your scheme. Don't give me that, Sally!"

Sally glared at him angrily, a hundred questions rushing into her mind. But before she could utter a word, before she had any time at all to find out what he meant, David appeared. Stefano stared at him, still as a stone.

David's cool glance took in Stefano's aggressive stance and Sally's bewildered and angry face. "Bianca needs your attention, Steve." His urbane observation was without expression. "If you will go help her, we can eat. I'd like to get started as soon as possible. I want to show our cook a bit of San Francisco today." He transferred his calm regard to Sally. "Breakfast about ready, cookie?"

Nothing in his manner indicated he had overheard his brother's incriminating words or her own inadequate defense. Sally threw him an uncertain smile, a craven gladness warming her. David reached out then, touched her flushed face with a gentle finger.

"Don't worry so much, *cara mia*. Everything is in good order." His smile charmed and soothed her, and dispelled her fear that he had overheard his brother's statement of their perfidy. She repressed a shudder, then turned hastily from him to the task at hand.

David stood there, his face unreadable as he watched her reactions. His expression was unperturbed.

"I've set the table," he murmured, a laugh in the words. "When will you be ready for us?"

"In about t-ten minutes, I should think," she stuttered, her equanimity destroyed by his nearness and his gentle gesture.

Dan Miller, the radioman, stuck his head into the galley. He had been introduced as they came on board the yacht. The other crewman aboard was Ron Wasson, the engineer.

"You're wanted, Dave. International call."

Rossi went with him. Instant businessman, Sally

thought wryly. David had received many international calls in the time she had worked in the office with him. They came from enterprises all over the world and had mostly to do with wine, although he had capital invested in other worldwide ventures, as well. Both David Rossi and the corporation that he headed were wealthy beyond the imagination of most of the general population, she had discovered.

Sally had the meal on the table in ten minutes. David returned with Stefano and Bianca in tow. The two members of the crew also joined the easy camaraderie of the delicious breakfast.

THEY CRUISED THE BIG BAY for the next three days, putting in at points of interest, lazing on the sun deck, listening to the marvelous sound system and just generally enjoying themselves.

Evenings they would anchor offshore from some restaurant that David or Stefano knew of and then ride to the dock in the powerful motorboat the yacht carried. The two crewmen stayed aboard and fended for themselves.

While they were cruising, David stayed on deck with the girls, as idle as they were in the warm sunlight. He teased them, played games with them and taught them to fish. He had decided Bianca must become fluent in the language of the land. So he set out to teach her idiomatic American-style English.

And he took on the task of teaching Italian to Sally. The three of them spent hours laughing at mistakes and correcting pronunciation.

While David seemed to be wholly content and absorbed in his self-appointed task of entertainment and instruction, Stefano sat apart. He seldom joined in the fun as he watched them with critical narrowed eyes. Indeed, his handsome face wore a permanent mask of sullen discontent.

Bianca tried her best to lift his spirits. He rejected her efforts with a sarcasm that wounded her and left her uncertain. David kept a quiet eye on him whenever he was around. Sally avoided him studiously.

She knew she must speak to him; she should find out what he knew about her reason for coming to the States. However, her newfound happiness in the sunshine of David's smile was too precious for her to take any risks with it.

She was a coward and she knew it. She despised herself but she was absolutely unable to ask him the questions she needed to have answered. Not that David gave Stefano any chance to corner her. He remained at Sally's side with a quiet persistence.

But Stefano wanted to talk to her in the worst way. Sally watched his subtle efforts. She stuck to David like a burr as Stefano tried more than once to maneuver her away from her husband and into a private conversation. But David would deftly remove her from his brother's influence each time the confrontation between them seemed inevitable.

Sally was sure the day of reckoning was near. There was little reason to try to hold it off. Yet she found herself extremely reluctant to be alone with him.

Her gratitude for David's constant attention added to her deepening love for him. But he was acting strangely....

The yacht carried an expensive and extremely complicated communications system on board. David received an inordinate number of phone calls each day. Miller would summon him to the cabin that housed the equipment. Most of the time David returned to the deck or wherever they happened to be with a mysteriously satisfied look upon his dark face. He did not mention his calls.

Sally had the definite impression he was up to something. Adrift in her euphoric fog, she couldn't be bothered to ask him what it might be. However, she did notice that he never took a phone call on one of the many instruments scattered around the luxurious yacht. Again, this fact didn't interest her enough to make her question him.

Sally basked in the glory of David's attention and spent her days in a kind of tormented daze. The weight of her love was an unfulfilled agony. It brightened her days yet made her nights into a restless painful experience. She wanted David quite shamelessly, although wild horses could not have dragged the admission from her. She only hoped her need was well hidden under the gaiety she adopted to see her through each day.

Saturday they anchored off a small island almost in the shadow of the famous Bay Bridge that linked Oakland to San Francisco.

David gave the two crew members a twenty-four-hour leave to be home with their families for the Easter festivities. He took them ashore sometime around four o'clock in the afternoon. As he returned to the yacht, the ship-to-shore telephone rang once more. Stefano answered, then called to David as he came over the side.

Sally lay on a thick colorful mat on the floor of the deck. She and Bianca were both in swimsuits, their skins already a golden tan from days in the sun. Swim wear had become their standard costume while the sun was high enough on these lazy spring days.

Bianca murmured about the chill and went to her cabin to change into something warmer. Almost seven months pregnant, she was really being very sensible. Stefano followed as she vanished.

David smiled down at Sally, obviously enjoying the picture she made in her brief swim togs before he strode down the deck toward the cabin housing the communications systems of the big yacht.

Sally kept her eyes on him and found she quite enjoyed the sensations the sight of his lithe athletic movement stirred in her. As her pulse fluttered in her throat, she closed her eyes, the thought of what might have been causing bitterness to gnaw at the pit of her stomach. If only she had learned to love this man soon enough, how different her life would be.

David had not entered the master suite during the whole time they had been aboard. As the days went by, she became more and more convinced he never would. Regardless, her love for him had been fed constantly by his closeness during these past few days. With nothing to distract her attention from him, she felt as if she were slowly approaching madness as her need for him grew. David, she was positive, knew what he was doing to her. He knew how he made her feel. She felt like a very small mouse being baited by an extremely intelligent cat. What was he up to now?

Her mouth twisted with a kind of tormented mischievousness. She wondered wildly what he might do if she went to him and demanded her conjugal rights. He would most likely pitch her overboard, she decided with a giggle she could not suppress.

He came back down the deck in time to catch the sound of her merriment. "Share the joke, *cara*?" His brow shot up as she refused with a quick shake of her soft curls. He sank down on his heels beside her, touched her on a smooth shoulder that was just turning an interesting shade of brown. "Go change, little one. You're cold. I have to pick up some very important people at the airport." His eyes sparkled with a secret happiness he did not share with her. "I'll take a cab and pick up the car at the yacht club."

"Will you be gone long?" Sally sat up and reached for her lacy cover-up. David took it from her and helped her into it.

"I'm not sure. Steve can take me ashore. I'll get back as soon as I can." He sounded casual, but something had stirred him. "I'll probably have a snack at the airport, so don't wait on me. I may be gone some time." His fingers lingered on her as he settled the flimsy jacket around her. Energy flowed from him with a force Sally felt clearly, but he ignored her questioning look.

Hating to be separated from him, she stared at him briefly, then lowered her lashes to hide the longing she was sure her face betrayed. The glow in his eyes caused her to forget her question.

David smiled down at her, then turned her face up to his with a gentle hand. "Don't be sad, little one. Things are working out well. I . . ." he hesitated then, and Sally's eyes flew open as a new note crept into his resonant baritone.

He stared deeply into the wide and dark blue eyes. Those eyes held an unconscious appeal the girl was not aware of at all. A flame glinted for a moment in the black velvet of his. He bent his dark head and kissed her with a gentle fire. Passion leaped through her, but he was gone before she could throw her slender arms around his neck.

Tears blinded her so she was unable to see clearly as he disappeared over the side, his half brother at his heels. She sat in a huddled misery as the motorboat purred into life and swept away from the yacht's side.

"Sallee!" Bianca's swift French fell upon her in a sparkling torrent. "You must not sit there so. You will have a death of cold!"

"I think I am going to die," Sally agreed ruefully. "But it will not be of the cold."

"Eh? I do not understand."

"Just a joke, Bianca." Sally stood with an inherent grace and dashed the tears from her eyes. Bianca watched with interest, but Sally left the deck hurriedly to have a long hot shower and change into a velvet skirt and silk blouse. Stefano would most probably wish to go ashore for dinner, she knew. She might as well be prepared.

She hoped he did not see fit to bring up the subject of Don Lang tonight, or of her apparent failure to contact the man. She decided to stick like glue to Bianca's side. Stefano seemed little inclined to bring the man's name into the conversation if either David or his wife were within hearing distance. With David gone, Bianca was her only deterrent. She went into the main saloon and joined Bianca, hoping against hope that her assessment of Stefano's reluctance was accurate.

Stefano came back and changed into beautifully tailored evening gear. He was really a splendid specimen of male attraction, Sally later realized as they walked into the spacious old dining room to which he took them. They had crossed the bridge and left Oakland far behind. He said the meal was worth the trip. The dining room was in an ancient and very plush white wooden hotel set far back into the foothills above Berkeley. White gingerbread lace gleamed in the softly floodlit windows as they approached in the taxicab that Stefano had hired. The grounds were lit up, as well, the whole scene extremely inviting.

Every woman in the place turned to notice Stefano as they passed to their table. Bianca clung to his arm, her little face proud and cool. She loved her man and was shyly happy he was so handsome.

Sally wondered wryly if she would always be so happy about it. Stefano, she thought, showed a slightly callous lack of feeling toward Bianca. It disturbed Sally. It would be easy for her to dislike him altogether, she decided.

Dining in the old hotel was an experience. Waiters hovered, attended to china, silver and spotless napery. They drank wine and water from fine crystal and ate food that melted in the mouth.

"I truly enjoyed that." Sally sighed, replete, as Stefano paid the taxi off and handed them back into the motorboat. "Thank you very much, Stefano."

"A little of the best is good for the soul," he intoned solemnly. "Especially if one has only one chance to enjoy it."

"Won't I have another chance?" Sally asked curiously, her attention arrested by an odd note in his voice.

"How do I know, dear sister-in-law? 'Gather ye rosebuds while ye may.'" And he turned his attention to steering the boat. Sally looked at him thoughtfully, a distinct feeling of discomfort causing a chill down her spine.

DAVID HAD NOT RETURNED when they reached the yacht. Sally said good-night and left them, unwilling to prolong her contact with Stefano, for she was suddenly very uneasy in his presence. She went to bed, where she tossed and turned, dozing, then jerking awake. The yacht was as quiet as a church, but she could not truly fall asleep.

The digital bedside clock said four when she finally became fed up. She got up and reached for her robe without turning on the bedside light. No need to disturb anyone. She tugged on her robe and slipped her toes into fluffy slippers, then headed for the galley.

She needed warm milk, she decided. Warm milk with chocolate in it. Then perhaps her restless nerves would calm, and she would drop off into real sleep.

She was in the dining room, her hand on the galley latch when she heard a distinct pop somewhere behind her. Transfixed, she stood still as she listened to the rising crescendo of a crackling roar. Her heart in her mouth, she turned and ran back the way she had come. She was halfway across the saloon when the door to the passage leading to the bedrooms blew open with a boom. "David! David! Bianca!" she screamed. The flames roared her only answer.

The passage was a leaping crackling inferno. Heat

reached out at her, seared her, forced her back across the saloon. Running out on deck, she was suddenly frantic in her need to find out if David had returned, to warn him, warn Bianca. She did not think of Stefano.

Flames licked her feet, and she glanced down at her burning gown. Reflex action sent her over the side. As her body hit the water in a perfect arc, the yacht exploded behind her, lifting her on a great swelling surge of water.

Sally trod water, a wild numbing fear sending tears sheeting down her face to disappear in the waters of San Francisco Bay.

CHAPTER FOURTEEN

SALLY SHOOK OFF the terrible apathy stealing over her, whipping water out of her eyes with a snap of her head.

The water was cold. She continued to tread water, her mind suddenly clear as crystal. It took about three seconds for her to recognize her danger, but she felt no panic as she accepted the clear logic of her rapid thoughts. She shed the garments that dragged at her, and once freed, she struck out for the flaming remains of the yacht.

She noticed for the first time the damp thick fog. It clung close to the surface of the water, swirled like dirty cotton wool about the burning ruined vessel. She swam with a grim competence as she headed for the far side of the craft. The motorboat should be there, fastened with its painter to the doomed yacht.

It wasn't.

As she floated in the water, the melancholy cacophony of foghorns calling to each other struck a chord of sadness deep within her consciousness. Only Stefano could have taken the boat. She had been alone on the yacht when it fired.

She trod water and thought of Stefano's cynical words. "If one has only one chance to enjoy..." he had said. And "gather ye rosebuds while ye may...."

Had he been gloating over her death? Had he arranged the fire? Set it, perhaps, and then taken Bianca and left the yacht, counting on the fact that she was asleep and would never know? She thought of her uneasiness when Stefano was around, of the odd feeling of dislike she had for him. The conviction grew in her. He had wanted to get rid of her. In some way her presence threatened him and his plans. And he did know something about Charles. His reference to the little boy had made it sound as if the child were a pawn in some detestable game they had been playing.

Anger such as she had never known grew in Sally and pumped adrenaline into her system. She would find her way out of this mess, find her way to land and get help. Not for one moment was she prepared to let David's half brother get away with his criminal act.

So she began to swim, launching her body through the cold water with a strong and determined crawl. She felt able to swim miles, her energy fueled by anger and a cold desire to find out if Stefano had planned to destroy her along with the yacht.

She would certainly owe him an apology if she were wrong, she thought grimly, but the conviction that her assumptions were correct grew with each stroke she took. When she got to shore, she would find David, and make him understand the necessity to check very thoroughly on his relative. It did not occur to her that David might be implicated in any way.

There was no rush of fireboats or rescue vessels toward the burning yacht. Sally realized the fog must be thick enough to hide the fire, even muffle the explosion from anyone more than a few yards from the doomed vessel. There was not much chance of anyone knowing of the tragedy until the fog lifted, or someone stumbled upon the yacht accidentally.

"You are in for a long swim, old girl," she told herself. "So just get busy and do it."

Sally was in good physical condition, but the length of the swim before her appalled her. She conserved her strength by resting with a slow untiring motion that aided her buoyancy. Hidden in the back of her mind was the awareness that she had no idea in which direction her long smooth strokes were taking her. She might be headed down the length of the long bay for all she knew. In that case, she would undoubtedly drown or be swept out to sea. She tried to get a bearing from the hoarse foghorns, but they sounded all around her, distant, tantalizing, and only confused her.

She had been swimming for some time. The fog seemed to lighten and become more translucent. She wondered if the sun were about to rise.

After a while she became aware of a new sound. She stopped, treading water, her arms feeling more like lead than flesh as she moved them in an attempt to keep her head well above water so she could listen.

It was a muffled sound, rhythmic. Hope flared, warmed her a little. She shook her head impatiently to rid her ears of invading water, listened again, then realized she heard the sound of oars being pulled with a steady tempo. The sound grew dimmer as she listened.

Sally screamed for help then. She repeated it, using

an intensity of pitch that tore at her throat. The fear that the fog would blanket the sound and make it impossible for the man who rowed the boat to hear her tore at her mind with icy fingers.

She stopped then, her tension such that her buoyancy was affected, and she swallowed water. The sound of the oarlocks did not come to her. She sobbed in instant terror, then mercifully she heard a man's call.

She answered and he called back. As she kept up the ragged sounds she was just able to force from her throat, Sally did not dare move. In this thick blanket hovering within inches of her head, it would be so easy for the boatman who searched for her to miss her.

Her surge of relief was little short of hysterical when the boat became a darker blotch in the grayness of the fog. She was crying as she was lifted over the gunwale of the boat and deposited on the shelf seat. She was completely unaware of her nudity as she allowed the fisherman who had found her to push her arms into the yellow oilskin he had divested. He wrapped her shivering body in it, made sure she was clinging safely to the seat, and headed with as much speed as he could muster toward the shore.

Sally sat huddled on the seat. Her teeth rattled in her head as they chattered uncontrollably. Great shudders racked her slender frame as she shivered with cold and delayed shock. She sat with her bare feet thrust among the man's catch of the day and did not even feel the cold and twitching bodies of the fish. The old man tied up at a quay as he bellowed for help.

It came. Sally was bundled in blankets. Impressions barely registered on her exhausted brain as she was hoisted in strong arms and carried into the fisherman's house, where it sat in aloof dignity among the sprawling vastness of dockside warehouses.

She was warmed, washed and dried and put to bed. The fisherman's dainty wife hovered over her like a ministering angel.

SALLY SLEPT THE CLOCK AROUND, not awakening until past eight the morning after. Rested and refreshed, she was greeted by an atmosphere of love, laughter and gentle humor.

The room was furnished with a spare loveliness, the deep lacquer of the few wooden pieces lustrous in the soft light filtering through the slatted blinds at the big bow window. The gleaming hardwood floor had been beautifully cared for. A single flower rose in restrained elegance from a vase on a low graceful table.

Suddenly memory of the events that had brought her here flooded in, and Sally stirred restlessly. The fisherman's petite wife peeped in upon her immediately, smiled a cheery greeting and vanished.

She returned in a few minutes with a tray. It contained a tea service for one, plus crusty rolls, butter and honey. "You must be starved, my dear," she spoke in a sweet, rather reedy voice. "Please have this, then there is a man, or rather, two men to see you."

She arranged the bed tray over Sally's middle, plumped up her pillows and helped the girl to sit up. She laughed in amusement and turned back the cuffs of the long-sleeved pajama jacket Sally was wearing. And then she perched on the edge of a chair she had placed beside the bed and waited for Sally to eat.

Sally smiled at her, broke the delicious warm roll and spread it with butter and honey. Ambrosia! Sally could not remember ever being so hungry.

"You are so kind," she said, smiling at the little woman. "Where am I, please? Do you know the wonderful man who rescued me?"

"Indeed I do, my dear." Sally was the recipient of a lovely shy smile. "He is my husband, Samuel Tsumo. Whatever were you doing swimming in the middle of San Francisco Bay at that time of night? We have not been able to understand where you came from. The nearest shore was a considerable distance away."

"I'm not sure where I started from." Sally buttered another bit of flaky roll. "But I think someone was trying to kill me."

"Oh, my dear! How awful for you! I am so happy you managed to get away. You must tell me exactly what happened, but first you must see my son. He is a physician, and my husband wishes him to determine if you have suffered from your exposure." She went toward the door, then stopped suddenly, turning back. Her features lit with a sunny smile. "How rude of me. I forgot you don't know who I am in my wonder at your presence here. Forgive me. I am Margaret Tsumo. This is my home. And here is my son."

She stood aside as a tall man with lean Oriental features entered the room. He greeted his mother affectionately as he raised his eyebrows at the girl in the bed.

"My son's name is Tyrus," Margaret announced with obvious pride. "Dr. Tyrus Tsumo." Her pleasure in her tall son was easy to see and understand. "He is a teaching professor of medicine at the university here and is quite good, I am led to understand."

Dr. Tsumo smiled sunnily at his mother and came to Sally's bedside. "You had quite a sleep," he commented. "Almost thirty hours."

"Oh, dear. So long as that?"

"Yes. How do you feel now?"

"My head is a little muzzy. Too much sleep, I expect. Otherwise I feel fine."

"Let me check you over just to be sure." His mother left, then he proceeded to examine her carefully, his smooth face intent.

"I think you will do," he told her as he finished. "May I know what happened? It is rather unusual for a fisherman to find a mermaid swimming in the middle of the bay at that time of the morning, you know. He is generally considered lucky if he just finds fish."

"I am ever so grateful to him." She laughed, her eyes dancing as she appreciated the joke. He smiled, but his eyes were serious.

"I'm not sure," Sally replied, sobering to his mood. "I think perhaps someone intended to end my attempt to be a mermaid rather permanently. I think he meant to kill me."

He considered her for a moment, then went to the door. "Danny!" he barked. "This is for you, I think. My brother, Daniel, is a cop," he informed her as he retraced his steps.

"Detective-lieutenant, if you please." A tall Oriental with handsome regular features came through the door followed by Margaret Tsumo. All three sat down and looked at her expectantly. "What is your name, little mermaid?" Daniel asked in the best policeman style.

"Sally Rossi."

"Hmm." He narrowed his long eyes, considered her thoughtfully. "I assume you are English?"

"Yes. At least, I have seen the remnants of a British passport. I think I am English, and I think I am Sally Rossi."

"Don't you know?" All three of them wore a startled expression.

"Yes, well, I expect I'd best start from the beginning."

She told them of the accident, of her amnesia, of the arrival of Stefano from Italy and of the trip on *Sea Breeze*.

"Your husband was not on board all evening?"

"No. He received some sort of important message just after he took the engineer and radioman ashore so they could spend Easter with their families."

"You were to dinner with this Stefano and his wife then."

"Yes. Stefano made me uneasy so when we returned to the yacht, I went straight to bed."

"Your husband had not returned?"

"I am sure he had not." How do you explain to a policeman you were so sensitive to a man's presence you always knew when he was around, even knew when he was not because you felt so empty, so alone? Sally did not even attempt it.

"Did you sleep at all?"

"Not very much, I'm afraid." She thought of the long hours she had been awake listening for the sound of David's return. "I finally decided I needed some hot chocolate to make me drowsy. That's why I went to the galley."

"Tell me about the explosion."

Sally looked at him uncertainly. "I am not sure it was an explosion. I heard a sort of loud pop, and when I turned back to see what caused it, the passageway door blew open, and fire just leaped out. Of course, there was a big explosion just as I jumped in the water. The fire spread so quickly it caught my nightgown and robe when I tried to yell at Stefano and Bianca to warn them. I jumped without thinking."

"Good thing you did." He eyed her thoughtfully. "Are you certain they were not on the yacht?"

"I cannot be positive, of course. I swam around the *Sea Breeze* almost at once. I thought I could untie the launch and use it. It wasn't there."

"Perhaps your brother-in-law received a message from your husband and went ashore to pick him up."

Sally shuddered. "I did not think of that," she acknowledged sadly. "If he did, I expect Bianca is dead. She could not have lived through the heat of the fire." A tear crept down her soft cheek. "She was a dear little thing."

Margaret Tsumo made a gentle sound, went to a chest of drawers and came back with a handkerchief. Sally took it gratefully and mopped her face. She smiled into the calm face of the detective. "Thank you for realizing Stefano may not have been guilty of

trying to murder me. I truly had not thought he may
have just gone to pick up David. Oh! I must get word
to my husband immediately. He will think I have
drowned!''

"Leave this to me." Daniel Tsumo glanced at his
brother. "Is she able to be up and about, Ty?"

"I should think so if she does not try anything too
strenuous. I absolutely forbid her to swim back
across the bay today. She must find a more conven-
tional method to go back from whence she came.''

"Waterskiing, perhaps?" Daniel suggested, and
Sally laughed, joining in the fun.

"Out!" their mother ordered. "Let me find our
little mermaid something to wear. She seems to have
lost her nice fishy tail somewhere and will need something appropriate to clothe those lovely limbs she is
now using.''

Daniel got as far as the door. He turned and
looked at the girl then, his eyes narrowed in the
thoughtful look Sally was beginning to realize as
characteristic of him. "You give me the impression
your husband is not capable of planning to murder
you. Is this true?"

"He would not." Sally's reply came without hesitation. She knew she was not in danger from David.
Nor had she ever been. He was an intelligent man, a
dangerous one when aroused, perhaps. But he was
not a violent man. Beneath his arrogant hauteur was
a warm and gentle individual who loved deeply and
well. His treatment of her proved it. In the long run
he had not even been able to maintain the hateful
twenty-four-hours-a-day surveillance he had sen-
tenced her to as he took her home from the hospital.

He had been unable to remain indifferent to the stress his actions had caused her and had changed. No, David was not capable of murder. And she loved him.

It shone in her face as she returned Tsumo's look. He turned from her, a faintly envious quirk to his sensuous mouth.

"I must go. I will leave you in my mother's impeccable care. Just don't let her bully you."

Margaret Tsumo smiled lovingly, her eyes on the blue black gleam of her son's head. "These great hulking children of mine are entirely out of hand. They give me no respect. I wonder if it is too late to take the rod to them? I have certainly spoiled them."

"You can be forgiven," Sally laughed. "From the size of them, they probably weighed as much as you do within hours of their birth. How did you manage to have such large sons?"

"They are rather nice, aren't they?" Mrs. Tsumo agreed complacently. "I must say I earned my husband's everlasting respect by producing such handsome monsters. He still treats me as something special. I've done little to disabuse him of his illusions."

They spent a morning filled with humor and laughter. If Margaret Tsumo's object was to divert Sally's attention from her traumatic experience, she was completely successful. Daniel called his mother in the late morning and had a long talk with her. Sally was not aware of the conversation. She spent several hours dressed in an exotic silk kimono wrapped around her slender form and held in place by a long smooth tie, with little matching slippers on her feet.

Her tiny hostess just smiled when she asked what she must do about clothing.

"Daniel is in contact with your husband. He will see about something for you to wear."

They had just finished lunch when a taxi drew up in front of the house. A woman got out, loaded her arms with boxes and came to the door, followed by the driver laden with more boxes. Sally's husband, the shopkeeper informed her, had ordered her here with a selection of outfits for her approval.

Sally selected black slacks that fit her to perfection, then chose a black silk shirt and a gorgeous V-neck sweater in a deep blue, soft as a kitten's ear, to wear over it. She also took a set of underthings, panty hose and a pair of short black boots that fit with blissful ease, but she refused to consider anything else.

"I have closets full of things," she told Margaret seriously. "I expect David will come for me sometime today. I shan't need more than this." She stamped her feet into the boots and stood, ready for action.

If Margaret's look was a little peculiar, Sally did not notice. She bustled the chagrined woman out the door and into the waiting cab, piled the unopened boxes she was carrying in beside her and waved the taxi off.

David did not phone and neither did Detective-Lieutenant Daniel Tsumo. Sally became restless and decided to go for a walk along the wharf area. Margaret Tsumo looked worried a moment. Then her face cleared, and she asked Sally if she would mind doing a bit of shopping for her as Mr. Tsumo had not yet arrived to do it as he usually did.

Sally tucked the money and the list into her pocket and set off down the waterfront.

It was a lovely afternoon, the sky a pale sunlit blue, the huge bay a cheerful mirror. Clouds drifted by in the soft April breeze. Sailboats danced on the ruffled water, and the cheerful trill of bird song cut through the busy hustle of the dockside activity.

Sally, clad in her superbly fitting slacks tucked into the short suede boots, covered the ground with graceful strides. The blue cashmere encircled her silk-clad shoulders in an arresting accent. She wore it draped down her back, the arms looped over each other and swinging with her lissome body.

The men she passed eyed her appearance with fine appreciation. Sally, deep in thought, did not notice. With the clear brisk air blowing the cobwebs out of her mind, she came to the very satisfying conclusion she must again tell David she loved him.

It did not matter what he did with the information, she decided. She knew very well he would never be able to wipe the past from his memory and start over or learn to love her again if he ever had before. She doubted very much if he had done so, even in the beginning. The attraction had been purely physical, she feared with a wry twist of her lovely mouth. He had been on the loose, away from home and caught in a time of rare self-indulgence. It was her own fault if she had agreed to remain on the yacht when he had taken it over. It was a little hard to bear when she thought of the probable reason she had been there in the first place, but what had happened had happened. It was too late to regret it now.

The thought of leaving Carla was one she did not

want to face. Even worse was the thought of never seeing David again, but the unexpected late-night swim in the bay had at least washed the indecision from her mind. She knew she had to go.

Her treacherous emotions had betrayed her. She loved David and he knew it. He was using her love for some purpose of his own, and she was powerless, trapped by her own feelings. She knew she was not able to handle the stress of her strong emotional attachment when he did not want her.

Tears in her eyes, she changed direction and climbed toward the top of the steep hill. For fifteen minutes she walked, unaware of interested looks she received as she faced a bleak future that could not include the man she loved.

The pavement underfoot became a stairway with widely spaced flat steps. A postman, coming down, his leather bag full of undelivered mail, caught her serious eye and smiled at her. Sally returned the smile, sighed and came back to earth to accept the reality of her situation.

She stopped on the steps and looked back the way she had come. The street swooped away from her, plunged downhill to the Embarcadero shopping complex where the bay stretched its limitless blue. Far across, mountains in varied shades of green rose against the horizon. The Embarcadero curved to her right with the busy Bay Bridge. To the right she could see Fisherman's Wharf with its clustering small-boat traffic.

Everything was so clean and beautiful, so full of sunlight and shadow, so right. How could her world have gone so wrong when it was obviously meant to be enjoyed, to act as an enhancement to her own sense of being?

Sally sighed and turned from the view to stare into the window of a sidewalk newspaper dispenser. The top paper, folded in half so its masthead was clearly visible, carried a banner headline: VITICULTURIST FACES MURDER CHARGE

David Rossi's arrogant lean features looked at her calmly from the large photo reproduction under the paralyzing words.

Sally stared at it through the glass as the color left her face. Her heart seemed to turn over with a horrible leap. Sally pulled the folded bills Margaret had given her from her pocket, realized she needed change to open the box and looked around wildly.

She dashed into the pharmacy behind her and stammered her need. The clerk watched her curiously as she snatched with trembling fingers at the change for the bill she had given him.

"May I help you, lady?" He had followed her to the door and came across the pavement now as she fumbled vainly with the coins. They would not go into the slots.

She looked at the young clerk in mute appeal, the coins in her outstretched palm. He chose a couple, inserted them, pulled up on the front of the box and handed her a newspaper.

"Thank you very much," Sally whispered, her eyes already speeding down the double column of print.

David was being held without bail while the police investigated the explosion and fire that had destroyed his yacht. His wife had been aboard and had not been founa. Neither had her body been discovered. His brother and wife had been aboard but had most fortunately escaped injury. This was due to the sister-in-law's sudden illness. She had awakened in the early-morning hours in severe pain. The brother had rushed her to the emergency room of a hospital in time to prevent the premature birth of their first child.

David's unsubstantiated alibi was being investigated. The arrest had been made when Rossi had appeared on the wharf. He had apparently been caught as he attempted to return to the scene of the crime. The police were awaiting him. They had received a tip from an unidentified source.

The young clerk put his hand on Sally's arm and looked at her in some alarm. "What is it, lady? You look as if you've seen a ghost. Can I help?"

"I need to have a taxi."

"I'll call one for you." He guided her carefully back into the store, sat her down in a chair near the prescription counter. "Hang on half a minute, and I'll get one here."

He went behind the counter and dialed quickly, his eyes on Sally's strained face. When he finished speaking to the dispatcher, he came back around the counter and knelt beside her, his finger flicking the paper.

"Someone you know?"

"He is my husband."

"But it says you were on his boat. . . ."

Sally did not understand it, either. David had ordered the clothes she was wearing to be delivered to her. He must have ordered them. How else would the woman have known her size, her tastes? Yet how was he able to order them if he was in jail? And how had he known where to send them?

Daniel Tsumo, her logic answered. But Daniel knew she was alive and well in his mother's house. So how could David be in jail?

The questions chased themselves around her skull in a great fury as she waited aeons of time for the taxi to appear. When it did, she scrambled into it before the driver could open his door to assist her.

"Take me to the jail where men are held for murder," she gave the tormented request through stiff lips. "Please, please hurry!" The thought of David behind bars, his proud arrogance humbled, cut her to the quick. She must get him out at once.

She paid off the cabdriver at the foot of the long marble stairs leading from curbside in front of the Hall of Justice. She had to use Margaret Tsumo's money. She would have to replace it later. The thought flashed through her mind that she did not know the address or the location of the fisherman's pleasant home. That would need sorting out later.

The cabdriver told her to turn right after she entered the hall. The offices and the jail were at the end of the hall. She ran quickly up the wide stairs, her head down as she concentrated on maintaining her footing.

She ran straight into a solid male chest. Arms grabbed at her and kept her from falling. She flung back her head with a murmured apology and looked straight into the amazed and hostile dark eyes of Stefano Rossi.

"Sally!" His hands tightened convulsively on her

arms as she attempted to step away from him. His face looked gray under his dark tan. "Where in God's name have you come from?"

The force of feeling in his question frightened Sally. In that instant she knew he thought her safely dead and had been glad. His eyes blazed at her, incredulous, hate filled, dangerous. She struggled, her quick sense of danger flaring up.

Stefano flicked a lightning glance around and took a gambler's chance. He dropped one arm, swung a short jabbing blow to her jaw and caught her as she collapsed. He picked her up then, her head lolling back against him, his other arm under her slack legs.

"She has fainted," he told a woman who turned to look at them as the movement caught her peripheral vision. "She does sometimes. I must get her home."

He sped down the steps with his victim, his attention concentrated wholly on his need to get his burden out of sight.

"Hey, mister!" The reedy voice followed him down the steps, but Stefano did not look back. "Hey, mister!"

He vanished around the end of the ornate stone balustrade, then ran toward the car he had left in the municipal parking lot when he had come to visit his brother.

The gray-haired old woman stared after him in exasperation, Sally's deep blue cashmere sweater in her twisted fingers. "This is a very expensive sweater," she remarked to the tall Japanese-American who had paused beside her, drawn by her agitated expression.

"May I?" He was almost rude as he took the garment from her arthritic hands. He shook it out, stared an instant, shock in his good-looking face. "Where did you find this?"

"It belongs to the girl who fainted," she told him. "She dropped it. Her husband is taking her home. Says she faints all the time."

"Did you see her faint? What did she look like?"

"I didn't exactly see her. She just sort of collapsed, and he caught her. That's when her sweater fell. I saw that."

"What did she look like?" he repeated with a driving urgency.

"Sort of blondy hair. Pretty. I didn't see her very well...."

The young man raced down the steps with a blinding speed, the cashmere still in his hands.

The old woman stared after him as he vanished around the balustrade and headed for the parking lot. She shook her head then over the antics of young people and went on about her business.

CHAPTER FIFTEEN

SALLY CAME TO, conscious of motion. She was in a car, and it was moving at a great rate of speed. She was slumped in the seat and very uncomfortable. She moved, tried to straighten and became aware of the fact that her wrists were bound tightly. She opened her eyes then and stared at the white handkerchief around her wrists.

Slowly she ventured to look at the driver of the car. Stefano Rossi. Sally was not surprised. She closed her eyes and considered her position.

Stefano had tried to kill her for reasons of his own, reasons that she had no way of knowing. Whatever those reasons were, they were strong enough for him to take ghastly risks in order to ensure that she did not suddenly get her memory back and reveal them to David or anyone else.

He had tried to kill her once. He must be going to try again. This time he would make certain she was dead. Sally faced the fact with a cold intelligence. She did not know where they were, or where they were going, but she would die before the night was out unless a miracle were to happen.

She lay quietly back against the seat and tried to think. Her wrists were so tightly bound she knew her hands would be useless until the circulation was restored in them. That left her with her feet and her head for weapons. Not much, but perhaps she could get a mouthful or two while he made a meal of her, she thought with grim humor. She must fight him as hard as she could as soon as he stopped the car, and she knew what he had in mind. Even though she had little hope for the outcome, she would still try.

They drove on for hours, it seemed to Sally. She had determined to maintain the appearance of unconsciousness as long as humanly possible, for she had an instinctive feeling that an unconscious person must be infinitely more difficult to deal with than a conscious one, should another person want information. She was not sure what kind of information Stefano wanted, but she decided to make his task as hard as she possibly could.

When they passed through a town, she peeped carefully through barely opened lids, her eye level just above the panel of the door upon which she leaned. Paso Mayacama, she thought with amazement. She was not sure, but when the car sped over a dipping twisting road that kept rising, she was convinced Stefano was on the way to Rancho Las Colinas de la Pantera.

Her heart was in her mouth when he pulled to a rough halt, the tires crunching off the macadam and onto a graveled shoulder. He switched off the ignition and doused the lights. The door slammed as he left the car. Sally slumped in the seat as he crunched around the car and jerked the door open.

Her weight had been against it. Sally was taken by surprise and slid out, hitting the ground with a force that drove her breath from her body. Stefano swore and picked her up roughly, his hands hard on her soft flesh. He kicked the door shut, then headed across the road, dragging her through the dark. Sally forced herself to stay limp with the greatest effort of will she had ever used.

He dumped her at the roadside with the same care he might have used on a sack of potatoes, then knelt down beside her. "Wake up, you little bitch!" His hands were cruel on her shoulders as he shook her mercilessly. Sally forced herself to remain limp. Her head flopped on her slender neck with all the resistance of a rag doll's. Light flared in her head, streaked behind her closed eyes.

He stopped suddenly, grabbed a handful of silky curls. "Wake up, I say! Now!" His open palm stung her face, and he brought it back across the other side of her face in a powerful backhand.

"Don't! Please don't!" Pain tore through Sally as the vicious slaps jarred through Alan Stern's careful repair job.

"Ah! That's better." He stared at her intently, trying to see her expression in the darkness. "Now talk to me."

"Why am I here?" she whispered. "What do you want?"

"I mean to know where Don Lang is, and what you two are up to, and I mean to know it right now."

"You tried to kill me."

"It was ill-advised. I know that now. I have to know about Lang and find out about his plans so I can stop them. It's just as well you did not die in the fire. You can tell me now." He laughed, a chill sound in the cool night.

"I can't tell you what I don't know."

"Oh, you know, Sally." Again his threatening laugh rang out. "You will tell me. You can count on it." He reached out, grasped her chin in a rough hand and forced her face upward. "David doesn't know you are still alive, does he?"

"What a silly thing to say." Sally grasped at the straw. "Of course, he knows I'm alive."

"No." Stefano's denial was unequivocal. "I had just been visiting him when you turned up and dropped into my arms. He was suffering like hell. He thinks his love is dead. Why is he in love with you, Sally?" His curiosity got the best of him. "Knowing my brother, I would have bet you were the last woman on earth he would ever have fallen for."

"Don't be ridiculous. David hates me. He hates me and will always hate me. And I can't blame him."

Stefano's harsh laugh jeered at the sad note in the words. "I find the fact you love him even more incredible. You've certainly changed, you thieving little whore. Now tell me about Lang."

"I know I am supposed to have returned to this country with him. I do realize I must have had some sort of relationship with him, but I just don't remember him, any more than I remember you—or David, for that matter," Sally offered, utterly sincere.

"You will remember. And you will do it now." He enunciated clearly as if this might force his will upon her. "Stand up!"

He dragged her to her feet and pulled her away from the road, his hands roughly insistent. Sally realized he was forcing her toward the lip of the cliff at the same instant that their location struck into her with an icy certainty. The scene of the accident. She remembered Stefano's close interest in her reaction when David had brought her here.

What was he planning? She wriggled as violently as a game fish on a hook but was unable to break his hold. The man swore vividly and wrenched at her, wrestling her to her knees.

"Look over, Sally." He fastened his fingers in her disordered curls as he thrust her out over the lip of the canyon. Sally recognized her helplessness instantly and became still in his grasp, her breath uneven in her fear. Her terror was hardly lessened by the fact that the canyon itself was just a dark impenetrable maw waiting to swallow her. "Talk, you filthy little slut! Tell me where Lang is!"

Sally struggled against the pain he was causing and the fear induced by the depth of the space over which she hung so perilously. She did not say a word. With a livid curse he jerked her to her feet and pulled her with him as he rushed back down the slope of the curving road.

"I know this place does something to your memory, Sally. I'm prepared to sweat it out until you decide to confide in lil ol' Steve." His unpleasant bark of a laugh sounded terrifying in some way, as if he were close to dropping over the edge and into some form of insanity. "When I get through with you, you are going to wish you had stayed aboard *Sea Breeze* and burned with her. And I'm the only one in this world who knows you are alive."

Not the only one, Sally remembered with heartfelt gratitude. However, she did not see for the moment how the fact that Daniel Tsumo knew she was alive, and who she was, could help her now. Margaret must have missed her long ago. She hoped Tsumo's mother would have lost little time informing her son that their guest was missing. There was small comfort there, however. She realized no one had a clue as to her movements. For all practical purposes, she had vanished after leaving the Tsumo home.

Her rising panic caused her to dig in her heels. She flailed at her captor with her bound hands, her lungs heaving.

Stefano laughed nastily as he jerked her off balance and shoved her. The downward slope of the road insured she must keep her feet moving in order not to fall. Sally trotted in the effort to remain upright.

It was difficult to maintain the stumbling run, but she managed. They ran downhill until they came to the point where the road started upward again. Stefano tugged viciously at her. The girl fell. Gravel bit into her flesh, tore at her clothing. The man ignored her gasp of pain. He plucked her off the roadside, then set her on her feet.

"We can climb down here. The ledge where they found you is right below. Get up." Sally wriggled in his hard grasp and aimed a kick at his shins. He cursed fluently and thrust the barrel of a weapon she had not known he possessed into her rib cage with a force intended to bruise.

"Get over the edge, Sally, or I'll shoot you right here. Go!" He sounded demented.

Was it best to be shot here or down on the ledge? Desperately she played for time. "I can't see!" she spat as she refused to give in to tears or her growing panic.

"You'll see enough, or you'll pitch yourself over the edge and break your damn neck. It doesn't matter to me!"

"Don't be stupid," she hissed at him. "I'm of no use to you if I kill myself before you find out if your theory is correct or not. I absolutely refuse to climb down into this canyon with my hands tied. It's just plain stupid suicide."

She held her breath, not sure what she would do if her sensible appeal did not reach him through his inflamed and passionate anger. Then she heard the snick of a knife being opened and felt the coldness of the blade as Stefano sliced at the rope where it looped between her wrists. She did not feel the prick of the knife blade as it skimmed the skin of her left thumb. Her hands were too numb. But when the blood did pump into the restricted arteries, she gasped and rubbed her hands together to help the restoration of circulation.

"Get over that edge, Sally!" Stefano yelled at her. "Climb down at once."

Sally went, responding with a primeval awareness that the man who issued the command was incapable of rational action. She clambered down into the yawning blackness, her heart in her throat, her hands and arms still numb and almost useless.

As she lowered her weight over the lip of the canyon, she tried desperately to pierce the gray gloom with frightened eyes. Somehow she slid and bumped her way to the safety of the ledge with Stefano just behind her. The ledge offered footing, at least.

Stefano pushed her ahead of him. She stumbled in the darkness, twice going to her knees as she fell across drifts of debris that the rains had loosened and caused to fall across the ledge. Suddenly the area was illumined by the pale glow of moonlight. Sally glanced up and realized for the first time a high cloud cover had been concealing the waxing crescent of earth's satellite. The glow was dim, but the angle was right. In the pale wash of the reluctant light a giant earth slide reared a formidable barrier across the ledge and into the canyon. Several trees loomed darkly on the impossibly steep slope as it dropped beneath the ledge. Sally stopped, glanced up at the barrier and shuddered.

"You can climb it. Get!"

"Why? Where are you taking me?"

"Back to the spot where the ambulance men found you, dear sister. Now get over that slide." His face looked wild in the faint moonlight, his skin taut enough to pull back from his teeth in a vicious animallike snarl.

"How do you know where they found me?" Sally pushed fear away with a determined effort and flung her defiance at him.

"David showed me when I asked. Get going, Sally. From what I've learned about your kind of amnesia, you need to visit the scene, and by God, you are going to do just that. Climb that hump."

Sally did it but not because of the overriding fear Stefano inspired in her. No, she scrambled over the treacherous unstable earth slide in a feverish effort to do exactly as he asked in the fervent hope that he might be right. She paid little attention to the rocks and stones she dislodged, which bounced down the steep slope to her left, pitched over the edge and

dropped far down to the river below. She needed to
see if Stefano's theory was any good. She scrambled
over the rock slide, chasing her elusive memory. *Oh,
God,* she prayed silently. *Let him be right.*

Stefano followed, loosing a frightening amount of
debris, as well. Then he was over, his boots on the
solid ledge beside her. He grabbed Sally's arm and
gave her a push. In another hundred feet the lip of
the ledge thrust out and sheered off in a straight drop
to the river.

Sally moaned as she dropped to her knees, dread
flooding through her as the ledge spread before her
another hundred feet or so, then disappeared into
blackness. Her head jerked back, and she stared up
at the dark wall of the canyon, where it towered
above her. A suspension of feeling, a numbness of
reaction, seized her. Her memory knocked at the
locked doors of her mind and tried to force its way to
the surface of her consciousness.

She screamed shrilly. Stefano's eyes glittered down
at her, but his hoarse exclamation of triumph was cut
off by a piercing hiccuping roar that split the air and
drove Sally's blood from her heart. She had no
chance to move. As the great cat launched itself from
the cave mouth hidden in the blackness ahead,
Stefano's foot reached instinctively, driving into her
back and sending her spinning against the wall of the
canyon. One hundred and fifty pounds of lithe and
agile mountain lion hit the man directly in the chest
and flung him back against the wall of debris he had
just struggled over.

The gun in his hand went off, reverberations clapping against canyon walls. The panther screamed

again, an unforgettable bloodcurdling ululation that squalled defiantly into the night. Long claws raked at the man. Powerful hind legs kicked in a vicious punishment. Stefano rammed the gun into the cat's open mouth and pulled the trigger as her clawed front foot swiped at his exposed soft neck and ripped it open.

They were both dead as the disturbed earth moved down and took them over the edge.

Sally lay against the cliff, trapped, as the tail end of the earth slide that they had triggered rained down and covered her slender body to the waist under a numbing weight of dirt and rock.

Sound of the slide bounced off the canyon walls, faded, to be replaced almost instantly by the chopping whirr of helicopter blades in motion.

Cars squealed to a stop high above her on the road. She raised her face from the rough surface beneath it and listened intently, her heart thundering in her ears and interfering with her hearing.

The helicopter hovered over the road. Men shouted urgently at one another, then a shaft of light beamed down from the aircraft. As the girl twisted her head to watch, the light, moving deliberately, came over the edge of the cliff and struck the ledge. Sobbing, she frantically moved her hands. The looming bulk of the landslide was so close she was seized with the fear that she might be missed.

A shout went up as a voice boomed out from the copter's sound system. "We see you, Mrs. Rossi! Just lie very still. We are sending a man down."

The girl put her arm under her blackened cheek and sobbed into her torn shirt sleeve.

Daniel Tsumo clung to the rope as he was lowered

from the police helicopter suspended overhead and dropped lithely onto a cleared spot on the ledge. He was at her side in an instant, long fingers stroking her hair with a soft tenderness.

"Don't cry, Sally Rossi. Everything is okay. Don't cry."

"Oh, Daniel!" The cry was wrenched from her. "It will never be all right. I am not Sally Rossi, and I have killed a man."

CHAPTER SIXTEEN

THE DETECTIVE'S FACE did not change. He smiled gently, and his expression was one of tender indulgence. "You may not be Sally Rossi, love. But you have never killed anyone. I will bet my badge on that! Who are you, then?"

"I am Megan Wynn-Jones." The whisper was almost lost in her sobs and the sound of men scrambling gingerly over the landslide. "I am Sally's cousin. She tricked me into coming to the States with Don Lang. And Carla. He had a gun." Her sobs drowned her voice a moment. "I thought he meant to use it so I fought with him. In the car. The gun went off and k-killed him. That's when the car went off the road and into th-this canyon. And... and the panther screamed at m-me."

"Shh, Megan. Shh." He took off his shirt, lifted her head with a consummate gentleness and placed it under her dirt-streaked face as half a dozen men skidded down the unstable rock slide to land at his side. "We'll talk later." There was a curious tinge of happiness to his voice as he stood and issued orders with a concise brevity.

The girl was extricated and put carefully into a flexible stretcher. They winched her up to the big copter and flew her to the hospital in Paso Mayacama. She was met by James and Marion Maclean as the helicopter settled into an area cleared for it in the hospital parking lot.

Maclean rushed her to X ray as he had her thoroughly examined for breaks in her bone structure. The cold slick table on which she lay tilted at crazy impossible angles and affected the girl strongly. She retched several times, and then to her utter horror she was sick.

Maclean stopped then, a frosty amusement in his canny eyes as he allowed Marion to clear up the mess. Marion washed her with quick gentle fingers and then wrapped her in a clean hospital gown.

"C'mon, sweetie. Let's get you to bed." Marion was careful to avoid the use of her name, the girl noticed.

"I am Megan," she told the nurse. "I am Sally's cousin."

"So I've been told." Marion locked the mechanism on a wheelchair, assisted the girl into it with smooth efficiency. "I am so happy I may just burst out into song. And you are my friend. The fact that you look exactly like someone altogether different can't change our friendship," she declared sturdily, pushing her patient through a large door.

The girl heard David Rossi's imperious command then as he demanded to see her at once. She watched him stride down the long passage toward her and felt her heart squeeze in a vise. The unfairness of her position hit her like a blow.

David. Oh, David, my love. My love, my cousin's husband.

He saw her as Marion maneuvered her down the

long corridor, and came to her with his long swinging stride. The expression on his pale tense face wrenched at her heart. Wordlessly he took over the wheelchair and moved her down the hall. After a compassionate glance at his closed uncommunicative features, Marion walked ahead of them.

The nurse pushed open the door of a hospital room and waited as they entered, then shut it, leaving the two of them alone.

David stopped the chair and walked over to the window, staring blindly out onto the hospital grounds. "You are going to be okay?" The question sounded choked.

"Yes," Megan answered simply. "Thank you. No broken bones. My name is Megan Wynn-Jones. Sally is my cousin."

"I know." He still stared outside. "I knew three days ago. Megan Wynn-Jones from Chichester, England. The well-brought-up only daughter of a solid family. Your brothers are both successful lawyers. I beg your pardon. I believe they are barristers, and that makes a difference in your country."

"Yes," Megan returned. She was sure she felt her heart break as she stared at the tense back of the man she loved. "Philip and Jerome are both barristers." David did not turn around.

"Your mother was a twin," he went on quite calmly. "Her sister married at the same time as your mother did. She had twin sons born the same year as your older brother, Philip, was."

Megan nodded wordlessly. How had he learned all this?

"You and Sally were born in the same month,"

Sally's husband continued bleakly. "And you always looked so much alike you might just as well have been twins. Right?"

He turned his dark glance on her then. Megan drew a ragged breath. She was unable to answer him.

"You grew up fighting Sally's battles, defending her and rescuing her from the results of her lack of discipline or restraint. She talked you into this piece of foolishness, and you didn't have the sense to resist." His smile was frosty. Megan shivered as she held his glance. "Part of the scheme was to kill you, I think, after you had done your job. Do you know what that was, Megan?"

"No," she whispered. "Sally only asked me to see that Carla was delivered safely. She...she didn't plan to have me k-killed."

"That remains to be seen." David's tone was cold and impersonal. "I happen to think differently. At any rate, I know now that you were the personal assistant to Ian Johns, the chief of a large and prosperous electronics firm. He just happens to be your fiancé. You are deeply in love with him from all reports." David's face was white now, his mouth set in grim lines.

No, David! her heart cried. *I don't love Ian Johns. I never loved him as I love you. My love, my cousin's husband.* The refrain tore through her, blocked her thinking and twisted in her chest in unbearable despair.

David left the window with an abrupt impatient gesture and came to kneel beside her, resting back on his heels. He lifted a hand, smoothed her burnished curls back from her woebegone face. "Am I right so far?" he asked gently.

Megan shuddered at his touch as she resisted the impulse to snatch at his hand and hug it to her. "How did you find out?" she whispered tautly.

"I had Tom Avila come and take some good photos of you, remember? Roger Dickson was there that same night and talked to you. He collected the pictures from Avila and left for London on the first plane out." There was a bitter edge to the voice she loved so well. "I sent him over to check Scotland Yard's missing-persons files." He shook his head sadly, a hard regret in the black depth of his eyes.

"Why?" she whispered.

"Because I knew I had made a terrible mistake."

"You knew I wasn't Sally?"

"I knew you weren't Sally," he agreed quietly. "I should have always known. All the signs were there. I was just too thickheaded, too stubborn, to see them. I must beg your forgiveness, *cara*."

Megan's heart flipped over at the familiar endearment. Did he use it because he did not wish to associate her with Sally? A faint hope sprang to life and wavered deep within her.

Remembrance of the wonderful shared experience high on the top of his personal mountain thrust itself into her consciousness, accompanied by her acute awareness of his change in attitude toward her on the long days the yacht had been used as a hotel.

Oh, David, were you wooing me then? But how could he have been? Even if he were at last positive she was not his hated wife, he still knew he was married. What could it all mean? She shook confusion from her, but before she could ask the questions trembling on her lips, someone knocked at the door. And faint hope died a natural death.

David rose from his crouch to answer the imperious knock. Marion followed Maclean in, casting David an apologetic glance.

"Everything will be great, young lady." Maclean was gruffly cheerful. "I just wish you would refrain from falling down that particular mountainside. It always manages to chew you up."

Megan laughed ruefully. "You are right, you know. I'm going to have to stay away from it."

"You're satisfied with her, Jim?" David demanded. "She'll be okay?"

"She will." Maclean thrust his fists into the pockets of his white jacket and surveyed her critically. "She's going to be a mass of bruises, though. There's not too much I recommend after having half a mountain fall on her. I'll want her here for several days, though, to keep an eye on her. Besides, she'll need a thorough course in physical therapy before I'm going to let her out into the wild world."

"I understand." David's reply was so noncommittal that the girl looked at him sharply. "Will that be all right with you, *cara mia*?"

She blinked at the endearment, and a tear crept out, rolling slowly down her cheek as she nodded. My dear, he had called her. Oh, if she only could be!

"I have some people here to see you, *cara*," he stated without inflection as Marion and Maclean left the small room. "I rather think you will enjoy seeing them. Shall I bring them?"

She nodded, her eyes a deep blue and drowned in sorrow as she sought vainly to suppress her unutterable need for this man who was her cousin's husband.

Caught in the misery of her impossible love, she was quite unprepared for the sight of the man and woman who entered the room at David's request.

"Mother. And Ian. How on earth..." Megan's glad cry rang out. A shadow passed over David's face and lingered grimly.

The woman ran to the girl's bed, and she was gathered into loving arms and kissed quite thoroughly. The man moved deliberately, plucked her from her mother's arms and lowered his blond head.

"Oh, Ian..." Megan surfaced breathlessly, the darkness of her blue eyes deepening as they flew to the man standing still as a stone in the doorway. His dark eyes sparked, angry, passionate. Then he turned on his heel and was gone.

Gone from her life forever, Megan knew. Her face stark with her misery, she turned her attention to the two people who had once meant the most to her. They still meant a great deal, but no one was as important as the man who had just left without a word. There was no comfort for her, no way to assuage her grief.

Ian Johns assessed her strain as she sank back into her pillow, his intelligent features twisted with a bitter regret. "Oh, Meggie, my love. I thought we had lost you for sure." Her mother smoothed her hair back from her forehead and clucked at the coldness of the skin under her fingers. "Whatever happened? You just vanished from the face of the earth."

"I know, mums. When I got to London with Carla, Sally was with this man, Don Lang. She begged me to take Carla to the States for her. She seemed terrified to do it herself, and yet she was determined to have Carla go." She sighed gustily. "You know, I have never been able to resist Sally when she gets herself in one of her pickles." She sighed as she remembered Sally's hysterical accusations against David Rossi, her very evident fear of the man who was her husband. She had not been able to understand it then, and she understood it even less now.

David was a strong and very adult personality, his passions controlled by a soaring intellect and a deep feeling for people. Sally had wronged him grievously, but Megan was convinced he had meant her no real harm.

Sally had always been her wild and uncontrollable cousin, spoiled by her two older brothers and a father with too much money, which he had used, quite ill-advisedly, to buy his only daughter's affection.

Sally's mother had died when her cousin was just a tot, so Sally had spent much of her early life at her aunt's house. The two little girls made a game out of confusing everyone they could. They had changed clothing until Megan's father forbade the fun as they approached teen age. Because of their uncanny similarity in looks, only their own families had ever been able to tell them apart in those days.

But as they grew older, and Sally became harder to control, Tevis Wynn-Jones had sensed his niece's total self-centeredness. He had not wanted Megan to suffer because she was mistaken for Sally and blamed for mischief that he was sure Sally would not avoid, so he had been vastly relieved when Sally had allowed her hair to grow and had bleached it to a silver gilt. The girls were then no longer mirror images.

Sally had grown up to be beautiful, spoiled and sexually attractive to the boys who flocked to her house as friends of her older brothers. Her father died when she was sixteen, leaving a daughter who was out of control and in possession of a great deal of money. It had not occurred to him to deny her access to that money until Sally reached the age of majority. She had gone through it before she reached twenty.

Accustomed to the trappings of wealth, the girl began to exploit her undoubted ability to attract any man she fancied. By using her sex and her beauty, she maintained her standard of living.

She had lived hard in the segment of society that made up the international set known as the beautiful people. Her brothers were unable to control her, and she steered a wide berth around her disapproving aunt and uncle.

When she had turned up in Chichester more than two years ago with six-month-old twins, the Wynn-Jones family had been completely surprised. Sally stayed two days, looked as if she was settling in as part of their household, then disappeared, not to be heard from again until last autumn. The twins had lived with the Wynn-Joneses two years as part of the family when Sally finally called.

Megan had taken her call from London, astounded to hear from her. Sally had sounded frantic, asked her to bring Carla with her and come to her at once as she was in deep trouble.

"I knew I should never have allowed you to go to London alone that day," Ian remarked bitterly. "I have been out of my mind, Meg. You just disappeared from the face of the earth."

"Sally promised to let you know." Megan was regretful. "I should have realized she would do no such thing, but we got to Heathrow at the last moment. I had no time to phone, myself."

"How did you agree to go, Meggie?" her mother's question was completely amazed. "You didn't have your clothes or your passport."

"The man, Lang, had a visa made out to Sally. He said he would get one for me, but he never did. I didn't know until later. I did have my passport. Sally had told me to be sure I had it. But she rang off before I could ask her anything about it. She had everything very well planned and even had an overnight bag packed for me so I could freshen up, she said. And she insisted on lending me her bracelet so I would look dressier." She sighed at her naiveté.

"How could you do it? Go off like that with a strange man?" Mrs. Wynn-Jones still looked incredulous. "I cannot conceive of such a thing."

"I know, mums. I was incredibly stupid." She plucked at the coverlet with stiff fingers. "Sally begged me just to take Carla to David Rossi. I was to catch a plane back to London the next day. They assured me of this." Her expression haunted, she looked at her mother. "I had to do it. Sally said she would send Carla with Don Lang if I did not go. And Carla was terrified of him. She screamed the house down if he came near her. And they gave me my return ticket, though I found I wasn't meant to use it."

"I don't see how you managed if you had a visa for Sally and your own passport." Ian looked at her fondly, his eyes skimming her tired little face.

"I handed my passport to Lang just as we dashed

up to passport control because Carla fussed and was crying. I got on that plane as Sally Rossi, but I didn't know it until we reached San Francisco. I began to be frightened then."

"Why on earth..." her mother jerked the words out, her lack of comprehension evident.

"Carla was asleep when we got to San Francisco. You know how she sleeps, mother."

Mary Wynn-Jones nodded. Nothing short of a major explosion in the immediate vicinity disturbed the child once she had gone off.

"Well, Lang insisted on carrying her from the airplane. That is when he handed me Sally's passport and visa. As I had to gather up the hand luggage and my handbag, I did not notice it until we were in the terminal." She took a deep unhappy breath. "It was then he threatened to kill Carla if I didn't use Sally's documents. He meant it, mums. It was in his face. It was horrible." As the scene flashed into her memory, she suddenly sobbed and covered her face with her hands.

Johns growled deep in his throat, gripped her shoulder. Megan pulled herself together and smiled shakily. "Lang insisted I hire the car in Sally's name. It was then that I really began to be suspicious of him. I asked him what he was planning. It was dark and raining, but he insisted on driving north to the ranch he told me was the house of Sally's husband. It seemed as if we drove for hours. I talked to him, tried to find out why he was so insistent that I pretend to be Sally." Megan's mouth went dry as she remembered.

"I was to deliver Carla to David, along with an

ultimatum. If David was ever to see Charles again, he had to deposit a vast sum of money into a numbered account in Switzerland. Lang gave me the number.'' She looked at them in torment. ''David had two days to comply, or they would kill Charles.'' She stopped a moment, breathing hard.

''All the time I was to pretend I was Sally. David had not seen her for two years. They were sure he would not know the difference. As it turned out, they were right. He never did know I wasn't Sally, not in all the months I spent in his home. He th-thought I was his wife.'' Some of the more explicit results of his acceptance of her identity seared Megan's memory.

Her mother saw her stress and patted her hand sympathetically. ''I am sure it has not been easy for you, child.''

''No, it hasn't.'' She brushed away a tear, stole a look at Ian's thoughtful face.

Megan sighed regretfully and got on with her story. ''Lang looked so ruthless, so violent. I began to realize he was being too frank with me. It frightened me. I asked him what he planned to do, and when he planned to take me back to San Francisco to catch my return flight. He laughed and assured me we would leave just as soon as I delivered the message to David Rossi. He—I....'' The girl found it impossible to go on.

Ian Johns, his face bleak with the knowledge that his fiancée had been living for some months with another man under the assumption that she was his legal wife, sat frozen to his chair. The possibilities did not bear thinking about.

But Mrs. Wynn-Jones was more concerned with what had happened to her only daughter. "What happened, Meggie?" she urged softly. "How did the accident occur?"

"It was raining," Meg whispered. "We were driving up this winding mountain road. I glanced down and just happened to see his gun thrust through his belt. The handle was sticking out toward me. I figured he meant to kill me after I had delivered Sally's message. I had Carla in my lap. I never should have been so foolish, but I snatched at that gun, and I got it. He...he just came at me, and the car went over the edge. That's all I remember."

Ian Johns was white with anger. "The bloody bastard. If I can get my hands on him—"

Megan looked at him with an inexpressible sadness. "The man is dead, Ian. He...he died in the crash of the car, the crash that caused my amnesia." She could not bring herself to repeat to the people who loved her the phrase she had forced out to Daniel Tsumo. They would talk, he had said. She did not think he wished her to tell anyone else she had killed Don Lang. She was not sure why he wished her to remain silent, but she was content to do so. She shrank from her recollection of the horrible incident on the winding wet road so many months ago.

"Why did he plan to kill you after you delivered Carla and the message?"

"I don't know, mother. I expect so they could enjoy the money without the worry of having David on their trail."

"Did Sally know his plans, do you think?"

"Oh, mummy! I hate to think she did, but she was

helping him. She must have known something. Is Charles safe?"

"Charles is at his father's home now." Ian moved back to the bed, his face taut with his own need for assurance. "You lived there, Meg. He thought you were his wife. You thought you were, too. You lived there all these months with him...." His voice trailed away on the unasked question.

"Oh, Ian!" Mary gave him a glance loaded with reproach. "Not now. The girl is still in shock...."

"It's a fair question, mother," Megan answered softly. She knew what she must do and did it very quietly. "The answer is yes, Ian. We shared the same bedroom." She let the information drift into the silence of the room, then steeled herself for the flare of rejection that flamed in Ian's gray gaze as he stared down at her, his face as white as a sheet.

"No." The sound tore from his throat and hung between them. "No, Meggie! No!"

God forgive me, the girl thought, her mouth twisted with stress. David had slept with her many times and made love to her only once. He had put paid to the possibility of her return to the gentle arms and the tender care of her fiancé when he had possessed her with such authority.

She knew she was incapable of ever again accepting love from another man. David was out of reach, but she would love him forever.

Ian dropped his head in his hands, his shoulders shaking. A sob caught in Megan's breast. She longed to go to this man she had been ready to marry, to pull his head against her, cherish and comfort him. Ian Johns was a fine man and deserved better treatment, but she was helpless in her love for David Rossi.

Her tormented eyes sought her mother's face. Mary got up and went to Ian, her fingers smoothing his hair. She was very fond of Megan's fiancé and hated that he should be made to suffer so deeply.

Fortunately, Daniel Tsumo appeared in the doorway then and gave her the excuse she needed. "We must go and find the accommodations David has booked for us," she reminded Ian gently. "I expect he was thoughtful enough to find us somewhere close to the hospital, but we should go now, I think."

As Ian stood, he focused bitter attention on the girl he loved. He wanted her under any condition, and it showed in his face. "It doesn't matter, Meggie. It doesn't matter at all. I love you."

Megan returned his pleading stare, her heart in her eyes. "It matters, Ian," she stated with the certainty of the passionate experience she had shared with David Rossi. "I wish I could say it does not, but in all honesty I cannot."

He disregarded the others in the room as he assessed the gentle rejection of his hope. "I can see it does." He swooped over her suddenly to plant a fierce seeking kiss on her mouth.

Megan raised her fingers to lips that quivered and watched him walk from the room. Her mother kissed her hurriedly, nodded at Daniel and followed Ian.

CHAPTER SEVENTEEN

Tsumo watched them go, his own face thoughtful, his eyes bleak. "Poor bastard," he observed mildly. "You hit him where he lives, Megan Wynn-Jones. He loves you."

"I know." A tear surfaced, slipped over. "I wish he didn't. Ian is too fine a man for one to treat so badly. If only I had never come here! It...it's ruined my life."

"Has it, Megan?" He looked at her strangely. "Why is that?"

Megan sniffed in a watery scornfulness. "I was happy before I came here, Daniel Tsumo!" she exclaimed testily. "My life was in control, and I liked it that way!"

"Did you now?" Tsumo's clever face was gently derisive.

"I most certainly did." She sounded stormy. "Ian loved me. We had planned our life. I was contented."

"And did you love him?" the detective asked, a quiet smile touching his smooth features. "Can you honestly say you did, little one?"

Torment touched her and caused her to draw a deep breath. "We were to be married," she retorted bitterly. "I was very sure Ian and I would have been happy."

"You might have been," he allowed easily. "Lots of women are when they settle for half a loaf. But Ian doesn't strike me as the kind to be satisfied with less than the best. If you didn't love him, you were headed for trouble, Megan."

"I suppose so," she whispered. She was confused and aghast as Tsumo's words forced her to recognize that she'd never loved Ian at all. She had valued him and had accepted his gentlemanly demands as proper and right. His love had been quiet and comfortable. It had never placed the severe claims upon her that David evoked by just looking at her. She sighed in defeat. "We were happy before I came here and met David Rossi. Everything's changed."

"Change is the name of the game, little lady. Don't be afraid of it. There isn't too damn much you can do about the past." A grin lit up his exotic and very good-looking features. "Inscrutable Oriental offers a quote from the Occident: 'Fear not for the future, weep not for the past.'"

Megan gave a little hiccup of amazement and brushed eyes that threatened to brim over. "What on earth goes on in the dark interiors of your police stations? A cop quoting a poet? Definitely out of character."

"Yeah. Police departments the world over started going to hell when we were allowed to learn to read. I want to talk to you about Don Lang, Megan."

Megan shrank into her pillows, her eyes filled with dread.

"It's all right, baby. Don't look like that. We found him, you know. Or rather, what was left of him." He smiled in gentle reassurance. "He was thrown from the car and wound up half a mile down-stream from the wreck." He paused and considered her stricken look. "Probably died before he knew what hit him."

"Did you find h-his gun?" Megan swallowed convulsively as she tried to sort out the impressions she retained in the dark reaches of her mind about the incident that had caused such a traumatic change in her life.

"What gun?" Daniel's smile was enigmatic and told her nothing. "We found no gun, nor did the remains show any sign of a gunshot wound."

"But I'm sure I shot him." Megan forced the agonized whisper out.

"I'm damn sure he needed to be shot," Daniel offered quietly. "You must have missed. How did it happen?"

"We were both seated on the front seat," Megan recalled. "Carla was crying. He'd frightened her badly a couple of times. When I absolutely refused to demand money in return for Charles's safety, he yelled like a madman. It was awful. He was yelling and the baby was screaming. He sounded so vicious I'm sure the tone of his voice terrified Carla. I was frightened of him, too." She drew in a long shuddering breath. Tsumo reached over and patted her hand as he gave her a reassuring smile.

"He'd shown me his gun, of course. I don't know how he managed to smuggle it through the airport security, but he showed it to me as soon as we were in the car he rented."

She paused to collect her thoughts and gave the policeman a tentative smile. "He pushed it into the waistband of his trousers, and I spent a couple of hours trying to figure out a way to get it from him.''

"That was just plain stupid, Megan. Never—but never—mess with a nut who has a loaded gun.''

"I suppose you're right, but I had to do something,'' she protested. "I was sure by then he planned to kill me as soon as I delivered the message and Carla. I figured I might not get a chance to tell David what he and Sally were up to. He was driving like a maniac and shouting at me to quiet Carla. He turned to me to hit either me or Carla. I ducked, and as I did, I saw the gun in his waistband. I didn't even think, Daniel. I just went for it.''

Daniel Tsumo nodded his understanding. "What happened then?''

"I had Carla in my arms, of course.'' Megan trembled at the clarity of her recollection. "He felt me pull the gun from his waistband. He came at me like a madman. I couldn't get away from him.'' She closed her eyes, her paleness attesting to the stress she felt. Daniel watched her closely, his own pain showing clearly.

"Th-the gun went off,'' she muttered raggedly. "H-he slumped against me.'' The tears rolled unchecked then. "The next thing I knew, we were going over the edge. I—I don't remember what happened then.''

"There was one hell of an explosion, and the car burned, but you and Carla fell out before that when it bumped off the ledge.''

Tsumo reached into his hip pocket, extracted a large white handkerchief. Megan accepted it with a watery smile of thanks and applied it to tears she could not control.

"You didn't shoot the s.o.b., Meggie. Much as he needed it, you missed him. He just lost his head and steered the car off the brink. Hard luck, but let's forget him. Okay?"

The girl stared at him. His face really was inscrutable. He looked at her blandly, and his expression didn't give away a thing. Megan sighed, decided she had no choice except to believe him. "Does that mean I won't be charged with h-his murder?"

"What murder? The stupid bastard was just fool enough to drive off the edge of a cliff. He killed himself. And inflicted grievous bodily harm on an innocent woman and child. He should be prosecuted, but he took the easy way out and died."

"Thank you for telling me. What happened to Stefano?"

Tsumo considered her carefully. "He didn't come out too well from his brush with that big cat. He killed her, but he died in the process. That ledge led to her lair, you know. She had two kittens there, probably a couple of months old. David thinks that is why she attacked Steve. A mountain lion does not usually attack a man unless she is defending her family."

"What happened to the little ones?"

"David took them home. He's feeding them. He's some kind of guy, is your David."

"Some kind of guy, but not *my* David." Megan shook her head at this man she had known such a short time but liked so well. Suddenly she remembered a terribly important fact.

"Why was he still in jail when you knew I was not dead?" Her whisper accused him. "I saw his picture—that terrible headline—in the paper. I was frantic. Why didn't you let him go, Daniel?''

"I talked the whole thing over with David and his attorney. We decided the best way to flush out the real culprit was to give him a little security. Hold Dave in jail, let the story break and see what happened. Don't forget, we were looking for Lang. Dave was sure he had a hand in the whole business. We were just getting our teams into action when you came up those steps and wrecked the whole damn thing. Well, almost. I had the good sense to come out of the building just as Steve made off with you." He sighed with self-mocking humility. "I'd like to think we did it because of outstanding police work, but it was just luck. If that old lady hadn't talked to me about the sweater she found, I wouldn't have known until much too late that Steve had you."

"What sweater?" Megan did not remember a sweater at all.

"The blue cashmere you dropped when Steve slugged you. He did slug you, didn't he?"

"Yes, but how could you have known the sweater belonged to me?"

" 'Cause I bought it especially to match those lovely blue eyes of yours, lady."

"You mean you sent over all those clothes?"

"I do indeed. And I did an excellent job of quick shopping, I thought. But the blue cashmere was my particular favorite. I thought you would look smashing in it. Did you?"

She stared at him in utter confusion. "But I thought David.... How could you know my size?"

"I knew." The brief statement said volumes. "I

took one look at you, Megan, and thought heaven had delivered you to my doorstep especially for me." He grinned ruefully. "Of course, I hadn't met David then. It's a good cop who knows when there is no contest. I'm a good cop."

Megan caught his implication and was momentarily speechless. She just looked at him.

Tsumo smiled at her, his eyes hooded. "But that blessed little old lady did come along and handed me the one thing I had really pictured you wearing. I had a tail on Steve in seconds. Ground units followed him out of town while I went to work on the brass. I was a model of fast efficient action," he declared with mock modesty. "I got Dave out of the slammer and got permission to chase you in that copter in something under a half hour. And that, my dear young lady, was nothing short of a miracle in the fine art of cutting red tape."

Megan grinned at him. She knew the delicate thread of affinity, the easy feeling of familiarity she had with this tall Japanese-American was special. In another time, another place, she could have learned to care deeply for him, and he knew it. The knowledge was between them as he sat there and gazed at her in a rueful manner as she wiped the tears from her face.

"I am sure there are very few pieces of red tape able to resist you, Daniel."

"That is absolutely correct," he informed her. "In this case, it was just as well. We really moved. We weren't five minutes behind you when the landslide hit."

"Do you know why Stefano was trying to kill me, Daniel?"

"Dave thinks he was convinced you were Sally, and he desperately needed to get rid of Sally."

"I thought he was hand in glove with her. That is what he intimated to me."

"Yeah. He was in on the original scheme Sally and Lang hatched up when they kidnapped the twins, or so David has found out. Lang snatched them with Sally's help. They went to Canada with them and left for England from there. Sally had money David had given her, and Lang had some he had embezzled. They dumped the kids on you and your folks, and just disappeared until they ran out of money or figured David was hurting enough to want his kids back at any price."

"Sally involved me because she was afraid to face David."

"Uh-huh. I expect Lang figured he could leave Sally's identification on you, get rid of you, and he and his girl friend were home free."

"I can understand that, but why was Stefano so afraid of me if he really thought I was Sally?"

"Well, Lang and Sally were the instigators of the scheme in the first place, we think. Steve just went along because he resented David's authority over him and wanted to get back at him. He went to Italy full of rebellion and resentment. Then he married Bianca and settled down. David gave him a good hunk of the business for a wedding present and promised him a partnership when his first child was born."

"He must have been afraid I was going to recover my memory as Sally and give him away, then. No wonder I was a threat to him. He thought I could wreck his life."

"As Sally, you would have done exactly that, according to Dave. Steve had reason to want you out of the way."

"I find it difficult to believe Sally is so bad, but I can't deny all the evidence that keeps piling up," she offered unhappily.

"It wouldn't make good sense to deny it, Meg. She's a real bad number from all accounts. She and Lang refused to let Steve off the hook. They told him he was in up to his neck and in to stay. He was frantic. He didn't want his deal with David ruined. We think he came over with the idea of stopping Lang, then hit the panic button when he couldn't find him. Personally I think they were setting him up as a future blackmail candidate. Poor bastard can't be blackmailed now. He had a very quiet funeral."

"He must have decided to get rid of me when he couldn't find Lang," Meg ventured, sad that he had wasted his life so recklessly.

"That's about it. He became convinced you did have amnesia, apparently, but he couldn't take the risk of having you regain your memory and spill the beans. I reckon he decided to force Lang's whereabouts out of you, push you off the cliff and then go find Lang. Sally was found in London, by the way. The police over there are showing more than a little bit of interest in some of her more unsavory exploits and companions. She is helping them with their inquiries, as the saying goes."

"I am very grateful to you, Daniel," she assured him solemnly. "I owe you my life. And I owe you for a very nice outfit, which I am afraid I ruined first time out, as well."

"Not to worry." His smile was gentle. "You'll be okay now. Just follow the doctor's orders and get out of here." He stood up to leave. "I've got to get back to the grindstone. You'll come to see my mother when you are well?"

"I would like that very much. Please thank her for me and make my excuses to her. I'm afraid I did not turn out to be a very satisfactory guest. I owe her money, too."

"Don't worry about it." His eyes lingered regretfully on her face. "Tell David for me that I think he is the luckiest bastard alive. If you ever get fed up with him, just let me know."

Megan looked at him sharply and read his message clearly. *It isn't a case of my getting fed up with him,* she wanted to protest. *Just the opposite.* However, she found herself unable to utter a word.

Daniel Tsumo smiled down at her wretched face. "Just take it easy, little one. The guy is crazy about you. You'll see." Meg made an involuntary sound of denial, and his smile gentled. "So long. Take care." He left then, a man who wished their relationship had been given a chance to develop.

Megan spent the rest of the day thinking about him and about Ian, her face sad most of the time. One man who wanted to love her and one who did. She knew all she would ever want was the one man who was never to belong to her.

DAVID DID NOT COME to see her and had not put in an appearance when Ian came by the next day to tell her he had to leave.

"I am sure you will be glad to see the back of me,

Meggie." He was aggressive in his hurt. "I expect I can't blame you for what happened, but I sure as hell don't like it. If I didn't have to get straight back, I'd be inclined to stay here and fight for you." He stared at her, his mouth a grim taut slash. "It's probably for the best I can't stay. I'll go now. Maybe I'll see you if you get back to England."

"Oh, Ian. I can't tell you how sorry I am. It just happened, you know. I hate it, but I can't help it."

"No more sorry than I, I can assure you." He smiled, a tight humorless grimace that emphasized the white line around his lips. "I'll go now, Meggie, before I get maudlin."

He bent over her, snatched her into his arms and gave her a rough kiss that punished, searched. Meg did not respond. He dropped her back onto her pillows and left, striding quickly away. His back was stiff with outrage and hurt.

Megan lay still and mourned his departure. What a mess she had made of her life. She was unable to see how she would ever go back to normal, but knew she must find a way.

Her mother came to see her and was not much help. She had moved out to the ranch, she told Meg. *Nonna* had invited her, and it was a chance to be with the twins for a few days until Megan was discharged from the hospital, and they could return to London.

For Megan was quite determined to go. Her determination grew as David continued to be absent. She had not set eyes upon him since he had witnessed Ian's kiss on that first day. As soon as she could persuade James Maclean to discharge her, she would go back with her mother. She knew she was ruined for life in Chichester, but perhaps she might go to London, find work there and learn to live with the ache in her heart.

Maclean had turned out to be particularly obstructive. Megan complained about it to Marion the day after Ian left. "I don't *need* to be in this blasted hospital," she informed the nurse in no uncertain terms. "But that mean old husband of yours just acts as if he can't even hear me when I tell him so!"

Marion laughed at her. "He has his reasons, Megan. Believe me, David will have his scalp if you are not still here, having a good rest, when he...." Her friend stopped the flow of speech and shot an oblique glance at her.

Megan stared at her in disbelief. "You are saying David Rossi has ordered Jim to keep me here in the hospital, aren't you?"

"I said nothing of the kind," Marion protested, going a little red about the ears. "You know Jim would never take orders about one of his patients from anyone, not even David."

"I know nothing of the kind," Megan retorted evenly, sure Marion had made a slip and was trying to cover it up. "Has he asked Jim to keep me here for some reason of his own? David Rossi has nothing to do with me, you know. I'm not his wife and never have been." Except for a gloriously insane few moments on a mountaintop, a part of her insisted.

Marion watched the tide of Megan's blush wash over her stricken face and sighed softly. "You love him, don't you, Meg?"

Megan swallowed convulsively, completely unable to stop the instant tears.

"Thought so." Compassionate arms wrapped around the girl's shaking shoulders, and Megan buried her face in the white uniform-clad embrace of her friend. Marion soothed her, told her everything was working out and jollied her. Megan concealed her depression and smiled. She knew nothing had changed, nor was it likely to.

HER MOTHER CAME THAT AFTERNOON along with *nonna* and Bianca. She was glad to see them. Bianca was pale, her small face puffy as a result of the tears she had shed. *Nonna* was tight-lipped, her grief concealed.

"I am unhappy about my grandson's death," she told Megan with quiet dignity. "It is natural. But I wish to offer you my apologies in his name for the trouble he has caused you. It may be for the best he is gone. David has explained all to me."

"Oh, *nonna*. You must not say such things. Of course you are unhappy. You loved Stefano."

"I did, but he was very wild. I cannot condone what he has done to you or the way he has treated Bianca. He always wanted his own way. He listened to no one. David tried very hard to help him, but Stefano was never easy."

"He was my husband and I did love him." Bianca's tears slipped down her cheeks. "But I see now that he would have been a bad father, I think. I am glad my child did not have to find that out. I shall tell my little *orfano di padre* what a good man his father was. Just like his Zio David."

Megan held out her arms, and Bianca sank into them, sobbing quietly into her shoulder. Her hands gentle, she pulled the widow onto the bed and soothed her.

"That is a splendid idea. *Nonna* will help you. You must not cry anymore, Bianca. It is not good for the baby you carry. You need to protect your little one by being strong and as happy as you can be under the circumstances."

"I can see that, Sallee—I mean Megan." She sighed into Megan's shoulder and raised her head. "It is so confusing to me. I liked you so much as my sister-in-law, Sallee, and now you are somebody completely different, a stranger I do not know. Yet you are still the dear person whom I learned was so kind and such fun. What am I to do?"

Megan laughed and hugged her. "I am the same person, one who thinks you are brave and pretty, and who loves you very much. The only thing changed is that I am not your sister-in-law."

The shadow of regret that washed over her face was clearly evident to the two women who were watching. Bianca scrubbed at her own face with a scrap of a handkerchief and went into the adjoining bath to splash water on it.

"You are looking well, Meg," her mother offered in an obvious effort to change the subject. "What does your doctor say about you?"

"Nothing." Megan's soft chin jutted aggressively. "He treats me as if I am going to break into a thousand bits at any moment when he knows perfectly well there is nothing wrong with me. And he absolutely refuses to allow me to leave this place," she complained bitterly.

Her mother cocked an eye at her, not in the least

bothered by her complaint. *Nonna* smiled a secret little smile.

Bianca, returning from the bathroom, understood Megan's discontented words, although Megan had expressed herself in English. She clapped her hands, her eyes twinkling unexpectedly.

"Oh, Megan, you have such a surprise...!" She put her hand to her mouth then, her eyes dancing with mischief. *Nonna* and Megan's mother fixed stern glances upon her, then laughed with her, unable to resist her merriment or her lovely flow of French that had tumbled out so spontaneously.

"What are you three up to?" Megan inquired testily. "Don't try to tell me you're not planning something. You have guilt written all over you in large shiny letters!"

"How can you possibly say such a thing?" her mother remarked calmly and then went on to speak of Bianca's pregnancy in great detail. Bianca was doing well. The doctor had assured her she was quite able to carry the child to full term.

Bianca was in a much more cheerful frame of mind by the time they rose to leave. She kissed Megan affectionately and promised to return when she was able. *Nonna* was equally affectionate. Meg sighed when they left. She would miss them when she returned to England, she knew.

MARY WYNN-JONES visited the hospital on a daily schedule. Franco brought her in each time, accompanied her to the room occupied by the person whom he had once known as his employer's wife to gravely pay his respects. He would leave then, to wait patiently until Megan's mother finished her visit with her daughter.

He was a perfect gentleman, Mary assured the girl. All of David's employees and family seemed to meet the elder woman's approval. She went into flights of rhapsody over the Ranch of the Hills of the Panther.

"But, mother," Megan protested after one glowing account of the beauties of the vineyards that was liberally sprinkled with her mother's assurance of how lucky she was to be a part of it. "I'm not a part of it. It belongs to David Rossi. He has nothing to do with me. He's married to Sally, remember?"

Her mother looked decidedly wise for a moment, then quickly masked the odd look she gave her. "Yes. Well, I've been talking to Marion, and I thought...."

"No, mum," Megan stated flatly. "David can't stand the sight of me. He hasn't been here for days. I'm going home with you as soon as I convince Jim Maclean he can no longer keep me here. Home with you. To England."

"David has not been to see you because he is in London," her mother protested mildly. "He went on the same plane Ian took. Business, he said."

Business! Megan bade her mother a careful goodbye and thought about that bit of news. Had David Rossi gone to London to meet Sally? For the police apparently knew where she was, according to Tsumo, Megan remembered with a pang.

Her mother had had no idea of Sally's whereabouts. Mary Wynn-Jones had told her as much when she had given an account of the events leading up to the trip that brought her here. She had not seen Sally.

An extremely large American had appeared at the door of the family home in Chichester, accompanied by an equally large representative from Scotland Yard. It had been early evening, and Megan's father had been at home.

The American, Roger Dickson, had shown them a beautiful photo of her and assured them she was alive and well in California. He had explained to her happy parents about the girl's accident, which had caused amnesia. Then he'd assured them she was in good health and asked if Mary and her husband would bring Charles and come to the States for a reunion with their long-lost child. Mary had agreed eagerly, but Wynn-Jones had been unable to leave just then. She and Charles left the next day, with Ian as a willing escort.

They were already in San Francisco when the yacht exploded. Apparently David had just picked them up at the airport at the time of the explosion.

"He took us straight to a hotel, you know," Mary informed her daughter. "He thought it best we try to get some sleep while he went to fetch you." Mary smiled gently. "I was so impatient at the time. I wanted to go straight to you, but he persuaded me to try to rest. It was for the best as it turned out. I don't think I could have borne up if I'd had to face the police who arrested him when he returned to the docks. As it was, we slept until almost noon the next day. Jet lag, David said. And when we awakened, that nice Daniel Tsumo had a man waiting to tell us the report in the newspaper was a mistake. You were alive and well." She sighed. "But it was all very worrying."

Megan hugged her mother. "I know," she murmured regretfully.

"I don't think for a minute you did it on purpose," Mary protested. "I can tell you one of the happiest moments of my life was when Dickson knocked on our door. I couldn't even take it in for a while. I called Ian at once. He was beside himself."

"I know, mums."

"Your father was in an absolute frenzy. He couldn't get away without wrecking the whole structure of the talks he had set up. He was ready to chuck it in when Ian persuaded him to stay and finish. Fortunately Ian was able to get away for a couple of days."

Mary looked regretful as she spoke of the man her daughter had expected to marry. Ian's offer to escort her to California must have been quite a relief. Tevis, Megan's father, handled some very delicate negotiations in the common market for Her Majesty's Government. There were occasions when he was literally unable to call his time his own. During these times the presence of Tevis Wynn-Jones was absolutely essential at all meetings. It was a fact her mother had dealt with for a number of years. And Megan was well aware of the demands on her father's time.

"Didn't Sally ever get in touch with you?" Megan asked, more to veer the subject away from Ian than to gain information.

"Not once. And we didn't know how to reach her. Tevis had already alerted some of the men he knows in Scotland Yard. They were working on your disappearance, so they knew all about you when Dickson put in his appearance. They were down in Chichester in two ticks." Mary sighed and shook her head. "I can't tell you what a relief it was to speak to him, to know he had actually seen you and talked to you."

"I am so sorry to have been so worrisome."

"Yes, I know, dear. I've been talking to you for years about the way you would always rescue Sally from her, er, indiscretions. I hope you have learned your lesson finally."

"Oh, I have, mums. If I've done nothing else, I've certainly learned that." But what a way to learn, Megan thought with a bitter little laugh at herself.

When her mother left, Megan's mind wandered restlessly. Where was Sally now?

Was David with her? And was he seeking a reconciliation? It was a possibility she hated to consider. And yet, why else would he need to see Sally personally?

If she faced facts realistically, she knew David had taken her to his mountain, believing she *was* Sally. He had acted like a man in love. It was entirely within the realm of the probable he had always loved her cousin. She was beautiful and extremely attractive to men. Why should she think David was immune?

There was an excellent likelihood that his apparent hate was inspired because he was helplessly in love with Sally. It would explain many things Megan had been unable to understand about his treatment of her during the time they both thought she was truly his wife.

David must love Sally, after all, no matter what she'd done to him. She was the mother of his children. Megan knew this was no light thing in the dark man she loved. And David Rossi was the type who would commit himself once. That woman would be the only one he would ever love. The thought was a dreary one. She could not bear the thought of him bowing his proud head to knuckle down to the kind of treatment he would undoubtedly receive from her cousin.

And then she thought whimsically of those last few days she and David had spent together. David had acted like her lover then. A man in love, determined to woo the one he wanted. His laugh, his gentle teasing, his touch, the way he looked at her under long lashes when he thought she was not observing him. All of these things!

Had she dreamed them in her need, her obsession with his every change of mood, her desire to be touched, to be held by him?

It was no dream. It was a ruined reality. Never again would she be able to love. She must face the fact that a home shared by the man she adored and children to cherish and care for were not for her. Sally's thoughtless action combined with her own stupidity in loving her cousin's husband had dashed those hopes.

MEGAN WAS GUILTY of crying herself to sleep more than once during her stay in the hospital. By the end of two weeks there, she was decidedly impatient with James Maclean. Twice a day she went to his prescribed sessions of physical therapy, picked at her food and fretted under the prolongation of her stay.

She waylaid him one morning with a fierceness that meant business. "I am perfectly well, James Maclean," she protested tartly when he had refused once again to release her.

Megan had risen early, taken a brisk walk around the hospital grounds in the delightful spring air. She wanted desperately to get away, get back to her own country, pick up the threads of her life and get on with it. She would have liked to see Carla and Charles before she left, but there was no way at all for her to go again to the Ranch of the Hills of the Panther. The panther's scream, the restoration of her memory, had made that impossible. But she had to get away, go home.

"Go to your morning therapy session, Meg. Then we will see," the doctor had finally temporized.

"You are a most annoying man, James Maclean. I don't know how Marion puts up with you. She may have made a mistake."

"I'm sure she did." He had grinned very unrepentantly. "But it's too late now, thank God. I've got her trapped by my fascinating personality, and she will never get away. So beware, my fine beauty. Don't attempt to influence her—" he leered hideously "—or you will never get out of here."

Megan could not help laughing at him. "All right, you horrid man. But I have to arrange plane tickets and things like that. I expect mother and I will stay in San Francisco a couple of days, but I do need to make plans and be on my way."

"I know. But you can't go until I give the word. So you had best be nice to me."

She stuck her tongue out at him. He had winked and went on about his business, leaving a very dissatisfied girl behind.

And she was still dissatisfied as she came out of her morning therapy session, her hair damp and clinging to her because of the hot packs she had been wrapped in and the exercises she had done. She stepped into the shower of her private room, gave her hair a quick shampoo and toweled herself as she left the stall.

She stepped from the tiny cubicle into her room and stopped, her breath leaving her glowing body. His long legs, clad in black slim boots and finely tailored black suede pants, stretched lazily in front of him, and a silk shirt, carelessly unbuttoned to expose his muscular throat, stretched across his shoulders. He watched her come from her shower.

CHAPTER EIGHTEEN

HIS EYES DEVOURED HER. "Get dressed, my love."

Megan stood and stared at him, anger rising in her like a bubble. She clutched the inadequate protection of the towel to her and fought an unsuccessful battle to stem her rage.

"How dare you?" she stormed. "How dare you come here after all this time, sit there as if you were lord of the universe and tell me to get dressed?" She was close to incoherence by the time she finished her impassioned protest.

Long lashes veiled the glitter deep in his black eyes. "You missed me."

"No, damn you. I didn't miss you. I just thanked God you were gone out of my life."

"Careful, *cara mia*. Don't push me too far. You sent your lover away." He stood then, a smooth dangerous movement, and towered over her. Megan quivered, stepping back instinctively to avoid being pounced upon.

"Ian was my fiancé, not my lover."

"Was." David's rough laugh was entirely self-satisfied. "He is gone for good, then?"

She threw a tormented glance up into his dark face. "Yes. Was. I could not go to him after what passed between us." Her flesh felt stiff with tension as she spat the tortured accusation at him. "He is gone, and I hate you for what you have done to me."

"*Pobrecita.* How can you be in such a temper when you share the same lovely memory with me? Get dressed, Megan. I want you to go with me."

"I shall not go," she replied with a reckless disregard of the warning in the depths of those brooding black eyes. "And speak English. I hate it when you call me names in Italian."

He reached for her then, a man who was not able to contain his passion. Megan dropped her towel and flailed at him, striking his hard chest with fists meant to punish. He laughed huskily, caught her hands and used them to pull her into his arms, his dark head swooping hungrily, his arms folding her slender naked body to the silken covering of hard muscle. Megan's convulsive movement ceased as she gave herself up to the wonder of his mouth on her own.

It was passionate, seductive, demanding and tender all at once. Its beauty overwhelmed her. She clung to him, her body, her mind, her spirit enthralled with the call of the man who held her.

He raised his head, the breath whistling into his lungs. Dazed, Megan stared up at him, her love laid bare in the great wide eyes she turned on him. He laughed huskily, then kissed her eyes closed.

"Don't look at me that way, you bewitching creature, or we shall never leave this room." His arms closed on her a moment, sweeping her tightly back against his aroused length. "Get dressed, *pobrecita*, before I commit untold assault upon your delectable person. And *pobrecita* is Spanish, poor little one. Not Italian."

"I stand corrected," the girl muttered in a distrait retort. She watched him warily as she sorted out silken underthings and pulled on a summery cotton dress in yellow that was splashed with great white daisies.

David watched her dress, leased passion glittering as his glance clung to her. He did not offer to leave.

What does he want with me, Megan wondered desperately as she brushed her short curls into order, then touched her throbbing lips with color. *He surely cannot expect me to go with him. He is my cousin's husband. No matter how much we are attracted to each other, he cannot ignore his marriage.*

And he must know I will not be his mistress. No matter how much I love him, how much he wants me, there could be no future for us.

David watched impatiently as she slipped her slender feet into strappy thongs and fussed with her handbag.

"*Cara*, my long-suffering patience is wearing thin. Come with me now, or I will not be responsible for my actions."

Megan took one look at the dark intense face and took warning. She went. David's hand fastened over her arm with almost a convulsive movement, and his fingers wrapped painfully tight.

"I'm not going to run away, David," she protested in a squeaky little voice she did not recognize.

"I made sure of that," he volunteered, his glance mischievous. "I threatened Jim with all kinds of dire consequences if he dare let you out of the hospital before I returned."

"Wait until the next time I see Jim Maclean. Keeping me here all that time! My mum wants to go home, but she can't without me. And where exactly did you return from, Mr. High-and-Mighty?'' she asked, knowing full well the answer.

He grinned at her, guided her toward the back of the hospital. His helicopter was parked there, shiny clean from a fresh wash and wax job.

"London, my love." He helped her into the glass bubble of the machine, returned her amazed look with a mocking little laugh. "And your dear mum, much as I like her, will just have to return without you. You are not going."

"I am, you know." Megan's outraged exclamation bothered him not at all. He swung into his seat, fastened their seat belts and reached for his controls, his face imperturbable.

"No," he stated flatly just before he sent the machine whirling into the air. "You are staying here with me. You belong to me, and I shall never let you go."

Megan had not recovered entirely from the thrust of that unequivocal statement by the time the glass bubble in which they rode swung across the ridge of the valley called Ta-La-Ha-Lu-Si and dropped toward the courtyard of Rancho Las Colinas.

David landed his craft, gave her an enigmatic look and came around to assist her. She unbuckled her seat belt and ran her fingers through her hair. He had landed on the tarmac outside the courtyard. She could see no one, but she had no chance to comment on the fact. He stood over her and held out his arms in a silent command.

"David, I will not live here with you. I will not be your mistress!"

He swore at her then and plucked her from the aircraft as if she were weightless. "Little goose! Will you shut up? You madden me with your ridiculous arguments, your lack of understanding."

"Put me down, you great bully!" The tenderness in his eyes startled her; it sent her heart into impossible efforts at acrobatics that hearts were not meant to perform.

He laughed at her, then kissed her with a thoroughness that caused her to cling to him as passion flared in her.

When at last he raised his dark head, she lay in his arms bereft of resistance, longing for more. She opened great violet blue eyes, blind to everything except the strong face of the man who watched her expression with such satisfaction. Her own love for him was written plainly on her face for him to see and revel in.

He smiled gently then, charm lighting his handsome features with a devastating effect. "You will come with me now, my Meg, and you will not argue with me for a full thirty minutes. Is that understood?"

"Yes, David. I will try."

He laughed and kissed her quickly. "Well, that is something." He put her down then but kept one arm strongly about her waist. "Come along."

He led the way to the patio arch and stopped at her sound of amazement.

The patio had been turned into a bower of flowers. White lilies and lilac twined up the pillars and were laced through the graceful black ironwork. A long aisle of interwoven lily and lilac stretched from the patio arch to an elaborate arbor of flowers and ferns. A man stood under the arbor, a book in his hand. Megan gave him a fleeting glance and realized she knew him: Grant Callum, the judge who had married James and Marion Maclean. They were with him, standing under the flower-entwined arch.

Her mother was there, too, beaming happily. And so were all David's relatives, the office staff and workers from the ranch, vineyards and the winery. They made a fair-sized smiling crowd as they stood on the sunlit patio, their attention centered on the couple who had just entered.

To Megan's joy, the twins were under the arch with the three adults. They looked positively angelic. Both were dressed in velvet. Carla wore a darling dress over many frilly petticoats that fluffed in white perfection beneath the soft white skirt. White flowers nestled in her shining black curls, and she held a bouquet beribboned with satin in her chubby little fists.

Charles was splendid in his black velvet trousers and jacket that matched his dark hair and eyes. He had not seen Megan for months, and her appearance with his beloved and newly found father caused his eyes to dance with anticipation. However, he was determined to do his job. He stood straight and solemn, a small velvet cushion in his hands. As ring bearer for the ceremony, he was ready with all the contained poise of any small child entrusted with a very important task.

Megan felt as if she might go into shock. The scene before her was fraught with an undeniable intent. She turned wondering and slightly incredulous eyes up to the man beside her. "What is this all about?"

she asked him in a choked whisper she had to force out.

"I've been a bachelor for three days," he mocked her gravely. "I don't like it, so I've decided I must marry again. You just happen to be the only available candidate. It was easy to arrive at the conclusion that you must be the only volunteer."

She swallowed quickly, got rid of the lump in her throat. The action seemed to bring tears that caused her eyes to glisten like rain-drenched pansies.

David growled at her, deep in his throat as he handed her his handkerchief. "You are in my power, fair maiden. Tears will get you nothing but a red nose. Most unbecoming in brides."

Before she was able to react to his outrageous statement, he turned her away from the waiting crowd. It was then she spotted her father approaching from a veranda at the side of the casa. She flew from David's arms straight into her father's embrace.

Nothing in her life had prepared her for the flood of joy she felt at that moment. Her parent kissed her, his hands gentle on her back. She clung to him for a lifetime of seconds, then turned her radiant face up to the man she knew to be responsible for this bliss as he approached.

"Thank you, David," she said simply.

He took her hands and drew her close, the intense glint with which he scanned her features drawing a blush into her soft cheeks.

"Will you marry me, *cara mia*?" He laughed tenderly at the play of emotion she felt no need to hide. "And I will tolerate no arguments for half an hour,

remember? You promised...well, sort of," he
allowed. "Besides, would you have the nerve to embarrass me in front of all these people? Think of the
consequences if I should lose that terrible temper I
am reputed to have, were you to be so foolish as to
turn me down."

"You are an absolute fool, David Rossi," she told
him. "I expect I must marry you to protect you from
yourself. We can't have all these people disillusioned,
can we? Most of them have accepted that lord-of-
creation image you manage to project so well."

He pounced on her, his lips relentless. "I should
have insisted you be silent for the half hour," he
taunted in mock dismay. "Come on, you infuriating
woman. Let's get married."

He left her in her father's care and went down the
flowery aisle with long strides that carried him to the
bower where Callum and the Macleans waited in
smiling patience.

And so it was that Megan Wynn-Jones, clad in a
sunny cotton dress sprinkled with large white daisies,
married David Rossi. No man ever looked better on
his wedding day than David in his suede pants and
black silk shirt. And certainly no man ever looked
more content.

James was best man, Marion acting as Megan's attendant. Solemnly Tevis Wynn-Jones gave his daughter into David's keeping.

Megan made her responses with a happiness that
throbbed in her voice and caused the man who slid
the diamond-encrusted band onto her finger to look
at her with a regard that chased rosy color into her
radiant face.

She blushed again as he kissed her at the end of the ceremony, trembling in his arms in a way he found wholly enchanting.

"We'll go soon, my love. Hmm?" His dark eyes danced with his challenge as he whispered the words meant for her ears alone.

The twins, restrained with self-importance over their part in the ceremony, broke away and launched themselves in an irresistible assault at "mum-mum" at that moment and saved her the necessity of replying to the imperious and passionate demand in his eyes.

Then the panther's kittens provided a diversion as they tumbled about the feet of the guests on the patio, pouncing, spitting defiance, executing a mock attack on Quito who watched their antics with the complacent look of an elder brother putting up with the antics of younger members of his family.

Somehow everyone soon had a glass in hand, and the contents were downed with plenty of goodwill. It was while the party was getting under way that David leaned down to her.

"Our half hour is just about up, Mrs. Rossi. Since I will not have you arguing with me before all these people, we must leave." He looked inordinately pleased with himself and quite determined to have his own way.

"David!" She was sincerely shocked. "How can you suggest such a thing? These are your guests, and you know it. We cannot leave!" There was no suppressing the thrill his use of her new title sent coursing down her spine.

"Argue, argue!" He lifted black eyes to heaven.

"Must I always put up with your opposition?" His glance was very tender as he laughed at her bemused face. Could he feel her glorious sense of anticipation? Megan tried to resist.

"In this case, yes. How can we leave now?" Her protest was remarkedly weak even to her own ears.

"How?" His brow shot up into the unruly mass of curls that had tumbled onto his forehead. "Like this." He grabbed her hand and ran lithely toward the patio entrance. By the time he reached it, he had the attention of all. He turned then and flashed them his charming smile.

"Adiós, amigos!" he shouted happily. "I'm sure you understand. Have fun!"

Swinging the astonished girl at his side into his arms, he sprinted across the courtyard to dump her unceremoniously into the helicopter. They were airborne before his astounded new wife recovered enough to voice a protest.

"David Rossi," she scolded with severe disapproval, "you are undoubtedly the most arrogant, undisciplined, outrageous—"

"Fellow who ever lived," he finished with laughter. "And I love you to distraction. Oh, Meg, I want you, need you so. I could not abide sharing you one moment longer with that crowd. Come with me. Be my love."

She cast a glance down onto the valley floor, then looked at him, her heart in her eyes. "I really seem to have Hobson's choice, don't I? And where are you taking me, Mr. David Rossi?"

"Ah, Megan. As if you didn't know!"

She did know. His mountaintop. She blushed, and

he laughed again, a sweet controlled sound in the chop of the helicopter's rhythm. How good it was to hear him laugh, she thought. He had seemed so grim, so different when she had first known him.

"Bianca tells me she is going to stay at the ranch at least until she has her baby," she offered in an attempt to steer her marauding thoughts away from her thrilling memories of that flat-topped mountain.

"Yes," David agreed. "It is best for her, I think. I am hoping she will stay on afterward and live with us at the ranch until she has settled her future, if you will agree."

"Certainly," Megan returned. "It must be shattering to lose one's love when one is so young. And then, she has the child to think of and to support, as well."

"She will not want for material things," David informed her easily. "Stefano was not a poor man, just a greedy one. He left a substantial estate, which she has asked me to handle. I'm glad to do it for her and the child."

He concentrated a moment on his controls, his face quiet. Megan sensed he was thinking of Bianca. She allowed herself to examine his dark face, wondering how she had ever thought him cold and hard. He was, she decided, the most caring man she had ever met. She had met many in her capacity as Ian's personal assistant. Successful men, assertive, arrogant, sure of themselves. They had never attracted her because she had known early in her dating years that most of them had turned off real feelings and lost touch with themselves.

By the time she had turned twenty, she realized she

wanted more than financial success from the man she married. Ian had come close to fulfilling her image of what a man should be. But he didn't begin to be the equal of the dynamic man beside her, Megan knew.

David was a successful man in a cutthroat world. His personality embraced all facets the world expected such a man to have, and much much more besides. He was strong where strength was demanded, yet he had not lost his ability to be tender. He was sure of himself, assertive, yet he recognized and cherished sensitivity in others and in himself. He was a born leader who was aware of the rights of those he led. Yes, David Rossi was quite a man, and Megan loved him to distraction.

The controls adjusted to his liking, he turned his attention back to his new wife. "Bianca is part of the family," he continued quietly. "I have been in touch with her relatives in Italy. They are content for her to stay here a little while if she wants to. They are convinced Stefano did not love her much, although they know she was besotted with him. That's understandable. He was a handsome devil."

"He certainly was," Megan agreed. "I couldn't like him. He seemed spoiled and quite ruthless to me."

"He was," David agreed without apology. "Dad and *nonna* both gave him his own way far too often. As a result he seldom took the trouble to notice if his actions affected anyone but himself." David slanted a self-mocking glance at her. "I had a devil of a time with him after dad died. Your cousin supplied a complication I really didn't need."

"I can well imagine. But you brought it on yourself, you know." The thought of David's affair on his yacht with Sally caused her newfound happiness to dim a little.

"No regrets, *cara*!" David's strong hand closed on her arm, command in his deep retort. "It had nothing to do with us." She shot him a glance, aware that he had read her distress.

"I think Steve married Bianca for the sole purpose of convincing me he had settled down," David continued. "He wanted to entice me into sharing the corporation with him. I had always planned to, and he knew it. I was ready to make him a junior executive when he got mixed up with Sally, and I was forced to send him to Italy. I hated to make *nonna* unhappy, but he was sincere in his feelings for my former wife, I think. I tried to break up the attachment before it ruined him, but I was much too late."

He laughed ruefully. "Once he even suggested I should divorce her so he could marry her. I would have done so. It certainly would have solved my own problem. But Sally had no more interest in Steve than she had in any other male body. She stuck to him longer than she did with most as a means of getting at me, I see now. Steve was always convinced she loved him, however. He was ready to do anything for her."

"Poor man." Megan shook her head.

"For that matter, poor Sally," David observed quietly. "She is driven by her own twisted personality and is a prisoner of desires she will never be able to satisfy. Anyway, I'm convinced Steve had no love for Bianca, and of course, she is too young, too unsophisticated, to have been any kind of sexual competition for Sally. Sally went to Italy from England as soon as she left my troublesome offspring in the care of your folks.''

"They were no trouble,'' Megan protested. "They were absolute loves. Mum and daddy could not have been happier during the past two years. They cared deeply for the twins. I dreaded the time when Sally might come and take them away.''

"No fear of that!" David declared crisply. "Thank God you and your folks were there to care for them. Sally didn't want them. She hated them and me. When I saw her in the solicitor's office in London, she told me she had put them into an orphanage whose name and location she had forgotten." His smile chilled his wife. "I failed to tell her Charles was home in California at that moment. She did not mention Carla, of course. Steve apparently had not been in touch with her. She didn't mention Lang, either, but she actually didn't give a damn whether the child was safe and cared for or not.''

"How did you find her, David?"

"Dickson located your family immediately through his inquiries at Scotland Yard," he answered. "Your mother left at once for the States, along with Charles and Ian, as you know. Dickson got in touch with me, of course. I was convinced Sally was up to something and would be in touch with your home. Your father agreed with me. He installed Roger as a family friend, so he was there and actually met Sally at the door when she came to collect Charles. She had become restless, of course, not knowing where Lang was and having no contact with Steve. I think she was determined to go ahead on her own and use Charles to force some sort of ransom

from me. Anyway, your father called me at once, and
Roger Dickson followed your cousin back to London.
I took the next plane out of San Francisco." He
grinned at her. "I shared it with an extremely unfriendly Englishman, poor devil."

"Ian."

"Ian. We were halfway over the Atlantic before I
could convince him I truly loved you and had not just
taken advantage of your convenient condition, Mrs.
Rossi."

Megan blushed on cue. "You did, you know."

"Ah. . . but not until I was driven to absolute and
utter distraction. No man should suffer as I had to
suffer, my little one. I knew and despised what Sally
was, and I could never forgive what she had done to
me, and yet I was falling in love with all that I hated.
I almost went out of my mind. . . ."

"Why did Stefano decide to come here with Bianca?" she asked hastily, unable yet to think of that
glorious incident on the mountain, and what it had
meant to her.

"He was deeply involved with Lang and Sally in
some scheme to wrench control of the corporation
from me, I think." David's mocking glance acknowledged her need to divert him. "We'll never know
what they had in mind. He panicked when Lang disappeared. Then when he arrived and found you unexpectedly on the scene, his fears were reinforced by
your refusal to react toward him as Sally would have
done. When he became convinced you really did have
amnesia, he had to get rid of you before you regained
your memory and ruined his chance with me. The
scheme he had dreamed up, or at least joined in with,

was probably washed up. He didn't want his share of the corporation lost to him, as well. So he had made his preparations to blow up the yacht at the first opportunity. When your mother and my son arrived at the airport, I left to get them and provided him with the perfect chance to stage the accident. In his worst nightmare he never envisioned you might survive."

"It. . . it's such a horrible thing. . . ."

"It is that, my love. Greed can make monsters of us all. Steve had nothing to worry about, had he but known it. Sally did not care whether he lived or died. She might have had a little interest in him if she ran out of an immediate source of ready cash, but she never mentioned him to me when I did see her in that London office."

"Did she. . . did you have to give her money to get the divorce?"

"I didn't have to, but I did it, *cara*. It was an easy and fast way to get what I wanted: you. And at the same time I was finally rid of the one element in my life I had never been able to handle to my own satisfaction. I expect I was a coward, but perhaps we all are at times."

"It's a wonder Sally agreed to anything. Unless you settled for some huge amount," Megan observed. She looked at him and knew he wasn't about to tell her more. "I only hope it was worth it."

He laughed at her. "You can be very certain it was, my love." His happiness was obvious. "I beg to inform you right now that I'm planning to draw interest on that investment for the rest of my life and beyond." Bold black eyes touched her soft features. The helicopter skimmed up the valley, the rising pitch of sound loud in the sudden silence. David increased the angle of the blades another notch. The machine climbed sharply.

"I went to the airport the night your mother arrived with the intention of bringing her and Charles straight back to the yacht as a surprise for you," he told her gently. "Much as I wanted to tell you everything, I was sure your mother's presence would restore your memory. I had talked with Mellon. He thought her unexpected appearance might just do the trick." His voice tightened, and he reached for her hand. "Ian came off that plane with them, and I thought my world had come to an end. I felt like killing him when Mary introduced him as your fiancé."

"Oh, David...."

His mouth twisting in a wolfish smile, he manipulated the controls of the big machine as it crested the edge of the mountaintop. He set it down with an easy skill, stopped the motors and turned to her, his hands reaching for her shoulders, his lips closing eyelids over the tears that suddenly blinded her.

"God, that was the worst thing that ever happened to me. I was absolutely incapable of taking them to you. I had to think. So I installed them in a hotel and wandered the streets of San Francisco for hours, wondering how the hell I was going to get them back to England without you ever seeing them. I found I had an overriding need to keep you blissfully unconscious of your past and the fantastic man in it."

"Ian is rather fantastic, isn't he?" She couldn't resist the impulse to tease this fiery man who had fallen so deeply in love with her.

"Damn it, Meg!" His lips met hers with exquisite

force. "Don't ever mention his name! When I think what you might have done when he turned up. . . ."

"How did you know I wouldn't?"

"After your accident there was no way for me to keep him and your mother from knowing the truth. I think I said goodbye to you when he kissed you there in the hospital."

"I knew that," she murmured into the warmth of his neck, her words muffled as she buried her face in that strong brown column. "My heart broke when you walked away. And you didn't come back even when Ian left. I was sure you were gone forever, that my life was over."

David pried her flushed face out of its hiding place. It was some time before he raised his dark head.

"I was sure God was in his proper place and all was right with the world when I boarded that airplane and saw Johns sitting in my section. It took a little while for him to get over his anger and tell me you would not be coming back to England to marry him. But I knew it as soon as I saw him. He looked at me as if he could have slit my throat without a regret in the world. Oh, Meggie!"

His arms slipped around her slender body, and he lifted her in the spacious helicopter, bringing her into his lap. His kiss was full of gentle passion. "I think the worst night of my misspent life was when Ian and your mother arrived in San Francisco." He shuddered and sighed against her eyelids, kissing them to keep them closed as he studied her features with an intent fierceness. "I finally went back to the yacht. I still didn't know how I was going to get rid of your mother and Ian, but I had decided I would, some way. And get rid of Charles, too. I couldn't figure any way at all to keep him with me and avoid an explanation of how I had recovered him." His deep voice took on a haunted quality. "I didn't want you to see Ian. I was afraid I might lose you to him. So I decided to say nothing and just go back to the yacht and spend the rest of the night making love to you." He sighed grimly at the little sound she made, but he did not inquire as to the reason for it. "God help me. I still hadn't figured out what to do, come morning and sanity." He didn't sound apologetic. "At the wharf I found myself in the hands of the police and charged with murder, thanks to the information my half brother had so conveniently supplied to them. I didn't even argue with them. For I thought my love was dead, burned in the total destruction of my own yacht. I knew what hell was really like then, *pequeñita*. Daniel Tsumo came to me the next morning and prevented me from going mad. He told me you were alive and well and in his father's house. The good *Dios* had saved you. Dan also said you were still an amnesia victim. I made a vow then never to ask for another thing in my whole life. You were alive and didn't know Ian loved you!"

Megan surfaced, rosy with his kiss, amusement in her eyes. "Never, David?"

"I already knew I loved you. What more could I ask?" He smiled, and her heart did its little flip. "I thought I could teach you to love me." His statement was imperious, certain.

"I loved you, but how could you have learned to love me when you thought all along I was Sally? You never changed your mind about her, did you?"

"No, Meggie. I never changed my mind about Sally. And you did manage to confuse me for a while, but it is hard to confuse a heart. Steve's sudden appearance made me suspicious for a while—I thought maybe you as Megan might have been in cahoots with him all along. But I soon realized how wrong that was. I knew what I was doing after a little."

She touched those sensuous lips from which she derived so much pleasure. "And what were you doing, David Rossi?"

"Falling irretrievably in love with a captivating small witch whose name I didn't even know." He kissed her exploring fingers with a fire that brought more color into her cheeks. "I even invented a name for you, remember, *cara mia*? I couldn't live with calling you Sally."

"You were taking a large-sized risk, Mr. Rossi," she told him pertly. "What made you think I would ever agree to marry you? I really probably should have decided against it...." She had no chance to finish that little show of independence. David growled at her and crushed her into his long frame.

"You didn't have a chance in hell of getting away, Mrs. Rossi," he declared fiercely. "I called Jim Maclean as soon as I cleared customs at Heathrow. I threatened him with murder and an instant consignment to the last outposts of humanity if he dared let you out of that hospital before I could get back to collect you personally. He was most understanding," he conceded sunnily. "Your mother and *nonna* agreed to help with my plans, too, as soon as I clued them in. By the time I reached San Francisco this morning, everything was arranged and in order, thanks to them.''

Megan risked a glance at his composed and complacent face. Never had a man looked more in control of his life!

"You are a self-satisfied male specimen, aren't you, my love? And more than a little chauvinistic, I suspect," she added for good measure, laughing at the offense her lofty words caused.

"Any time you can call me your love in that tone of voice, I am self-satisfied." He kissed her into silence, then stared down at her possessively.

Megan surfaced, breathless. "Oh, David, you must stop kissing me so thoroughly. I shall disgrace myself miserably if you continue. I'm so happy I—I want to c-cry."

David tilted her face upward and searched it carefully, his dark eyes glowing. His delight at what he saw was written in his expression. Megan gasped a little and started to speak, but David forestalled her question.

He laughed and plopped her back into her seat, face stern against her protest. "No more questions, no more talk. I absolutely forbid it. Here I have spent endless hours and energy trying to prepare this surprise for you, and you haven't even looked at it."

Megan looked then. The mountaintop had been converted into a dreamer's paradise. A roomy cabin, its windows sparkling in the late sun, stood on a brushed tile patio, its peaked A-frame as tall as the oak beside it. Lounge furniture, as well as yellow and green cushions thick and inviting, sat about on the patio. A fireplace stood in one corner of the paved area, its shiny grill ready to be used.

David came around, plucked his silent companion from her seat since she seemed unable to make a move. "Well, little dragon. I am pleased to have found something at last that is able to render you speechless. Shall we go look?" His teasing mocked her silence.

She threw him a speaking glance and ran from him to explore the house. Clapping her hands, she danced across the tiled floor, then stepped up the one level to the adorable dining area. It was separated from the kitchen by a tiled counter top with a storage area cunningly fitted with wine bottles slanted so that the contents rested against their corks.

The kitchen was a maiden's ideal, the cupboards completely stocked with pans, utensils and groceries. Megan gave it little time as she sped up a little circular staircase to the upper floor.

The wall over the downstairs living room was only waist high, the light from the two-story window serving both the downstairs and the big bedroom. A beautiful tiled bath opened off the bedroom.

David followed her as silent as she was. She turned to him, wordless, and he came to her then, his fingers trembling as they encircled her, slid her zipper down her back.

He undressed her with a slow urgency that acted on Megan with the power of an aphrodisiac. He watched her through lashes he kept lowered, his hands gentle, his mouth drugging as he used them to arouse her.

Megan lost her consciousness of everything except his presence. She lived a lifetime in those few minutes before he laid her upon the big bed, his hard length a desired anguish he withheld from her until she was frenzied with her need. When he moved to take her, their shared passion engulfed them in an overwhelming tide. Their hearts, their minds, their bodies, acted as one.

David buried his face in her hair then. If there were tears in his eyes, she did not see them. She relaxed on an outgoing tide of ecstasy, content to be pressed into the side of this man she loved so well.

If David had any more reasons for loving the woman in his arms, he kept them to himself as they drifted into that wonderful renewing sleep of perfect love fulfilled.

EPILOGUE

FIFTEEN MONTHS LATER Megan Rossi lazed on the cushions of a puffy lounge chair in the warmth of her sun-drenched patio.

Bees went busily from flower to flower, their droning flight a sleep-inducing accompaniment to the lilt of bird song. Quito had left on an enterprise of his own, and the twins were not due from their nursery school for another hour.

She smiled as she thought of those two active little imps. They were well on the way to becoming accomplished linguists. They spoke Italian and Spanish with fluency equaled only by their English. And their French was more than passable. Already they were both reading English well, absorbing the written word with all the drive of thirsty little minds bent on finding out as much as possible.

Not bad for five-year-olds. David would soon have to come up with many more interesting things to keep them stretching their lively little intellects. She only hoped the child she was carrying would have the same degree of intelligence.

She smiled gently at her thought. As if any child David Rossi fathered could be anything but intelligent. She allowed her thoughts to wander to the man who was her husband, felt her awareness sharpen and her senses begin to tingle as they always did when she thought of him.

David Rossi, his wife had discovered, was a unique human being. He was a man who was true to himself, true to his most intimate feelings and possessed of the ability to translate these in such a manner that he could share them with her. He managed to reject and ignore any attempt to force him into preconceived patterns and, in doing so, was able to be spontaneous and unashamed in his sharing with her.

He laughed when he was happy, shed a tear if he felt like it and gave love that was free from the need to manipulate. He had made their life together a perfect whole, unencumbered by guilt or artifice.

Their love was a constant source of wonder and beauty to them. It nurtured and sustained while it was ever constant, ever growing. Megan knew it was the central magic of her life.

She was almost three months pregnant now and anticipating the birth of their child with a vivid happiness. Surely her cup runneth over.

Nonna came through the big front door and crossed the patio to her. The old lady sat down in the chair under the shade of the big umbrella whose fringe fluttered gaily in the warm breeze, and smiled at her grandson's wife.

"You are so brown, Megan. It becomes you. You seem to glow."

"David says it is only because he has had his way with me and has finally managed to give me a child." Megan laughed, ready for *nonna*'s slightly shocked look. She had made herself a secure place in *nonna*'s affections by loving David so completely, she knew.

She loved the old lady's sense of humor and often teased her gently as she was now.

"David is inclined to say all sorts of things his grandmother should not have to hear." She smiled in mock dismay. "You do look lovely, even so."

"Thank you, *nonna*. It is only because I live in such a place. The Indians showed much wisdom when they named the valley beautiful. Ta-La-Ha-Lu-Si has such an intriguing cadence."

They sat for a few moments in companionable silence. "Are you all packed and ready to go, Meg?" *nonna* asked presently.

"Yes. David went up to the mountaintop to make sure everything was in order. He wouldn't want anything to happen to it while we are in Europe."

"You love that mountain, don't you?"

"I can't tell you how much it has meant to me," Megan murmured happily. "It is heavenly up there. And I love being alone with David. If all newlyweds had such an idyllic retreat and could learn to know each other in such a beautiful setting, I'm sure there would be fewer divorces."

"Perhaps." The chopping sound of the helicopter's blades came to them. Both Megan and *nonna* squinted into the sky in an effort to catch a glimpse of the returning machine. "I shall miss you while you are gone," David's grandmother went on.

"I know you will." Megan smiled in understanding. "However, it is only for six weeks. Bianca is very anxious to visit her family and show off Annetta."

Bianca's rosy little girl was beautiful. With Stefano's curls and snapping tawny eyes, she was the picture of health and entirely irrepressible.

Bianca had blossomed under the love and care she had received from her American family. And her association with David had brought her out of her shell, given her confidence in herself. Megan thoroughly enjoyed the younger girl's company and had been pleased when David suggested they have a long vacation—go to England to see her folks, then on to Italy to visit Bianca's relatives and his, as well, so that the Italian branch of the family could become acquainted with his new wife.

The twins were going with them, but *nonna* did not feel up to the stress of the journey. Nor did she wish to be so long away from her beloved home.

Megan heard the helicopter hover, then land. She straightened unconsciously in her lounge, her long tanned limbs, her glowing body, tensing with the expectancy of seeing the man she loved. She did not hear *nonna*'s chuckle as she watched him stride gracefully through the big arch, his lithe form erect and beautiful.

He dropped a kiss on his grandmother's soft cheek, then scooped his wife up, unabashed passion flaring in his dark eyes. "You're so beautiful," he murmured as he kissed her.

Megan trembled a little, unable to prevent her instant response to the strong and unmistakable call of his masculinity.

"You grow more outrageous every day. Do you know that?"

He narrowed his black eyes as he watched her color rise and felt her instant answer to his touch. "Are we ready to go?"

"Yes." She lowered her lashes, hid her thought

from him. "As soon as the twins get here, we can eat and change. Everything else is ready."

He slid a firm brown hand under her chin and raised it. Megan refused to cooperate, and his arm tightened around her.

"Look at me, *pequeñita*." When she ignored the soft command, he put her on her feet, his arm an unrelenting band around her slender waist, his fingers a soft insistence on her skin. Unable to help herself, she raised her tangled lashes then.

David caught his breath at the expression in her eyes, his heart thundering an answer to the beat of her own. He growled deep in his throat.

"I suppose you're starved to death and can't possibly wait to eat?" His whisper was pitched for her ears alone as his lips nuzzled into her silky hair.

Megan's speaking glance gave him the answer he sought with such confidence. He kissed her then, and passion shot through her, left her clinging madly to the firm anchor of his wide shoulders.

"Nonna," his satisfaction was plain in the thickened timbre of his voice, "will you please see to the children? We must go shower and change. And Megan does not seem to be hungry at the moment."

Never had food had less appeal, but once in the privacy of their rooms, Megan turned to him in protest.

"Whatever will *nonna* think of us? Coming up to our rooms...." Her blush was properly rewarded with a kiss that drank thoroughly of the sweet promise in her response. "Running away from our responsibilities in the middle of the day...."

Restless long fingers were busy, intent upon reaching silken skin and arousing an abandoned fire as they did so.

"Ah, my love. I am sure *nonna* would agree that I am your first, your greatest and your most demanding responsibility."

My most wonderful one, as well, David's wife knew some time later as she snuggled drowsily into strong arms that tucked her closer to the muscular male body she was learning to need so much.

Never had any woman been more fulfilled. And never had any man made any woman happier. The realizations faded as she drifted into sleep, her cheek pillowed in the hollow of a shoulder it fitted perfectly.